Praise for

THE GLADDY GOLD MYSTERIES

"This is one sassy and smart series with a colorful gang of senior sleuths." —*Mystery Scene*

"Beyond the skillful blend of Yiddish humor, affectionate characters and serious undercurrents... picks up speed and flavor with some twists worthy of Agatha Christie's archetypal dame detective, Miss Marple." —*Publishers Weekly*

"What gives the book its warmth is the way Lakin has turned this group of friends into a family who are there not only for the fun and laughter but also for the heartbreak and tears." —*Romantic Times*

"Young and old, Jewish, Protestant, atheist, all will love this tale told with clarity, wit and interesting characters. This is a must-read mystery."
—iloveamysterynewsletter.com

"An entertaining cozy mystery series with a set of lovable and oddball characters. The mystery has a puzzling plot with twists and turns that will surprise readers.... Retirement takes on a new meaning after spending time with Gladdy and her gladiators!"
—Freshfiction.com

"Rita Lakin shows a real flair for comic mysteries.... The plotting is expert, but the background color of life among older retired people is wonderful (and sometimes very poignant)." —*Connecticut Post* Forum

"This is a **funny, warm, absolutely delightful** tale . . . a must read." —*Mysterious Women*

"An unforgettable romp . . . Lakin's characters are zany, her writing is **witty and crisp,** and anyone who's ever visited one can attest that her peek at life in a Jewish Florida retirement center is portrayed both accurately and tastefully." —*Cleveland Jewish News*

"**Wonderful dialogue and a touch of romance** enlivens this delightful breeze of a tale."
—*Kaw Valley (KS) Senior Monthly*

"**Sassy, funny and smart** . . . Lakin sprinkles humor on every page, but never loses respect for her characters."
—*New Hampshire Senior Beacon*

"**It is a tribute to Lakin's talent that she is able to mingle comedy and murder successfully.**"
—*Dade County Jewish Journal*

"If getting old is this much fun, maybe I won't mind! **Miss Marple, move over** . . . Rita Lakin's witty romp through a Florida retirement community is just the thing for what ails you!"
—Parnell Hall, author of the Puzzle Lady mysteries

"So who knew a retirement community could be so dangerous—and so much fun. . . . Lakin handles her characters with **dignity, compassion and love,** while allowing them the full extent of their eccentric personalities." —Vicki Lane, author of *Old Wounds*

"A truly original voice. **Great fun from start to finish.** Plan to stay up late." —Sheldon Siegel, *New York Times* bestselling author of *The Confession*

About the Author

Fate took Rita Lakin from New York to Los Angeles, where she was seduced by palm trees and movie studios. Over the next twenty years she wrote for television and had every possible job from freelance writer to story editor to staff writer and, finally, producer. She worked on shows such as *Dr. Kildare, Peyton Place, The Mod Squad,* and *Dynasty,* and created her own shows, including *The Rookies, Flamingo Road,* and *Nightingales.* Rita has won awards from the Writers Guild of America, the Mystery Writers of America's Edgar Allan Poe Award, and the coveted Avery Hopwood Award from the University of Michigan. She lives in Marin County, California, where she is currently at work on her next mystery starring the indomitable Gladdy Gold. Visit her on the Web at www.ritalakin.com.

ALSO BY RITA LAKIN

Getting Old Is Murder

Getting Old Is the Best Revenge

Getting Old Is Criminal

Getting Old Is To Die For

Getting Old Is a Disaster

Rita Lakin

A DELL BOOK

GETTING OLD IS A DISASTER
A Dell Book / January 2009

Published by Bantam Dell
A Division of Random House, Inc.
New York, New York

Cover art by Hiro Kimura
Cover design by Marietta Anastassatos

ISBN 978-0-440-24388-5

Printed in the United States of America
Published simultaneously in Canada

www.bantamdell.com

OPM 10 9 8 7 6 5 4 3

This book is for Leslie Simon Lakin,
my amazing daughter-in-law,
with Love and Gratitude

Baby Boomers: the Third Act, or, Encore Careers

Act One:

Even though I didn't know it at the time, I followed every trend.

I was born in 1947.

In the 50's I was the perfect student in school.

In the 60's I was the perfect teenager.

Then in the 70's the perfect hippie.

Act Two:

By the 80's I became the perfect yuppie. By then I was married. It was all about money and spending.

In the 90's women's rights! I divorced and started my own corporation.

Act Three:

I married the right man. Now the two of us spend our time being useful to others. We began our encore career. We opened a bed-and-breakfast to bring pleasure to people in a beautiful place. I thought I was such a rebel all my life, but now I know I'm just a variation on what 70 million baby boomers have done with their lives.

—Guiamer Hiegert, co-owner with her husband, Gary, of the Lost Whale Inn, Trinidad, California

Introduction to Our Characters

GLADDY AND HER GLADIATORS

Gladys (Gladdy) Gold, 75 Our heroine and her funny, adorable, sometimes impossible partners:

Evelyn (Evvie) Markowitz, 73 Gladdy's sister. Logical, a regular Sherlock Holmes

Ida Franz, 71 Stubborn, mean, great for an in-your-face confrontation

Bella Fox, 83 The "shadow." She's so forgettable, she's perfect for surveillance, but smarter than you think

Sophie Meyerbeer, 80 Master of disguises, she lives for color-coordination

YENTAS, KIBITZERS, SUFFERERS: THE INHABITANTS OF PHASE TWO

Hy Binder, 88 A man of a thousand jokes, all of them tasteless

Lola Binder, 78 His wife, who hasn't a thought in her head that he hasn't put there

Denny Ryan, 42 The handyman: sweet, kind, mentally slow

Enya Slovak, 84 Survivor of "the camps" but never survived

Tessie Spankowitz, 56 Chubby, newly married to Sol

Millie Weiss, 85 Suffering with Alzheimer's

Irving Weiss, 86 Suffering because she's suffering

Mary Mueller, 60 Neighbor whose husband left her; nurse

Joe Markowitz, 75 Evvie's ex-husband

ODDBALLS AND FRUITCAKES

The Canadians, 30–40-ish Young, tan, and clueless
Sol Spankowitz, 79 Now married to Tessie
Dora Dooley, 81 Loves soap operas; Jack's neighbor

THE COP AND THE COP'S POP

Morgan (Morrie) Langford, 35 Tall, lanky, sweet, and smart
Jack Langford, 75 Handsome and romantic, Gladdy's boyfriend
Oz Washington, 36 Morrie's friend, also a police detective

THE LIBRARY MAVEN

Conchetta Aguilar, 38 Her Cuban coffee could grow hair on your chest

OTHER TENANTS

Barbi Stevens, 20-ish and
Casey Wright, 30-ish Cousins who moved from California
Yolanda Diaz, 22 Her English is bad, but her heart is good
Stanley Heyer, 85 Original builder of Lanai Gardens
Shirley Heyer, 80 His wife

INTERIM TENANTS PHASE TWO

Abe Waller, 85 Stanley's friend
Louise Bannister, 60-ish Femme fatale of Phase Six, interested in Jack

Gladdy's Glossary

Yiddish (meaning Jewish) came into being between the ninth and twelfth centuries in Germany as an adaptation of German dialect to the special uses of Jewish religious life.

In the early twentieth century, Yiddish was spoken by eleven million Jews in eastern Europe and the United States. Its use declined radically. However, lately there has been a renewed interest in embracing Yiddish once again as a connection to Jewish culture.

bubbala	endearing term for anyone you like, young or old; a tasty egg dish
bar mitzvah	at age thirteen a boy becomes a man after a ceremony accepting responsibility and religious law
kasha varnishkas	cooked groats and broad noodles
kibitzer	one who gives unwanted advice
kvetch	whine and complain
mezuzah	tiny box affixed to right door frame containing parchment with 22 lines of Deuteronomy

nachas	joy, especially from children
nosh	small meal
tsouris	trouble
schmegegi	buffoon, idiot
schlep	drag, carry, or haul sometimes unnecessary things
schmear	to spread like butter
Shabbes	Sabbath
tallis	prayer shawl
Torah	the five books of Moses—Talmud law
yarmulke	traditional skull cap worn at all times by observant Orthodox Jews
yenta	busybody

Building Q-Quinsana
mailboxes & elevator
IDA 319
GLADDY 317
SOPHIE 314
TESSIE & SOL 216
CASEY & BARBI 118
DENNY 119
IRV & MILLIE 114
ENYA 219
EVVIE 217
BELLA 216
HY & LOLA 214
MARY 314
mailboxes & elevator
Building P-Petunia
Lanai Gardens
Jack Langford lives in Phase Six.
L.H. MAESTRO

Getting Old
Is a Disaster

The construction worker embraced the storm, letting the torrents of rain sting his face and soak his denim jacket. His hard hat offered little protection. His sopping tool belt weighed him down. But he was content to be the last man on-site. He knew how to finish a job.

The dim work light flickered with the splatter of the raindrops. Bolts of lightning illuminated the wooden billboard staked across the construction site: Lanai Gardens Modern, new one- and two-bedroom garden apartments. Three acres of lawns, Six Phases pools, recreation rooms. Fort Lauderdale at its finest. Opening September 1958.

A few more minutes and he'd go home. To a hot shower, his bottle of whiskey, and the news on the radio. He was always fascinated by the news in his reluctantly adopted land.

Meticulous and compulsive, he was annoyed that he could not find the shovel that he'd last seen near the tall piles of gravel. He debated whether to keep searching. Never mind, he told himself. He would dig it out of the mud tomorrow in the daylight. All he had left to do was tarp over the rest of the tools that were too large to be put in the shed. Then, home.

The booming thunder kept him from hearing the stranger until the man was standing before him, wrapped in a huge black greatcoat with a wide-brimmed gray felt hat obscuring much of his face. The construction worker startled, his boot clanging into a pile of pipes. Then he relaxed. Probably someone lost, needing directions.

The stranger didn't move as he watched the construction worker lay the last corner of the tarp down.

"Are you lost?" the construction worker finally asked.

For a moment the stranger didn't answer. "No, I am not lost."

The construction worker straightened, bracing himself, forming his huge hands into fists. He always had a knack for smelling danger. "What do you want?"

"I want you to die," the stranger said with unchecked bitterness. "Now."

A huge bolt of lightning lit up the site and at the same moment they both saw the hard staff and sharp blade of the missing shovel less than five feet away, sticking up in the mud. The two men lunged for it. The stranger got to it first and raised the shovel high, preparing to charge, but the construction worker was too quick for him. He grabbed at the shovel, twisting it, pulling it away, using his more massive body to throw the stranger off balance. The stranger held tight, desperate to regain control.

Lightning and thunder were as witnesses to this dance of death. Huge earth movers stood as silent observers as well. The stranger grappled mightily in his battle to keep standing. But he fell. Then the construction worker fell. Rolling, tumbling, neither losing his grip on the shovel. Mud blinded them, covered them, slowing their movements, but hatred and the realization that only one of them would survive kept them going. Raw animal cries belched from their throats.

* * *

Several minutes later, the victor lifted his eyes to the sky so that the rain would rinse them. When he could see, he bent down and stared at the dead man's face. He smiled grimly, then glanced around, determining his next move.

The work light barely silhouetted the killer as he ripped off his clothes and exchanged them with the victim's. It was a difficult, tedious job. The clothes were soaked. The fit was bad. Carefully he searched his own pockets, making sure not to leave any evidence.

Then suddenly he saw it. And with a shudder, he

understood. He stared at the man's body as if memorizing something.

He dragged the dead man along the sodden gravel until he came to a plywood-framed trench. His rage returning, he kicked the body, edging him closer and closer to the hole, until the dead man tumbled and fell in. He picked up the shovel. Over and over, he pitched mud and gravel in on top of the dead man, and finally, anger spent, his body heaving with exhaustion, he stopped. He spit into the dirt and walked away.

1

Home

The airport van pulls up between the Phase Two buildings of our Lanai Gardens condominium complex. It's a mild September evening with just a bit of drizzle coming down. I'm home at last.

I sigh happily, getting out of the van. We are back from New York and I'm so glad to be on home ground again. At the same moment I wonder—where will we all go from here?

The girls and Jack pile out. I call them girls although there's not one of them under 73—my sister, Evvie, and our three friends, Bella, Sophie, and Ida. They're also my partners in our three-month-old private eye business.

My on-again-off-again boyfriend Jack Langford, now definitely on for good, graciously pays the van driver, since the girls manage to fumble through their purses long enough, with sheepish smiles, for Jack to take up the slack. He's immediately commandeered into lugging suitcases for each one of them. Suddenly my girls are helpless? Next year's birthday presents should be smelling salts in case they decide to take up fainting. But Jack good-naturedly carries Bella's bags, along with my sister Evvie's, up the elevator in the P building, to their second-floor apartments. Then he's down again and racing across the courtyard to schlep Sophie's and Ida's things up to the third floor of building Q. The girls are always one step in front of him, rushing to unlock their doors—their idea of being helpful.

I wait downstairs for the troop movements to cease. I can foresee that there will have to be some rules and regulations as to how much they use and abuse my guy now that we are officially an item. What a relief that the girls are finally happy about our relationship, after fighting it for so long. Or are they? We shall see.

Tiny Bella is all atwitter. "It's so nice to have a man around the house," she trills off-key, hanging over her balcony and waving down to me.

"I could get used to it," Sophie calls out from across the way, patting her skirt down, trying to smooth the creases out of her lime-green velour traveling outfit as Jack lugs her stuff into her apartment.

Ida insists on carrying one of her own bags, so she picks up her small carry-on. "I'm not helpless. Yet," she tells Jack as she grudgingly allows him to wheel the other case—which, from the way it is listing to one side, looks like she packed an elephant inside.

Some of our neighbors stick their heads out to see what's going on. Not a surprise. They always stick their noses into anything anyone does at any given moment. Newlyweds Tessie and Sol Spankowitz pop out of Tessie's apartment on the second floor of Q. Is it my imagination? The reluctant husband, Sol, looks like he shrank since he got married. Not like the Sol we knew as The Peeper, who scared all the women with his lecherous snooping. Super-sized Tessie looms over him, eating pistachio ice cream from a gallon carton.

Naturally Mr. Know-it-all, Hy Binder, appears in a flash, on the second-floor balcony of P. And right behind him is his parrot. I mean his wife, Lola.

"Look who's finally blown back into town," he calls out. "So how was the Big Apple? Anybody get mugged?"

"Yeah," mimics Lola, "anybody get mugged?"

Bella, standing two doors away, beams at the two of them. "No, but we were in a parade and got a medal. We had a fabulous time."

Sophie has to chime in, calling across, "And look who we met up with in New York. Our very own Jackie."

Uh-oh, here they go. My entire life will now be spilled out of the girls' eager mouths into our neighbors' ever-inquiring minds. But what can I do? I love them even though sometimes I want to paste duct tape across their lips.

Years ago, our husbands all dead—or in Evvie's case, divorced—we formed a new family unit sworn to care for one another through thick and thin. Mostly it's more thick than thin. We are an odd combination—mixed nuts is what Evvie calls us. My smart, fast-talking sister is also my best friend. Then there's Bella, our sweet, diminutive shadow, who follows us everywhere; roly-poly Sophie, who sees herself as a fashionista, mad about clothes; and last but definitely not least, Ida, our curmudgeon and self-proclaimed man-hater.

Bella is breathless in the face of everyone's attention. "Have *we* got a big announcement to make."

Even Ida is grinning.

By now Jack is at my side, puffing a bit, and as the new male alpha dog of our little pack, he decides to nip this bud off quickly. "Ladies," he calls out. "We've all had a very busy day. Time to get some rest."

"Yes," Evvie says with a tad of sarcasm, "let's get some rest." I can't believe my eyes. Immediately they scamper inside their own apartments, waving cheery good nights as they do. Doors one, two, three, and four—closed and not opened again. I hold my breath in case one of them changes her mind. Jack and I stand there and wait. And finally the looky-loos retreat, too. It seems as if the show is over. But I know better. They'll all be peering from behind their venetian blinds to see what we do next.

My very tall darling bends down to whisper to me, "I can feel their eyes burning holes in me."

"Not to worry," I tell him. "They'll get bored as soon as their favorite TV show comes on."

"What do we do now?" he asks. "Do you want me to come up with you?" A reasonable question since now we are officially a couple.

"It might be a better idea if we go to our own places alone. Let's meet tomorrow and figure out a plan of survival."

"Good idea. But I don't care if the yenta brigade is watching. I *am* going to kiss you good night."

I'm so lucky to have this wonderful man. For a brief moment I let myself think of the life-changing events that occurred when we were in New York. It will take a while for me to absorb the truth about my husband's murder so many years ago. But it was Jack who gave this truth as his finest gift to me. It has finally brought us together—forever more, I hope.

And Jack kisses me. Beautifully. Lovingly. I cling to him, not wanting the kiss to end.

From somewhere I hear a low smattering of applause.

* * *

Jack, suitcase in hand, walks to his building in Phase Six, his jacket collar turned up against the drizzling rain. He hears a sugary voice calling out to him from the third floor.

"Hi, honeybun. Up here."

He glances up to see Louise Bannister waving a

handkerchief. His upstairs neighbor is a flamboyant widow in her sixties, who, because she's a bottle redhead, is under the illusion she's a Rita Hayworth lookalike playing Gilda. As she leans over, her Chinese red robe reveals—as Jack assumes she planned—much cleavage.

"Welcome home," she says breathily. "We missed you while you were away."

"Thanks, Louise," he answers quietly so as not to disturb the other neighbors. She's hard to take, his overwrought femme fatale neighbor, but Jack has to admit that Louise is a darned good bridge player.

His eye is caught by two men coming toward the building. Both are dressed in the Orthodox Jewish tradition: black hat, suit, and vest; full beard and mustache.

Louise calls cheerily. "Abe, Stanley, look who's home."

To Jack, the two men, both in their eighties, seem an odd pair, but they're always together. Abe Waller squints, peering through his Coke-bottle eyeglasses, and nods in recognition. Stanley Heyer smiles openly and waves in greeting. Whereas Abe is big and burly, Stanley is small and feisty. Abe speaks rarely, and smiles little. Stanley is garrulous and upbeat.

"Well, gotta go, boys," Louise says, straightening. "See you soon, hon." She winks at Jack before turning to go back into her apartment.

"I can hardly wait," Jack says under his breath.

"Good trip?" Abe asks.

"Very," Jack answers.

"Just in time for some heavy rains," Stanley comments as he plucks a few dead leaves from a hibiscus bush nearby.

Jack smiles politely. Everyone knows that Stanley was one of the original developers of Lanai Gardens back in the late '50's. Apparently he liked it so much, he moved into one of the apartments himself when they officially opened.

The two men separate and go their own way. Stanley crosses the courtyard to building Y and Abe walks into his ground-floor apartment in Jack's building, Z.

Jack's finished gathering his mail and is about to head up the stairs when he hears another voice behind him. Dora Dooley pops out of her first-floor apartment. The petite eighty-one-year-old soap opera addict is always cold, and wears a bulky sweater and wool scarf no matter the weather. "It's about time you got back. My garbage has been piling up."

"I'll take care of it in the morning, Dora. I promise," he says in his usual patient voice.

Welcome home, he thinks ironically. Women to the right of me, women to the left of me. It's not going to be easy having some kind of life with Gladdy around here with all these clutching women.

* * *

The phone has already rung four times. Each of the girls called me to do what they always do: say good night, make plans for the next day, share last-minute thoughts of any kind. Bella is last. Finally, peace and quiet. It's wonderful.

The phone rings again. It's Jack this time. "I've been trying to reach you, but the phone's been busy."

I sigh. "It's a tradition."

"I can't stand not being with you. I wish it was morning already. Maybe I should wait until dark and sneak over. No one will see me."

"That's what you think. The native drums will beat your arrival. Got a better idea. Meet me at the bus stop at the main gate. Six-thirty A.M." This time he sighs. "Six A.M. all right. Until tomorrow, my dearest. I love you."

That night, I have a dream. In it, I see Jack sitting on the beach waving a Mai Tai at me. He's in swimming trunks wearing a big floppy sun hat and aviator sunglasses with a big grin on his face. He waves to me to join him. The girls and I are dancing around a maypole. All of them are sewed on to me with huge colored ribbons. As we dance I try to get their ribbons off. I want to pull free, but they won't let go of me. The music goes faster and faster and finally we all fall down.

I wake up in a sweat. I don't need Dr. Freud to tell me what that nightmare was about.

2

Mata Hari Explains It All

I am sitting at the bus stop in front of the main gate of Lanai Gardens, on Oakland Park Boulevard, at six-thirty A.M., waiting for Jack. It rained last night. Lucky thing I brought along a towel to dry the bench. But it's a lovely morning. It's been a long time since I got myself up this early. Nice to hear how quiet things are before the mobs of people start their day.

Someone has planted a new grouping of camellias in a wired fence in front of the big Lanai Gardens sign and I am enjoying admiring them. So far two buses have attempted to stop for me but I waved them on.

It's about a six-minute brisk stroll from my apartment to here, maybe ten from his. I look at my watch. I know Jack will be on time. Sure enough, here he comes at a sprint down the long road from Phase Six.

He hesitates at the strange sight of me. I give him a great big smile. He drops down next to me on the bench, puffing slightly. "Morning," I say.

"For a moment I thought it was Halloween. What's with the Mata Hari outfit?"

"You like the black hat with the veil? And the huge dark glasses? I picked them up at a garage sale years ago for a costume party."

"So, I take it you're in disguise?"

"You bet I am. I snuck out the back way behind the buildings. Nobody looks out those windows because all they'll ever see are the garbage trucks. You might consider the same route going back. If you want any privacy, that is."

"Is this the life you predict for us from now on? Sneaking around Dumpsters? Getting up at dawn? Meeting at bus benches?" He grins. "It's a little kinky, but if that's what turns you on."

He lifts the hat off my head and places it beside me. "The better to see you with, my dear," he leers. Then kisses me, and I kiss him right back. I feel like a teenager again, sneaking out to meet my boyfriend.

Another bus starts to slow. This time Jack waves it past. I didn't know we had such good public transportation around here.

Jack turns my shoulders so I am facing him directly. "I have an easy solution. Let's get married. After the girls get over the shock, everything will become wonderfully boring. They'll get used to us being together."

"Nice plan, but it won't work."

"Why not?"

"Maybe that's what I'm afraid of—the getting-used-to part. See how fast the girls got you to pay the cab bill and carry up their suitcases? Soon you'll graduate to 'Jackie, won't you please run down to Publix and get me a jar of Hellman's mayonnaise?' Or 'Jackie, I can't plug in my iron,' or 'Jackie, could you change a lightbulb for me? I just can't reach the socket.' Never mind they've been doing all these things for themselves for years before Mr. Easy Touch came to town."

Jack laughs and pulls me close and kisses me again. "You forget what I did last night. I just needed to snap my fingers and they jumped at my command."

I shake my head. "Foolish man. You just imagine you've got control."

"No, I know I have."

"You won't believe me? I'll prove it. We promised we'd have a celebration dinner when we got home. Okay. Tonight at the deli. It's what I like to call show and tell. After that, you'll understand what you're in for."

For a few moments we snuggle together, exchanging kisses and waving buses on. Early-morning traffic on the six-lane street is getting heavier. Maybe we'll die from the exhaust coming out of all those vehicles. Right now, I don't care. This is bliss.

"Yoo-hoo, Gladdy, Jackie!"

We turn around and, yes, here they come. My darling, predictable girls. They climb out of a car, thanking a neighbor for the lift to the main gate. They manage to pull a huge picnic basket after them. They are all smiles.

"You left so early, you didn't have time for breakfast," says Bella, placing the basket next to us on the bench. "So we put together a feast from all four of our almost-empty fridges."

Sophie says, "Just a little snack, a little cheese, some apples," as she pulls them out. "A *rugallah* or two. Some hard-boiled eggs..."

Ida adds, "Naturally a few bagels and cream cheese. Already *schmear*ed." She removes these, along with plastic silverware and napkins.

Evvie grins wickedly at me, enjoying the look of horror on Jack's face. "We even brought a thermos of coffee and cute little plastic cups. Just like a family picnic in the park."

"Don't bother getting up, Jackie," comments Ida. "We're fine just standing here."

I add my own evil grin as I ask him, "Shall I pour, dear, or will you?"

He grimaces. "How did you find us?"

"Piece of cake," says Ida. "Tessie was vacuuming the venetian blinds in her Florida room and she saw Gladdy sneak out. You know what an early riser Tessie is."

Evvie had this to add: "Denny was driving back from the flower market with new plants for his garden when he saw Gladdy sitting at the bus stop."

Bella giggles. "Lola was beating her rugs on the landing railing when she saw Jack run by."

My sister smiles ever so sweetly at me. "So we put one and one and one together and we realized two people we know and love were up early and we thought how nice it would be to bring them breakfast."

"How kind," I say, tossing an equal dose of saccharine back at her.

Another bus pulls up and we hear the whoosh of the pneumatic door opening. I see the expression on my sweetheart's face as he eyes the lowered steps to freedom.

I say, "Don't even think about it . . . Jackie."

3

The Pool

It is still early in the morning. We've had our impromptu breakfast at the bus stop bench. Jack went back to his condo. The girls and I have done our exercises, such as they are—a little walking, a little stretching, a lot of kvetching. Now we're ready for the pool. We're waiting for the "regulars" to arrive for our usual nine A.M. meet. Definition of swim: Ten minutes spent getting in the water, inch by inch, to get used to what they describe as excruciatingly cold. The pool is kept at 80 degrees, so don't ask. Then walking and talking as we slosh our way across from side to side in the shallow section.

Now we're sitting around one of the patio tables, its umbrella shielding us from too much sun, and using the time to go through all the private eye business mail that piled up while we were solving crimes in New York. We are job efficient. Sophie opens each envelope. Bella takes out each letter and flattens it for easy reading. She hands all bills to Evvie, who is our bookkeeper. We all read, discuss, and decide which pile to place the rest of the missives in. Our stacks include: boring, crackpots, whiners, just plain stupid, junk mail, and maybes.

Sophie holds up a letter. "Here's one from a guy who wants to know if our agency can find him a girlfriend. He says he's eighty years old and still a stud muffin."

"Hah!" says Evvie. "Boy, is he unclear on the concept. This is not a dating service."

Sophie crushes the letter and puts it in the "stupid" pile. "I'm sorry Jackie had to leave us right after our nice meal. How could his head hurt so bad that he had to lie down?"

Evvie laughs. "Gee, I wonder."

Poor Jack. The girls crowding over him on the bench was a little much, and the dropped bagel crumbs on his shirt were kind of irritating, but the last straw was when Bella, in her eagerness to serve, spilled orange juice all over his lap. I'd tried to warn him.

"What about this one?" Bella says, holding up a letter. "Her husband goes to the park every day, then gets lost and can't find his way home. She says he doesn't have Alzheimer's, it's just his short-term memory that's shot."

"I feel like we're Dear Abby with these letters," Evvie comments. "What does the woman want us to do? Pick him up every day and bring him home?"

Bella looks up, surprised. "How did you guess?"

"Tell her to get him a dog," Sophie suggests. "One with a good sense of direction."

"Or put a bell around his neck so his wife can find him." Bella giggles.

Ida says, "Listen to this. A woman in Margate says men keep stalking her and the police won't believe her."

"Men?" Evvie asks. "More than one?"

"Does she give any other information," I ask, "like her age?"

Evvie says, "The woman writes she's fifty-five and still a heartthrob." She glances at the enclosed photo, then passes it around for us to see.

"Maybe we should send her photo to that first guy whose letter we read," says Ida. "I smell a possible romance here. Heartthrob meet stud muffin."

Everyone giggles.

Evvie studies a newspaper article someone sent in a folded sheet of paper. "Hmm," she says, "get this. It's from last week's *Broward Journal*. While we were away." She laughs. "You're gonna love it. 'Grandpa Bandit eludes police again. A gray-haired elderly male has robbed six Fort Lauderdale banks to date. Bank officials and police, who arrived quickly on each scene, are baffled as to how the bandit has made his escape time after time.' Wow. And what about this?" She holds up the clipping for us to see. "Someone scribbled across the article with a heavy black marker. It says, 'Catch me if you can, girls!' "

This gets everyone's attention. "Girls?" Ida says. "He means us? How does he know who we are? Is that his way of hiring us to find him?"

Bella looks bemused. "But how will he pay us if we don't know who he is?"

"Well, he could afford it from his loot when we catch him," suggests pragmatic Sophie.

"But why would he want us to catch him?" Ida says. "I don't get it."

Evvie pulls something else out of the envelope. "Well, look at this!" She holds up a tiny green feather.

"I wonder what that's for," Sophie muses.

A green feather? A challenge to us to catch him? Why? I'm intrigued. "Put that one on our 'maybe' pile," I say.

"Someone's coming," Bella says. "I guess the pool gang is starting to arrive."

Evvie looks up and scowls. "Oh, no. Here we go again. I thought he'd have moved out by now."

Shuffling toward us is Evvie's ex-husband, Joe Markowitz. His head is bowed. It's sad to see what a broken man he's become, so unlike the virile, exciting soldier Evvie married after the war. Evvie has still not forgiven him for his sorry treatment of her during their marriage and she won't budge from her position. She hadn't seen him in more than fifteen years when, to Evvie's surprise and annoyance, Joe recently turned up and rented an apartment in Phase Three.

Joe reaches our table. "Hi, Evvie. I heard you were back. I just came over to say hello."

There's a stain on his shirt, which is buttoned wrong. And his shorts are badly wrinkled. His clothes look shabby, like he's given up caring. So unlike the meticulous dresser he used to be.

Evvie stiffens. Her tone is curt. "Okay. Hello. And good-bye. We're busy here."

I shoot her a look to tell her to lighten up a bit. She shrugs at me, meaning she doesn't want to. All our lives my sister and I have talked in body shorthand.

"Take a load off," Sophie says, offering Joe a chair that she pulls from an adjoining table. Evvie is not pleased.

"May I?" he asks pathetically.

Evvie gives him her shoulder. A very cold shoulder. More like ice.

He hesitates, then sits down. No one speaks. The girls pretend to busy themselves with opening envelopes as Joe stares hopelessly at Evvie.

Finally, Evvie's had enough. "Well? Speak your piece."

"I thought I could take you out to breakfast. I'd like to talk some things over with you."

"I've already had breakfast," she says loftily, not giving him an inch. "Anything you have to say, you can say in front of my beloved sister and my dear friends."

Ouch... when the drama queen wants to play mean, nobody does it better.

Joe stares at her with a hangdog expression. She

turns away. Joe stands up. "Maybe at a more convenient time."

The rest of us are silent when he leaves. Nobody will look at Evvie.

"What?" she says testily.

"Get up," I say. My tone is to remind her I'm the older sister. "Your parents brought you up with some manners. Go and say something kind to that poor man."

Evvie stands and puts her hands on her hips. "Or what? You gonna spank me? We're grown-ups now."

"Then act like one."

We glare at each other. Then she stomps off like a kid having a tantrum.

The girls applaud me. "Back to our mail," I say, but I'm glancing over my shoulder at Evvie catching up with Joe. He's obviously surprised and pleased, but trying not to show it.

I can barely hear their voices. "I'm sorry I was rude," she says, obviously not meaning it.

Joe shrugs. "Beggars can't be choosers. I accept your apology. But I bet Glad put you up to it."

Evvie has the decency to blush.

Joe says, "She always was nicer to me."

Isn't that the truth? Evvie, in true sisterly loyalty, humphs. "Look, Joe, I just want to say, even though you've moved here, there's no reason for you to hang out with me. I have a life and it doesn't need you in it."

"I'm sorry you feel that way. I'll try to stay out of your hair," he says sadly.

"That's that, then. See you around."

I turn around quickly, so Evvie wouldn't see me spying.

Evvie walks away and heads for her usual seat around the pool, her shoulder still stiff. I assume her attitude is as kind as he deserves.

* * *

"Oh, goody, here comes the gang," Bella announces. She sweeps the piles of mail into a basket and heads for our appointed lounge chairs, which are around the three-foot-deep pool mark. These seating arrangements have been set in stone for years.

Sure enough, as if a bell rang, the usual denizens begin to arrive from all directions. The Canadians stake out their camp at the deep end, near the diving board. Hy and Lola plop down on their chaises, near the shallow end. Tessie and her new husband, Sol, who used to swim in Phase Three, take their seats next to the couple.

Barbi Stevens and her cousin Casey Wright are across the pool, directly opposite them. They immediately start rubbing sunblock on each other's bodies. My girls watch with fascination, knowing the "cousins'" secret sexual persuasion.

Oh, but here's something very new since we've been away. Irving Weiss arrives with Mary Mueller. They are carrying snacks, towels, and books to read. He now has a chaise next to hers. Irving, whose life has changed radically since his Millie went into an Alzheimer's unit at a local nursing home—Irving, who's always avoided the sun like a plague—now has become a worshipper?

There are the usual morning greetings.

As I walk past them to join Evvie at our usual spot, I have to ask. "How is Millie?"

Mary's eyes tell me what I know already. But Irving is still in denial. "Mary drives me over there every day. I stay all afternoon by her side. She seems to be doing a little better each time I see her. Sometimes I think my Millie recognizes me."

I look around. I can see there are mixed reactions to this new "couple." I know everyone feels compassion for Irving, but there are negative responses to his spending so much time with Mary. Mary must be lonely, too, since her husband left her. Speculating on what they are doing or not doing together? I shake my head. What do they want from him? That he should sit in his apartment and cry all day?

Everyone settles in. Tessie drags a reluctant Sol into the pool. She splashes him playfully, he cringes, then she takes off, doing laps. Hefty as she might be, Tessie is lightness itself as she swims laps up and down the pool.

The Canadians, the "snowbirds" who come each year during the winter, read copies of their back-home newspapers and chat quietly amongst themselves.

Lola immerses herself in one of her endless collection of romance novels. Hy always leers at their lurid bodice-revealing covers. I bet they secretly turn him on.

Casey and Barbi have their laptops open and their hands fly across the keys.

Mary reads medical journals. She used to be a nurse and even though she's retired, she likes to keep up. Irving stares into space. By his mournful expression, he must be thinking of Millie.

The girls are already in the pool. Ida and Evvie are doing kicking exercises along the edge. Bella and Sophie are humming little ditties from old musicals or other songs they remember, wiggling their fingers in time as they walk back and forth in two feet of water—their idea of strenuous exercise. I recognize the tune as "Tiptoe Through the Tulips." Tiny Tim, of course.

Hy, like some bird of prey, peruses the group, looking for mischief. His wicked, paunchy face lights on me. The perfect target. Not that I don't expect it. I hide behind my new Janet Evanovich mystery. Her books always make me laugh out loud. I brace myself. With Hy on the attack, there will be no laughter from me this morning. Only aggravation.

"So, Gladdy," he calls out, loud enough for everyone to hear. "What's the big news announcement? Bella dropped a spicy tidbit the other day. You and Jack Langford maybe ready to tie the knot?"

Trust me, I don't have to say anything. My girls will do all the talking.

Sure enough, they hop out of the pool, dripping and smiling, ready to reveal my secrets to one and all. Except for Evvie, who will try to remain loyal . . . until she, too, will succumb to the great idol, Gossip.

Sophie starts it. "Well, you know they broke up."

Bella: "And then they made up."

Sophie: "And broke up again."

Ida: "Get to the point already. They are definitely an item and plans may soon be in the making."

I pretend to read my book, but it's impossible to concentrate. I have to keep alert for damage control.

Barbi and Casey look amused. The Canadians always listen to our repartee; to them I imagine it's something like going on safari and watching the baboons at play. Terribly droll, what?

Bella blathers on. "Gladdy doesn't have a ring, yet, but maybe . . ."

I shudder. I cannot bear the idea of my very private life being thrown to the hyenas. I pull my floppy sun hat farther down on my face.

Sophie adds, "We're hoping to hear dates being mentioned . . . soon."

Ida says smugly, "A formal engagement might be announced one of these days."

Sophie jumps back in. "With a great big party possibly to follow. We think."

Hy is chafing at the bit. He jumps up, his annoyance running over. "So? So? This is your idea of news? Maybe this. Maybe then. Maybe soon. Maybe later. It's like pulling teeth getting facts out of any of you. Gladdy, 'fess up."

Everyone turns to stare at me. I bet I'm doing a

perfect imitation of a deer caught in the headlights of a two-ton semi. I remain in that trance, hoping it will be over soon and they'll turn on somebody else.

Evvie grins, knowing how much my silence is annoying Hy. "Believe me, you'll be the first, or maybe the last, to find out."

Lola the puppet bounces up and down with joy. "You can tell us. When's the wedding date?"

That's it. Time to stop this. I turn to Hy, smiling insipidly. "So, Hy, no joke today? I sure missed your jokes while I was away."

What can I say? It's either that or me, and I want out of the spotlight.

Hy bows like the bantam cock he is, and holds his arms aloft, embracing everyone with his largesse. "Funny you should ask. I'm reminded of this joke. I look around me, and I see couples. Newly married couples." He indicates Sol and Tessie, who simper back. "New sorts of couples." He looks toward Irving and Mary. Irving looks embarrassed. Mary throws him a dirty look. "And now love has resprouted. Phase Six melds with Phase Two."

That's aimed at me. I smile, though it's more like a grimace.

Hy pulls Lola up. I guess this routine needs a stooge.

"There's this loving couple, see? Let's call them Hy and Lola." He grins.

Isn't he the clever one? Meet Romeo and Juliet of Transylvania.

"They're sitting on the couch in front of the TV and suddenly Hy puts his arms around her."

Hy does just that. He pinches Lola for a response, and by golly, she says, "Oh, darling, how nice."

"His arm moves down her shoulder to her waist." His actions continue to follow his words.

I pray he doesn't make his story X-rated.

He pinches Lola for the next response. I guess they've been rehearsing.

She goo-goo-eyes him and says, "I love it, darling, keep going."

Hy, the man and the character, is now moving down toward her bony hips. Believe me, I'm holding my breath. He wiggles his fingers along her legs.

"Oooh, aah," she gurgles. "Don't stop."

His hand is moving dangerously close to no-man's-land. I grin, amused by my thought.

Hy, the narrator, says dramatically, "And Hy stops."

Lola moans like she's got indigestion or something. But I think she is trying to act out ecstasy. "Ooh, my precious, why did you stop?"

Hy lifts his hand aloft, using his sunscreen as a prop. "Because I found the clicker."

There is a long moment of quiet. Then, as one by one we get it, the applause builds to a smatter.

I hope this dangerous duo of daftness isn't going to be a regular act.

Suddenly there is a huge cloudburst and rain starts to fall. Hoorah, saved by the weather. We all grab our things and run home before it becomes worse and we get soaked.

* * *

But when I reach my apartment, it hits me—what was different about the pool scene today. Someone was missing. Enya, our concentration camp survivor, who is always there, reading a book and never talking to anyone, didn't show up. She never misses a day. I hope nothing happened to her while we were away.

* * *

It was all confusion. Driving rain and impenetrable fog. Bodies pushed every which way, prodded by bayonets, useless struggling, nowhere to run, lights zigzagging, pinning them down, their pathetic screaming turned into wailing. Clutching their loved ones, their soggy flesh herded, smashed together until they were one mass of seething humanity. Hopeless.

Enya wakes up. She knows she should get up, but she can't. Her body *feels* paralyzed.

The nightmares have come back.

4

Dance Around the Dumpsters

Jack covers his ears against the noise of the garbage trucks as they empty the trash behind my building. It's early afternoon and once again I've snuck away from the girls to be with him. We have yet to get enough time alone to make some plans.

"I thought you were kidding when you said we should meet here," he shouts.

Between the clatter of the garbage trucks and the heavy traffic on this back road and the ambulances that speed by in a direct route to the hospital across the way, we can hardly hear each other.

"Well, I figured no one would think to look for us in this place, but then again, I thought we were safe at the front gate," I yell back at him. "You've already learned there's hardly any way to have a private conversation around my girls."

"We're not in jail, you know. We could have met off the premises." He grimaces as one of the trash men heavily drops the lid of the Dumpster nearby.

"Yes, but we have a visitor coming soon, so it wouldn't have been convenient. Guess who."

"Somebody I know?"

"Intimately."

"Really? Morrie?"

I nod. He looks at me, surprised. "My son, the cop, does house calls? I'm impressed."

"Well. Not quite. He's giving a lecture in the main clubhouse on avoiding senior scams and I asked him to drop by afterward to chat with us about an odd letter we received from the man who calls himself Grandpa Bandit.

"I've already filled him in on the phone about the challenge thrown down to us. Naturally, Morrie's interested in the article sent to us with the man's handwriting on it. He's coming by to pick it up. Care to listen in?"

"Sure. Why not."

I give him a hug. "So, quick, let's get to our own agenda. We need a plan."

"I have a plan. We go out to dinner. Afterward, we go to my place. Plain and simple."

"You mean I sneak away and come over? I can walk this back route most of the way." I pause. "Wait, that's a problem. I have to tell someone where I'll be. If they keep phoning and I don't answer, they'll panic."

"That's not what I mean. No more hiding. Tell them you will be with me tonight. All night."

I am pleasantly surprised and a little shocked. "Are you sure you want to go so public? You may regret it . . ."

He tips my chin up so I can gaze into his eyes. Those gorgeous blue eyes that I want to sink into. "Chicken," he says sweetly.

He knows what I'm thinking. He always knows what I'm thinking. We have yet to consummate our love. Not for lack of trying to find an opportunity, though.

"Be brave, my sweet," he continues. "Since you won't marry and make an honest man of me, then you have to deal with being a fallen woman."

"Are you sure?" I ask tentatively.

"Yes!" he cries out dramatically. "Shout it out. Be strong. Who cares if the whole world knows!"

"Gladdy. Jackie. Hello down there." We hear Bella's lilting voice from up above. We look and she is half-hanging out of her Florida back room window on the third floor. "Morrie got done early and he's already here. We're waiting for you two lovebirds to finish sparking."

Sparking? I haven't heard that obsolete word since the 1930's. Is Jack really turning purple, or am I imagining it?

He sputters, "How do they do it? How do they always know where we are and what we're doing?"

I grin. "They just do. That's what makes them such good private eyes."

I call up to Bella, "We're on our way."

I start to walk toward the front of the building.

"Come on, Jackie, your cover's blown. Now's your chance to tell the whole world, including your son, that we're sleeping together tonight."

* * *

Young, handsome Detective Morgan "Morrie" Langford is waiting for us, seated at a patio table on the lawn, with my girls gazing at him adoringly. Which makes him most uncomfortable. He is dressed casually for his lecture today. Chinos and a cotton plaid shirt and a tie, instead of the usual suit.

Whenever I gaze at him, I see the young man my Jack used to be. Many a proud grandma in Lanai Gardens has shoved photos of their unmarried granddaughters into his unwilling hands, hoping to make a match. He hasn't ever followed up. Very wise, I'd say. I've seen some of those granddaughters.

Spotting us, Bella and Sophie immediately jump up and take each of Jack's arms and cuddle into him. They lead him to an empty chair. Poor darling—trapped again.

Morrie is clearly surprised to see his father being greeted so familiarly. But before Morrie can open his mouth, Jack waves his arms at him, warning him. *Don't ask. I'll fill you in later.*

Our police detective shrugs. I guess he isn't used to seeing his dad flustered.

"Hand Morrie what we've got," I tell Evvie in my business voice. She takes the article as well as the envelope and offers both to him.

"Thanks," he says. He briefly glances at the article, then places the papers in his shirt pocket. "We'll look into it." He changes gears. "So, girls, how are you all?"

"Wait just a minute. Not so fast," I say. "After all, Grandpa Bandit reached out to *us*."

"Don't bother your pretty little heads. It's minor stuff."

I persist. "Maybe we can help you catch him."

"Don't waste your energy. This is small potatoes."

Evvie chimes in. "But according to that newspaper article he's robbed six banks. Isn't that a big deal?"

"This is police business," Morrie says severely, obviously trying to end the conversation.

Don't bother our pretty little heads? Translation: We should mind our own business. What a put-down. Yet again our earlier successes as private eyes mean nothing. And why? Because of the usual prejudicial attitudes—we're old, and assumed senile. And invisible. Who would take us seriously? Even Morrie still doesn't get it—and he's seen us in action. But that's precisely why we succeed—people don't see us as a threat. They assume we've lost our marbles. That's why they're careless of what they say around us. And then we nail them.

"But it's our case," Sophie says stubbornly, as she refills Morrie's glass of iced tea.

He's just as stubborn. "You have no case."

"Yes, we do, now." Bella says sweetly. She

reaches over to pick an imaginary bit of lint off his shirt.

Morrie is getting hot under the collar. "You have no client. A client meets with you face-to-face."

Bella smiles at his naiveté. "Now, isn't that silly? If he met with us, we'd know who he is."

Sophie jumps in. "Yeah, and we wouldn't have a case anymore."

"Where is it written that he hired you?" Morrie crosses his arms, determined not to let us steamroll him, which we are about to do.

Ida points. "In the article that you just pocketed. In his very own handwriting. He wants us to catch him, not you."

"Yeah," says Bella. "If he wanted you to catch him, he'd have written to you."

Morrie's face stiffens. Jack shakes his head, trying to signal his son. I can tell he's warning him to get out while he can. But Morrie blunders on. "So where's your retainer?"

Bella smiles. "Silly. We work on a handshake deal." She stops to think about what she's said. "That is, we'll shake his hand when we find him."

Morrie is behaving oddly—for him. He's usually not so nervous around us. He's hiding something. I wonder what's going on. I can tell by Jack's expression he has the same impression.

"Look," Morrie blurts as he stands up, "somebody is pulling your leg. Somebody you know sent you the clipping as a gag."

That stops us for a moment, then Evvie glances at me, both of us remembering. "Take a look in the envelope," she says. "You missed something."

Puzzled, Morrie opens the envelope and sees the tiny green feather. By the way his face goes from tan to red to gray, we've hit gold.

"That wasn't in the newspaper, was it?" Evvie says knowingly. "That's the information the police kept back."

"Bingo," I say. "Your bandit has thrown down his gauntlet, so to speak. In fact," I add, "do us a big favor, since we're so old and helpless, mail me a list of the banks that our client robbed, and their addresses."

Morrie is sputtering by now. "Wait just one minute..."

He's right, of course. The police don't want civilians pursuing cases on their own. They want cooperation and information, not meddling. Or interfering in a way that might compromise their investigation or their evidence. It's not just the bandit who's thrown down the gauntlet; so has Morrie, wanting us to keep out of it.

We are at an impasse.

Jack says, "Son, why don't you and I grab a cup of coffee and let the girls do what they are so good at—finding out anything and everything they set their minds to."

With a last glance at me, he winks and the two men take off. That is, as soon as Jack can get Sophie and Bella to let go of his arms.

I call after him, "Jack, you have an announcement to make. Remember?"

He grins. "Enough excitement for one morning. Later."

I laugh. The girls want to know what's so funny. I give them the same answer: "Later."

5

Early Birds

The girls are not happy. They're dressed for going out but so far they are getting nowhere. We stand in front of my building waiting for Jack to pick us up. It rained all day and there are puddles everywhere, so we are grouped in a tight circle under the eaves, where the ground is dry. Sophie's pantsuit is a study in peach. From top to toes, she is every shade imaginable. Even to her latest hair dye, sort of peachy brown. Bella is also monochromatic—all in pale gray, which matches her hair as well. The two of them color coordinate whenever we go out. Evvie, on the other hand, is in one of her many flamboyant caftans—a riot of color, no pastels for her. Her hair is still red, but the gray is coming back slowly. Ida—well, Ida dresses as if she's standing under a thundercloud. Very dark. Plain. No frills, no jewelry for our Ida. I'm in my usual beiges, tans, and whites, with a coral blouse and silk scarf.

We are already late. Bella couldn't find her glasses. Sophie couldn't decide between her beige flats or her peach sandals. It's already four-thirty, and I told Jack to be here by four. It's our first outing as a couple with the girls and I'm nervous enough about the outcome. The girls are already grumpy, not a good sign.

Much tapping of feet and glancing at watches. Finally Jack's vintage Cadillac casually pulls over to pick us up, just before five.

"Hi, ladies," he says, getting out and opening all the car doors. The girls climb in, not looking at him. Ida mumbles, "It's about time."

Jack looks at me and I shrug and say, "Go ahead, ask it. I know you're dying to."

"Why does anyone want to eat at four-thirty?"

"You'll see." I realize that Sophie and Bella have already scrunched their way into the front seat, so I don't get to sit next to my "date." I struggle to fit myself in back with Evvie and Ida. Thank goodness the Caddie is large and roomy.

* * *

We stand on the long, long, long, long line snaked around the strip mall parking lot adjacent to our favorite deli, the Continental, and apparently everyone's else's, too. Ida taps her foot. Bella, as usual, peers into every store window as we pass. Evvie is using my back as a desk, scribbling her latest movie review for the next issue of her Lanai

Gardens newsletter. Jack stands next to me, his shoulders slumped, his eyes glassy. The line is hardly moving.

I gesture at the crowd. "Now you know. Short lines at four. Chaos after five."

Sophie adds, "And the prices are lower."

Bella pipes up, "And the kasha varnishkas sell out fast."

"I am more than willing to go somewhere else and pay whatever extra it costs." Jack is sweating. He takes his jacket off.

"No way," says Ida. "We refuse to be beholden to you. We are independent women and pay our own way."

"At least Evvie is smiling," he says, grasping at straws.

Evvie looks up from her notebook. "That's because I'm writing about George Clooney, that hottie."

After yet another ten sweltering, humid minutes, we finally get inside.

I see Jack glance around. He whispers to me, "Not many men here."

"You need reinforcements?" I ask.

"I might." He squeezes my hand. "I'd love to kiss your cheek but I don't want to embarrass you."

I laugh. "Honey, in this place, embarrassment knows no bounds."

We get our favorite waitress, Velma, formerly of Flatbush, Brooklyn. Thin as a blade of sawgrass. Greasy hairstyle circa 1950's, very puffy and large.

Nickname: Motormouth. The girls like her because she always makes sure to give them big portions of dessert. She is thrilled to see us.

As she shoves the menus at us, she says, "So where you guys been? I thought you all died."

"Not yet," Bella comments mildly. The girls are used to Velma's hyperbole.

"We took a vacation." Sophie bites off a chunk of sour pickle from a dish of coleslaw and assorted pickles already on our table.

Velma, not much of a listener, runs along her own track. "Boy, you missed some excitement around here. Edna Glatz from Hawaiian Gardens choked on a bone and almost expired before our very eyes."

"No!" Sophie and Bella chorus in horror, as Jack attempts to concentrate on the three-foot-high plastic menu.

"If it wasn't for our manager, Mr. Kay, who knew the Heimlich maneuver, we would have a dead duck on our floor. Instead of on a plate." She chuckles at her joke.

I can see other customers waggling their fingers to get Velma's attention, but Velma loves to talk and is on a roll. "And one day Mary Lou Feeney's great-grandchild upchucked on their table, all over the *plat de jour* and her new flowered sundress. Don't ask."

"Could we order?" Jack asks morosely.

Velma is pulled up short by this interruption of her news report. She pretends to do a double take, as if seeing him for the first time. She turns seductive. Her idea of sexy is batting her eyelashes.

"I didn't notice you have a man with you. And who is this Mr. Gorgeous?"

Jack blushes. I can tell that he's sorry now that he opened his mouth. Here we go.

Ida can't resist. "Meet Gladdy's intended. Jack, meet Velma."

Nor can Bella. "We're here to celebrate."

"Gedouddahere!" Velma screeches with excitement. She flashes a huge mouthful of horsy teeth at me. "Congratulations! This calls for an announcement!" She picks up a glass and a spoon and turns to the rest of the room. I grab her by her apron strings and tug hard. She turns back.

I glare. "No announcements. Please."

Velma reluctantly replaces the glass and spoon. She sniffs loudly. "I guess I'll take your orders now."

* * *

Dinner manages to glide along without too many annoyances. Sophie sends her chicken back—"Too tough." Ida complains her brisket is stringy. Evvie doesn't take her eyes off me while I'm looking at Jack and Jack is looking back at me. Usually I can read my sister's expression, but not tonight. Everyone's cheerful but there is an underlying tension. Kind of like waiting for the other shoe to drop. I am on edge wondering if Jack is going to make his promised announcement about my going home with him tonight. I'm hoping he doesn't.

The checks arrive. Velma gives them out one at a time, making goo-goo eyes at Jack when she hands him his. The girls get into their usual discussion about tips. They pull out their little tip chart and make their decision. Velma always gets their best. Twelve percent.

Jack says, "I really do want to treat all of you."

I add, "And I agree. In honor of our celebration tonight."

"Nonsense," says Ida. "I told you, we pay our own way." She reaches into her purse and takes out her share.

Bella follows suit, digging down into her pockets. She pulls out crumpled-up dollar bills along with many, many coins, which she counts aloud.

Evvie hands him her check and folds her hands. She smiles sweetly at Jack. "I don't mind being treated on occasion."

Sophie grapples through her purse. Then again. And again. She throws up her hands in disgust. "I can't believe it. I left my wallet at home."

"Shh," Bella cries out. "I lost count. Now I have to start again." With that she flails her arms and accidentally knocks her pile of coins onto the floor.

Jack gallantly stoops down to pick them up.

While he is down there on his knees, reaching under the table, a drumroll sounds. More like someone banging on a pot. Even though it's still light outside, someone is flashing the light switches off and on. And a huge chorus of voices begins to sing, "Happy engagement to Jack and Gladdy, happy engagement to them . . ."

Jack, caught on his knees as if he is in proposal mode, practically cracks his skull leaping out from under the table.

All the diners in the restaurant burst into applause.

I shrug at Jack and point to the huge strawberry cheesecake lit with candles that Velma holds aloft as she comes toward us.

* * *

The bill is finally paid. By Jack. Why am I not surprised? The girls are about to stand up, when Jack announces. "Ladies, I have something to tell you."

I gasp. I can't believe he's actually going to do it. All eyes look to him expectantly. "Glad won't be going straight home tonight. I'll drop you all off, then Gladdy and I will go to my apartment."

Sophie and Bella don't get it right away. When Bella does, she blushes. Ida's head drops down as she rips what's left of the bread on her plate into little pieces. Sophie giggles. Evvie slyly smiles.

The awkward silence that follows is broken by Mr. Kay, the manager, who walks over to our table and hands me a plain white envelope. "Mrs. Gold, a gentleman gave this to me on his way out and asked me to deliver it to you."

I open it as the girls begin to come out of their comatose state. Inside is a plain white piece of paper folded in thirds. As I take it out a small green feather flutters onto the table. I pick it up as I read from the scrawled note, " 'Getting old ain't for sissies. Catch me if you can.' " There's more but the girls are already on their feet. I shove the note and feather in my purse and stand.

Bella fairly swoons. "Another note from the Grandpa Bandit!"

To Jack's astonishment, we all race for the door. Once outside we look around the parking lot.

"Look!" Evvie shouts.

We see a hand waving to us from the darkened window of a senior pickup van leaving the shopping center. We hurry to the curb, but are too late. Evvie quickly grabs her pen and takes down the model and license number of the van.

Back in the restaurant again, we question the manager. But all Mr. Kay can say is he was an old guy with gray hair. Figures.

6

Jack's Place

From Jack's grinning and whistling, I gather the girls didn't throw him off as much as I feared. I guess the letter from the bandit with its green feather cushioned the shock of his announcement.

We dropped the girls off at Phase Two, thinking who knows what thoughts as they stared after us. Jack parked his car, and now we stroll, hand in hand, toward his apartment building. All I have brought to this evening's adventure is my toothbrush. I wish I'd had time to put on something slinky (not that I have much in that line). Or even a dab of perfume. But never mind, it's a beautiful evening. The storm clouds still hover, but the sky has striations of reds amongst the deep purplish-blues. And I'm with my darling man.

Jack swings my arm with his, like some happy five-year-old on his way to a party. "See how easy this will be?" Now he's the party clown putting on a smiley face for the birthday girl. His mood is contagious. I feel like a kid, too. I am fairly skipping along with him.

We hurry upstairs to his apartment on the second floor. Jack turns the key in the lock. I glance around discreetly, relieved to see that no one is watching. The grounds are fairly empty since it is dinnertime for most people—those who don't live by early-bird-special rules.

Jack's voice goes singsong. "I know what you're thinking."

I laugh. "I know you know."

Once we're inside, he makes a demonstration of double locking the doors. Dramatically, he pulls down the blinds in each of the rooms. "No one and nothing will spoil this evening. I give you my promise."

"And I'll hold you to it." I watch his shenanigans with delight. He's so good to be with. I feel so blessed. I also feel a little nervous about where this is going.

He turns off the phone ringer with a flourish. "There! We are alone in our little pleasure-dome cocoon. Nothing will disturb us."

With that he grabs me and kisses me, holding me tight to him. It's a wonderful kiss, and the hug that goes with it feels like it may go on forever. I hope it does. We finally come up for air.

"Need a drink for courage?" he asks me.

"No," I whisper, trying to catch my breath.

We zigzag our way to the couch. "Shall I tear off

our clothes before or after we make it to the bed?" Jack says this as he's unbuttoning his shirt.

"Wait," I say eagerly. "We need to exorcise old demons."

"Go on, exorcise away." Jack kicks off his shoes.

I am worried. Not so much about the act we intend to consummate—well, that, too, a little. My concern is, what will interrupt us this time? Something has on every other occasion. I have to voice it out loud. "May I remind you that in Pago Pago, just as were about to have at it, we received a fax that changed our plans immediately . . ."

"How could I forget?" Jack gestures expansively with his hands. "No fax machine here. No problem."

"And our silly fight that kept us apart for so long."

"Over and forgotten."

"In your New York hotel room, the phone rang, once again interrupting us with important news that had to be dealt with instantaneously."

"Phone's turned off. No news can find us."

I listen. The silence is wonderful.

"Nothing's going to intrude. I'm telling you."

"It will. I know it will."

"Nonsense." He pulls me down on the couch. Then onto his lap. "Thank God."

"Why 'Thank God'?"

"Because I don't need Viagra."

Kiss. Kiss. Ummn, more . . .

"Lucky us to have each other."

I snuggle closer into his arms. "No girls to interrupt."

"No thinking about the girls allowed. Shut it down."

"Done."

More kissing and murmuring of silly nothings. How happy can one be? His body fits so well with mine. I let myself sink into the pleasure of the moment. It's been so long...

The doorbell rings.

We freeze.

I moan, "No..."

He echoes my "No," then shakes his head. "I will not answer it."

We both jump up so quickly that we bang heads.

The doorbell rings again. Jack mutters irritably, "I am absolutely not opening that door."

The ringing is now followed by knocking and then a seductive female voice calling, "Come on, Jack, I know you're in there."

Now it's Jack's turn to moan.

Another voice is heard. A high-pitched one. "It's seven o'clock."

And yet another female voice, a wispy one. "I brought the cards."

Jack gets off the coach. I roll over into a sitting position, straightening my dress as best I can.

He whispers to me, "Don't move, they'll go away."

"Who are they?" I ask.

"My bridge partners."

A few moments later, Jack's cell phone rings from a side table, once again startling us. Jack snarls. "They aren't giving up." He glares at it as the phone keeps ringing, then finally it stops.

We wait breathlessly. Silence. He smiles at me, sensing victory, then grimaces as the pounding on the door begins again.

We look at each other. No use. Jack says, "One thing you can say about bridge players, they are tenacious!"

Moving to the door, he runs his fingers through his hair and turns on the lights. "Damn, damn, damn..."

He struggles with the double lock, cursing. When he finally opens it, there is an immediate flurry of activity. One woman, nice-looking, in her fifties, wearing navy blue sweats, lugs in a small square folding table. Two other women carry packages. One of them, a redhead wearing a rather sexy sundress with a jungle/tiger print, moves easily to the kitchen. The one following her is taller and big-boned. Even though they see me sitting there, none of them has the decency to be embarrassed.

The sexy voice calls out, "We brought all the snacks this time because we knew you didn't have time to shop."

The taller one adds, "Mostly pretzels and chips."

As if in a trance Jack helps the woman in blue sweats unfold the card table.

I sit up straighter on the couch, trying to look

casual and relaxed although I am neither. I'm actually frustrated and annoyed. I cross and recross my legs. This can't be happening again. It can't. Is this some cosmic joke?

Finally the trio turns to stare at me. The sexy woman stands much too close to Jack, who looks beyond sheepish.

"Hi," says the sexpot. "I'm Louise Bannister." With that dress, I expect her to growl.

The tall woman says, "I'm Carmel Graves, from one flight up."

And blue sweats waves cheerfully. "I'm Carol Ann Gutsch from two doors down."

"My bridge partners," says Jack, shamefacedly. "Tonight's our usual game night. I guess I forgot."

I get up from the couch and move on shaky legs. "I'm Gladdy Gold," I manage to say, my voice breaking. I can't even look at Jack. "I was just leaving," I stammer.

"No, don't," Jack says, holding tightly to my arm. He faces the trio of card players. "I'm terribly sorry, but I made other plans tonight."

"So I see," says Ms. Bannister, assessing her competition. "I wish you'd called. I could have made other arrangements and not wasted my evening."

Carol Ann behaves as if someone ran over her pet cat. "I was so looking forward to tonight. I circled it three times on my calendar."

Carmel also seems crestfallen. "Maybe I could still make it to the movies if I can find someone to drive me. I don't see too well at night."

They look to Jack, waiting. What a bunch. The man-eater is trying to make him feel guilty because such a hot tootsie could have filled her dance card over and over again.

Carol Ann is making him feel even guiltier about her lonely night ahead, and Carmel is playing the "I'm so needy" card. Jack doesn't have a chance.

I touch his shoulder and shake my head. I say to the group, "Please, don't let me upset your plans." I give Jack a quick peck on the cheek and leave.

* * *

As I hurry toward the stairwell, Jack is suddenly behind me. "Gladdy, wait."

"Let me know who wins." I can barely stifle my sarcasm.

"I am going to insist we play another night. Come back in. Please." He tries to pull me into his arms, but the mood is gone. Talk about totally.

"I can't. Not right now. I have a splitting headache."

Jack tries for a smile. "Can't you see the humor in this?"

And I do. I laugh softly. Jack joins in. He says, "You think there's some conspiracy keeping us apart?"

"Probably. Go back inside before your harem girls melt into a pool of self-pitying tears. And beat the hell out of them. In cards, I mean."

He kisses me.

I warn him, "And watch out for the tigress in there. She's out to devour you."

I'm still laughing as I dash down the stairs.

Suddenly, the skies open. It's raining and of course I didn't bring an umbrella. Then I realize I left my toothbrush at Jack's. I slosh my way home, my feet getting wetter and wetter in my open heels. All the way I am giggling and muttering like a madwoman. "I cannot believe this, I absolutely, positively cannot believe this . . ."

7

Enya in Trouble

Enya thrashes about in her bed in the throes of a terrible nightmare.

Closer and closer. They are coming at last. There is no place to hide or to run. Huddled in their bedroom, the four of them cannot look at one another because the truth will be revealed in their eyes—they are doomed. Eyes, eyes. She sees his *eyes and the terrible scar. Why is there no help? The pounding rain will drown them. They are hammering on her door. No escape.*

* * *

As I dejectedly arrive back at my building, I am surprised to find many people holding umbrellas and standing around. I look up and see Ida on the balcony of our floor, staring across the courtyard parking area to the building opposite. She is holding a newspaper over her head against the rain. I turn to find out what's caught her interest.

Denny, our handyman, dressed in rain gear, is standing in front of his apartment, staring up at the second floor. Evvie and Bella are on the walkway in front of Enya's apartment, 219, at the end of their floor. At the opposite end of the landing, Hy and Lola are standing in their doorway, whispering and gesturing.

Evvie is pounding on Enya's door. "Enya. Open up. Please?" Bella huddles right behind her.

I am up the stairs in moments, joining them. "What's going on? What's wrong?"

Evvie glances at me, surprised. "What are you doing here? You're supposed to be with Jack."

I'm not about to go into detail about bridge players barging in on us and trumping our love scene. "Never mind that right now. Why is everyone outside?"

"We heard Enya screaming and then it suddenly got very quiet. We're trying to find out what's wrong but she won't open the door."

I try the bell, with no response. We attempt to peer into her kitchen window, which is next to the door. There is some ambient light, but no movement. I take out my cell phone and dial her number. It rings five times. Finally a small soft voice answers. "Who's there?"

I sigh with relief. "Enya, it's Gladdy. Are you all right?"

"I need to sleep. I can't sleep."

"Please let us in. Just for a moment. Okay?"

She hangs up. I do, too. After a few seconds the door slowly opens. Enya, wearing an old gray chenille bathrobe, barely peers out. She looks haggard and frightened. I speak gently to her. "May we come in?"

She nods. Evvie turns to all the onlookers to signal things seem all right.

Ida calls from across the courtyard, "I'm on my way."

Bella backs away. "It's fine," Evvie tells her. "Go back to your place and rest." Bella, relieved of having to deal with something possibly frightening, does so.

The show is over. The onlookers return to their apartments. The rain stops.

* * *

I can't remember the last time any of us has been inside Enya's apartment. Years and years ago. And only briefly. She is a very private person and wants to be left alone. We've tried to include her in events, but she politely refuses. While her husband, Jacov, was alive, he brought her to all the seders we had and the Hanukkah parties. But after he died she didn't pretend anymore. She wanted nothing to do with celebrations, religious or otherwise. She's eighty-four now but it seems that, as far she's concerned, she died with her entire family in 1942.

Her home is laid out as all of our apartments are: tiny entry hall, equally small kitchen, dining area and living room next, and bedrooms off to the side. But unlike the rest of us, who've decorated our homes to our taste, Enya has kept hers sparsely furnished. She has never bothered to adorn it in any way. She still has the few pieces of basic furniture she bought years ago when she and Jacov moved in. There is no artwork on the walls. However, there are books, magazines, and newspapers everywhere—both in English and German.

Ida arrives and joins us.

Enya is shaking, though the apartment has the heat turned up high and the weather outside is warm and muggy. Now that I can look at her more closely, it seems as if she's aged overnight. We crowd the spotless kitchen. Evvie immediately starts boiling water for tea. I find a shawl on one of the kitchen chairs and wrap it around Enya's shoulders. Ida brings in a throw blanket from the living room couch. She places it across Enya's knees.

When the water is ready, Evvie prepares a pot of chamomile tea. She has to hold the cup for Enya, who can't control her tremors.

"This will warm you up," Evvie tells her.

"It was a terrible dream. It woke me."

I ask, "Do you want something to eat?"

"No, I only want to sleep and I can't anymore."

Anymore? That sounds ominous.

"Why not?" Evvie asks gently as she pours a little more tea.

Enya clutches the shawl tightly around her and bows her head. She doesn't want to speak, but we wait. Finally she lifts her head, her eyes glazed, as if we aren't there. "There was a storm the night they came for us."

She stops, lost in her troubled thoughts.

"A storm?" Evvie prompts. "Like the rain tonight?"

She shakes her head. "No, so much worse. They pulled us out of our home, without coats or hats and clutching only a few small personal things. We sat in the open trucks, wet and shivering."

Evvie, Ida, and I look at one another, distraught. She has never spoken to any of us of the horrors her family went through. Jacov did when she wasn't with him. But that was so many years ago. Why now? It's as if I'd asked the question out loud.

"I haven't had these dreams for such a long time." She shudders. "It's the storm. I can't bear the rain."

I remember Jacov telling us that Enya was a college professor in their native Prague. He was an architect. They were both married to other people, but they lost everything and everyone in the camps—Enya and Jacov were the only survivors in each of their families. They met in America after the war.

"I'm so tired." Enya pushes the teacup away and lays her head on the kitchen table.

We are at a loss to know what to do to help her. "Do you want me to call your doctor?" I ask.

"No, no doctor," she whispers.

Ida leans down and says softly, "Come back to bed, Enya dear."

She helps her up and Enya doesn't resist. The three of us walk her down the short hallway and into her bedroom. There is only a small light on the wooden chest of drawers next to the double bed, but it is enough for us to witness a shocking sight.

The entire wall opposite the bed is covered with photos and papers. From top to bottom, old, crumpled, torn family photos and documents. Jacov's smiling face and his equally smiling first wife in a marriage photo. Various happy shots of their four children before the monstrosity that took their lives. Enya's collection of her dead—her husband and two children, standing in front of an obviously expensive house, the two little girls in ballet outfits. Documents, possibly in German. Maybe marriage licenses. College degrees. School report cards, it's difficult to tell. The personal things they took with them that managed to survive.

The remnants from a country gone mad. Reparations finally offered for that which was irreplaceable.

Evvie and Ida help Enya into bed, then join me and share my shock. I can see it in their faces and they in mine. *This* is what Jacov and Enya looked at night after night from their marriage bed? The guilt of the survivors, so they would never forget? God have mercy on their souls.

Enya, almost delirious with exhaustion, cries out, "They're coming for us. Hide! Hide! Something bad is coming, something very bad!"

We rush back to her side. Ida covers Enya with

the blanket, then turns to us. "I'm going to stay with her."

I look down on this tortured woman thrashing in her bed and I am in tears.

* * *

When Evvie and I walk outside, it is raining again. Pouring. The wind now raging. I walk her to her apartment, two doors down. Hug her and kiss her good night. She offers to give me an umbrella, but I tell her not to bother, it will only blow away. Besides, my feet are already wet.

I run across the courtyard, head down against the wind, getting soaked, of course. Was it only this morning Jack and I got up at dawn and met at the bus stop to rendezvous? What a day filled with dramas! The girls showing up with breakfast and interrupting us. The gang at the pool interrogating me. Morrie telling us to mind our own business about the Grandpa Bandit. The crazy dinner at the deli, and let's not forget the bridge players showing up at Jack's apartment. With Enya's nightmares to end this stressful day, I want only to throw myself into bed and pull the covers over my head and sleep.

In my apartment I attempt to towel dry my hair. And try to think about this emotional seesaw I'm on. But I am beyond tired.

Suddenly I remember that the bandit's note had more to say—we forgot about it when we ran out of the deli to chase him.

Once again I call upon Scarlett O'Hara to guide

me in times of tension. I dig the envelope out of my purse, and without reading the rest of his note, I toss it on the kitchen table and head for my bedroom.

I'll think about it tomorrow.

8

Damage

Rain poured relentlessly all night, amid dramatic displays of thunder and lightning. The winds raged, making eerie sounds in the darkness—creaking and groaning as if the buildings could bear no more.

In the morning, Jack glances around as many of the residents of Phase Six group themselves in front of Z building in the early light. They seem a sorry collection, most still in pajamas and robes, shaking their heads, surrounded by the mess all over the grounds, and studying the building that is clearly in trouble. Z for Zinnia, Jack reminds himself. The rain has finally stopped, but the wind still howls and his neighbors all stand hunched over—even the palm trees are bending over. Windows have been blown out. The elevator has been seriously damaged. Carmel Graves reports the roof leaking in her third-floor apartment.

Stanley Heyer is also here. Right now, he is pacing back and forth in front of his crumbling creation.

Dora Dooley and Louise Bannister stand on either side of Jack, clinging to him. Carmel Graves huddles into herself, staring up at her damaged apartment worriedly. A Canadian couple, Larry and Sylvia Ulan, look on with concern as well. Residents from building Y across the way lend sympathetic mutterings.

"Seems like the roof took a beating last night," Stanley comments. He'd already sent his roofer up there this morning to investigate.

"I was so scared," Carmel says. "I thought the whole building would cave in on me. I hardly slept a wink."

"Me, neither, all that thunder and lightning right on top of us," adds Louise, leaning closer to Jack as if needing his support—far too close for comfort.

Stanley makes notes in a pad he holds. "Fortunately, it looks like you people got the worst of it. The other buildings report very little damage."

"Lucky us," comments Louise.

"And notice the cracks along the sides," Sylvia Ulan adds, pointing. "This place is falling apart at the seams." Her husband nods in agreement.

"Well, I'll get on it right way," Stanley says, "but I got to warn you, with all these storms lately, there's hardly a worker available. My roofer told me he's already backed up into late October. I'll see who I can round up."

"Please hurry," Sylvia says, nervously clutching her husband. "Do what you can."

Stanley shakes his head. "Fifty years these buildings are standing. Never a big problem. Now this. Let's hope the storms don't get any worse."

The group slowly disbands, but Louise doesn't seem willing to let go of Jack. "Wanna come up for a cup of coffee?"

"I would love to, Louise, but I've got to get going. I—"

"I'll take you up on your offer," says Dora.

Jack tries not to grin. That's not what Louise had in mind. She never stops trying.

"Forget it," Louise says sharply. "I've got too much to do." With that she flounces off.

Dora shrugs. "What a ding-a-ling. Well, I got my soaps waiting for me. Who needs her swamp mud coffee?" And she's off.

Jack looks up again at his damaged building and shakes his head. Not a good sign. He wonders how Gladdy's building held up.

The way things are going around here, when will they ever find time alone? He's got to think of something.

* * *

The girls are fairly jumping up and down with excitement. Having finally read the rest of Grandpa Bandit's note this morning, I discover he intends to rob another bank. Today! This very afternoon, in fact. I quickly called the girls to an early-morning meeting at our usual patio table under our favorite palm tree. Our poor tree lost many a frond during last night's storm, Except for trash blown everywhere, though, our buildings didn't suffer too much damage. But because of the heavy wind, now starting, we change our minds and go back inside to my apartment instead.

First order of business is to check on Enya. Ida says she slept fitfully, but she is up and about this morning and seems in better spirits. So hopefully her nightmares will stop.

I know I have to call Morrie and give him a heads-up about the bandit. But based on his unfriendly attitude about this case, first we must make our own plans. Grandpa's going to hit the SunTrust on Oakland Park Boulevard, according to his note. Fortunately, we are familiar with that corner—we shop there often. Naturally Morrie will tell us to stay away, but we intend to find a hiding place nearby so we can watch Grandpa in the act. How can we resist?

Sophie reminds me that one of our favorite delis, the Bagel Bistro, is right across the street, so we agree to use that as our observation point. I advise the girls to dress in subtle colors so we won't be noticed. Sophie beams at that; she can hardly wait to coordinate her outfit.

"Grandpa's got to know we'll tell the police. How's he going to make his getaway with them there?" Ida wonders. "He must have a reason for wanting us to know his plans. This is going to be trouble for us, I know it." Always the cynic.

"Maybe this time they'll catch him," Bella says.

"And we get the credit for leading them to him." Sophie looks up from polishing her nails. Her newest color is Burnt Orange to match her latest hair dye.

Evvie smiles. "Wanna bet he eludes them again? He has to have an escape plan. I'm dying of curiosity to know how he does it."

The girls listen as I talk to Morrie on the phone. "No article this time. He wrote a real letter. Yes, I'll read it to you. He says, 'Today I'm hitting another clueless bank, this time SunTrust, between two P.M. and four P.M. Oakland Park branch. He also says, 'Getting old ain't for sissies,' and once again he writes, 'Catch me if you can, girls.' That's it."

I listen, and shake my head. I say, "Yes, Morrie, even though it's clear now this is our case, we'll stay away," with as much sarcasm as I can muster. Then I add, "And don't forget to send us the list of banks he's already robbed. Yeah, yeah, I know, it's in the mail. Sure."

When I hang up Bella does a little dance in anticipation. "This is gonna be so much fun!"

After the girls leave, I call Jack. He tells me about his damaged building and I catch him up on our bandit.

"Did you call Morrie?" he asks.

"Of course I did."

"And did he tell you to stay away?"

"Naturally."

"And you aren't going to listen to him, are you?"

I think a moment—do I lie or tell the truth?

Jack answers before I weigh this decision about honesty in relationships. "You're going. I know you are."

"Don't tell Morrie," I beg.

"I would never mix in with your business tactics, but you can guess what I'm thinking."

"I know . . . I know," I say, feeling guilty.

We both change the subject at the same time and, saying the same thing: "I missed you last night."

* * *

The girls and I meet at my old Chevy wagon at one o'clock. We're hoping to get there a little before Morrie and his cops arrive. As agreed upon, we are all in pastel shades or light grays and tans. Except Sophie. Her idea of subtle is a bright yellow slacks outfit with a bright yellow ribbon in her hair. She's carrying a huge yellow flowery purse.

Ida shakes her head in disgust. "You look like a lollipop!"

Evvie says, "More like a deranged canary who escaped from her cage. Where's a cat when you need one?"

Sophie sniffs, annoyed by our attack on her judgment. "The walls in Bagel Bistro happen to be painted in sunshine yellow and I'll blend into the woodwork perfectly. So there!"

Huh. No arguing with Sophie's logic. We're on our way.

When we arrive at Oakland Park Boulevard, first we oh-so-casually check out the front of the bank and then take a brief stroll inside, searching for anyone who might look suspicious. Every gray-haired man is to be examined. There are senior citizens, but only four male gray heads. I snap my fingers and the girls get it. Each follows one of the men only to return moments later, saying that all four got into their cars and drove away.

"One of them almost hit a telephone pole backing up," reports Ida, "but let's not get into a discussion of how some seniors drive."

So, we hightail it out of the bank and over to our hiding place.

The deli is packed with the lunchtime crowd, but we're lucky—there's a table for four in a corner at the window with a perfect view of SunTrust Bank directly opposite. We drag over another chair so the five of us can all squeeze in. It's then I realize Bella isn't with us.

Evvie nudges me to look out the window, and there's Bella, still across the street, bent over, dropping money in a small cup. An elderly legless man, wearing a large torn straw hat, holding pencils, is propped up on a wooden block with skate wheels. It is a small drama. After Bella puts her money in his cup, he hands her a pencil. She shakes her head and steps back. The legless man says something to her and waggles the pencil at her. Finally she gives in. She takes her pencil and crosses the street.

Dear kind Bella, I think. There's no way she'd take the pencil and prevent him from another sale.

We are in a deli, so naturally everyone wants to eat. But I warn them not to take their eyes off the bank. Happy chomping commences as we watch the busy parade of passersby go back and forth and in and out of the bank.

Sophie points animatedly. "Look, there's Morrie."

Morrie walks past the bank with his good friend and fellow detective Oz Washington and several other men in plain clothes. The legless man tries to sell them a pencil, but they ignore his efforts.

The men spread out. Morrie and three others enter the bank. Oz and the two men with him cross the street and move to the left of the deli.

"Oh, oh. They're searching all the stores!" Evvie grabs me by the sleeve. We all watch as the three men disappear from sight. Bella guesses Oz is going to the lamp-shade place next door.

"They're having a ten-percent-off sale," she informs me. We wait nervously. Moments later they appear again, and suddenly I have a sinking feeling.

I bark, "It looks like he's coming in here. Everybody hide your face." We use napkins, menus, half-eaten sandwiches, squirming to look invisible—but sure enough, as Oz walks up and down the restaurant searching for gray heads, he reaches our table and naturally recognizes us. He is his usual gorgeous self—café-au-lait skin, wavy black hair, and a smile to break your heart.

Caught! This was a dumb idea, picking a place so close to the bank. Oz and I exchange glances. For a moment, I hold my breath. Oz winks and walks past us.

We wait motionless until he and his men are safely past our table.

Ida whispers, "Why didn't he say something? Such as 'Get out of here'?"

I exhale in relief. "I think he likes us. And I bet he doesn't tell Morrie that he saw us."

Two o'clock comes and goes. So does three. Luckily the restaurant has cleared out and nobody needs our table. My eyes are smarting from watching so intently. People enter the bank and exit the bank. But nothing. No robbery. Finally my watch reads four. I can see Morrie, Oz, and their guys take off. Oz glances in our direction and shrugs. Morrie looks annoyed.

Sophie is disappointed. "Grandpa lied to us and sent us on a wild-duck chase."

"Goose," Ida says.

"Who are you calling names?" Sophie huffs.

I calm everyone down. We gather our things, throw our trash into the proper receptacles, and leave. But when we turn the corner to where I parked my car, lo and behold, there's a familiar white envelope stuck in the windshield wiper.

"He *was* here," Ida says, grabbing for it. Sure enough, inside, there's his trademark green feather. We all peer over Ida's shoulder as she reads.

" 'Hi, girls, this was only a test. Just wanted to see if you were on your toes. Next time, weather permitting, will be the real thing. Speaking of getting old, did you know if you were age fifty on the planet Neptune, you'd only be three months old?

By the way, loved the yellow outfit. And enjoy your other friend's new pencil.' "

We all gawk at Bella. The pencil! Grandpa's disguise was the old man pretending to be without legs, and Bella spoke with him!

"What did he say to you?" Evvie demands.

"Who?" Bella doesn't understand why we're all staring at her.

Sophie practically yells, "You were talking to Grandpa!"

"How could I talk to my grandpa? He died in 1937."

"Oy," says Evvie. "Grandpa Bandit sold you your pencil."

Bella now takes it out of her purse and looks at it in amazement. "He did?"

My turn to ask a question. "The two of you had a conversation. He said something to you. What was it?"

She thinks for a moment. Short-term memory is a problem for her. Ask her all about that grandpa who died in '37, and I bet she'd have a volume to tell.

"I said . . . I said, 'I don't want to take your pencil. Save it for your next customer.' And he said, 'No, please take it, and maybe you want some more for your friends.' "

"Double oy," Evvie says.

Grandpa knew she's one of us. And knew where we were hiding. All the while, he was laughing at us.

Bella is unhappy. "I didn't want to give him

more money so I didn't take any more—" She stops at the expressions on all our faces. "What?"

Ida is a study in aggravation. "Why didn't you tell us? We would have had him."

"At least describe him for us," I say.

Bella thinks. "I couldn't take my eyes off the folded pants with no legs. And he had that big hat. I never looked at his face."

Ida is disgusted. "Never mind. Let's go home."

We all plop into the car. Bella is still mulling it over. "So how can he rob banks without legs?"

No one bothers to answer her.

She huffs in her own defense. "Anyway, I can always use another pencil."

9

Looking for Clues

Today is library day—might as well go while the sun is briefly out, since threatening clouds hang overhead yet again. Even though my girls love to read, somehow they are always too busy to come with me and pick out their own books. So I find myself overloaded with their books to return and a list of what they want next.

I drop Sophie off at the nail place along the way. She chipped a few bits of polish while we were on the stakeout for Grandpa Bandit yesterday. I still find it amazing that whole stores devote themselves to applying nail polish—and where was it I read that now nail polish is supposed to be bad for you?

Evvie is at home working on a survey article about hurricane shutters, for her community newspaper. Should residents buy their own or should Lanai Gardens order them for all?

Bella is at her knitting group at a neighbor's apartment. Ida is teaching a class on pie-baking in the club room. So I'm on my own. Which, frankly, I enjoy.

I asked Jack if he wanted to join me, but he was busy with the men at Phase Six, dealing with building problems. They are taking roof measurements for the roofer, who they hope will be coming soon.

That's equally fine with me, since I'll get to visit with my librarian friend, Conchetta.

When I arrive, Conchetta is busy with an elementary school group on a field trip. I wave and head for the stacks to gather books. Another Carl Hiaasen for me—his Florida comedy mysteries are hilarious. He sure does have a monopoly of this state's underbelly of weird characters. Another Sandra Brown for Sophie. Another Catherine Coulter for Bella. Ida loves Michael Connolly. And Evvie, that frustrated entertainer, gets to read an autobiography of Marnie Nixon.

Amazing how these writers keep churning new books out every year. I wonder how they can do that!

I stop in my tracks at the bank of computers. One of these days I'm going to have to give in and learn how to work the darn things and keep up with the rest of the world.

I stack my take-out books on a reading table, glance at the instructions posted on the desk, and poke a couple of keys. The screen goes black. So much for my foray into cyberspace.

Conchetta comes to my rescue. "*Pobrecita,* the machine chewed you up and spit you out?"

I smile. "Something like that." We hug. Sweet, chubby Conchetta is a huggy kind of person. "Did I break anything?"

She plays with the keys, and like magic the screen comes to life again. "Let's say you put it to sleep."

I tell her, "I always have that effect on machines."

"What were you trying to find?"

What the heck. Might as well. The machine's here and I have someone who can work it. "How would you look up Grandpa Bandit?"

"First, I Google—" She looks at me. "You're kidding? Grandpa who? Wait a minute, I did read something about that name. He robs banks?"

"That's the very grandpa I mean." I fill her in on our new client as she listens incredulously.

She claps her hands. "I love it! He wants you to catch him. I wonder why."

I hazard a guess. "Maybe he feels guilty but can't turn himself in? Reminds me of a movie where the killer scrawled on a mirror, 'Stop me before I kill more.' You think Grandpa wants us to stop him from stealing?"

I tell her about yesterday's adventures.

While we talk, I watch Conchetta whiz along the keys. She says, "Let's check out some articles. Maybe pick up a clue. Here's one."

I look over her shoulder as she clicks on an article from a local paper, featuring an interview with a Ms. Sarah Byrne, of Plantation, who was the bank teller Grandpa held up in the Wachovia East Broward Boulevard branch robbery. The reporter on the scene comments that "Ms. Byrne was in such a state of hysteria from the horrific experience that she was sent home immediately to recover. She was unable to give the police any details about the notorious bandit, who has been plaguing local banks for the last six months. This was the sixth bank held up by the man the police call Grandpa Bandit. Many descriptions have been given by onlookers, but no two people have agreed on what he looks like other than that he is old and gray-haired."

I smile. "Well, next step for Gladdy Gold and Associates is to attempt an interview with the young, frightened bank teller."

"And of course you will report everything you learn to me?" Conchetta says.

"Naturally."

The elementary school kids are now charging the desk with their chosen books, their shiny new library cards out and ready. The two librarians behind the desk have their hands full.

"Sorry to leave you," Conchetta says, "but I better help out."

"You've already helped me." I wave good-bye and head for the door.

I hear an imperious voice call after me, "Just a moment, Mrs. Gold." It's Conchetta, putting on a tone of authority in front of the gawking children.

"The moment you walk out you will set off the alarm."

Oops. I forgot to check out my books. I look with chagrin at the mob at the desk and dutifully go to the back of the line.

10

The Bank Teller

The five of us face the very young Sarah Byrne as we all sip lemonade. We have our most solicitous expressions on in respect for Ms. Byrne's recent painful encounter.

"I hope you're feeling better." This from Evvie.

"And not crying a lot anymore." Bella offers her sympathy.

"Are you under a doctor's care?" asks Sophie.

Our witness perches daintily on a small tapestry bench opposite us. We are sitting on flowery chintz couches and spindly antique chairs. Her house is charming and beautifully kept up. Sarah, herself, is petite and pretty and nicely dressed, in white slacks and a black tee. Her curly blond hair is tied back in a white ribbon. And she is barefoot.

After we found her address—in the phone book, amazing these days—we called her. We explained who we were and what we wanted. She said she was more than happy to have us come and visit.

Now she stares at us in confusion. "What are you talking about? Why would I need a doctor?"

"Was it because of the shock of being robbed?" Ida wants to know.

A smile forms on Sarah's face.

She's smiling? Odd. "We read the newspaper account of your leaving the bank in hysterics," I tell her.

She walks over and refills our lemonade glasses. "That's a good way of putting it! Hysterics? Oh, yes, I left in hysterics. I didn't know whether to laugh or cry, so I did both."

Now we're the ones looking puzzled.

"You know why I invited you ladies over? Because I'm upset about losing my job. Because I miss my work. Because none of my old friends at the bank have the guts to call me. The bank fired me. I didn't push the panic button fast enough."

"Was that because you were frightened by being in danger?" I ask.

"Danger? But was I really in danger? I'm not sure. This was the weirdest thing that ever happened to me in my whole life." She pauses as she rolls her head in a stretch. "Are you really private eyes? You're really looking for Grandpa?"

Evvie answers Sarah's question with dignity. "We certainly are private eyes. Who did you think we were when you gave us permission to come over?"

"I didn't know and I didn't care. I wanted the

company. I thought you were a bunch of old ladies who were bored and nosy. And, by the way, thanks for the pineapple upside-down cake."

"Hmph," mutters Ida, baker of said cake.

Sarah drops to the floor in front of us. "Mind if I do a little yoga? I missed my class today."

Why not, I think. This is turning into a bizarre little episode. Next thing, she might want us to do push-ups with her.

"Start from the beginning," I say. "Please. The whole robbery incident."

We all lean forward as she twists her legs around in a way that I never thought possible outside of the circus.

"Okay," she says. "It was an ordinary day, maybe a little quiet. This old guy comes to my window."

Fashionista Sophie interrupts immediately. "Do you remember what he was wearing?"

"Honey, I remember every little thing about him."

I tap Sophie, indicating that she shouldn't interrupt.

Sarah twists into another improbable position, resembling something like a figure eight. "He was about five foot four, thin, wearing gray pants and shirt and a Miami Dolphins baseball cap. He had on huge sunglasses with white rims, making it very difficult to see his face. He had kind of a Groucho Marx bushy mustache. Looked like a paste-on to me. And a big Spider-Man Band-Aid on his cheek. I only realized later that all that stuff was to keep me from really seeing anything of his looks other than the tufts of his gray hair sticking out."

Bella pulls her chair even closer so as not to miss a word of this amazing story.

Sarah continues, "He carried a small tote with the SunTrust Bank logo on it. He opened it up and pulled out a bag from Mickey's Deli, the one that's right across the street from where I work."

We are listening with open mouths. Her attention to detail is fascinating.

"He took out a rye bread sandwich and unwrapped it."

Now Sophie can't stand it. "He was going to eat his lunch?"

Sarah shakes her head. "He then tells me he got turkey but told them to hold the mayo so it wasn't too messy."

Bella is gaga over what she hears. "What wasn't too messy?"

"His gun, wrapped up in the sandwich," Sarah says. "He insisted it was a real gun, but frankly, I wasn't sure."

"You gotta be joking," Ida says. "He's holding up a bank with a gun wrapped in a turkey sandwich?"

"I kid you not," Sarah says, giggling. "Here I am being robbed by an old guy dressed like a clown, carrying a gun in rye bread. I didn't know what to think. I was so weirded out, I didn't know whether this was a joke or serious."

We're all giggling now.

Ida pours herself more lemonade. "Then what?"

"Then he says, 'Give me five hundred and fifty dollars and forty-six cents or I shoot.' My hands were shaking; I could barely count out the money. He tossed it into the sandwich bag, thanked me, and tipped his baseball cap."

We are speechless. Finally Evvie says, "That's it?"

"Oh, I almost forgot. He dug out a small green feather and said, 'Robin Hood's my name, robbing banks is my game.' "

Sarah does another complicated yoga move then gracefully stands up and stretches.

Bella and Sophie applaud.

I've heard some strange stories in my lifetime but this takes the cake. "Did you tell all of it to the police?"

"I did indeed, but I don't think they believed me, what with all my nervous laughing."

I have to ask. "Why did you give him the money?"

She thinks for a moment. "That's a good question. Maybe it's because I thought he was adorable. Maybe because he reminded me of my grandpa. And because maybe he was loony enough to be carrying a real gun. I tell you, ladies, I was a nervous wreck."

She performs another long stretch. "And when I finally remembered to hit the panic button, he was already racing out of the bank."

11

Another Teller Tells Another Story

Pallie Finchum is a very different experience from Sarah Byrne. No laughing here. This one's a straitlaced bank teller who reminds me of an old-fashioned schoolmarm. Maybe it's the tight brown bun perched on the top of her head or her starched black suit. She's in her fifties, thin-lipped, and very unfriendly. She, too, had been mentioned in an article after one of Grandpa's robberies. We called her. She refused to speak to us, so today Evvie and I track her down at lunchtime. The others stay home because I tell them five of us stalking her would be ridiculous.

We wait for Finchum to leave the bank. Noon, right on the dot. She then enters Fuddruckers directly across the street. That's a surprise—the noisy youth-oriented restaurant doesn't seem her style. We manage to get a table right behind her.

She orders a chicken salad and iced tea. We order a couple of hamburgers and Cokes. We let her read her book and eat in peace. While she sips her tea and before she pays the check, we get up and sit down next to her, Cokes still in hand.

Naturally she's startled. Very quickly we introduce ourselves and remind her that we'd tried to make an appointment. When she recovers from her shock, she says, "Get away from me or I'm calling for help."

"Please," I say, "just a few minutes of your time. We need to talk to you about the old man who held you up."

"It's none of your business."

Evvie smiles. "Actually, it is. He's our client." And she hands Finchum one of our business cards. I remember how Jack surprised me with these cards as a "new business" present. I've given out about eleven so far. These cards will outlive me.

The woman accepts it with the same attitude she might have shaking hands with an alligator. "Your client? That's preposterous."

"Maybe so, but it's true," Evvie tells her.

"Prove it. Tell me what he looks like."

I don't know quite what to say since we've never met our client. Nothing fazes Evvie, though; she jumps right in. "Don't play with us. You don't know what he looks like, either. He's very secretive about his appearance. He usually wears a disguise. I'm sure he was wearing one when he walked up to your window. The only thing he lets people see clearly is his gray hair."

Miss Bun-on-top-of-head pauses, but she's not giving up yet. "You'll have to do better than that. Tell me something you know that only the police and the bank and I know."

Evvie, former budding actress, is in her element. "Gramps, our master of disguise, comes up to your window and shows you his gun, wrapped in a sandwich. Usually turkey, and he holds the mayo so it won't be messy."

This information startles Finchum. She weakens a bit. "It wasn't turkey."

"All right, already," Evvie says, pretending annoyance. "So what was it? Pastrami? Baloney? What?"

Pallie Finchum finally relents. She leans over and whispers, "It was corned beef on a Kaiser roll."

"How much did he demand?"

"Forty-four dollars and seventy-eight cents."

I'm surprised by this but I don't show it. "And," I add, "he showed you the green feather and called himself Robin Hood."

The bank teller sighs. "That's exactly what happened. My life has been hell ever since. My manager says I can never tell this story to anyone. So do the police. Why would I want to tell anyone? It was too embarrassing. But I did tell my mother. I live with her."

"And?" Evvie asks.

"She was so upset, she wanted me to quit. How can I quit? I need the money."

She stands up from the table. "I have to go back

to work. This robbery has ruined my job for me. Now my manager watches me all the time."

And with that she leaves us sitting there.

Evvie look at me. "First it was five hundred something and now forty-four and change. What in blazes is that about?"

"One of the first things I'll want to ask 'our client' if we ever catch up to him." I stand up. "Time for another meeting to figure out what we know."

* * *

We're in the clubhouse with the door locked and a sign tacked on that reads PRIVATE PARTY. KEEP OUT. We need to use the chalkboard. Outside, the wind is blowing, rattling the windows and door-knob, promising a new storm. Inside, we are cozy. Evvie pops some popcorn for us in the community microwave.

We list on the board what we know and what the police know.

"Keep calling it out," I say, chalk in hand.

Evvie: "He's always in a disguise, with distractions, so nobody really gets a good look at him." She hands out paper cups filled with popcorn and we nibble as we chat.

Ida: "He goes to the nearest restaurant and buys a sandwich to hide his gun."

As I write, I add, "He probably gets the sandwich at an earlier time or the cops would have caught him by now."

Sophie: "The two amounts of money he robbed

were different. I'll bet they're different in each bank. That's pretty weird."

Bella: "Maybe he gets bored and changes it. Or maybe he forgot what he asked for last time." She ponders this. "I know I would."

I look at the chalkboard, where I've copied out the list of six banks that arrived in today's mail. Frankly I didn't think Morrie would really send it. "I bet when we visit these banks, we'll find some kind of restaurant nearby. And that will be the sandwich wrapper of the day. He's toying with the banks and the police."

Evvie says, "Morrie probably knows in his heart that we can solve the case and is depending on us."

"Maybe," says Sophie. "I bet the cops are all frustrated because this old guy keeps foiling them."

Ida adds a clue. "I checked on the shuttle van that Grandpa got into the other night when we had dinner out. The driver said Grandpa didn't belong to the Golden Era Retirement Home, but he admitted the old guy tipped him for a ride with them."

"Did the driver describe him?"

"No, he never really looked at Grandpa."

Sophie says, "I like that he calls himself Robin Hood and leaves the green feather. He steals from the rich to give to the poor."

I'm not so sure of that. "Maybe yes—maybe no. We'll ask him when we find him."

The wind outside is picking up, rattling the windows of the building. "Everybody got their flashlights ready if the power goes out again tonight?" Evvie is always on storm duty. She gets the appropriate number of nods.

"Bella," I say, "you look puzzled."

"I still don't know how he can rob a bank without legs."

Ida throws a handful of popcorn at her. "Get it through your head already. He has legs. He hid them under the box he was sitting on."

She pouts. "It looked real to me."

"Which brings me to a few puzzling questions," I say. "Didn't Morrie tell us that the police warned all the local banks about him? So, why were the tellers surprised?"

Evvie refills my popcorn cup. "And how does Grandpa make his getaway?"

Ida says, "I'm guessing he hides things nearby, in his car. Or in a backpack. What we saw was a legless-man routine. I wonder how many other getaways he has in his bag of tricks?"

Evvie adds, "What I want to know is how he knows us—does he live here in Lanai Gardens? Is he someone we see often?"

"And we should pay attention to this map," I say, indicating the Fort Lauderdale map I've taped to the board. I used a marker to circle the locations of the six banks. Grandpa has hit so far—all within a five-mile radius of one another. "Within this same area there are at least three more banks that haven't been robbed yet. I wonder where he'll hit next time? We also need to figure out if there is a pattern to how often he robs and if there is a similarity to the time of day..." My cell phone rings, interrupting my daunting list of next steps. It's Jack. I tell him what we're up to. I turn so the girls won't see me blush as Jack informs me he's coming to my apartment tonight for our next attempt at a "sleepover."

"What was that about?" Evvie asks when I hang up. But I'm saved from having to answer her question when a loud burst of thunder and lightning hits right above us.

I quickly erase the board. Everybody hurries to the door. Evvie tosses suggestions as we go: "Keep safe. Pull the blinds. Stay away from windows."

We race back to our apartments, holding hands. But I'm not thinking of the amount of rain or the velocity of the wind or Grandpa Bandit— I feel warm and fuzzy at the thought of my own thunder and lightning show on for tonight.

12

Let's Try Again

It's after midnight. The weather outside is wild—the worst storm we've had in many seasons. But indoors we are comfy. Jack and I are wrapped in a blanket and stretched out on my couch in the living room, in front of a romantic fire sizzling in the fireplace. Candlelight takes the place of the power we no longer have. Wine warms our insides. Our clothes are still on, but in much disarray.

"I really missed you," Jack says, nuzzling my neck.

I nuzzle him back. "It's only been three days, silly."

"It felt like a week to me."

"What have you been doing?"

"Helping out. Stanley Heyer's been leading a group of residents from building to building, looking for damage from all the recent rain. And what mischief have you and the girls been up to?"

"Trying to find our Grandpa Bandit. He's very elusive."

We kiss. Then kiss again. Our hands are exploring. Our breaths shorten. No need for words. I am happy to realize that even at our ages sex is still an active urge. And to think I was sure I would never have these tingling feelings again.

The candles are burning down. The room grows dimmer. Our bodies are well heated. I am softly moaning with pleasure. Jack indicates the bedroom. He's ready. I'm ready.

As we get up there's a knock at the door.

We stare at each other in utter disbelief. It can't be happening again.

"Someone's knocking?" Jack asks incredulously.

"Impossible. On a stormy night like this? Must be a branch hitting the door."

"Or maybe a whole tree falling down on the building," he suggests jokingly.

The doorbell rings. Then there is the sound of a key turning in the lock. In the near-darkness we see the door open, and a small apparition enters. At first I don't recognize it—it's all bundled up with rain jacket, large floppy rain hood, boots, and a broken, upturned umbrella.

It's Bella. She flings the soaking-wet umbrella to the floor, drops the rain jacket from her shoulders, and kicks off her boots. She is wearing her favorite lobster and squid pajamas; her hair is in curlers.

Her teddy bear is tucked in under the waistband of her jammies.

She slogs toward me, shaking her damp head.

"What are you doing here, Bella dear?" I ask gently.

She walks through the hallway and into the living room without stopping.

"The storm is scaring me. I don't want to be alone." Her voice is slurry and sleepy.

"But, Bella! Dear, you live next door to Evvie. Why did you walk clear across the courtyard to my building? It's dangerous out there."

She doesn't even look at me as she moves through the living room. "I tried Evvie. But she was sleeping so soundly she didn't hear the bell. I used the key, but she double-locked the door. So I came to you."

With that, she enters my bedroom.

Jack and I stare at each other. Jack whispers, "She has keys to all your apartments?"

"Yes, we all do, in case of emergencies."

"She didn't even see me."

"That's because she forgot her glasses." I smile weakly.

We tiptoe into my bedroom. Bella is already snuggled up in my queen-sized bed, comforter tucked under her chin, sound asleep. Her teddy bear rests on my pillow.

I can't help it. I start to giggle.

Jack scowls. "This is funny?"

The giggle becomes a laugh. "My turn to say 'Can't you see the humor in it?' "

Jack sighs, then gives in to a wry smile. We tiptoe back to the living room and sit down on the couch. "Shall we continue where we left off?" he asks dolefully.

I giggle again. "You know what this reminds me of? Being seventeen and having a date in the living room and trying to smooch while my parents were sleeping in the next room. No way. I mean, horrors, what if they woke up and saw us?"

"And now you have this woman well into her second childhood in your bed and you still can't make out."

"What if she wakes up and heads for the kitchen to get a glass of water or something?"

"You said she can hardly see without her glasses. She'll never notice us."

"It won't work." I sigh. "I'm sorry, Jack."

"I know," he says, sighing, too. "I guess I should head for home."

"No. Stay. It's awful out there." I leave him standing there while I bring him a blanket and pillow. "Should I tuck you in?"

"Sure. Why not. Want to read me a bedtime story?"

I swat him playfully.

"And, darling Gladdy, I'll make sure to leave very early in the morning so Bella won't even know I was here. Okay?"

We kiss good night. As he rolls over in an attempt to get all of his over-six-foot-tall body comfortable, I head for the bedroom to my unexpected sleepover guest. Behind me I hear Jack mumble,

"How far do we have to go to be alone? Tell me. I'll book us a flight anywhere. Just name it."

I pretend to count off names as I call back to him. "Timbuktu. Bimini. Lower Botswana." I can't resist using the new computer terms I overheard in the library. "Google Travelocity and pick somewhere."

13

The Next Morning

As I drink my morning coffee, I have the TV on low. I don't want to wake Bella. The newscasters making small talk agree that it was quite a storm last night, with winds up to twenty miles per hour. The screen shows image after image of downed trees and flooded streets and highways backed up for miles.

My original houseguest, Jack, did what he said he would: He woke up very early in the morning and snuck out. What a comedy of errors. I looked in on him around three A.M., during a bathroom trip. It's the first time I'd ever seen him asleep. His long legs hung over the couch. Poor thing, he looked so miserable, yet adorable. He probably thrashed around half the night trying to fit his body into that small space. Oh, well, one of these days I'll get to see him sleeping in my bed. I'm really looking forward to it. Waking up next to him—how wonderful that will be. To see him sitting opposite, having breakfast with me, is something I will treasure. Though the way the fates have had it so far, who knows when that will happen.

I'm sitting at my kitchen table, enjoying my fantasies, when Bella walks in. Talk about another kind of adorable. She stands there in her cute PJs, rubbing her eyes and holding her teddy bear. I can picture Bella as she was as a child, in that same posture. Sweet and gentle. And as usual, confused.

Bella asks, "What are you doing in my kitchen?"

I smile at her. "No, you mean what are *you* doing in *my* kitchen."

She looks around, realizing that indeed she is in my apartment. "I don't know. How did I get here?"

She sits down and I pour her a cup of coffee. "Don't you remember coming over here last night during the storm?" I indicate the cluster of rain gear that we both can see in the adjoining hallway.

"I did?"

"You tried Evvie's door but couldn't open it, so you sloshed across the courtyard to me."

She blows on the top of the cup to cool her drink. Bella likes her coffee lukewarm.

We sit there quietly sipping and enjoying the silence and comfort of longtime friendship. Suddenly Bella perks up, remembering:

"I had the funniest dream last night. I was in a strange bed and some man was standing over me, looking at me. Isn't that weird?"

I cough, sputtering my coffee slightly. "That's quite a dream. Did you recognize this stranger in the night?"

"No, it was too dark. But I think he was nice."

* * *

The sun is out, although it's weak and weary. Black thunderclouds darken the horizon.

Ida is at her mailbox when Bella and I exit the elevator. She looks Bella up and down, eyebrows raised. Bella is still holding her teddy bear. "Are those your pajamas you're wearing under all that stuff?"

"Don't ask," I say.

Bella blushes, and hurries across the courtyard to her building, where she passes Evvie talking to her ex, Joe. Before Evvie can comment, an embarrassed Bella scampers into their building's elevator with her eyes closed against curious expressions on anyone else's face.

Evvie and Joe are standing near Joe's old Ford V8. He's parked, with his door open, right in the middle of the street. I can hear their voices clearly.

"I don't want them," Evvie says loudly.

"Why not? They're just flowers." Joe is obviously frustrated, but trying to stay cool.

"So, what's the occasion?" My sister busies herself reading her mail.

"Does there have to be an occasion? All right,

maybe it's a peace offering so you'll stop treating me like dirt under your shoe."

She snorts. "As far as I'm concerned, this war is still on."

"How about amnesty?" he begs. "After so many years."

"How about you shut your car door before another car bangs into it?"

As he does so, Evvie is aware of me looking their way and she beckons me to hurry over—I suppose to get her away from Joe yet again. As I cross the courtyard, I see Denny busy sweeping up last night's mess. Many of my neighbors are brushing leaves, and whatever else the wind brought, off their parked cars and balconies. Palm fronds and debris clog the street. Trash barrels are overturned. Denny waves to me and I wave back.

Joe is holding a lovely bouquet of flowers, which he is attempting to pass to Evvie, who refuses them. I hate being put in the middle of the two of them.

We exchange good mornings. I wait to see how this will go.

"Lots of rain last night," Evvie comments.

"Plenty of wind, too," says Joe.

I can play the same game. "Nice flowers," I comment.

Joe eagerly says, "Evvie's favorites. Pink roses."

Ms. Contrary has to say, "That was twenty years ago. Now I favor yellow."

My sister, queen of the put-down.

Joe turns to me. Here it comes, me-in-the-middle. "Gladdy, tell her to have dinner with me. She keeps turning me down."

"I have no need to go out. I already have a dinner planned," Evvie says haughtily.

"Like what?" Joe demands.

"Like my leftover pot roast from last night."

Joe sees this as a possible break. "Then maybe I can share it with you?"

She shrugs. "Sorry, only enough left for one."

Just then Enya appears in front of the building. Seeing us standing there, she moves in our direction. Joe pushes the flowers into my arms. "I give up. Stubborn broad. Here, you take them." And he gets in his car and drives off. I give my sister my stern look of disapproval, but she doesn't care. She still won't give her ex an inch.

Enya manages a feeble smile for the two of us. "Thank you for your kindness the other evening."

"You're very welcome," Evvie says.

"Are you feeling better?" I ask. She still looks very fragile to me and she clutches a worn black sweater to her, as if she isn't able to warm up.

She shrugs. "It helps when the sun is out." She leans over to smell the roses I now carry. "Such loveliness in an ugly world." She shudders, then frowns. "I still can't help feeling something very bad is coming."

"You mean another storm?" Evvie asks. "We've never had a hurricane hit Fort Lauderdale, so you needn't worry."

She pulls her sweater tighter. "A different kind

of storm. A storm like no other. Something evil is coming." Then she forces a smile. "Don't listen to me. I'm just a silly woman with a lot of fears."

I look at Evvie, then at the flowers, and then at Enya. Evvie nods. I hand the flowers to Enya. She is surprised. "Please take them," I say.

Evvie adds quickly, "I'm allergic."

Enya smiles and reaches for them gratefully.

Evvie pinches me and indicates I should turn to see something.

I do. It's Jack coming briskly toward me. Enya, her nose smelling her flowers, walks off to go on her usual morning stroll.

Evvie winks at me, then heads for her apartment. I go to meet Jack halfway.

"Hi—" I start to say, but he instantly interrupts me.

"I'm already packed."

I gaze at him, startled. "Are you going somewhere? You didn't mention—"

Again he interrupts me. "*We're* going. I made us a reservation in Key West. Tonight. Throw a few things in a bag."

"You really took me seriously? You actually picked out a place?"

He takes my arm, and marches me toward my building. "You won't need much. I don't expect we'll be leaving the room too often."

With that he playfully pats me on my backside. "I'll pick you up in an hour."

14

Key West

The girls can't believe Jack and I, based on a few minutes' discussion, are actually going down to Key West. I can almost hear one of them say, *Just like that, you go on a trip? Without us?* But with Jack standing right there, they hold their tongues. Roughly 180 miles away, approximately a three-hour drive. I can't believe it, either, yet here I am. Everyone is standing in a tight cluster when I appear downstairs with an overnight bag. Jack's vintage Cadillac is parked right in front, with its trunk open and his duffel bag very much in sight. I watch my girls as they watch me hand Jack my case and stare at him placing it next to his.

No guessing what the two of us intend to be doing on this trip—the answer is as plain as the blush on my cheeks. I look at their faces, trying to read what they're feeling. No one says anything but

Bella is grinning. Sophie pinches her in excitement. Ida is scowling. Evvie is absolutely poker-faced. When will I ever feel comfortable about this couple thing and my girls? Maybe only when we finally marry—ha!

Needless to say, others are watching the Jack and Gladdy show, too. Ever-present Hy and Lola stand on their second-floor landing, whispering to each other. Lola giggles. This should give them an entire afternoon of speculation and innuendo. I'm surprised they aren't waving a sign that says FALLEN WOMAN.

Jack sees me gazing at them. He grins, and whispers, "Scarlet woman, babe. I keep proposin' and you keep dozin'."

The girls wave as we head out. We pass Mary and Irving in Mary's car. I am sure they're heading for the hospital.

What little sun we had before disappears. The first raindrops begin to fall.

* * *

I'd been to Key West many years before, but this trip will definitely be different, very different. I'm going with a man who loves me and wants to be alone with me. I look over at him adoringly. He catches my glance and winks at me. I feel this tiny little shiver up and down my back. I can hardly wait until we get there.

I look at Jack and then at the sky. *Threatening* is the word that comes to mind. Jack senses my concern. "Don't worry," he says, "I checked the weather report. All systems go."

We pass Miami. Jack thoughtfully packed a picnic lunch, so we munch turkey/cranberry sandwiches, brownies, and bottled water without stopping.

Leaving Homestead, we get onto US One, the Dixie Highway, which takes us all the way down to the Keys. I sigh. Only forty-three bridges and 110 miles to go. Rain threatening. Clouds black and grumbling.

First town coming up will be Key Largo. How can I not think of Bogart and Bacall steaming up the sheets in that famous movie of the same name? I look at my macho Bogart type driving happily along with a big grin on his face. But then again, I remember that movie also featured the worst hurricane in the United States up to that time. The Keys were very badly hit. The sky above us gets darker and more foreboding. Jack whistles some tune I don't recognize. Maybe it's the theme from *Titanic.*

"It's starting to rain," I say, "in case you haven't noticed." I singsong the child's tune: "Rain, rain, go away. Come again some other day."

"What's a little moisture," he says cheerfully. "Won't spoil our indoor sports."

"You have a one-track mind."

"And why shouldn't I, since we've been derailed so often."

By the time we reach Islamorada, the rain is seriously coming down. And the wind has picked up.

"Would this be a good time to tell you I really can't swim?"

"Swimming is not on the agenda."

"And I'm afraid of sharks."

"Who isn't? But we won't be swimming, ergo we won't have to worry about sharks."

I wish I had his confidence. "Maybe we should get a room closer in. Long Key is just right up ahead."

"Nah. Key West is great. Why, if you get bored we can visit Ernest Hemingway's house and see all the cats that live there or Harry Truman's Little White House or maybe even ride a dolphin..."

I reach over and pinch his arm.

"Wise guy. But the weather does look ominous."

"Not to worry. To an ex–navy man who rode out the storms in the North Atlantic, this is nothing."

"Nothing can turn into something," I say, still nervous. "You never told me you were in the navy."

He leans over and gives me a peck on the cheek. "There's a lot you don't know about me."

That's for sure. Now I'm getting the macho view of my man against nature. I hope nature doesn't win.

By the time we pass Marathon, the wind is howling and the rain is pelting down. It's hard to see out the windshield. Many cars are on the road, but they are going in the opposite direction.

Jack is still whistling. I close my eyes and pretend I'm asleep. But that's even worse. My imagination continues to paint dire scenarios.

* * *

I feel like I'm going "up the down staircase" as we fight our way through the heavy wind up the steps to the Brown Pelican Inn. People hurry past us, obviously on their way out, lugging their suitcases. Nervousness is written on their faces.

I would like to admire the charm of this pale yellow faux-Victorian B&B, but I can't tell much for the downpour.

"Lots of people leaving in a hurry," I say, trying to look at Jack, though I can't see his face clearly.

"Good," says Mr. Cheerful. "We'll upgrade to a better class of room."

At the desk, the checkout line is longer than the registration line, which consists of us! I stand next to him and leave it to the admiral to get us settled.

The manager introduces herself as Ms. Teresa LeYung, petite with long, lovely dark hair and almond eyes. She looks to be in her thirties. I timorously ask what the latest weather report is.

"Last report I heard, the storm was heading toward Puerto Rico, possibly south toward Cuba. But it will be bouncy here. Storm should subside by midnight. Not to worry." She's upbeat, but I detect concern in those pretty eyes. Jack is right; she offers us the bridal suite. No extra charge. Apparently the Midwestern newlyweds had changed their minds and canceled their reservation. Am I imagining it that the manager's hand is shaking as she hands Jack the key?

"You will keep us informed?" I ask.

"Absolutely," Ms. LeYung promises.

As we head for the elevator, I glance around the lobby quickly. It is a lovely place, done in good taste with French antiques. A few tourists are milling around having drinks, looking relaxed. So why am I still worried?

* * *

I admire our "bridal suite"—all white satin and peach lace with Laura Ashley delicate lavender floral drapes and bedspreads. It overlooks Mallory Deck, a huge outdoor party space where people gather by the hundreds each night to view the glorious sunsets over the ocean and be entertained by carnival performers. The ocean is an angry battleship gray. There are no cruise ships parked there this time. There will be no sunsets tonight. No people dancing the night away.

Jack hefts the voluminous basket of fruit, cheese, and wine. The ribbon reads, "Congratulations, Mr. and Mrs. Jim Lawler."

He reaches for a slice of pineapple. "I'm sure the Lawlers won't mind."

"I don't know," I say, "maybe they'll come for it tomorrow. We've gotten this by default."

The playful ex–navy man puns, "Yeah, 'de fault' being that those Midwestern wimps are no-shows, so the goodies go to us."

I sigh. "Keep making jokes. Then how come so many rats left the sinking craft? I sure hope you were never a captain in the navy—you know, the guy who always goes down with his ship."

"Nonsense. I've been in worse storms than this. Remind me to tell you about the time I was with a convoy in the North Atlantic in December near Greenland. Now, that was a whopper."

He bites down happily on the pineapple, licking the juice on his lips. It's a very sexy sight and I almost succumb to his mood. Almost.

He remains in amazingly good humor. It must be the storm turning him on, it couldn't be scaredy-cat me. I take my little overnighter to the bed and start to unpack. He's at my side in a flash. "Never mind. Unpack later."

He sits me on the bed, then slowly lowers me to a lying-down position. I can smell the slight lavender perfume on the delicately patterned Laura Ashley spread. Above my head I stare directly into the top-floor skylight. I wonder why a Victorian has a skylight. I wonder if the glass will hold. And whether there'll be a tsunami. Can the ocean climb three stories high? I ponder dozens of disastrous events as Jack leans over me and with his wonderful body blocks out the sight of the window.

For a few moments, I am able to get with the program.

Until I hear a cracking sound. Followed by an immediate crash of thunder. Jack either doesn't hear it or ignores it. He kisses me slowly, deliciously, his body tight against mine. I am torn between passion and terror.

Not a time for me to make jokes, but... "Did the earth move for you?" I ask.

He laughs. "Not quite yet for that, honey. Soon. I promise."

"Well, it is for me, sweetie. In fact, the whole room is shaking now. And not only that, but there must be a leak in the skylight."

"What skylight?" He turns his head just in time for a drop of water to land on his cheek.

"The one right above us, which just might totally collapse on us any moment."

Within seconds, Jack is off me and the bed. He pulls me up with both arms. "Why didn't you warn me?"

We rush to the windows and, clinging to each other, watch the storm rage. No more little squall—this is bad news. We can no longer see the Mallory Deck. What few sailboats were tied to the docks, bouncing about like toy toothpicks, have disappeared and there is nothing but bleak grayness everywhere.

The sounds of the storm are so loud, we barely hear the shouting and the frantic knocking on the door. Jack opens the door to the wide-eyed Ms. LeYung. She looks to be red-faced from having run up the three flights. She can't hide her state of panic.

"News from the National Weather Service. The winds have shifted and the hurricane is coming directly at us. Delta force winds, type four, at more than 150 miles an hour are predicted. They're giving us twelve hours' notice, but they think it will hit sooner. We've all got to evacuate!"

I automatically salute. "Aye, aye," says the ex-navy man's "mate," who is envious of Mr. and Mrs. Jim Lawler, in whatever warm, dry place they might be.

We grab our bags and race down the stairs after the manager. Other guests are running downstairs as well. Ms. LeYung is muttering, "Oh, God, I was here when Wilma struck. It was horrible."

In the lobby we meet up with the rest of the frightened guests. Ms. LeYung gives last-minute instructions to her staff, who are hurriedly pulling down the hurricane shutters all over the B&B.

"I'll be right back," she tells the working crew.

She starts for the door. Jack stops her. "Wait. Don't you want us to help?"

She shakes her head. "Thanks, but don't worry. We'll all get out of here in time."

We join the guests anxiously waiting at the front door. "Follow my car," she tells us. "I'll lead you to the shortcut out of the city."

* * *

Bleak. All I'm aware of are bleak- and angry-looking clouds covering the sky. Jack struggles to see out the windshield. The car is rocking as he fights to keep it in control. Frankly, I'm glad I have no view. I don't want to watch the destruction that might be happening to all these beautiful little towns along the Keys.

Other cars also rushing from the Keys pass us, dangerously close.

"I'm an idiot," Jack says. "Putting you through this."

"You said it, I didn't." I lean over to kiss his cheek. "But you're my idiot and I still love you. Besides, how could you know the winds would shift?" I pretend to put a good face on it. "Isn't this exciting?"

Jack is glum. "Not the kind of excitement I had in mind."

"All is not lost. I've learned a lot of new things about you, Mr. Navy Man. Stubborn. Opinionated. Risk-taker..."

Jack cringes. "Don't say another word. And what I've learned about you is that you're loyal, though foolishly so, and brave."

I don't want to ruin his opinion of me so I don't contradict him.

I peer out, barely able to see from one side of the very narrow causeway to the other, thinking grim thoughts. To the left of us, all of the Gulf of Mexico. To the right, the entire Atlantic Ocean. Water lapping hard on both sides reaching out to connect in the middle. Coming closer and closer to our car. Eager to have at us and suck us in. Forever.

"Brave" me, hiding my eyes with sunglasses, shuts them and keeps them that way for most of the ride home.

15

Getting Ready

It takes us nearly five hours to make it back to Fort Lauderdale. The farther north we go, the less ominous the weather, but no doubt there's a real hurricane chasing our tail. Everywhere we look the escalating wind is heaving debris, forming bizarre kites in the sky.

Drivers on the road rigidly lean forward into their steering wheels, clutching them with all their strength. They're a study in fear. Everyone is speeding home or in any direction that might get them out of town as fast as possible. Their vehicles are rolling from side to side. Already, small-weight cars have overturned, some blown onto the shoulder. Jack's car radio repeats the same announcements over and over. The Atlantic Hurricane Center reports that as of four-thirty P.M., the storm has intensified, and that now the east coast of

Florida is in severe danger. Ocean waves at Miami Beach were kicked up by the Category Four storm. Winds are gusting at 160 miles an hour. By now the expensive beach hotels had been evacuated. The waves had already destroyed five houses and damaged ten others. So far, the hotels are still standing. The news comes at us at a staccato beat, breaking up occasionally, but the message is loud and clear: Fort Lauderdale will be next, hit hard with a hurricane for the first time ever.

When we finally pull into Lanai Gardens, exhausted, we see more of the same. People driving out and away; others boarding up windows or scurrying to and fro with last-minute preparations. For the first time I'm sure everyone wishes we'd put up hurricane shutters. But in all these years we never needed them.

Jack parks the car in front of my building. It's a parking spot belonging to someone else, but this is no time to worry about the rules. As we get out I hear someone cry, "They're back, thank God!"

I look up to see Ida, hands clutching a jacket to her chest and neck, her hair bun unruly. Perched on our landing, she frantically waves at us. We hurry upstairs, not bothering to use the elevator, heads bowed, the wind pushing at our backs.

Ida throws her arms around me. "We didn't think we'd ever see you again. They expect Key West to be hit in a few hours!" I think of the lovely Ms. LeYung and hope she gets out in time.

Ida pulls us into my apartment.

What a sight before us. Every light in the apartment is on. My highboy, the tallest piece of furniture I own, has been pushed against my living room windows. The rest of the windows were obviously hurriedly boarded up. Denny is finishing up last-minute hammering. His girlfriend, Yolie, acting as his assistant, is handing him nails. My floors are covered with mattresses and sleeping bags. The couch and chairs are circled in and around the sleeping bags. The dining room table is sky-high with snacks. The air, oddly, is filled with delicious smells.

Evvie runs to hug me. "Thank God you're all right. I was so afraid you wouldn't be able to get back in time." Her hug is tight, I hug her back. We hold on to each other for a few moments. For the first time I allow myself to think of what might have been, had we left any later.

"Welcome to Hurricane Central, Operation Gladdy's Apartment," says Ida. "We decided to use your place because it has the least amount of clutter."

Bella adds, "So we could be able to fill it with the biggest number of people."

"And because if you returned very late, you'd be able to find us." This from Sophie.

"What's going on? Do you have a plan?" I ask. Jack stands close to me, holding my hand.

"You bet we do," Evvie says. "Every building has made sure no one is left alone. People are staying together in groups. We have a telephone outreach so we can check on one another, and we know where every person is. That means we all have the phone numbers of the apartments with groups staying in them. For as long as the phone lines stay up. About five to eight people have been placed per apartment."

"Yeah," says Bella, seated cross-legged on one of the mattresses. "The stores ran out of candles and flashlights so we're all sharing everything."

Sophie adds, "Everyone brought food from their apartments. And we figure before the power goes out we're cooking all the frozen food."

That explains why I smell pot roast. And chicken, too.

Bella adds, "And we made a ton of ice cubes to keep the stuff in the fridge from spoiling."

Evvie looks shyly up at Jack. "Sorry your vacation trip was ruined."

"Me, too," Jack agrees stoically.

It's already getting much darker outside. I can tell from the tiny slits of sky showing through the rough plywood boards.

Denny and Yolie walk carefully over and around all the stuff on the floor. "Best I could do this fast," he tells us.

The girls hug the two of them and thank him in unison.

"Where are you and Yolie staying?" I ask.

"With Sol and Tessie and Mary and Irving in Irving's apartment." Yolie nods for emphasis. They head out the door, into the wind.

Evvie calls after them, "Be careful."

They wave and with heads down, holding hands, they run to the stairs.

Out of curiosity, I ask, "Where are Hy and Lola?"

Ida grins. "Home alone. They insisted on being by themselves."

Evvie looks at Jack. "You'd better get back to your place while you still can." As she says this, she hands him a sheet of paper.

I look at Evvie, upset. "What are you talking about? I want him to stay with us."

Jack glances at the list. He looks at me. "I guess I better go." He hands the sheet of paper back to Evvie.

"No," I say quickly. "That's ridiculous. We need you here. I want you here."

Jack shakes his head. "Evvie's right. My building has a number of women who live alone. Our Canadian neighbors all went home days ago, so Abe Waller and I are the only men left. He'll need my help. They must be frantic waiting for me to round them up into my apartment and I can't let them down."

I grab the list and look it over. I know they are right. Evvie looks at me. "I'm sorry," she says.

Jack gives me a quick hug and turns to the girls. "Take good care of one another."

With that he gets hugs from them and a chorus of "We wills."

With a last kiss for me, he hurries out. Before I shut the door, he calls to me, "We'll keep talking on the phone until the lines go down. I love you."

I shout, "I love you, too." But it's drowned out by the wind.

When I go back in, I notice for the first time that my bedroom door is closed, as is the screened-in Florida room.

Evvie sees my look. "We have all the furniture up against the screens to protect the inside as best we can, but I doubt it will help . . ."

"What about the bedroom? Can't we use that?"

"Of course, but right now our other houseguest is napping. Enya is also in our group," Ida reports.

I look around the room once more. Each mattress and sleeping bag has a pillow and someone's clothing on it. "That's pretty darned good organizing in so short a time," I say. I look at the faces of my girls. They are frightened but excited, too. And trying very hard to act brave.

"Thanks to Evvie," says Ida. "She mapped out this plan in her last newsletter."

I blush. I've been so involved with Jack; I'm probably the only one who hadn't read it. I look apologetically at my sister. She smiles knowingly.

Sophie adds, "The minute the TV said we were going to get hit, Evvie was on the phone organizing every building. Within an hour everyone was set."

Evvie comments, "A lot of people went to schools and community centers but we all voted to stay here."

Suddenly there is a loud smashing sound outside. We all jump.

Enya rushes out of my bedroom with sleep-encrusted eyes. "What . . . what happened?"

Ida puts her arm around Enya. "We don't know."

Sophie joins Ida and embraces the shaking Enya. "Anybody hungry?" she says. "The pot roast smells ready."

Enya sees me and comes to hug me. "You're back safe."

I nod. "We'll be fine. Try not to worry."

"We have three kinds of potatoes to choose from," Evvie says, starting for the kitchen. Everyone follows. "Five different veggies and three meats."

My tiny kitchen will have to hold all of us.

There is a poignant cry from the living room floor. It's Bella, struggling to get on her hands and knees. "Somebody help. I can't get up!"

We rush to her aid.

Partners, all of us. Through thick and thin. God help us through this night.

16

A Night to Remember

We are all pleasantly stuffed, which helps make what's going on outside almost bearable. The girls are stretched out in the living room in nightgowns and robes, leaning against pillows, walls, and couch backs, contentedly watching a classic movie. Each of them has a flashlight at her side.

It's dark out and the storm rages around us. Every time there is a banging somewhere, we stiffen. But we are determined to keep things light, to soldier on.

Enya stiffly sits away from us on a chair at the dining room table, eyes closed, still dressed. She is somewhere else, lost in her troubled thoughts. She clutches her cup of tea, already cold.

I am in the kitchen cleaning up the mess we made at dinner. I had offers of help, but it's much easier for one person to move around in the small space. Besides, I need something to take my mind off the storm. I watch my girls and Enya through the small pass-through opening. Poor Enya, she seems almost in shock.

Believe it or not, the girls voted to watch this TV rerun of *A Night to Remember.* Evvie, our movie maven, explains that this is the famous black-and-white English version of the disaster. It came out in the 1950's. The girls are mesmerized by the almost documentary style of the sinking of the *Titanic.* I guess watching another disaster is better than thinking of the one we're in right now.

Bella giggles.

Evvie asks, "What's so funny? We're watching a serious movie. They're about to hit the iceberg."

"I can't help it. Two nights in a row I get to go on a sleepover." Bella burps, and then giggles again, holding on to her expanded tummy. "Maybe I shouldn't have had three different desserts, but how often do I get to eat peach pie, chocolate cake, and strawberry shortcake in the same night?"

Ida huffs. "You didn't have to stuff yourself."

"Well, it was gonna spoil."

"So what," Ida answers. "It's disgusting watching you pig out."

Sophie grins. "I'm with Bella. I loved having all those different main dishes. I vote Evvie's cabbage rolls were the best."

"Thank you ever so much," Evvie says modestly.

"And besides," Sophie adds, "what if we're stuck

here for days and run out of food? We might need to feed off our own fat—I read that somewhere."

"But where's that adorable Leo DiCaprio and the cute English girl?" Bella wants to know. "Where's the love story?"

Evvie corrects her. "That's the much later version, in color. This one is from the point of view of a young man who worked on board."

"No kissing, no naked painting?"

Evvie shrugs. "Sorry."

A Night to Remember is interrupted for another update on our own catastrophe.

Sophie groans. "Just before my favorite part, where the captain starts shutting down the emergency doors."

"We interrupt this broadcast for a special report," says the announcer. And now for the third time this evening we are getting a repeat of the same fifteen-minute documentary. *The Eleven Worst Florida Hurricanes in History* flashes on the screen, once more preempting our movie.

This program has been playing in between the actual on-the-spot news reports happening on our own streets. "Here we go again," mumbles Evvie, sitting next to a lamp; she'd been trying to read a book and watch the movie at the same time. "If it isn't another depressing news flash, it's this thing. They're ruining our movie."

Ida is knitting. Sophie and Bella are holding up skeins of yarn, forming them into workable balls for Ida.

I keep playing over and over in my head the trip

Jack and I took to Key West to be alone. I think of the warm feelings I felt for him. I wish Jack had been able to stay with us. I want his nearness and his comfort.

The phone rings. I set out for the bedroom to answer. It's probably not any of our families. We've spoken to a few of them earlier. My daughter, Emily, worriedly called much earlier from New York and so did Evvie's Martha. We assured them that we are fine. But are we?

Sophie's son didn't call, but she's not surprised—her jeweler son in Brooklyn is very selfish and uncaring. I can't go into what Ida is thinking. She has family but there is a huge rift that she refuses to speak about, and she never hears from them. As for Bella, as she says, she's an orphan. And Enya, well, there is no family left for her anywhere since the end of the last World War.

I'm sure it's Jack on the phone. He's already called twice. As long as the phone lines stay open, I feel connected to him, and I need this connection, to know he's safe.

In the background I hear stentorian tones: "In 1919 Key West was hit by the most powerful hurricane in its history. The storm killed more than eight hundred people. In 1926 . . ."

I shut the door to block it out. "Hello, dear, everybody still in one piece?" I ask, keeping my voice cheerful.

"About the same. Except for a few battles about who gets to control the TV, the ladies are holding up. Of course, Dora keeps wanting to tell us what's happening on her soaps and all she's worried about is will she be able to see tomorrow's episodes."

"And what about dear Louise?" I say icily. "Is she still pretending to be terrified, so she can hold your hand?"

Jack laughs. "Meow," he says. "You're jealous. Admit it."

"Maybe a little, since she's the one with you right now."

There is a pause. "I wish it could have been otherwise."

"Shh, take care of your little harem." I pause. "Just keep her out of your bedroom."

Jack laughs. "I promise to restrain myself."

I hear a deafening sound from his end of the line followed by a woman's scream, then, "Jack, get over here quick! I need you!" I recognize Louise's voice.

His voice tightens. "Something's happened. Better check on it. Hold on, be right back."

I listen with the phone glued to my ear. I hear women's voices crying out all at once. They sound terrified. But I can't make out what they're shouting.

Jack's phone goes dead.

I try redialing, but no luck. I can't get through. A copy of Evvie's list is on the dresser. I dial Abe Waller's number. Surely he'll know what's going on in their building. The phone continues to ring. But no one answers.

I try Stanley Heyer across the courtyard. His

line is busy. In a panic I call the next number on the list, of someone in the Y Building. A man named Charles answers. I've never met him. I ask him to look out through the slats in his window and see what's happening in Z. He does so. He reports back that all seems okay. Lights are still on. I thank him and hang up.

I want to run out the door and get over there now! But I don't dare. It's not possible anyway. I'd never make it. Maybe it's nothing too serious and the women were overreacting. Maybe, I pray . . .

I go back into the living room, sick with worry, but I don't intend to say anything. My group's scared enough, and there's no sense causing a panic until I know more. I pull myself together and try to hide my dread. The moaning and groaning sounds, mixed with whatever things are smashing outside our door, add to my fears.

The girls are mimicking what the announcer is saying. They've memorized these words from earlier broadcasts. "In 1928 Okeechobee; 1935 the Keys; 1960 Donna; 1964 Cleo. Betsy, Andrew . . ."

"I wish they'd name a hurricane after me," Sophie says wistfully. "This year we're gonna get Arthur, Bertha, Cristobal, Dolly, Edouard, Fay, Gustav . . . who makes up those names anyway? And why do they make them up in advance? They have names picked out all the way through 2012." She counts on her fingers. "Twenty-one names. Does that mean they're expecting twenty-one hurricanes to hit this year? Oy."

Ida says, as she untangles a knot in her yarn, "I

read somewhere that three different ancient civilizations all predicted a comet would hit the world in 2012. That's the day we're all supposed to get killed, so why sweat it now?"

Sophie groans. "Why do you always have to be such a truthsayer?"

"You're trying to say *soothsayer,* but you mean *naysayer,*" Evvie corrects.

"Whatever."

Ida makes a face. "I'm only telling you what I read."

Evvie climbs over the sleeping bags to find the remote, when suddenly the TV switches to one of our local broadcasters. He's huddled inside a restaurant doorway, clutching his mike, his hands shaking, his voice quivering. Behind him a group of onlookers peers into the camera, too frightened to make faces the way people usually do when they manage to squeeze their way in front of the camera.

"We are in Melina's Greek Diner on University Drive right off Oakland Park Boulevard. We can hardly believe our eyes. The corner streetlight fell moments ago and the street sign just . . . blew away!"

The camera shifts and now we are witness to what's going on outside the door, from their point of view, as the announcer continues to report. We see what he is saying.

"We are on generator power, as all lights are out in the entire neighborhood. Trees are tumbling haphazardly down the streets as water from broken mains turns this usually busy intersection into rivers!"

"Those poor people," Bella says. "How are they gonna get home?"

Even as the newsman continues to speak, the lights in my living room flicker and everyone responds nervously.

On the TV, we see fire trucks racing by, sirens screaming, gushing up huge puddles as they pass the cameras. "The store windows are exploding," the announcer's frantic voice shouts. "Everyone, move back!"

Sophie gets up on her knees and points at the TV. "Oh, no, across the street, look—there goes Bagel Bites!"

Bella utters a small scream. "A car just floated by. Did you see?"

We watch as a wrought-iron bus-stop bench at the corner falls over. The announcer is fading in and out. Their generator light is dimming and we can hear people screaming as the front glass panes blow out. The sounds and sights are terrifying. Suddenly the picture is gone.

A voice tells us, "We now return to our original broadcast..." And *A Night to Remember* is back on again. Just in time to see and hear people screaming and running for the lifeboats as the *Titanic* starts taking on icy water.

One by one the girls turn away from the screen. Our real disaster has trumped the movie. They are all silent. Enya moans, shaking her head from side to side. We all turn as strong winds whistle eerily through the uneven slats on the windows.

Evvie mutes the TV. "Enough," she says. "Let's do something else."

"Like what?" Sophie asks.

"I don't know. Talk about stuff. Somebody pick a topic," Evvie answers.

I jump in, wanting to get their minds off what just happened on streets that are barely a mile away. "How about telling a funny story about yourself."

They look at me, blank expressions all.

After a few moments, Evvie says, "Okay, I'll start."

With that, Bella and Sophie start passing out candy and other assorted junk food.

When we are all settled, Evvie begins. "During the war I got a job singing in this bar in Brooklyn. I was only sixteen but I lied about my age. And on a Friday night, after one of my sets, this old guy sidles up to me and tries to pick me up. He uses the corny line, 'Hey, girly, haven't we met before?' and I look at him and I look at him and finally, I say, 'You know, we did meet years ago.' Now he's getting all heated up. He says, 'Yeah, where? Did we have a hot old time?' And I tell him, 'We met on Boynton Avenue in the Bronx. I was a kid and you were my babysitter. Herby, you old cradle robber, you!'

"Herby was so embarrassed, he backed up and ran for the door. I yelled after him, 'How come you're not in the army?' "

The group is entertained and distracted. Bella claps. Evvie turns to see my frown.

"You sang in a bar when you were sixteen and you never told Mom and Dad?"

"Oops," says my adventurous sister, grinning at me.

Sophie raises her hand like a kid at school. "I got one. I got a story."

All eyes turn to her.

"Remember when we all had to wear girdles?"

There are sighs of uncomfortable memories at that. Bella comments, "We had to wear them every day. Even if we only went to the mailbox."

"Even if we were skinny," Ida comments.

"I was the Corseteria's best customer," continues Sophie. "One day I saw this picture in the paper of a crowd of women burning their bras."

Ida nods. "In the sixties."

"Well, I was living in a cute house in Long Island at the time and I took all my bras and girdles out to the burn barrel in the yard and set fire to every foundation I owned. However, I didn't take into account that the rubber in the garments and the plastic stays would start the smelliest fire you could ever imagine. The fire trucks came and my neighbors hissed at me. When Stanley came home that night, he had a fit. 'Why, why, did you do it?' he screamed.

"I put my hands on my hips and said, 'Because I'm a feminist now.' He looked at me and screams, 'Well, you're a *fat* feminist, so put your girdle back on.' "

The girls and I are awash with laughter. I even see a tiny smile appear on Enya's face.

Bella waves at us. "Me, too. Me, too. Could I tell a sex story?"

We look at her in amazement. Bella?

"Must you?" says Ida.

"Go ahead," says Sophie, patting Bella on the back. "Ignore the man-hater."

Ida, on the other side of her, shoves her elbow sharply into Sophie's side.

"Ouch," Sophie cries.

Bella manages to stand up. "Well," she says in her wispy little voice, "my Abe never undressed in front of me. And I never undressed in front of him. He went into the closet and I went into the bathroom."

Incredulity on every face. The things you don't know about your friends. We push forward to hear better. Even Ida.

Bella continues, "I must say I was curious about what he did in that closet, so one night I got in with him." She beams. We wait, openmouthed.

"And?" Sophie says to encourage her before her short-term memory loss kicks in and she loses track of what she's saying.

"And from then on we had the best sex ever in that closet."

Sophie screams with laughter. Evvie and I join her. Even Ida loses it. And Enya is actually smiling.

Bella adds in all innocence, "I must admit, we did smell like mothballs when we got out."

"I love this," Evvie says. "Speaking of sex, you wanna know the first time I did it?"

I squint at her. "I'd certainly like to know, big mouth."

"Well, if you feel that way..."

"I could live without any more of your stories," says Ida.

Sophie pinches Evvie. "Come on, tell us."

"Okay, now that you've twisted my arm, so to speak. We were in a phone booth. In Times Square. On VE Day."

Need I say the girls gasped at that? My sister, what a bold young thing she was. And I—I was always the well-behaved one. How boring, I think now in retrospect.

Evvie looks at me and giggles. "Don't worry. I was with my husband. Joe had just come home from the war."

Our laughter fades as suddenly there's another crashing sound close by and the lights go out.

17

Uninvited Guests

We are in a total state of panic. I feel the girls scrambling to get off the mattresses and sleeping bags, bumping into one another, crying out in fright.

I grab my flashlight. "Find your flashlights and turn them on."

"I'll light the candles," Evvie says.

"Enya, where are you?" My light finds her standing up next to the table. She waves her arms at me to indicate she is all right.

I crawl on my knees until I'm able to stand: "I'll check the phones." I make my way, cautiously, along the walls to the kitchen. Just what I was afraid of. "Can't get a signal," I call out to them.

Evvie says, "Try the cell." I pick it up from the kitchen table. "That's dead, too," I tell them. All I can think of is not regaining contact with Jack. I can't stand not knowing what is happening over there.

Evvie tries to calm everyone. "Come on, stay down and form a circle and light up the center with our flashlights. Let's pretend we're camping in the woods and we're sitting in front of a fire telling ghost stories."

Sophie says eagerly, "Should I get some hot chocolate and marshmallows?"

Ida groans. "Enough with the food, already. Besides, we don't have marshmallows. And we won't be able to heat up the hot chocolate. Can't you make believe?"

"Ugh," Bella says, hugging herself. "Too many insects. I hate the woods." She slaps at her arm as if something bit her.

Ida huffs. "We're making this up, silly. Stop slapping."

"I don't like ghost stories," Sophie says. "They scare me,"

Evvie is exasperated. "All right. All right. We're not in the woods, we're in Sawgrass Mall. Shopping."

"Ah," says Sophie, "that's better. I could use a couple of things."

We move around, trying for more comfortable positions. The storm's roaring sounds are terrifying, the winds are howling. The building feels like it's actually shaking. I can hear dishes rattling in the kitchen.

Sophie shrieks as she hears a cracking sound above us. "Maybe we should have gone to a second-floor apartment. What if the roof caves in and blows us all away?"

Ida looks up fearfully. "If we were on the second floor and the roof caves—then the third floor will fall on the second floor and we'll all be buried alive!"

"Are we going to die?" Bella asks plaintively.

"Are you ready to go if we do?" asks Ida, curious.

Evvie gets angry. "What kind of dumb question is that?" She looks nervously at Enya, who seems not to be listening.

Sophie pipes up, "When they asked my deaf aunt Fannie if she wanted to go, she said, 'You bet!' She thought we were talking about going to the Hamptons."

Leave it to Sophie to break the tension. But then she asks, "Does anyone believe in an afterlife?"

"Not me," says Bella, "not 'til I know there's a there there."

Sophie continues, "My dead cousin Sooky once came back to me in a dream. She said, 'Don't bother, stay where you are, it's nothing much.' "

Enya speaks softly. "I wanted to die when they took my husband and children."

It's very quiet for a while after that.

Evvie locates the battery-operated radio and turns it on. She fiddles with the dial until she finds music.

"Maybe we should all try to sleep," I suggest. "Or at least rest."

The music is basic elevator stuff, but perfect for

this occasion. Enya returns to the bedroom. The girls lie down. And one by one we settle into our makeshift bedding. Evvie hums along to songs she recognizes, sometimes singing the words with that beautiful voice of hers.

As I'm lulled to sleep, I can even believe the storm is lessening. I close my eyes and think, Jack, please be all right.

* * *

A horrific pounding awakens me. Because of the boarded-up windows I can't tell if it's still night. I think I'm having a nightmare, but I finally realize the pounding hasn't stopped and voices are shouting. We all begin to stir.

Evvie is up first. "Someone's trying to get in," she says fearfully as she climbs over us to get to the hallway. I'm right behind her.

"Get out of the way," I say, "when the door opens."

And I'm right. Once Evvie unlocks it, the wind slams the open door against the wall behind her. To our astonishment, Hy and Lola practically fly inside. The whooshing sound of the wind behind them is mind-boggling. It takes the four of us to get the door shut again.

Everyone is up now, even Enya, who hurries out of the bedroom. All of us stare at Hy and Lola as they drop down to their knees on the floor of my hallway, panting.

What a sight they are. In robes and pajamas,

with ropes wrapped around their bodies. They are soaking wet.

Sophie runs to get towels. Evvie quickly dashes to put up hot tea. But then she remembers we have no electricity. She reaches for the one pathetic quarter bottle of scotch which has been in my cupboard seemingly forever, and pours two glasses.

"What happened?" Ida asks.

The couple can hardly catch their breaths.

Hy manages to croak out his words. "The plywood didn't hold. Our living room windows shattered and the winds raged in and threw our furniture all around. It was so strong, it knocked us down. We had to get out of there."

They tug off their sopping-wet slippers. Evvie hands them the scotch. Hy downs his quickly. Lola, trembling, sips hers.

"Lucky we had ropes in our front hall closet," Lola says, crying with relief that she is safe, "or we'd be dead now."

"We crawled on our hands and knees through the cars, using them to shelter us. We made it across the way, tying the rope to fenders, telephone poles, streetlights, whatever we could hook on to and pull from," Hy adds.

Ida doesn't understand. "Why didn't you go to Irving, right under you?"

Hy says, "We tried, but with all our banging, they didn't hear us. We saw the candles in your kitchen window so we hoped you were still up."

Lola sips gratefully. Color starts to come back

into her face. "It must have taken us an hour to get here."

Hy reaches over and pats her gently. "It only seemed like it, toots."

She shudders. "I thought the wind would pick us up and . . . and toss us away . . . like rag dolls."

I find a selection of bulky sweaters and sweats and the two of them go into the bathroom to change.

When they come out, toweling their hair, and in an assortment of my clothes, they sit down at the dining room table and we surround them anxiously.

Evvie asks what we all need to know: "What's going on out there?"

"I don't know," Hy answers. "It was hard enough trying to keep our eyes open to see our way, and we had to bend our heads down against the wind. But I could tell a lot of our cars are damaged."

Lola moves closer to Hy, shuddering. "It was so pitch black. No light anywhere. Like the end of the world."

He puts his arm around her, comforting her. This is a Hy we've never seen. Caring, even strong. And brave. A kinder, gentler Hy? Perhaps we've been unfair to him all these years.

* * *

After a makeshift breakfast of cold cereal, milk, and juice (kept cool by the now-melting ice cubes), everyone is feeling a little better. The wind seems to be dying down. The worst might be over. Our battery-operated radio informs us that the storm is moving southeast along the Atlantic Coast, back toward Puerto Rico and Cuba. But it's still not calm enough for us to go outside.

No one is sleepy anymore. We lounge around the living room, listlessly waiting for it to be over.

Sophie moans. "I wish the TV was on so we could watch something."

Evvie comments, "Our *Titanic* movie is over by now."

Sophie complains, "But I wanted to see how it ends."

Ida is sarcastic. "You know how it ends. They all live happily ever after."

Sophie is miffed. "They do not. Most of them drown." She hits Ida on the shoulder and Ida hits her back.

"*Dummkopf*," says Ida.

"Meanie," retorts Sophie. "I don't care. I'd watch anything right now."

Ida scoffs, "Why bother? There's never anything of interest besides the news, which is always depressing."

Evvie agrees. "No kidding. It's all dreck. Garbage produced by kids and watched by kids. And cable—the language, the violence, the filth. It's almost enough to turn you against sex. Disgusting stuff. Is nothing sacred anymore? No wonder kids today are a mess."

Even I have to put my two cents in. "I don't know why they don't have a senior cable station.

We're nearly forty-eight percent of the population now. Where's our representation?"

Sophie jumps in. "Maybe that rich guy—what's his name? Turner, who Jane Fonda used to be married to? I like his channel with old movies. He could afford our idea."

Bella rhapsodizes, "We could watch really grown-up love stories, with seniors falling in love and with clean language. That would be nice."

Evvie murmurs, "I wouldn't mind some dirty language myself."

Lola adds, "Grown-up family dramas where wise grandparents are listened to, for a change, so their silly children and grandchildren would learn some lessons."

"And fashion shows with mature-bodied women modeling," chimes in Sophie. "I'm sick of seeing all those bulimic girls who look like they just threw up."

"And those stupid sitcoms where everyone acts like morons." Evvie is in her element. "Our senior network would have intelligence and class. We'll be seen as sensible people living happily in this, the third act of our lives."

The girls applaud her little speech.

Hy, lying comfortably across one of my couches, comments, "Never happen."

We turn to him. Evvie, hands on hips, demands, "And why not?"

He gets up, stretches. "Those lovely shows you predict? Think of the commercials that will keep interrupting." Hy, frustrated show-off that he is, gets up and acts them out with gusto. "Here's the sponsors of your quality shows: Hey, you oldsters, get your Depends diapers so you won't embarrass yourself in public. One size fits all. Is that a bulge in your bottom? Or are you not glad to see me?"

Now he prances in between the pillows. "Teeth dropped out? How about our gluey dentures? Bald, but for us, not by choice and definitely not a fashion statement; hair transplant anyone? Need orthopedic shoes? Hearing aids that never work? Varicose veins. Knee replacements. Hip replacements. Pacemakers. Walkers. Wheelchairs. Rascal scooters when you can't walk at all."

We watch him in hideous fascination as he hops and skips through the bedding on the floor.

"Assisted living at End of the Trails Retirement Home. No waiting. Vacancies every day. Estate planning—don't bother; the kids will fight over everything. Reverse mortgages—get thrown out if you linger too long. Come and pick your own satin casket. Initials optional. Go choose your cemetery plot. Every one with a view. Overlooking the golf course."

Now he's jumping up and down, with his hand over his groin. "Gotta go, gotta go. Gotta go. Oops, too late." He squats.

"Enough already," shouts Ida, throwing a pillow at him. "You're disgusting."

"Yeah? And how about Viagra, that little blue pill that gives you a thrill." He winks. "Gets you up when you're feeling down."

Lola gently says, "You might try them yourself, dear."

"Quiet, toots, who asked you?"

Evvie is seething. "Are you through yet?"

"How about prunes for your constipation and Imodium for your diarrhea? And let's not forget Vicodin and Digoxin and Detrol and fifty others. You think we got a lot of pill sponsors already, just wait..." Hy is finished. He takes a bow. "How about all that?"

"How about we throw you back into the hurricane," Ida says.

"Hey, who else is gonna sponsor you old relics? It ain't Mercedes and Versace and Helena Rubenstein. *Bupkes,* that's what you old broads will get. *Bupkes*. No one cares about what you want to watch!"

I sigh. That's our old Hy, back again by unpopular demand.

I leave the living room with everyone screaming epithets at him. Entering the kitchen, I'm surprised to see Hy has followed me. As I drink a glass of water, he grins. "Like the show?"

"You were pretty disgraceful."

"Yeah, ain't I always, but I sure took everybody's mind off the hurricane."

Touché.

18

Aftermath

We are awakened by the sound of people shouting. And sunshine peeping through the uneven slats of my boarded windows. I can't believe I actually fell back asleep, especially since Hy's snoring nearly drove me crazy. But he did look cute cuddled up with Lola.

I jump up from my mattress, grab my sneakers, and quickly shove my feet into them. In the hallway, I open the front door carefully, then, realizing it's safe, I pull it wide. In moments, Sophie, Bella, and Lola, awakened by my activity, follow behind me as I hurry outside onto the balcony. Sophie and Bella cling to each other, jumping up and down. It's really over. Blessedly over. And we'd survived.

We see our neighbors down below, walking around, surveying the damage. What a mess it is. Most of the cars were hit. Some crashed into one another, some landed on roofs of others. Trees have fallen. Telephone poles are down. The street is a sloppy mess of wet trash. Broken glass is everywhere, and plywood slats that failed and fell. My neighbors wear boots and walk carefully amid the rubble, calling out to one another.

From inside, I hear Evvie say, "Phone's still not working. Power's still off."

Hy, in my kitchen, is complaining, "I'd kill for a cup of hot coffee."

Tessie and Sol, downstairs, in robes, wave up to us. She calls, "Everybody okay?"

Sophie calls back, "We're good. How's your group?"

"We're still here."

I can't stand the suspense. Why isn't Jack looking for me? He would have rushed over by now. I start down the stairs and yell back up, "I'm going to look for Jack."

Evvie calls, "Wait for me."

Still wearing the clothes we slept in, looking utterly disheveled, we hurry down what's left of our cement staircase, which, thank goodness, we can manage by holding on to the dangling wrought-iron rails. Behind us we leave the others dazed and bewildered, heading for their own apartments to assess what has happened during the night.

* * *

We cut through Phases Four and Five, pretty much the same scene we just left. Stragglers wandering around looking for friends, going to neighbors' apartments to check the damage. The buildings are still intact, except for broken windows and destroyed Florida rooms; many of our screened-in porches didn't make it.

When we round the corner to Phase Six, I stop and cry out, "No!" I can't believe what's before me. Building Z—Jack's building—has collapsed! Evvie sees it, too, and grabs my arm. We start running as best we can through the debris.

A small group of people stand in front, staring and talking quietly. I look across the courtyard. Building Y is undamaged. But in Jack's building, the third floor has caved in onto the second floor, where Jack's apartment is... Was. I can't see his apartment. It is crushed underneath the floor above. I remember Ida's chilling remark. I'm frantic. I finally see people I recognize. One of Jack's bridge partners, Carol Ann Gutsch, is there. As is Abe Waller. Carol Ann is crying. A woman I can't identify has her arms around her. Carol Ann's clothes are torn and her face is cut and bloody. We run over to them.

My voice is shrill, I hardly recognize it. "What's happened to the people in there? Where's Jack?"

Abe clutches at the yarmulke on his head as if to make sure it is still there. "We don't know. When I came outside I found Mrs. Gutsch here on the ground."

Carol Ann shakes her head, waving her arms impotently, crying harder.

I can barely let myself look back up. My God, are they still in there?

Abe continues. "We were lucky." He points to his far-corner first-floor apartment, which is about all that's left standing of the building. "Our people were able to escape when the building started to fall."

Evvie, who knows the list, says, "Jack also had Louise Bannister, Dora Dooley, and Carmel Graves staying with him."

I want to shake Carol Ann until she tells me what I need to know. I cut in. "What about Jack and the other women? You have to tell me what happened. Please."

Her words tumble out through her tears. "All I remember is we were sleeping on the floor in the living room. Then the crashing noise started above us and the ceiling began to cave in. Jack yelled for us to run. I was nearest the door and I got out first. I dashed to the steps as fast as I could. I was so afraid the steps would be gone, and I'd be trapped, but they were still there. I tried to look back, but I couldn't see with all the dirt and pieces of the building falling. I could hear Dora screaming, and Carmel crying that she couldn't find the door. I made it downstairs and ran into the middle of the street and I fell down. That's all I remember. I must have passed out. By the time I came to"—she indicates her neighbors—"they were bending over me—"

I interrupted. "But Jack and the others. Did you see them again?"

Carol Ann shakes her head.

A man holding a towel to his bleeding head

says, "I live in building Y. I saw something. After Z building fell I ran back home to grab my flashlight. When I finally made it out again, I saw a car drive out. Amazing that any of the cars could be running."

I feel hope. "Maybe someone picked them up." I look around. "Does anyone have a car that hasn't been hit?" I'm miserable when all I see are heads shaking and all I hear is them mumbling no.

Suddenly a piercing scream comes from behind Jack's building. We all run. The easier way around the building is from the side of Abe's apartment, which had the least damage. Oh, God, I fear the worst. Will all their dead bodies be lying there?

When we turn the corner, we see a young couple standing there staring down into what seems like a very deep pit where part of the building used to be. The man has his flashlight illuminating downward.

"What is it?" the man with the towel asks. "What did you find?"

The young man says, "We were heading to look for our friends in Phase Four and we took the back way because it was less of a mess, and we almost fell into this hole."

The young woman can barely stutter. "There's a dead body down there."

Abe's group crowd around, but I cannot move. Evvie holds on tightly to me. I shut my eyes.

"You're not gonna believe this," the man says. "It's someone dead, all right. But it couldn't have happened last night. That's a skeleton down there!"

19

The Hospital

It takes a few moments for me to process the information. A dead body. Buried deep. A skeleton. Thank God it can't be Jack—that's the only thing I care about. So where did he go? It had to be the hospital. Someone was hurt, or he would have come to me.

The hospital is right across the street. But Oakland Park Boulevard might be impossible to maneuver. We can take the shortcut through the back of Lanai Gardens. I grab Evvie and pull her with me. "Come on, we've got to get to the hospital! Now!"

We race through mud and dirt and rubble and more milling people stunned by what has happened to their lives in one night. The hospital seems not to be too damaged, but it's chaotic. Outside, dented cars that can still be driven are parked haphazardly; nobody bothers to use designated areas today. The streets are silent except for sirens. Probably every police car and fire engine is out and about today.

Inside, it looks like a war zone: Crowds of bloody, battered people are waiting to be helped. Crying relatives look bewildered and shocked. I try to get the attention of someone at the check-in desk, but it's mobbed. I'm not alone trying to locate lost people. The harried woman behind the desk, dressed in sweats, hair uncombed, who must have rushed over this morning, makes it clear she has little information yet. We will all have to wait.

Not my Evvie. She grabs my arm and we head for the stairs. We have all of us, one time or another, been here. We know the place backwards and forwards. We also know most of the staff. Most of our doctors use this hospital facility. We head for Emergency.

It, too, looks like a war zone. Bandaged heads and bodies everywhere. People lying on gurneys, waiting to be seen. Nurses and doctors hurrying from room to room.

"Let's split up," Evvie suggests. "Signal when you find them." She refers to the whistle we invented when we were teenagers and would lose each other in department stores.

I go from cubicle to cubicle, sometimes seeing people I know, asking if anyone has seen Jack. No luck at all. It's almost surreal, our friends and neighbors all at once in such a situation.

I have a preposterous thought—I wonder where

Grandpa Bandit is. Is he somewhere nearby? Never mind.

I'm at the last possible section, dismayed and frustrated, when I hear Evvie use our familiar whistle. I follow the sound around and about the nurses' station until I find her.

And Jack.

As I run toward him I see immediately that he looks all right. Unharmed. Dirty, disheveled, cuts and scrapes on his face, but definitely still in one piece. He sees me and runs to meet me. We kiss and hug. I feel like we're in a scene in a romantic movie.

"When I saw your building . . ." I begin.

"I couldn't leave my women charges to come to you. I was silently sending you messages and hoping your ESP was working."

We kiss again. "Is your gang all right?" he asks.

"Yes, we were very lucky."

He brings me to poor Dora Dooley, who is thoroughly miserable. "I broke my arm," she tells me. "I'm waiting for someone to put on a cast. And the TV isn't working. I could be watching my soaps!"

Poor one-track-mind Dora.

Then we check on Carmel Graves, who is swathed in bandages. "I feel like a mummy," she says with humor.

"Where's Louise?" I ask. "Is she all right?"

"She's fine," Carmel says, pointing. "She's over there visiting people she knows."

"Did you see Carol Ann?" Jack asks.

Evvie says, "She's okay, just shook up. She's with Abe."

"Thank God," he says. "I knew she got out, but I couldn't find her in the dark."

Carmel smiles at me. "He's quite a guy, your boyfriend. He carried Dora over his shoulder and held on to me tightly with his other arm. And with Louise hanging on to his jacket and staying very close, he got us out of there. I don't know how he did it. It was totally black and we only had my flashlight, which needed new batteries and was almost useless."

She and Jack smile at each other. "Some Boy Scout I was," Jack says. "First thing happened I lost my flashlight."

* * *

When we return to Jack's building hours later, having left Dora and Carmel with some friends, he is astonished at the damage. "That we got out alive is a miracle," he says. "And you tell me there's a skeleton?"

I take him around the back. By now there is a sizeable crowd circling the fissure in the ground and yellow tape has been hung to keep people away. A couple of police cars are parked nearby.

"Dad!" We turn to see Jack's son, Morrie, rushing toward us. Father and son hug. "Thank God you're all right," Morrie says.

"I asked every policeman I saw at the hospital if anyone had seen you," Jack tells him. "Then I ran into Oz Washington and he told me you were safe."

Morrie hugs me, too. Hard. Clearly he was worried about me, bless his heart.

"What's going on here?" Jack asks.

Another voice is heard. A familiar one. "That's what I want to know!"

I turn to see Stanley Heyer. The sprightly eighty-five-year-old comes hurrying toward us with, as usual, Abe Waller. Poor Stanley. A few days ago he thought it was just a roof that needed repair. Now he'll have his hands full with all of Lanai Gardens to deal with. He stares down into the deep crevice where the skeleton lies.

Morrie says to him, "We need to get the body out and do an autopsy, but obviously this is not a priority today, with the city in so much disorder. Can you tell us anything that might help?"

Stanley looks at the bones soberly. "One thing is clear: He or she is in the substructure of the building. I can tell from the cement and what's left of the framed trench around him. This poor soul must have been buried under the building before it was completed."

"Oy, such a terrible accident," Abe says, shaking his head dolefully.

"If I recall," Stanley says, "we were having many storms around that time, too. I guess he or she might have fallen in."

"Or," says a bystander, "maybe a person dug a hole in their apartment and threw someone in. On purpose."

Onlookers react with shudders at this gory imagination.

Stanley smiles ruefully. "That would be very hard to do. Since we have no basements, that person would have to dig through his living room floor. Everyone would be aware of the mess and the noise."

Some agreeing nods at that.

My probable future stepson, Morrie, says, "Speculation will have to wait until we know more. Meanwhile there's a whole city to take care of. I'll have a team on the scene as soon as I'm able."

I glance over at Abe Waller. His head is bowed, his lips move in prayer. Next to him Stanley Heyer seems deep in thought.

20

The Meeting Will Come to . . . Disorder

Two days after the hurricane a meeting of Phase Two has been called. The clubhouse is filled to the brim, including residents of other Lanai Garden Phases, who are here to help. I've been told that seated in the rear is a group of people who no longer have livable homes.

In front, I sit with Jack and the girls. Except for the Canadians, who left before the storm hit, all of the Phase Two condo residents are present.

We gaze around, nodding to friends and neighbors, many in bandages. Most of us look disheveled because we still don't have hot water.

When Evvie is sure everyone is seated, she wends her way up to the podium. As our Phase president and secretary, she thanks everyone for coming and indicates our guest speaker, who comes forward.

"This man needs no introduction. We all know him, since he has made it his business to know us. Before he retired, he was president of the Heyer Construction Company, which built our beautiful condominium apartments. He loved his creation so much he moved in, living here since 1958, when Lanai Gardens was built. Over the years this kind man has been a familiar sight, carrying a loaf of challah and a bottle of Manischewitz whenever a moving truck arrived and new people came to live here. He would personally greet each one that happy day with bread and wine as a symbol of friendship.

"For fifty years he has been our best neighbor and now, in our hour of need, our leader steps up to the plate to help us. A big hand for Stanley Heyer."

Stanley gets his deserved applause as we stand up to show our respect. Evvie returns to her seat next to me.

Waving his arms for us to stop and sit back down, he takes the battery-powered mike, which squeals, piercing everyone's ears. "You all know I've been meeting with each Phase about this terrible disaster. The very good news is that though many were injured, nobody died. The bad news is that our beautiful homes require a lot of work. I don't need to tell you how hard it will be to get help, with the whole city in disrepair."

Much murmuring at this. I think to myself how lucky we are to have a man like this in our midst.

The mood among the residents is despair, but Stanley will give us hope.

"It will be a long haul. But out of bad comes good, and neighbors will reach out in whatever way they can to help one another rebuild. Everyone in Lanai Gardens who has a construction skill, please sign up to help. Every Phase president will start a list of those who have a service of some kind to offer. Today Evvie Markowitz will start the Phase Two list."

Barbi and Casey raise their hands and stand up. Barbi speaks: "As many of you know, we own a computer research service. We deal in accessing information, which can be very helpful in getting services for those in need. We will explain our company's many uses to those who wish to contact us."

Casey adds, "We're available to anyone free for the next three months."

They sit down, to much applause. Evvie writes their names on her Phase Two list.

A woman I've seen before, from Phase Four, jumps up. She is colorfully dressed in what looks like a gypsy outfit. "Let me introduce myself. I am Madame Margaret Ramona, once known on the stage as the woman with a thousand identities. If you want to have your tarot cards read and find out what is in store for the future, get in touch with me. Free. For a while," she adds quickly.

Evvie leans over and whispers, "She stole that idea from Lon Chaney."

Ida puts her two cents in. "Like who cares. What a character."

Many other hands go up. Evvie speaks from her seat. "Meet me later and I'll get you all on the list. For now, let's let Stanley wrap things up."

The hands go down and Stanley speaks again.

"Thank you, one and all, for your generosity. People have opened their homes to their friends and neighbors whose apartments are unlivable. And today, we meet here to continue the same in your Phase.

"By now nearly everyone has been relocated. There are only a few still in need of lodging." He indicates the group in back. "Good friends, please come forward."

All eyes fix on the people who move up front, bunched together. There are seven in all. Among them, in front, are Dora Dooley and Abe Waller, looking forlorn.

Stanley puts his arm around Abe and says to the audience, "I, myself, wanted Abe to live with us, but with my large family, there is no room."

I whisper to Evvie, "Where's Louise? How come she's not up there?"

"I've been meaning to tell you. You won't like it, but she's relocated to your building. And worse, on your floor."

"What!"

"Shh," says Evvie. "Later."

"Looky, looky who's there," Ida says, poking Evvie. "Your ex."

Evvie spots Joe Markowitz in the back of the group, hiding behind a larger man.

"What's he doing there?" she asks, chagrined.

Ida says, "I heard his rental apartment was taken back by the owner, to do repairs."

Evvie quips, "Maybe they ought to put him up on an auction block and sell him off. To the lowest bidder."

"Don't be nasty," I say.

Sophie says poignantly, "Who's gonna want Dora? Or Joe? By now all the nice neighbors have been taken."

A woman rises. She introduces herself as Fran Duma. "My parents went back home to Quebec. Their apartment, P218, is available for as long as needed. They were apprised that Mr. Waller needed a place and I'm authorized to offer it to him."

Evvie and I exchange surprised glances. I say, "That's the apartment between you and Enya."

Abe walks over to Fran and bows to her as she hands him the key. "Please thank them for me."

While people are commenting, Jack suddenly gets up from my side and starts to move. I tug at his jacket to stop him. "Where are you going?"

He looks at me, his face blank. "I need a place to stay."

Startled, I say, "What are you talking about? You've moved in with Morrie."

He shakes his head. "He's got enough on his mind. I'll only be in the way."

I whisper, "Jack, cut out this nonsense. Please."

He shrugs. I hold on to his jacket.

People stare from me and then to Jack, as if at a tennis match. And a buzz goes round the room.

I say, "This is crazy."

He says, gently removing my hand from his jacket, "I'm being practical."

He moves toward the front. I feel myself turning red.

Even my girls stare at me, bewildered. He keeps going. Joe, grinning, makes room for him at his side.

Evvie pokes me, amazed. "What's Jack doing?"

"I wish I knew."

There's a moment when all stare at Jack, who's joined the people in need of lodging.

A hand flies up and a high-pitched voice calls out, "I have an extra bedroom. I'll be glad to share with Mr. Langford."

The room turns to Louise, now standing, looking sexy in some kind of slinky outfit with giraffes on it. How does she do it? With a smashed-in apartment how did she get a new dress? She takes out a house key and waves it. "Q317 is available, Jackie!"

The room erupts in shocked excitement.

Sophie hisses, "That brazen hussy!"

Bella says, "That brazen hussy just told us she's gonna be your next-door neighbor!"

Sophie gasps in alarm.

Evvie pokes me. "Do something!"

I can't believe Jack is putting me in this position.

I mumble, "I'm going to kill him when we get out of here. I ought to let Louise have him."

Tessie nudges Sol in delight and she begins clapping. Others join in. Mary and Irving turn and glare at her.

Hy can't resist and calls out, "Okay, any other offers for Jack Langford, very tall, handsome ex-policeman? A valuable man to have around the house."

A woman in the rear shouts, "He can put his shoes under my bed anytime."

Lots of laughter at that. The buzzing gets louder.

Evvie, furious, jumps up, stalks to the podium, and bangs the gavel. Stanley moves off to one side, confused about what's going on.

Evvie growls, "Let's have some order around here."

"Hey, Evvie," Tessie shouts. "How about Joe? Your ex needs a place to lay his tired head."

Joe perks up at that and smiles widely.

More enthusiastic clapping. If there's one thing my Lanai Gardens neighbors love, it's to turn rowdy. Especially after the tension of the last few days, laughter is a relief.

Hy fuels the fire. To the cadence of clapping, he stamps his feet and recites, "Evvie and Joe. Evvie and Joe."

Lola, ever the dutiful wife, adds, "And Gladdy and Jack!"

Louise yells, "Hell with that, I have dibs on him!"

That's it! I'm out of here. I march from my seat

to the exit as Evvie bangs the gavel and shouts, "Meeting's over!"

The last words I hear come from Dora Dooley. "Hey, what about me? Anybody got a TV with batteries?"

* * *

Jack catches up to me as I'm crossing the small bridge behind the pool. "Gladdy, wait!"

I call over my shoulder, "Haven't you humiliated me enough for one day?" Below me the ducks quack as if they are a chorus to my misery.

He tries to touch my arm but I pull away, on the move again. "What new quality did I learn about you this time? Mean-spirited? Someone who likes to embarrass women?"

"I was trying to get your attention."

"In front of fifty people?"

"I've tried and I've tried. I keep proposing and . . . nothing."

I stop running and turn to him. "And that . . . that performance was your way of wooing me?"

He shrugs. "The act of a desperate man. What can I say? I was waiting for you to ask me to move in with you. An act of God gave you a great big signal. The decision was made for you. It's *beshert*—meant to be. How about this poor guy who just lost his apartment—everything he owns, gone forever. How about this being a perfect time to say, *Gee, Jack, why don't you move in with me?* You could help me shop for new clothes. I'm terrible at it. I don't even have a coffeepot, and this was your opportunity to say, *Jack, darling, think of the breakfasts we'll have together.* And the lunches and the dinners. We could spend our days together looking lovingly in each other's eyes."

I think of all the same fantasies I've had and I feel awful. I feel like such a bad person. "But . . . I thought you wanted to stay with Morrie."

"Yeah, right. I'd much rather be sharing my son's one-bedroom house on his lumpy couch in the living room, and taking away his privacy at the same time."

"But . . . but Sophie and Bella are staying with me. They're still frightened and don't want to be alone."

"They're not alone. They have each other. Or they can bunk in with Evvie or Ida. Or any of the fifty willing people at the meeting. Any more excuses?"

He gazes at me imploringly. I think of the man I accompanied to Key West with such love light shining in his eyes.

"None." I melt into his arms. "What a fool I am."

He hugs me tightly. "And now all of Lanai Gardens knows it."

"It will take a little while until I get Soph and Bella out."

"I'm known for my amazing patience."

We kiss long and deeply. "Say it," he says. "Come on, it will only hurt for a minute."

I look into those gorgeous eyes. "Jack Langford, will you live with me?"

He lifts me up and whirls me around. "It's about time, babe."

And once again, the sound of applause, as who knows how many of the fifty are outside the clubhouse, *kvell*ing at our love scene.

Jack bows to them, then attempts to pull me into a run. But I stop him. "In my hurry I left my sweater in the clubhouse."

He says, "Go get it and meet me at my old building. I want to see if anything's happening." He takes off, and I attempt to pretend indifference as I pass my amused audience.

* * *

I expect the clubhouse to be empty, but as I'm about to step inside, I see Evvie and Joe. From the look of them, they're in the middle of an intense conversation. I should leave, but can't stop myself from listening.

Evvie is shouting, "What are you trying to do to me? I'm having a nice retirement, and you barge in."

Joe speaks softly, pleadingly. "Do you want me to get down on my knees and beg? I will if you want me to."

Evvie softens slightly. "No, I just want you to go away and leave me alone."

"And I want to make up for what I did to you in our marriage."

She backs away slightly. "So apologize already and get it over with. No, don't even bother. I accept your apology in advance. So, go back to New York."

"I hate the weather, I can't take the cold anymore."

"I'm sure our daughter will make sure you're nice and warm."

"No, I can't go there . . . I mean, I won't. I don't want to do that anymore. It's a small house. They need their space. It's not fair to them."

"So go live with *your* relatives. I'm sure your sisters will be thrilled to have you."

His voice climbs higher a notch. "I don't want to, Evvie. I want to be with you! I need you, Evvie. I love you!"

This stops my poor sister in her tracks. She gasps in astonishment. "Joe, please . . . don't." Then angrier, "Don't you dare say that to me!"

I back away from the door. I can't bear watching anymore.

21

The Skeleton

I hurry to meet Jack at his building. By now, what's left of the structure is yellow-taped. In the sharp sunlight, I look up to the crushed second floor. It looks even worse than it looked on that first gray morning. I shudder to imagine what might have happened.

He's not in front. I become aware of people hurrying to the rear, and I follow them. There's quite a crowd hanging around behind the yellow police tape, including Stanley Heyer and Abe Waller. I see Jack, and I join him, not wanting to miss a thing.

I watch the cops. Besides Morrie Langford and Oz Washington, there's a medical examiner and a team of police. They're all in hip boots, what with the ground still muddy from the storm. The sun is out, but it's weak, barely illuminating the scene.

The cops have brought their own powerful work lamps.

At the bottom of the cave-in, which seems to me about five feet deep, a couple of the gloved policemen carefully bag the skeleton and place it on a pulley.

Once the remains are hoisted out, the cops gather up what else might give them clues as to what happened to this person so long ago. They send up bag after bag of their findings. Other cops carefully lay the items down on a large tarp on the ground. We try hard to see what's there. Looks like a few scraps of fabric. Some shredded, sodden pieces of paper. When they retrieve a gray mass of something that looks like metal, Stanley gasps.

Oz and Morrie turn to him. "Something?" Morrie asks.

Stanley is shaken. "It looks like a piece from one of the helmets my men wore on the site."

Oz lifts the yellow tape for Stanley to enter. "Come and take a closer look," Oz tells him.

Stanley nervously moves toward the wretched-looking items on the tarp. "Yes, it could be."

Now Oz and Morrie talk in lower voices, but my hearing is sharp and I hardly miss a word.

Oz comments, "The cloth looks like it might have come from a plaid shirt. We'll know better when we have it analyzed at the lab."

"Remind you of anything?" Morrie asks Stanley.

He sighs. "Yes. One of my workers went AWOL the day before we poured the concrete."

Morrie says, "It could save us a lot of trouble if you can remember his name."

"Johnny Blake. When we first saw the skeleton, I had a hunch and went through my old records. He was new on the job. My foreman, Ed Luddy, hired him while I was away on business."

"Could you describe him for us?" Oz asks.

Stanley shakes his head. "That's what I'm trying to tell you. I never met him. By the time I returned, Ed told me he hadn't shown up one day. I didn't think anything about it since we hired a lot of itinerant types who took off the moment their part of the job was done."

"Where's Ed Luddy? We'd like to talk to him," Oz says.

Stanley says, "Dead nigh on seven years. Lung cancer got him."

"Anyone else still around who might remember?"

Stanley manages a wry smile. "You're talking to an eighty-five-year-old man. Do you imagine any of those other men are still with us?"

The cops place the bags and tarp in a van. Morrie and Oz remove the equipment they brought. Morrie hands Stanley a card. "You think of anything else, call me. I'll be in touch with you after the lab work is done. Might take a while."

The show is over and the onlookers scatter. Morrie and Oz come over to us.

Oz says, "Are congrats in order? Hear you two lovebirds are setting up house together."

I look at my love, amazed. When did he have time to report this news update?

"True," says my Jack proudly, putting his arm around me. Showing off now that he's captured his prey. Me.

"And I was so happy with you living with me," Morrie jokes. "So was my girlfriend. She loved having you around on her nights over."

Morrie winks, and I of course turn and blush. I grab Jack's hand and pull him away with me. He and I walk back to my place, hand in hand. All around us is a new kind of chaos. Tow trucks haul away battered cars. Resident men clear the streets of rubble, filling all available Dumpsters. Resident women come in and out of apartments, tossing damaged items. Everyone calls out to friends and neighbors. Who was lucky to be spared? Who wasn't? Cheerful voices and resigned ones.

Lanai Gardens is determined to rise again, and I've also got a new future to look forward to—living with Jack.

22

Days of Adjustment

All in all, damage to Fort Lauderdale was less than expected. With the exception of Z building, thankfully no apartments were destroyed. But major repairs may take at least a year. Life will be different from now on.

With the changes going on around Phase Two, you almost need a scorecard. What's good and not good: We have electricity again. Though the phones are erratic, cell phones are working overtime.

We did reach our families and everyone knows we are fine. They were sad that Jack lost his apartment, but delighted he is going to live with me. The unspoken question is—when's the wedding?

I get through to Conchetta, and learn her large family suffered only minor damage. She informed me the library will open again after the volunteers finish picking up all the bookcases and reshelve the salvaged books and tape the broken windows. No mail delivery yet. Some cars are operational and those are busy carrying neighbors to and from the places they need to go. Mine is still functional, but it reminds me of a big hunk of metallic cottage cheese, irrevocably dented. Publix, our big supermarket, is a mess, but the sign outside promises the store will be open for business soon. Our banks are open. Sophie bemoans the loss of her beauty shop—gone for good.

What's obvious is a sense of excitement with all the comings and goings. No lolling about the pool these days (the bottom is cracked). We are a beehive of productivity.

As I wander about I catch many snippets of conversation:

Hy and Lola moan about no glaziers being available to replace their apartment windows. "I can't sleep with that draft," complains Hy.

"And I can't sleep with that draft from your mouth complaining about it," says his much-put-upon wife. Seems to me like the dutiful wife is cranky from sleep deprivation."

Bella explains how she managed to get stuck with Dora Dooley as a roommate: "I don't know how it happened. She just followed me home. What could I do? So I let her in."

Evvie: "You never heard of 'just say no'?"

Ida: "You won't get her out again."

Sophie: "It'll take forever 'til they rebuild Z building."

Bella: "Oy!"

Dora, popping out of Bella's front door, announces, "I need a recliner. Why don't you have a recliner? How am I supposed to sit on a straight chair to watch my shows? And I need a *blanky* to keep me warm. And why don't you have sweaters? I'm freezing in there."

Bella, eyes like saucers, hurries back inside to wait on her demanding roommate.

* * *

Later in the day, Ida and I watch from across the courtyard as Evvie, Bella, Hy, and Lola greet their new second-floor neighbor with welcoming gifts of casseroles. Abe Waller is suitably grateful. He opens the door to his borrowed apartment, which is next to Evvie. Just then, on the other side of him, his other neighbor, Enya, appears, to see what's going on. Head lowered, she shyly says hello. Abe bows to greet her. Enya quickly retreats inside.

Their attention is drawn to the elevator as an excited Joe, lugging a bulging suitcase, comes out.

"Hi there, everybody," he says cheerfully. "Here's your other new neighbor."

All pivot to watch Evvie's response. But Evvie gives nothing away. She opens her door and hurries inside. Joe nods to the others and follows after her.

"He looks like a sad-eyed puppy," Ida comments to me.

* * *

From my balcony, another day: I'm with all the girls, and hands on hips, we watch Louise move into Q317, the apartment next to Sophie, which is only one apartment away from me. And three away from Ida. None of us is smiling as she turns her key in the lock and gives us a bright phony smile. "Anyone play bridge?" she asks, knowing damn well what the answer is. The only one on the floor who does is—my Jack. If he dares to play bridge with her, I'm going along. I can play dummy. Yeah, right. Ha-ha.

This evening Jack is moving in—with nothing but a toothbrush and some hurried shopping for a few necessary items. Tonight my life changes forever.

* * *

I clean up my apartment. Well, sort of. Dirt is everywhere, on everything. The slats on the windows couldn't keep out what the fierce winds blew. The washing machine room is working 24/7.

I do the best I can. The markets are low on fresh food. My first dinner alone with Jack will be catch as catch can. The girls are solicitous. They are aware of tonight's importance. They offer what goodies they have in their refrigerators.

Sophie and Bella call me just about every hour on the hour, for constant moral support. Bella spends a lot of time in Sophie's apartment because Dora is driving her crazy.

I wonder how Evvie and Joe are doing. It's two days now. Haven't seen her or Joe. I hope they aren't killing each other.

I dress up for dinner. Do my hair. Lather on the

makeup. Then ten minutes later, I wipe off most of the makeup. Back to simple beige slacks and a white cotton shirt. I don't know how to behave. An old song pops into my head. Was it Sammy Davis, Jr., who used to sing "I gotta be me"? But who is "me" these days?

It would be nice to sit in the Florida room and have a drink before dinner. But my sunroom is a mess. The screens all blew out; furniture is strewn every which way. I guess now I should call it an open porch. Trouble is, everything is broken in there. My bookshelves, my reading lamp, my stereo, my family photos. All smashed. Most of it will have to be thrown away. Besides, all I have in the fridge is some lemonade. So much for the cocktail hour.

I hear a knock on the door. Then it opens. All kinds of silly things run through my head. I gave him a key, but I guess he felt he needed to warn me. What do we say to each other? How am I supposed to act?

I hurry to the hallway. There he is, holding a small bouquet of flowers and a bottle of wine. He has on new clothes—tan windbreaker, tan khakis, and a navy blue sports shirt that goes wonderfully with his eyes. He grins at me. "Hi, honey, I'm home."

I laugh. I play back. "Hard day at the office, dear?"

He puts his gifts down on the small hallway table and grabs me and hugs me. "I couldn't find a florist with any flowers, so I picked these in the park. As for the wine, I grabbed the first bottle I could find. I hope you like cheap sangria."

We stand there looking at each other. "So, what do we do next?" I ask.

Jack emotes from the movie *Marty*: "I don't know, Marty, wadda you want to do?"

He walks me into the kitchen and peeks into the pot to see what's cooking. "News flash," he says, "I have a job." He picks up a spoon and dips into my pot of chicken soup. "I'm no longer retired."

"Tell me," I say. We each grab a bowl and fill it with soup. He carries the bowls to the dining room table. I bring the salad, napkins, and salt and pepper. For a touch of festivity I light the two candles that are on my table.

"I've been recruited. Along with a lot of other retired cops. To help keep law and order. And how was your day?"

As he digs into my hearty soup, I begin to tell Jack all the gossip going round.

It's like we've been together for years. And it feels wonderful.

* * *

I sigh happily. Here we are enveloped in one another's arms on the couch, finishing off the really bad sangria. Soft music plays. We have been talking nonstop since dinner. It's nearly midnight and my eyes are closing, but I never want this evening to end. What is wondrous to me is that Jack and I are already close friends, before we've even gotten to the sex. Though not for want of trying. I smile, thinking of the irony.

I look at him. He looks at me.

"Dare we?" he asks.

I know he's referring to heading for the bedroom.

"We're covered," I tell him. The girls won't call—they know I'll kill them if they do. Our relatives know we're safe. "Unless we have a sudden new hurricane, or the building burns down, all systems are go."

Jack is funny. I love his humor. He begins to tiptoe to the bedroom, stopping each moment to see if it's all right to take the next step. He takes another, still smiling and looking back at me. I can't help laughing. He's so cute. Can one call a man in his seventies cute? But he is—playful, upbeat, a happy man at heart. He makes my spirits fly. I begin to follow in his footsteps.

The doorbell rings, piercingly. Again and again.

The phone rings at the same time.

"What the hell?" Jack says.

"Maybe it's Halloween and we forgot the candy" is my exasperated response.

"You grab the phone," he tells me, "and I'll get the door."

Since I can see the door from the kitchen phone, all at once I know the news. My girls are standing there, faces pinched. Joe is with them. Evvie says, terrified, "Millie escaped from the hospital."

And on the phone it is Mary, informing me of the same thing. "Irving is hysterical. We're going out to look for her. We need every car that's working."

I tell her, "Yes, we'll be right down."

Jack and I grab our jackets and follow the girls to the stairs. As we run, Jack asks, "How could she get out of an Alzheimer's facility?"

Ida informs us, "When the electricity went off, the locked doors opened. They assume she just walked out."

"Did anyone call the police?"

"The nursing home did," Evvie says. "They've only just called us. We don't know how long Millie's been gone."

Downstairs Tessie and Sol and Mary are already in Irving's car. Ida, Evvie, Joe, Bella, Sophie, and I squeeze into my car and Jack's. Denny's truck holds him, Yolie, Hy, and Lola. The battered vehicles squeal as dents scrape against tires, but at least we are still able to drive.

With relief I think—thank God Jack and I still had our clothes on.

23

A New Worry

The gated nursing home in Margate is located on a half acre of grounds with wooded areas. The local police grimly tell us they've covered every inch of the facility, every room inside, every outbuilding. And are still at it. They suggest we surround the area outside the gate.

Though the nursing home itself is very quiet, a small group of staff greet our scruffy, anxious gang of fifteen. The home personnel are beside themselves. A Mrs. Stapleford, who seems to be in charge, reports to the shaking Irving, "We thought everyone was secure. It wasn't until eleven o'clock bed check that one of our staff realized that Millie had stuffed pillows under her blanket and was gone."

Another nurse says, "Nothing like this has ever happened here before."

A third says, “It’s unbelievable. Those doors are heavy. How could she have had the strength to open them? We only just got our electricity back an hour ago.” She cannot look at Irving and turns away.

Evvie asks, “When was the last time you saw her?”

“When we distributed meds at seven P.M. We left her lying in her room. Since the hurricane, our patients seem more comfortable staying in their rooms.”

Jack comments, “So she could have gone out anytime since seven, but before the electricity came back on.”

The nurses nod. What we are all thinking is she’s been out there on her own for maybe five hours. God help her.

Practical Mary asks, “What would she be wearing?”

The night nurse says, “Just her nightgown, I’m afraid. Her slippers are still under the bed. Her robe is still in the closet.”

Irving sobs at that.

Mrs. Stapleton suddenly remembers. “Oh, we left each patient with a flashlight. She must have taken it with her.”

For some reason, that fact gives me hope. I don’t know why.

“Then what are we waiting for?” asks Tessie.

* * *

Once outside the gates, the hardier ones of us spread out on foot, the rest pile in the back of

Denny's truck. Denny drives very slowly, for his passengers' safety and for them to be able to search. I'm glad Evvie remembered to bring the flashlights we used so much just a few days earlier. Our "on foot" group agrees to stay close, two or more, never alone. The plan—to meet back at the gate every half hour on the hour.

Through the dark neighborhoods, we call out Millie's name. We look in every yard, every empty doorway, ever mindful of hostile neighbors and dogs. Dogs do bark and neighbors come out, but no one has seen anything. We travel from street to street, Denny's truck and our waving flashlights the only movement in the night.

Joe and Evvie are with us. I notice Joe reach out to take her hand. She hesitates, then lets him.

"Haven't seen you in a couple of days," I say, making small talk, even though my eyes are darting every which way. "How's it going?"

"Things are fine, just fine," says Joe.

Evvie grunts. "Why can't he learn after fifty years to put the toilet seat down?"

Joe huffs, "Where is it written it has to be that way? You women make all the rules. What difference does it make? Up. Down. Up. Down."

"The difference is," she says tightly, "at night, half-asleep, in the dark, when it's up, I fall into the toilet, you idiot!"

"Over here," Hy shouts excitedly. We race to the sound of his voice. But when we get there, sadly it is a homeless person sleeping in a large brown carton in an alley.

We regularly trudge back to the gate. Hour after hour, we forge on, but with no luck. No Millie anywhere.

We are exhausted and cold. The police suggest we go home. They will continue on. They'll call when they find her, they tell us optimistically. But Irving shrivels up into himself. He has lost hope.

* * *

We gather in front of our two buildings. Even though it is near dawn, no one seems to want to go to bed. Yolie, bless her heart, has made pots of coffee for us. Irving sits at the picnic table and we surround him with our love—each of us taking turns insisting that Millie is an amazing woman. A survivor. Courageous and beautiful. But in our hearts we are talking about the Millie we knew years ago. Before that plague came upon us older people.

Abe, wakened by hearing us, has come down to join us. He leads us in a prayer for Millie. I watch the sky, about to turn into day. It will be a beautiful one. Mother Nature has trampled us, done her dirty work, and now she teases us with sunshine. Until she has another mood swing—as Hy calls it, Mother Nature with PMS—and gives us another blast of misery.

We swivel at the sight of a vehicle turning into our Phase. A taxicab pulls up and the driver gets out.

"I got a passenger in back," he says, not even showing surprise that this group of people is sitting outside at this odd hour. "Picked her up when she flagged me. Hey, I got an old mom, too. Felt sorry for her. I was going to drop her off at the police station, but she insisted she knew where she lived."

He opens the car door and Millie graciously steps out, one hand holding up the hem of her white cotton nightgown, the other holding her flashlight, still on. Her face lights up in a smile at the sight of us.

The cabbie asks, "Somebody gonna pay the tab?"

24

The Earth Moves

What a night! But all's well. Irving informed the police and the nursing home that Millie is with him. She doesn't recognize Irving or anyone else, but her bed is familiar to her and all she wants is to sleep. Last night's Gang of Fifteen, as we are calling one another, will take turns watching Millie as the others rest. Jack and I bow out.

* * *

Well, here we are. Six A.M. In my bedroom at last. We throw ourselves on top of the bedspread, still in our clothes, kicking off our shoes. Jack mumbles before he drops deeply into sleep, "How do I *not* make love to you? Let me count the ways. Pago Pago. New York. Key West. My bedroom. Your bedroom . . ."

The last thing I remember before I pass out, too—Jack is snoring and I'm laughing.

* * *

I think I'm dreaming. But I'm not. My eyes peel open and I see the clock. It's eight something. We are moving in slow motion. He helps me off with my clothes. I help him with his. Clothes are tossed. We kiss. I suggest a shower to get rid of last night's grunge. He doesn't care. He suggests later. Together. Arms and legs entwine. I don't know where one of us leaves off and the other begins. We are still tired, so our movements are unhurried. We are whispering nonsense as our bodies respond, ignoring our words. I say, "It's been such a long time." He says, "It's like riding a bike." I say, "I never rode a bike in the Bronx. My mother wouldn't let me." He says, "I have a bad back, it could go out any second." I tell him about the arthritis in my knees. "I might cry out in pain." We name all our old-age ailments. He tells me, "I have battle scars." I say, "I'll show you mine, if you show me yours." I giggle. He says, "We'll work around them." What we are doing to each other has us sizzling. We moan in pleasure. He says, "I think I hear the phone." I say, "No damn way." He says, "Kidding." We are no longer talking. We are in the moment, in the second, enveloped in bliss, peaking to rapture.

"The earth finally moved," I say afterward.

He says, "It's about bloody time."

25

Stanley Asks a Favor

It's our first morning of living together. Getting up was hard to do. Coffee was an incentive but lovemaking was the more intense craving. Will I ever again think of the shower as just a place to wash? Our bodies might be aging, but our spirits are young. And willing. And capable. Forget the gymnastics of our youth; this is a whole new experience of experimenting with what we still can do.

Breakfast is at ten-thirty. And I silently thank my girls for giving up their early-morning phone call ritual. I'm still in my robe. Jack is dressed in one of the two outfits he owns—the one he didn't wear yesterday. We are on our third cup of coffee when the doorbell finally rings. I wonder which one of the girls it will be. Or perhaps all of them.

To my surprise, Stanley Heyer stands on the

threshold, holding a small brown paper bag. "May I come in?" he asks.

Of course I let him in. I'm embarrassed, to say the least. Our first visitor, and it turns out to be the most religious man in all of Lanai Gardens. Can he see the blush on my face? But the little man seems not to notice.

"I brought bagels." He hands the bag to me.

I thank him and we tell him to sit down and join us. As I'm about to pour him a cup of coffee, he shakes his head no. I try to offer him a bagel. He says he already ate. He is being polite. My kitchen isn't kosher.

He begins, "You are probably wondering why I'm here."

Jack says, "Whatever the reason, you're most welcome."

"Allow me—the good news. It will take a while to clear the rubble, and to secure the building so it will be safe to enter, but then you and your neighbors will be able to get into your apartments again to gather up whatever has not been destroyed. I've already informed the others in Z building."

Jack is properly grateful. "That's a relief. Hopefully we'll retrieve important papers and not have to make endless reports to endless government agencies."

I agree. "Especially since the lines will be horrific."

Jack shakes Stanley's hand. "Thanks, you're a godsend."

Stanley accepts this shyly. "I wouldn't say that."

He sits up straighter in his chair. "However, I've just come from the police station with disturbing news. They finished the autopsy. The poor man's head was bashed in. They found bone fractures in the skull. And on some parts of the skeleton. No accident. It was murder."

"How awful," I say.

Jack asks, "Will they investigate? The department is overloaded and I doubt they have the manpower or the time."

Stanley nods. "You hit the nail right on the head." He clasps his hands together on my table. "Who knows when or if they'll ever find out anything. That's why I'm here. Gladdy Gold, I want to hire you to investigate."

I'm surprised. "I don't know what to say."

"Listen, let me tell you what I know." He grimaces. "It's true what they say about old age. I don't recall what I did yesterday, but I can remember fifty years back like it *was* yesterday."

I nod in agreement, but don't respond, not wanting to break his train of thought.

"The crime happened about this same time of year. The weather was stormy. We were late laying in the foundation. So many delays in the construction. So much mud. Men leaving for warmer climates and other jobs because they couldn't wait any longer for the weather to change. A lot of aggravation, but I won't bore you with my *tsouris*.

"As I said, my foreman, Ed, had hired a new man during the week I was in Chicago. Family situation. A relative in trouble. Ah, I digress. I already mentioned the worker's name was Johnny Blake. Ed told me he was a large man, a good worker, but he didn't talk much. He told Ed he came from Tampa. Somewhere near the Gulf. The day I arrived home, the storm was at its worst. But the next day, we had a break in the weather and we decided we had to get the foundation done. Fast. Ed was surprised Mr. Blake didn't show up for work. He believed Mr. Blake wasn't the type who would walk just after getting a job he needed. Besides, his locker still had his things in it.

"But we had plenty of other problems on our plates and I assumed the man would come back for his stuff one day, so I stored it. And I forgot about him. Until now."

"Do you remember what was in his locker?" Jack asks.

"Yes. But I didn't find out until after the job was done—when we closed down our on-site work office, I remembered it. I opened the locker, but there was very little in there. A change of clothes. Another pair of work shoes. A denim jacket with a wallet with a few dollars, and a key in the pocket. And a Christmas card signed 'your sister Lucy.' I thought it was odd that he left those items, but I was too busy to give it any more thought."

Jack and I look at each other. "So," I say, "it can be assumed the key was his house key and Mr. Blake wouldn't have left without his wallet before going home that night."

"Anything might have happened," Jack comments. "Maybe it was an attempted robbery. Or someone thought he could steal equipment and this man, Blake, tried to stop him."

"Do you still have the things from his locker?" I ask.

Stanley smiles. "Does not a pack rat save everything? I am such a pack rat. Actually it's in a storage locker that Esther has been asking me to empty for years." He shrugs, guiltily, as if to say "You know how it is."

Jack says, "Get whatever you have to the station. They have a good forensic lab. His stuff might be of some help."

"I will," Stanley agrees. "Then maybe it will prove to my wife that I'm not just a *shmegegge*."

I laugh. "No way are you a fool, Mr. Stanley Heyer!"

The phone rings. I excuse myself and answer. It's for Jack. I hand him the phone. He listens briefly and tells me he's wanted down at the station. They have work for him.

Jack kisses me good-bye. In front of Stanley. But Stanley is lost in his thoughts.

"See you tonight, gorgeous," Jack says, on his way out.

Stanley gets up. "I should not take up any more of your time. But my conscience is bothering me that I didn't look into this. He must have had family—this sister Lucy—who never knew what happened to him. At least let me make it up to them. Find out who they are and let me inform them."

He looks at me with an expression of pain. "I

won't sleep well until I know I have done my duty to the poor man."

He looks so forlorn standing there beseeching me with his eyes.

"I'll try, Stanley. I will."

* * *

Needless to say, the girls are standing right outside my door as Stanley leaves. They waited until Jack left and now the coast was clear. They greet Stanley as they rush inside.

"So? How are things?" Sophie cuts right to the chase as she sits down at my kitchen table and helps herself to a bagel. "We just happened to see Jack leaving."

Bella adds, grinning, "And he was whistling."

"Things are just fine," I answer, taking cream cheese and butter from the fridge and setting them on the table. One severe look from me means this subject is off-limits and that's that.

Ida leans against the kitchen door and gives me one of her raised-eyebrow looks, but I'm telling nothing.

"I wish I could say the same," Evvie kvetches as she pours her own cup of coffee. "Joe is making me nuts. 'Should I fix the venetian blinds? Should I take down the boards in the Florida room? Should I do this, do that?' I wish he'd leave me alone."

Bella huffs. "I'll change places with you in a minute. That Dora is driving me up a wall. Why don't you have strawberry jam? What kind of apartment doesn't have cable? Could you run to the store right now, I need my pills . . ."

Sophie jumps in. "I told Bella to ask for rent."

Bella says, "And what does my new boarder say? Her checkbook is in her apartment, her destroyed apartment."

Sophie again: "So we tell her she can always go to the bank."

Bella: "And she says her bankbook is gone, too."

"I hate to break in on all your miseries," I announce. "But we have a new job."

The girls stop, mid-chewing. I have their immediate attention and I fill them in on Stanley's assignment.

Ida asks, "How can we find out about something that happened so long ago?"

"Especially with practically no information at all," Sophie comments.

Evvie says, "First stop, our girls in Gossip. If anybody can track someone down, Barbi and Casey can."

"Wonderful," says Bella. "At least it will get me out of the apartment."

"Ditto," says Evvie.

26

Goings On

We watch Irving and Yolie bring Millie out of his apartment. Millie smiles brightly and waves to us even though she doesn't remember who we are. It's heartbreaking to think back on the dear lady she once was. Always positive and interested in everything around her. A good friend when you needed one. She and Irving were crazy about each other. Now here is this shell of a person; her vacant smile has no substance behind it.

As much as Irving wants to keep her home, Millie needs round-the-clock hospital care. As wrenching as it is, Irving must take her back.

We all take turns hugging a giggling Millie, trying to put a good face on how we really feel.

Just as she is about to be helped into Irving's battered car, she swivels, startled, as if she were waking from a dream. She looks around, suddenly seeming to know where she is. "Irving?" she says, reaching out to touch him. He jumps, shocked. It is Millie again, come back.

One of us gasps. I think it is Sophie, but I don't turn to see. We are mesmerized.

Millie clutches at Irving's shirt. "Don't let them put me in a box. Promise!"

He leans his head into hers. "I won't. I promise." Through his tears, he hugs her.

Then, as if a light went off, she is the Alzheimer patient once again. Lost and bewildered. Irving and Yolie help her into the car.

Irving sobs. "It's like losing her all over again. She was so happy to be home."

We stand there silently, as we watch the car pull away.

* * *

We remain near Irving's apartment tearfully, arms around one another.

But suddenly Tessie says, "Look, there's Bingo Bob. He's back at last." Bingo is the nickname of our mailman, who spends all his free time with his wife in the bingo parlors. Well, it's something to take our minds off Millie.

We hurry toward our mailboxes. Hooray. It's been days and we've missed our mail delivery. He tries to fill the boxes while the girls are eagerly grabbing their mail out of his hands before he can even insert the envelopes.

"Neither rain nor sleet can stop the U.S. Postal Service," Bob emotes in his high-pitched voice.

"Yeah," says Ida. "But a hurricane can."

"We're very glad to see you," Sophie says. "How are you doing at bingo?"

"The Indian casinos are shut down 'til further notice," he reports grimly. "Even the churches are too busy these days."

Sophie groans. "Now, that's bad news. I was looking forward to playing."

As I flip through my mail, a familiar square white envelope catches my eye.

I beckon the girls to join me. Away from listening ears. We head for our usual picnic table. Sure enough, it's from our old friend Grandpa Bandit. I rip open the envelope.

Ida comments, "I wondered if we'd ever hear from him again. What's the old geezer got to say this time?"

I read, " 'Happy you all survived the storm. Back to business—if we don't get hit with another hurricane. First I got to get my car running. Getting old is not for sissies. But the good news is: The older you get, the more money your old junk will be worth on eBay. Further instructions to come.' "

The familiar green feather is enclosed.

Sophie stamps her feet. "The postmark is Fort Lauderdale. He lives in Lanai Gardens. I just know it. Let's get a list of all the cars that need fixing." She stops, realizing how impractical that is, since all the cars were affected.

Ida says, "But who could it be? He doesn't sound like any of the men who live here."

Evvie shrugs. "Even with six Phases, we haven't met everyone. It's easy for someone to keep a low profile."

Bella says, "Round 'em all up and we'll drill 'em 'til we suss him out."

We look at her, amused at her vehemence. "Yeah," says Ida, "great idea."

As we head out for Gossip, I glance up, to see Enya moving along on her balcony, toward the laundry room, carrying her basket. I wonder if she's had a chance to talk to her new neighbor, Abe. Evvie looks to me and winks. I know we share a feeling. Maybe these two people can reach out to each other—they, who have known so much pain, and have history in common.

27

Neighbors

From outside, Enya hears the sound of the whirling dryer. With her basket firmly placed under her left arm, she opens the door with her right. She moves toward a vacant washer and stops abruptly.

Abe Waller is standing near the dryer, his empty basket on a plain brown wooden chair under a small unframed mirror. This is a utilitarian room with just the basics: two washers, one dryer, and a sorting table. The room is steamy and too warm. There is no air-conditioning in here. But one small louvered window, half-open, lets in a small breeze.

She is taken aback to see him, immediately uncomfortable. She hopes her new neighbor doesn't feel he has to speak to her. For a moment she is motionless, but poised to flee. Enya's eyes glance downward, to avoid looking directly at this large, overwhelming man. He is new to the building and won't know she does not make small talk to anyone, let alone strangers. She starts to leave, saying, "I'm sorry. I didn't know the room was occupied."

Abe wipes the sweat from his forehead with a handkerchief. "No, please. I am moments away from completion. Do not let me disturb you. The machine is yours to use."

She returns, opens the door of the empty washer, her back to him so he will not see her personal garments.

He, too, turns away, toward the small mirror. He takes off his Coke-bottle glasses and wipes the steam from them. Enya looks up and sees him reflected in the mirror. Then, not wanting to embarrass him, she quickly looks downward again.

The dryer comes to a halt. The room grows silent. As Abe removes his dry laundry, he attempts small conversation. "It was very kind of the people to allow me to use their place."

She pours soap powder in, and chooses the wash she wants, then places the quarters into their slots and turns the machine on. As she upends her garments into the machine, she says, "Yes. Mr. and Mrs. Duma are nice people. Very quiet."

"I promise to be quiet also."

She looks up at that, discomfited. "I did not mean—" She breaks off.

"I am not offended." He finishes removing his dry clothes and places them on the table and starts folding with great precision. "Forgive me for my forwardness, but your accent... May I ask where you are from?"

"So many years in this country, I don't lose it. I am from Prague originally. And you?"

"From Munich." He pauses. "That was a long time ago."

They are silent for a few moments, absorbing this information. She places her empty basket onto the bench. She tries to hide how tense she is, even though he seems a gentleman.

Abe finishes folding. He lifts his basket and moves toward the door.

As he passes her, he looks down at the numbers on her left arm. She immediately gasps, trying to hide them with her hand. She is not used to people staring at them, but then her eyes are drawn to just below the wrist of his long-sleeved shirt. He, too, has the damnable numbers.

Their eyes meet for the first time. Hers, watery and weak. His covered with strong glasses. He says very softly. "We are members of a very exclusive club, *ja?*"

Her head barely nods.

He opens the door and bows. "Good day, Frau Slovak."

28

Gossip

"Any luck?" I ask Barbi and Casey as the girls and I return. The cousins needed a couple of hours to research our new assignment. The girls were happy about that since there is a deli nearby that they like and we had a leisurely lunch.

Now we seat ourselves on the usual white chairs around the white table in the totally white room. Since this isn't our first visit, we no longer react to the strange working conditions of this all-white high-tech office located in a strip mall.

Barbi starts. "Given the fact we're dealing with dates so far back, even so, we did find quite a number of Lucy Blakes in that time span in the Tampa area . . ."

Casey continues, "Having a relative named Johnny, who was deceased, narrowed the options down to very few. We'll print out what we have."

I enjoy watching the two women as they swivel their desk chairs around and slide across the room to their twin computers. The girls continue to be awed at these two unusual women who we know are pretending to be cousins.

"So," asks Ida, making conversation, "are you getting any clients since the hurricane?"

"Just one other, so far," Barbi answers, reaching for the paper coming out of the printer. "One gal, kind of a character, wore a weird, lumpy outfit, wanted to know about cities in Georgia. Ones that didn't get bad weather."

They come back to where we're sitting. And hand us copies.

"Got a hit on a Lucy Blake Sweeney. In Tampa."

Casey says, "Could be a fit. She's seventy-seven years old. Actually written up recently in the local paper—something about a strike at a local fishery on the Gulf."

"Well, that's a place to start," says Ida.

Barbi says, "Just thought we'd check some obits for that era. Blake's a common name and these are the two nearest 1958. A John Adams Blake died in '59, but he was age sixty."

"Wrong year and age," says Evvie.

"And this one, John Willis Blake, age twenty-seven. Could be the right age, but he died in March. Six months earlier than what you're looking for. Small obit notice, no information about any remaining kin.

"That's about it," says Barbi.

Sophie is excited. "Why don't we call that Lucy

woman anyway? Maybe they didn't have a body and just had a funeral because they thought he was dead."

"Wait," I say. "We can't just call and say, 'You don't know who we are, but by the way, your brother didn't die when you thought. We found your brother's skeleton, and he died here.' This is a long shot."

Ida says, "But it's all we have right now."

Evvie says. "What if our skeleton isn't her brother and we just stir up a lot of confusion?"

Bella jumps in. "And what if she has a heart attack because we scared her out of her wits?"

I hold up my hands to stop the flow of what-ifs. "I need to talk to Stanley and ask how he wants us to handle this."

* * *

We thank Casey and Barbi and head back home. The noise level in my car's a crescendo.

Bella says, "Why don't you take Dora for a while?"

Sophie says, "You shouldn't have taken her in the first place. So why should I get stuck with her?"

"But I can't stand it anymore. I thought I was deaf, but she's deafer. The TV is blasting me out of my apartment. Ida, maybe you'll take her for a while?"

Ida sneers, "Over my dead body."

Evvie says, smirking, "Don't look at me. Unless you'll trade her for Joe."

Bella blushes. "I'm a single woman. I couldn't live with an unmarried man in my apartment. That would be a sin."

It takes a moment for her words to sink in. *I'm* the single sinner living with an unmarried man. Joe and Evvie don't count because they were once married.

"Bella!" Evvie says agitatedly.

She looks around, confused. "What? What did I say?"

It gets very quiet. We reach Lanai Gardens and I park in any old spot. We no longer have assigned spaces, what with the abandoned wrecks not yet cleared away.

"Well, it's good to be home," Sophie says to cover the uncomfortable silence as we climb out of my car.

I'm not about to touch Bella's line with a ten-foot pole.

* * *

Once back in my apartment, I call Stanley and tell him what we'd found out. He listens to the information and says that he wants to think about our next step.

I try to nap, one of my favorite pastimes. There's something about drawing the shades and lying down on my bed and closing my eyes midday that is so appealing. I usually drop off the instant my head hits the pillow. Not today. First, my bed has new meaning for me. I think of Jack lying next to me every night from now on. His reaching for me and pulling me close and then our sleeping together like two well-worn spoons. I never thought I was lonely until he moved in. Now I know how much I'd been missing.

How brave women are who live alone, whether by choice or not. We all put a good face on it, but it's never easy. Not easy raising children alone. Not easy having to bear all the responsibility in life with no one to share it. And hardest of all is to face that empty bed at night. We make peace with our lot, whatever it is. It's that or go mad. But lucky are those who find true love and companionship. As I did with my first husband. And now, with this wonderful man. I am twice blessed.

Why all this philosophizing that won't allow me to sleep? It was Bella's remark. I know she didn't mean it to hurt me. And it didn't. But it made me remember that one should never take good fortune for granted. Life has a habit of whisking it away on a whim. How well I know that.

My mind reels round and round. After an hour, I give up trying to nap, get up, and go into the kitchen to make a pot of tea.

I concentrate on preparing dinner as I sip my tea. Well, this is another piece of the puzzle of living alone or not. Ordinarily I just throw something together for myself, and quite often munch from a carton, just standing in front of the open fridge.

Now I'm back to planning meals, shopping for food, and cooking. Even though it's fun to see my man enjoying home-cooked meals again—who knows how many cartons *he's* eaten out of—I put this on the con side of the column. The pros are enormous, but still . . .

A timorous knock on the door, or did I imagine it? No, I have a visitor. There's Bella standing outside, carrying a covered dish with something that smells wonderful.

When I let her in, she waits in my hallway, tears forming. "I'm sorry. I didn't mean what I said in the car."

She walks into the kitchen and reveals her gift. "I baked you a peach pie, your favorite. I'm a very bad person."

With that I put my arms around her and tell her she is anything but. "I'm actually glad you said it. It made me think."

"No, don't try to make me feel better. I love you and I love Jackie and I even loved his dead wife, Faye. I wouldn't hurt any of you for anything." Now the tears are rolling down her face.

I grab a dish towel, the closest thing, and hand it to her. She dabs at her eyes.

"Come on, sit down, and join me in a cup of tea."

"No, I can't. I won't. Jackie will be here soon and you have to get his dinner ready. Please say you forgive me."

"I forgive you, honest."

She hands me my towel and heads for the door. "You can give me back my pie tin anytime. I'm in no hurry."

With that she's gone. Okay, sin forgiven. But there it is, the unstated contract, meals to be made.

Is he going to expect me to do that every single day? Wait just one minute . . .

* * *

Jack walks in. I'm in a frenzy of cooking. He comes up behind me and kisses the back of my neck. "What smells so fabulous?"

"Pot roast, baked winter vegetables, potatoes au gratin, and a huge tossed salad with balsamic vinaigrette, and peach pie à la mode for dessert."

"Yum. I'm already drooling," he says as he now kisses the top of my head. "No more eating out of open cans standing in front of the refrigerator. Ever again."

I wheel around, spatula in hand. "I have two questions for you. Will you marry me? And do I have to do all the cooking?"

29

An Evening at Home

What a splendid evening. Jack is so thrilled about my finally using the *M* word, he is eager to prove he doesn't only love me for my cooking skills. He demonstrates how much he loves all my skills. Okay, I get the point.

Some couples create prenup agreements about money, real estate, and jewelry. Ours is about chores. Which ones we hate to do and which ones we actually enjoy. We have fun making lists. And we fool around before, during, and after. He's perfectly willing to do half the cooking (he says he makes a mean lasagna) or we can go to restaurants anytime I want. Ditto on housework. (He loves ironing. Huh? Who loves ironing?) As well as taking clothes to the cleaners (fine with him) and food shopping (together—we'll make it enjoyable).

Checkbook reconciling. Banking (he likes it, he can have it), and so on and so forth.

What we are in total agreement on is that we are both willing to share the sex. Ha-ha-ha. Little joke there.

"Glad," he says to me as we microwave popcorn for an evening of watching old movies on TV. "No spreading the word yet. Not until I put an engagement ring on your finger."

"I don't need a ring to know I'm yours."

"Well, I need it to keep the other guys away."

"Yeah, right, there's a line of them from here to Publix, just waiting for you to dump me."

The popcorn dings in the microwave. "Showtime," I say, kissing him.

We've both seen *Miss Congeniality* at least three times. That's the Sandra Bullock movie where she goes undercover at a beauty pageant. We throw lines out before the actors get to speak them. And chortle and giggle at the remembered scenes.

A moment of unhappiness seeps through. I wonder what Evvie and Joe are doing. Was their dinner table just another combat zone? Are they watching the same movie—Evvie, who I know loves this movie, and has seen it with me the last three times? Are they in different rooms? Left to laugh all alone? Or not laughing at all? In a perfect world those married couples out there would give up their old foolish battles that no longer matter, and as that '60's hippie slogan goes, "Make love, not war."

* * *

Evvie hears the front door open and she can sense Joe walk in and hover behind the couch where she is sitting. "Can't you find something to do and not bother me?" she says without turning around.

She's settled comfortably in her living room in front of the TV, watching *Miss Congeniality,* and she doesn't intend to let Joe spoil it for her. It's one of her favorite movies. She takes a sip of her tea and then a bite of her chocolate chip cookie, not looking at him.

"I could go to bed, but you're on the couch."

"Sit in the kitchen and read a book or something."

"I wouldn't mind seeing the rest of the movie with you." Before she can cut him off, he says, "Please, Ev. Let's stop this fighting. Can't we have a truce?"

For a moment she doesn't answer. "Come on and sit down, then." She grudgingly moves over to make room for him.

He quietly sits down next to her. Then a moment later, "Evvie, I need to talk to you."

"Only at commercials." She pulls at her cotton skirt to make sure his leg isn't touching it.

"It's a commercial now. I have to tell you something. I've been meaning to tell you since I moved in."

"Say it fast. There've already been six commercials. The movie will be back on in a minute."

"I didn't tell you the truth about why I moved here."

Evvie's eyebrows raise. "So?"

He hesitates, then leans over and whispers in her ear.

"What!" she shrieks in response, turning to stare at him.

"I can't stand saying it out loud. Please don't make me repeat it."

She looks at him, stricken. "I don't know what to say."

"Please don't say anything. Let's just watch the movie. I beg you."

They sit there side by side, but Evvie no longer sees what's on the screen.

* * *

Our movie is interrupted by the phone. As I go to answer it, I ask Jack to tell me later what I'll miss. We both laugh at that.

It's Stanley again.

"I couldn't wait," he tells me. "I had to call the woman, you know, the sister?"

"What did you say to her?" I sit down at the kitchen table. This might take a few minutes.

"I didn't say too much. I told her I needed to talk to her about her brother, Johnny. Something that happened a long time ago. She sounded very nice on the phone and naturally asked what it was regarding. When I told her it was too complicated and took too long to explain, she said she'd be glad to meet with me. I'm surprised she gave a stranger her address."

"Sounds encouraging. When are you going?"

"Well, I had it in mind that maybe you would

come with me? A woman along would make her more comfortable. I hope it won't be a waste of our time, but I feel I need to know."

In the background I hear Jack laughing out loud. I wonder if it's the scene where Sandra Bullock jumps off the stage and takes a flying leap at the startled Texan carrying a gun. "If you think it would help. When?"

"I was thinking tomorrow. We could hop on a plane and fly across to Tampa very fast. I already looked up flights and we could leave by nine A.M. And I MapQuested where she lives."

"Very organized, Stanley. All right."

"Thank you. As my dear mother used to say, *A katz vos myavket ken keyn mayz nit khapen.*"

"Sorry, Stanley, my Yiddish isn't that good. You'll have to translate."

"Literally it says, 'A meowing cat can't catch mice.' But what it means for us is that we can't just talk about doing something, we've got to go out and do it."

I say good-bye and hang up and happily get back in time. I didn't miss Texan-with-the-gun scene after all. I snuggle under Jack's shoulder, prepared to enjoy the rest of the movie with, dare I say it, my husband-to-be.

30

Gladdy and Stanley Take a Trip

I enjoy my short early-morning plane ride with Stanley Heyer. Despite being acquainted with him for more than twenty years, I really don't know him that well. I'm familiar with the fact he's been married to Esther for a very long time. That he has two grown children, and now three grandchildren. And that he takes his religion very seriously.

Maybe it's my guilt over Stanley's being aware of my living with Jack that makes me blurt out we are getting married. Talk about Jewish guilt. Well, there's also Catholic guilt and Protestant guilt. And on and on. But I find it amusing that at seventy-five I want this pious man to think I'm still a nice Jewish girl.

He is thrilled. Naturally he asks the expected question: "So when's the wedding?"

"We haven't gotten that far yet, but hopefully soon."

"A good man, Jack."

"I know." Now I'm sorry I brought it up. I'm always embarrassed answering personal questions. I change the subject. "Tell me about Esther. How is she?"

His face lights up. "Fine. Fine. I'm blessed to have a loving wife for fifty years. What more *nachas* could a man want?"

"How did you meet?" The countryside down below seems so wonderfully peaceful. How ironic. Not that many miles away from where we are overwhelmed with the damage done by the hurricane.

"Interesting you should ask. It was 1959. I had joined the neighborhood temple. On my very first Shabbat, after services, a beautiful girl with long curly red hair and big brown eyes was introduced to me, but I was too shy to say more than hello. But I saw her step outside alone and I worked up the courage to ask her if I could walk her home. My excuse was that a young lady should not have to walk home alone in the dark. She said she always came to services with her friend, but her friend was sick tonight. To my amazement, she agreed." He smiles broadly. "And one thing led to another."

"That's a lovely story."

I stare out the window for a few minutes more. I'm enjoying this difference in the lush Florida landscape when one gets away from the east coast beach cities. I turn to Stanley.

"And Abe Waller?" I say, just to make conversation. "You and he have been friends for a very long time."

"Yes. Best of friends for more than forty-nine years. That's another good story to tell. It's about six months later. I come home one night from temple and I see a man standing in Phase Six, looking from one building to the other. I ask, 'Can I help you?' He says, 'I'm thinking of moving here. Is it a good place to live?' I smile. 'A good place to live?' I say he asked the right customer, the man who built it. I extol its many features. He looks at the yarmulke on my head. He hesitates for a few minutes, as if he's gathering up courage to ask. 'Yes, you must be the right man,' he says. 'You would know if we are near a good synagogue.' " Stanley makes a wide gesture with both his arms, almost knocking his club soda off his little tray table. " 'Have I got a synagogue for you!' I tell him. With that, I insist on taking him upstairs for a cup of tea and to meet my beautiful Esther, who is already pregnant with our first child." Stanley's eyes tear up. "It was then I saw the tattooed numbers from under his shirt cuff. Those numbers from hell."

He shakes his head as if to push away the memory. I hold in my own tears.

With a quivering voice, Stanley continues. "He lost his whole family to the camps. Esther and I and the children became his family."

We stay silent and deep in our own thoughts, until the captain announces our plane is about to land in Tampa.

Stanley manages a small smile. "Oy, I talk too much."

I pat him on the shoulder. "Thank you for sharing this with me."

* * *

"Okay," says Ida, as the girls turn the corner to Phase Four. "This is where she lives. Though I'm telling you, this is a stupid idea."

Sophie sulks. "You said it fifty times already. You don't have to go with us."

"I do, because if I didn't, you'd do something dumb and Gladdy would be mad at me for not looking after you while she was away."

Bella is annoyed with Ida, too. "I wish Evvie had come with us."

Ida says, "She can't. She's with Joe. Something about having to take him somewhere."

To spite Ida, Sophie knocks forcefully on Margaret Ramona's ground-floor door.

The woman opens it and greets them with that cigarette hoarse voice of hers. "Welcome, welcome. Madame Ramona and all the spirits bid you come in."

Ida rolls her eyes. Once again the "Madame" is wearing large flamboyant clothes. Ida wonders at it, because the woman's hands and feet seem thin. She wears a lot of makeup on her pointy-chinned face. And has an unsightly big pimple—why doesn't she do something about it? Her long gray hair has pink ribbons entangled in it. Weird broad, Ida thinks.

Madame Ramona leads them through her living room, heading for the Florida room in the back. Bella pokes Sophie, indicating the paintings on the wall. Ida shakes her head in disbelief. Each of them is painted on a black velvet backdrop and has a gold velvet frame. Elvis Presley with a guitar. Michael Jackson holding a teddy bear. Liberace seated at a piano with a lit candelabra. Shirley MacLaine in a spaceship.

The Florida room looks like no other they've ever seen. You would never know it was meant to be a sunroom, since it is painted all black, even the windows. The only light comes from white candles on a black chest. Four chairs surround a small table that is covered with a bloodred fringed cloth. On the tabletop is a crystal ball, which Madame Ramona turns over, making imitation snowflakes swarm about a Christmas tree. Next to the crystal ball is a deck of cards. Oh, yes, and an ashtray filled with cigarette butts. Bella and Sophie ooh and ahh. Ida smirks. A phony, no doubt about it.

"The spirits bid you welcome and wish you to sit down."

Sophie and Bella plop down immediately. Ida continues to stand, making sure she knows where the exit is if they have to make a quick run for it. She studies "Madame" for a moment. What's with the smug smile? Ida wonders.

Sophie attempts conversation. "So, is it true you come from Canada?"

"Shhh!" demands Madame Ramona. "You are disturbing the spirits." She quickly starts dealing from the tarot deck. "Queen of Wands," she intones melodiously, as she slaps that card down. "There is a woman in your life who holds power over you. The wand represents electricity."

Bella whispers to Sophie, "See, I told you she'd know about Dora Dooley."

"Shhh!" Madame Ramona hisses again.

She deals another card. "Ahhh. The Fool. There is someone else in your life. You think he is a fool, but it is he who fools everyone." She turns over another card. "The Magician. Yes, he deals in magic. You will understand his kindness someday. Now you see him, then you don't." She whisks that card away.

Sophie and Bella stare, transfixed, even though they have no idea what she's talking about. Ida just keeps shaking her head.

Madame Ramona continues to deal. "The four of Cups. The Magician gives you a clue with this magical number. He says to think four."

Suddenly she reshuffles the cards and places the stack facedown in front of her. She shoves a cigarette into her mouth with one hand as the other hand snakes out. "Ten dollars. No checks."

"What?" squeals Sophie. "You said at the meeting the readings were free."

"That special offer ended yesterday." Her hand stays open.

"Go back to before," Bella says, upset. "What about that Queen of Wands? You know. Our queen of the remote. Our problem. We need you to tell us what to do with her watching all that TV."

Madame Ramona shakes the crystal ball dramatically, and when the "snow" settles down, she says, "The crystal ball has three words for you: *Pull. The. Plug.*"

She gets up, indicating it is time for them to leave.

"That does it!" Ida is incensed. She takes a one-dollar bill out of her purse and tosses it at Madame Ramona.

"You owe me nine more," Madame shouts, lighting her cigarette and coughing at the same time.

"Sue us," Ida says as she pulls both girls out with her.

Outside the door, Bella begs Ida, "Don't tell Gladdy. Please."

* * *

Lucy Blake Sweeney lives near the waterfront. This isn't the Tampa tourists see. These mean streets have seen hard times. Stanley and I knock at the door of the run-down cottage that is desperately in need of paint. The woman who answers is wiry and haggard. But her denim clothes are clean and her hair is combed. Her demeanor suggests she could be quite a scrapper when necessary.

Stanley introduces the two of us and Lucy invites us in. She looks sideways at Stanley's yarmulke and black outfit. She must be wondering what this man would want with her.

We sit at the edge of her rickety living room couch at her suggestion. "The springs sometimes just up and bite your . . . bottom, so be careful." Out of courtesy, she is watching her language.

She sits opposite us on the only chair in the room, a straight-back plain wooden one.

She leans forward. "I gotta admit you got my interest piqued. Ya want something to drink? I got some Cokes and beers."

Stanley answers for us. "No, thank you. We don't want to take up too much of your time."

She shrugs. "Been laid off again. Time's a'plenty right now."

"About your brother," Stanley begins. "We don't know whether or not we've come to the right place."

"I'll let you know."

He nods. "Your brother, Johnny, died many years ago. Very young."

"So far yer batting a thousand. The dummy went and left me alone. He was twenty and me nineteen. Never said where he was going, just told me he had to wander. I had no money. No support anywheres. He was all I had for a family." Her eyes tear in memory. "But what does that have to do with you? Don't tell me you're from some bank and you just found a life insurance policy that's been lost for nearly fifty years."

I say gently, "Sorry. No."

Stanley continues. "There is no easy way to say this, so I shall just say it. We come from Fort Lauderdale and we have just suffered through a hurricane. A building fell down and we found a skeleton underneath." He pauses.

She shakes her head. "Now you lost me. What has that to do with me?"

Stanley seems tired, so I speak. "We think it was your brother."

Lucy gets up and slaps her thighs, amused. "Boy, are you in the wrong place. My Johnny is buried right here in the church cemetery, not five blocks away. And believe me, there's no doubt but that is his body in that there casket."

Stanley starts to get up. "Mrs. Sweeney, I'm sorry we bothered you for nothing."

"Wait," I say. "Would you fill me in on what happened to him?"

Stanley has no idea why I'm asking. Frankly, neither do I. I'm going on pure instinct.

"I don't mind," she says. "I haven't thought of the poor lad in years." "I only found out later that he'd taken a job on a freighter that came all the way from Argentina. Guess he wanted to see the world." She takes a photo off a chest of drawers and shows it to us. "That was my brother. Tall, skinny, long drink of water, he was, with big dreams."

Stanley and I exchange glances. We are both remembering that the foreman, Ed, described his worker as "large, even heavy." Definitely the wrong man. Out of politeness, we wait for Lucy to finish her story.

"Anyways," she says, "the kid always had bad luck. He wrote to tell me he was on that ship and I was so excited finally hearing from him. The day his ship pulls into port, not eight blocks away from where we're sitting, I wait and I wait and there's no Johnny. Later on, I find out he fell overboard."

"Somebody see him fall?" I ask out of curiosity.

"No. The shipping company lied to me. They denied he fell from the ship. Insisted they signed him out that last day. But how could I believe a boy raised on the docks would just fall off of one? I knew something was screwy." She hangs her head, sadly. "He washed up on shore a month later."

We sit a few minutes longer, but there's nothing left to say. Lucy shows us to the door. Stanley takes out his wallet and offers her some money for her time, what with her being laid off.

Lucy rears back, insulted. "I don't take charity." With that she slams the door on us.

Stanley and I walk to the nearest cab stand. "Sorry I dragged you along on such a wild-goose chase."

"That's all right. How often do I get to travel to these exotic places?"

"My pleasure." He smiles and follows me across the street. "So what now? Who is the dead man? Will we ever find out?"

31

Dead End

As we sit at our usual picnic table late that afternoon, I report to the girls about the trip to Tampa. Behind them I can see yet another dump truck dragging away one more load of wrecked furniture. After I give them all the details, I say, "I guess he was the wrong Johnny Blake after all."

I pause. My brain is trying to come up with something.

"What?" Evvie asks.

"Something that woman in Tampa said to me that I'm trying to remember." I shrug; nothing's coming to mind. "And yet, the body was washed up a month later. After being in the water so long, how could they have been sure it was Blake? I'm driving myself crazy."

Evvie says, "Unless Morrie's lab can come up

with something from the bones, we may never find out who was buried there."

"Speak of the devil," Ida says as she points to Stanley walking toward them with Morrie in tow.

"Look who I found on my doorstep," Stanley says.

"I just dropped by to see how your repairs are going." Morrie gives the girls one of his delightful shy smiles. They eat it up. I can almost read their minds—they've got to find a girl for him.

"Going slow," says Sophie looking at Bella, both thinking of Dora. "Way too slow."

"I do have a report for you. From the forensics lab."

Ida says, "We were just talking about that."

The girls lean closer to Morrie to hear.

"My guys were so intrigued about having such an old skeleton on their table, they got right to work. Unfortunately I don't think it will help us find out who he is, but it tells us who he was not."

Evvie comments, "Sorry to hear that."

Morrie continues. "The bones tell us he was definitely male, approximately five foot seven inches tall. Probably between thirty and thirty-five years old."

"It doesn't match my foreman's description of a large, almost heavyset man." Stanley doesn't hide his disappointment.

"It doesn't match Johnny Blake's height or age, either," I say. So much for my water-logged theory.

Morrie shrugs. "Sorry, they can't get much closer than that."

Stanley says, "Then we have indeed come to a dead end."

Our group is about to disband, when Joe shows up. He doesn't say a word. Evvie hurriedly gets up from the bench. "Gotta go. Need to pick up some groceries for dinner."

She moves quickly away. I look after her, wondering what is happening. Something is new with those two. It's unlike Evvie not to confide in me.

Stanley is about to head back to Phase Six, when Abe walks by carrying a shopping bag. Stanley looks surprised. "I thought you were coming to the family dinner tonight."

Abe smiles. "Would I miss a dinner at your home? Not to worry. I'm bringing along some noshes." Abe indicates Morrie, who is about to get into his car. "Any news on the skeleton?"

Stanley absently bends to pull a weed out of a crack in the driveway. "I think we're never going to know."

Abe tries to comfort his friend. "Maybe it's for the best. You have enough on your mind without this worry. Let the past keep its secrets."

"Gladdy." I hear my name being called and I turn around.

It's Jack, home from his work down at the police station. He waves to his departing son and Morrie waves back.

"Grand Central Station around here." Jack kisses my cheek. Bella and Sophie grin at that, vicariously enjoying our happiness.

I explain. "Pre-dinnertime gathering. Happens

every evening around now. Just look up. Lots of noses peering out of windows to see the comings and goings."

"Sounds familiar. Like my Phase Six. Seemed like you were having a party."

"More like a wake." I take his arm and we head for my place.

I see Louise Bannister leaning over the railing of the third-floor walkway, watching us. I keep up a light banter so Jack won't look up.

At the mailboxes next to the elevator, I check my mail. What with leaving so early this morning, I'd forgotten. "Well, well," I say, looking at the familiar white envelope.

Jack looks at the envelope, too. "Not your Grandpa Bandit again?"

I open it up, and there's the green feather. "Guess so." I glance at it and wait as I see Sophie and Ida nearing us, heading for their apartments. When they are close I wave the letter, then read it out loud. " 'Hello, ladies. Things are seldom as they seem. Skim milk masquerades as cream. I'm back in business. It's going to be the Lauderdale S and L on Hallandale. Getting old means life is too short for us to save for a rainy day. The good news for me is that their alarm system works only half the time. And don't expect lunch. There's no deli around. Won't tell you the time. Tuesday's the date. Don't want to make it too easy-peasy. Or, then again, maybe I won't show up and this is a wild-goose chase.' "

Ida growls. "This is the last straw. We're gonna get him this time."

* * *

No moon shines in Enya's apartment. The curtains are tightly drawn. Blackness everywhere except for the small candle that burns on the table at the opposite wall, above which hang the family pictures. Of all the dead children. The shrine will be lit as long as Enya lives.

In her "bed of nails" Enya flings her tortured body from side to side. Over the decades she has managed to strangle most of her memories out of her conscious mind. If she hadn't, she would never sleep. She would go mad. She has prayed for death many times, but her prayers were not answered. None of her prayers were ever answered.

Now these memories from hell seep back into her dreams, forming beads of sweat on her face. She sees rivers of blood. A barking German shepherd, his gums slathered with spittle. A body, like something crucified, plastered across an electric fence, the zigzagging lights patterning a macabre dance as the man dies hideously. The coward. She spits with venom. How dare he take the easy way out, her husband?

More twisting, clutching at her pillow, holding on for dear life. Dear life it is. Here he comes, *Oberführer,* as she will learn to call him. And fear him with every fiber of her being. It's him! She screams aloud while staring into the deadness of his eyes.

There is a sharp ringing and a banging noise. She awakens, aware of her body pounding itself against the backboard of her bed, which hits the wall behind her over and over.

Her phone is ringing. It's Evvie. "I just walked by your door and heard some noise. Are you all right?"

I'll never be all right, Enya thinks. She sits up. "I'm sorry. Forgive me if I disturbed you."

"Do you want me to come over and stay with you?"

What for, she thinks, leaning her exhausted head back against the now motionless headboard. Nothing will wash away this sorrow. "No, thank you, dear. Just a bad dream."

"You phone me if you need me. I'll come and sit with you anytime you want. Promise?"

"Yes, I will. Go back to sleep." Sleep easy, you people in this country who take for granted the peaceful lives you lead. You have no idea.

Enya stares at the shrine across the room. The light flickers back at her. No, my precious ones, I will never forget.

* * *

Evvie puts down the phone in her kitchen. The call upsets her. Enya sounded so very sad. She takes off her jacket, then heads quietly into the living room, where Joe is asleep on the couch. Evvie walks over to him and looks down, watching him breathe. He seems so helpless lying there. She bends to fix his blanket.

Her presence wakes him. "How was the lecture?" he asks sleepily. He squints at the clock on a side table. "It's late."

"We went for coffee after."

Joe looks at her, not knowing what to say or do as she continues to stand there.

"Joe. Comfort me. Please."

He hesitates for a moment, not sure she means it. He sees the tears in her eyes. Then he jumps up and puts his arms around his ex-wife. Together, they head for her bedroom.

* * *

Where his kitchen wall backs the kitchen of his neighbor, Abe Waller sits at the small table, vaguely aware of the sounds coming from next door through the walls. He sips his scotch and stares grimly at his bible. Maybe he should move out. This crying of hers is not good. Too many memories, he thinks. I don't need this.

32

Grandpa Bandit Strikes Again

We go over last-minute instructions as we wait for the bank to open. Standing in the parking lot behind the bank, we are a group ready for action. We are well organized this time. Since Grandpa knows who we are, we wear assorted disguises—hats, scarves, sunglasses, etc. Eight can play at his game—one of him and seven of us.

We have our own extra crew of volunteers, since Jack and Joe have joined us. But they defer to me as team captain.

"Everybody have their whistle at the ready?"

The girls nod eagerly as they feel for the whistles round their necks. They are hyped for this day of possible excitement.

"Cell phones?"

They all pat at where said phones are located on their bodies.

"Remember not to use them unless necessary. Joe, here, has volunteered to be rotating messenger. He'll go around to each of you to find out if there is something you need."

Joe smiles happily at finally feeling like he belongs. He gets to spend a day with Evvie, which obviously thrills him. Evvie is still not giving anything away. I guess she'll tell me what's going on when she's ready.

Out of the corner of my eye I see my Jack looking amused and pleased at watching his woman in take-charge mode. Another check on the pro side of his balance sheet. He isn't threatened when a woman is the boss. He winks at me. I bet he knows what I'm thinking.

"Everybody know her assigned exit?" Each of the girls has an exit to guard.

Bella raises her hand. "I don't know where the northeast corner is."

"I'll escort you," says Joe willingly.

I continue. "We know how Grandpa likes to trick us, so be on guard. And he might just wait for closing time, hoping to find us weary and careless."

Ida puffs her chest out. "He won't get by us this time."

"Just keep in mind, he knows what we look like. But then again, he might be someone we know, so be alert."

Evvie looks sternly at Bella and Sophie, who are giggling. "He'll look for the weakest link."

Bella sighs. "That could be me."

Sophie pats her on the arm. "I'll watch your back, *bubbala*. If you faint or something, I won't let you fall." They grin at each other.

Evvie and Ida roll their eyes at the *two* weakest links.

"Don't forget to take turns for lunch breaks." Oh, yes, we have backpacks with food and drink—this army always marches on its stomach.

"And remember, Jack and I will be constantly on the move, visiting each of your checkpoints. We plan to walk in and out of the bank as pretend customers. Later we'll use the desks we were offered and playact as bank employees."

When we told Morrie, he believed it was another false alarm. But when I told him Grandpa *had* been there the last time, he took it a little more seriously. He promised he'd warn the bank officers so they'd be prepared. But his tone told me he thought we're wasting our time.

The bank managers have thoughtfully provided chairs at all the doors so we "elderly folk" have a place to rest.

It's ten A.M., the bank is open, and we join the waiting group in front.

The girls march in, heads high and spirits good. The bank is in pretty good shape despite the hurricane of ten days ago. A few taped-up windows are all I notice as I look around.

"Look alive," I instruct them. "Get to your battle stations."

Everyone is eager. Even the bank employees, all

of whom know what's going on, share in our anticipation. I don't expect any action right away and we don't get any. Eleven A.M. comes and goes. Joe walks over to where Jack and I are playing at being bank officer and customer.

"Message from Sophie. She says her feet hurt."

I sigh. "Tell her to take off the stiletto heels and put her sneakers on."

Joe salutes and heads for Sophie at the northwest door.

An hour later, Bella, taking a turn as a customer while Joe mans her post, walks in with a poodle. She stops to "chat" with me at my desk.

"Where did you get a dog?" I look at the froufrou white standard poodle covered with purple bows.

She giggles. "A lady outside loaned it to me when I said I wanted to impress someone." She turns and waves to the dog's real owner, standing at a desk where she is filling out a bank form.

By two o'clock everyone's beginning to sag. I shrug and say to Jack, "I can tell the girls are getting bored."

"Yes," he agrees, "too many bathroom breaks. And lunch breaks. And lolling about on chairs."

"Dangerous time, and I bet that sly old codger is depending on it."

At two forty-four, all hell breaks loose when we hear what sounds like gunfire coming from near the bank-vault area. The place is in a sudden uproar. People yelling in fear, running out, pushing and shoving others out of their way. Total panic.

Guards rush toward the noise, guns drawn, as all attention is on what's happening. In moments, the guards have the culprit on the floor and cuffed. From where I stand I hear him shout, "Leave me alone. Don't shoot!"

I stay at my post, but not my girls. They run to see what's going on. I suddenly have a funny feeling the real show is somewhere else. I scout all the tellers for unusual activity.

Joe and Evvie show up, out of breath. Evvie announces, "It's a teenager setting off firecrackers."

"No Grandpa, I bet," I say.

"Doesn't look like it." Evvie starts to catch on.

The thin, wiry boy, wearing gang-style low-riding pants, is being dragged away yelling, "Don't hurt me. Some old guy gave me ten bucks to do it as a gag!"

The noise level is high, almost high enough to muffle the alarm going off. But not quite.

Jack and I exchange glances, then he starts running toward the front door. He tells Joe to try a different door.

A shout comes from the teller farthest from where I am. "Help. Stop him! He's getting away!"

We are flummoxed. People are running every which way. Get who? We didn't see any of it. We have no idea where Grandpa went. Everywhere it's total chaos.

Sophie and Bella come running, all at sea.

"I was so scared," says Bella, shivering.

"I thought we were going to be shot dead,"

Sophie says, waving her arms agitatedly in front of her face.

I scowl at them. "It was Grandpa, diverting our attention. And it worked. You all left your posts."

Evvie, Sophie, and Bella hang their heads in shame.

"Did anybody see anything?" I ask, knowing the answer. A lot of shaking heads. They were all watching the action with the kid. As I was. I should have known.

"What do we do now?" Evvie asks dejectedly.

I say, "We can all run outside and look around, but don't bother. He's far away by now. That shrewd old geezer has beaten us again."

Jack and Joe come back in, shaking their heads. Jack says, "Too many exits, too many streets to follow."

Joe agrees. "Just a lot of people milling around to catch the action. Easy for him to lose himself in that crowd."

At that moment Morrie walks over to Jack. "I just got here. Fill me in."

Jack walks off with his son. "See you back home," he says.

We stand there not knowing quite what to do. I count heads. Someone is missing. "Where's Ida?"

* * *

At the sound of the firecrackers, Ida looks in the direction of the noise, as does everyone else. But she stands her ground. Peripherally, she realizes that someone has just run out her exit door—a man wearing a windbreaker and a blue baseball cap. Everyone is running toward the sounds. This guy is running from. Quickly she races outside in pursuit. She has a vague memory of something else as the person runs by, but she doesn't know what.

Her exit door leads to a quiet side street. She looks both ways. The only person she sights is the back of a woman, carrying a Macy's tote bag, strolling away from her. The woman has long gray hair with ribbons. She is about to put on a big floppy yellow hat. A woman who looks vaguely familiar. On impulse Ida hurries after her.

Ida smiles as she catches up. "Well, fancy seeing you here. Madame Margaret Ramona, I presume?"

Madame Ramona turns an icy stare at her. "Do I know you?" She keeps walking.

"Of course you do. I was the one who paid you a dollar for your phony tarot reading."

"Which was very rude of you, cheapskate."

Ida keeps up with her. She glances toward the tote. "Been shopping?"

"Yes, and it's none of your business."

"Been banking as well?"

"No."

"Well, you just missed a bank robbery."

"Really. How thrilling. I'll read about it in the papers tomorrow." Madame Ramona turns a corner, takes her keys from her pocket, and moves quickly to where her Honda Civic is parked.

Ida makes a grab for the woman's tote bag. "Love to see what you bought."

Ida is fast, but Madame Ramona is faster. Ida manages to pull one thing out—a Florida Marlins navy blue baseball cap—just as Madame Ramona shoves her forcibly toward the wall. She climbs quickly into her Civic. Ida struggles to regain her balance.

As the car whooshes past her, Ida shouts, "Now I know what I saw when you ran past me—I'd know that pimple anywhere!"

With that she runs back toward the bank, blowing her whistle!

33

Gotcha!

We meet up with Ida, still blowing that whistle, standing next to where our cars are parked in the rear of the bank. We surround her, the girls all talking at once.

"What?" asks Bella. "Where's the fire?"

"What are you doing out here? All the excitement was in there," says Sophie.

"Did you hear the firecrackers?" asks Joe.

"I caught Grandpa Bandit," she announces proudly, twirling a blue baseball cap with her finger.

We all look around. Nothing to see but parked cars and hurricane-damaged backs of buildings. Ida grins from ear to ear.

"What! You kidding us?" This from Sophie.

Ida raises her hand. "Scout's honor."

"So where is he?" Evvie demands.

"Grandpa drove off in 'his' car."

"You let him get away?" Bella asks.

"I had no choice. Grandpa knocked me down."

I ask, "Are you hurt?" I can't figure out why Ida emphasized the *his*.

She's still grining. "Nope."

What's going on? I wonder. But Ida is having a good time with this and she's going to do it her way.

"How did you know it was him?" Joe asks.

"By the pimple on 'his' face."

"Huh?" That comes from all of them. Ida can hardly contain herself. She does a little jig. Evvie chews her nails in frustration. Bella and Sophie are just flummoxed.

I ask the practical question. "Did you call the police?"

"No, not yet," she says. "Later will be soon enough."

Evvie, even more annoyed, asks, "What's so funny?"

"You'll see."

"You know who he is, don't you?" I ask.

"We all know 'Grandpa,'" she says, accentuating the name.

"Spit it out!" chorus Bella and Sophie.

She looks directly at the two of them. "Didn't Madame Ramona tell us we were chasing a magician? Didn't she say we thought he was a fool, but he really wasn't? And four was a number to remember?"

The two of them slowly nod their heads in unison.

"She told us all about him. I wondered how she knew," Ida says.

Evvie, puzzled, asks, "Isn't she that weirdo with all the flamboyant clothes? What's she got to do with this? When did you learn all this . . . this magician stuff?"

Ida says, "You drove off with Joe the morning Gladdy was on her way to Tampa. We had a tarot reading at Madame Ramona's."

Bella's feelings are hurt. "You said you wouldn't tell."

"Well, now I have to."

Evvie glares at Bella. "What for? What silliness were you up to?"

I say, "Never mind that. Where is Grandpa Bandit?"

"Let's go ask the Madame." Ida turns to Joe, since she knows we have to leave Jack's car. "Onward to Phase Four. Magic number four."

"Wait a minute," I say. "You're taking us to the man who just robbed the bank? Don't you think we should get Morrie? And Jack?"

If Ida smiled any harder, her teeth would hurt. "Trust me," she says.

* * *

We follow Ida as she leads us to a ground-floor apartment. Evvie glances at me as if to say "What is going on?" I shrug. I don't have a clue.

Bella is quaking. "I don't want to go back in there."

Sophie whispers, "Me, neither. She's crazy." They cling to each other.

"Yeah," Ida says, "crazy like a fox."

We all crowd behind Ida as she pounds on the door. No response. She rings the bell, and then pounds on the door again. Still nothing.

Ida shouts, "I know you're in there, 'Gramps.' Open up. We're not going away, even if we have to stand here all day and all night."

The peephole finally opens and we see an eye. A voice whispers, "You have a reading with the Madame?"

Ida demands, "Just open the damn door."

"I won't," says the voice.

"You will," says Ida.

Evvie shakes her head in wonderment.

"Get out of here or I'll call the police," yells the hoarse voice.

Ida puts her hands on her hips. "Why don't you do that? And ask for Detective Morgan Langford. His stepmother is standing next to me."

I shoot her a look.

"To be," Ida adds.

A silence, then we hear many clicks of many locks and finally the door opens. To our surprise, a rather tall, skinny man—in his mid-sixties, I would guess—is standing there, in an undershirt and shorts. He's almost bald, with just a ring of gray surrounding his scalp. "You can only stay a few minutes," he tells her. "Madame has a client coming very soon."

"Can the act," Ida says, pushing her way in. We follow Ida into the living room. This is her show. Bella and Sophie linger behind. Evvie and I have not been here before, and we stare about this room, fascinated by the velvet paintings.

"Sit down," Ida demands.

We all hurry for seats. I find myself seated on the couch under Liberace and his candelabra. Evvie and Joe land on a love seat under Michael Jackson. Bella and Sophie huddle in the hallway, obviously hoping for a quick exit.

Ida shakes her head in disbelief. "I meant for *him* to sit, not you."

Joe smirks. Evvie hides a smile. I'm speechless. The bald-ish man sits down opposite us, on the edge of a straight chair, nervously picking at a large red pimple. He's seated under Shirley MacLaine, who looks down on him from her velvet spaceship.

"Tell them who you are," Ida demands.

"I'm . . . I'm Madame's boarder."

"And when you put on your outfit, which always has big ruffled blouses, and you pull out of your pants a colorful skirt, and then add your long gray wig with ribbons, you're also chubby Madame Ramona." She twirls the blue baseball cap in front of his face.

Eyes open wide at that. Even mine. Bella gasps.

She turns to Evvie. "Give a quick look around for a Macy's tote bag." I watch clever Ida as she watches the man, whose eyes immediately dart to a closet in the room. “Try that closet,” Ida says, pointing. He starts to get up, but Ida pushes him back down.

Evvie retrieves the bag from the closet and upends its contents onto the floor. Out falls the windbreaker. The big sunhat, dark sunglasses. The long gray wig and the frilly blouse and skirt. And a wad of money. Ida tosses her the blue Marlins cap. “That goes with it.”

The old man looks chagrined. Evvie turns to him and recites his own lines back to him, “Things are seldom as they seem. Skim milk masquerades as cream. Gilbert and Sullivan.”

He tries for an impish smile at me.

I say, “Why did you do all this? Why the green feather?”

He remains quiet. Ida says, “You might as well tell us. They’ll get it out of you at the police station.”

“Yeah,” says Bella, from the hallway, suddenly brave. “You might as well, ’cause you’re no good as a psychic. Your advice didn’t work. Dora’s still in my apartment!”

Evvie and I look at him, and he shrivels up, realizing he just gave himself away. So that’s how he did it.

There is a knock on the door. The man jumps up. Ida pushes her thumb into his chest. “Stay down.” She walks into the hallway. Sophie and Bella move out of her way. She peers out the peephole.

A voice outside asks, "Izzy here?"

Ida, confused, replies, "Is who here?"

The voice repeats, "Izzy. Izzy here?"

Our thief says, "He wants me. I'm Izzy."

Ida shuts the peephole, and opens the door to let the visitor in. He is a small, nervous man in shabby clothes. He is bent over, carrying a cane made from a branch of a tree. And he's quite old. His watery eyes squint to seek out "Izzy." "Sorry," he says in a shaky voice, "but I don't mean to intrude when you're having a party."

"It's all right," the man we now know as Izzy says.

"I'll just get what I came for and leave. You got the money?" the newcomer asks pleadingly.

Izzy gets up. Ida doesn't stop him. He goes to the tote bag on the floor and takes out the cash. He hands all of it to the man. "It's time?" Izzy asks him.

"Doc says I can't wait any longer." He hugs Izzy tearfully. "You're a saint. God bless you. Otherwise, I'm a dead man," he explains to us.

With that he turns and heads for the door. "Happy birthday," he announces, making an assumption, and leaves.

I jump up. "Wait a minute, that's stolen money . . ." I stop. Do I grab the money out of the hands of some pathetic sick man? Who might die?

The girls all look to me, aghast. Breathlessly awaiting my decision.

I sit back down. I'm glad Jack wasn't here. I sigh. Let the police unravel this later.

Izzy also sits down again.

Ida says, "Izzy. Are you going to give us a last name with that?"

No reply. Only silence.

Finally I say, "The green feather. You're playing Robin Hood? Steal from the rich, give to the poor?"

He corrects me. "Steal from the young, give to the old. Who takes care of the lost old people?" he asks. "The ones under the radar. Who cares if they live or die? They live in places you would run screaming from. They eat cat food when they can get it. They have no one. Then they get sick. And then they die. Alone. I pay for their needs the only way I can. The fourteen hundred I stole today is for his gallbladder operation. I steal only what I need for each individual case."

That explains the odd amounts.

"But why don't these people go to the proper authorities for help?" Evvie asks.

"Yeah, sure. *These* people don't know from how the system works. They don't know from papers to fill out. They're barely able to read. Or even see the fine print without any glasses. Folks who barely function at all. Old and infirm. Where's the health care for them? I do what little I can do."

I ask, "How long have you been doing your"—I grope for a word—"your charity work?"

"Many years. Since the day my sister died of a brain tumor because she didn't have any money to pay for doctors." He chokes up. "I had no way to save her."

Evvie walks close to him. "I don't get it. Why did you write to us? Did you want us to capture you?"

He glances up to her and shrugs. "Maybe I'm tired. Maybe . . ." Then he grins mischievously. "Maybe I was bored and I needed a little excitement. Pit myself against you to see which of us is smarter. I found out you were helping older people, so maybe I just wanted to reach out—one old professional to another."

I hear Bella and Sophie sniffling behind me.

I don't want to say it, but I know Jack would have. "But what you do is against the law. It's a federal crime to rob banks."

He cries out to me, "It should be a federal crime in such a rich country for only the wealthy to afford health care. It's enough to make a man turn into a Communist." Abruptly, he grins at me playfully. "Better he should be a bank robber."

He's getting to me, but I keep on. "We have to turn you in or we're aiding and abetting a criminal."

"No!" Sophie cries out.

What a terrible dilemma. My girls are in anguish. I feel awful, too. Evvie reaches out to touch my hand.

Ida comments, "And Madame Ramona was your cover."

"An escape method. I knew the cops would never think Grandpa was a woman." The imp in him can't resist. "Now, aren't you sorry you only gave me a dollar?"

Sophie jumps up. "Wait just a minute. You weren't wearing a dress when you posed as the guy with no legs."

Bella sighs. "I wish someone would tell me how you did that."

He smiles. "I wasn't robbing the bank that day, either. I was there to watch how you operate, so I stayed a guy."

Bella says happily, "I still have your pencil."

I look to Evvie and Ida. "I don't know what to do."

"Don't sweat it," Izzy says. "I'll go quietly. But can I put some clothes on?"

"Of course," Ida says quickly.

He heads into his bedroom and Ida follows him to the door. He grabs some clothes from the bed and waves them at her as he enters his bathroom.

We wait for him in the living room. I see tearful faces and listen to the unhappy murmurings around me.

"Do we have to turn him in?" Bella wails.

Ida says stiffly, "We have no choice."

Evvie says, "I wish he had never written to us."

Bella asks, "Do you think we'll get a reward?"

"Don't hold your breath," says Ida.

Evvie helps Ida pick up Izzy's disguises from the floor as they repack the tote bag. Wait 'til Morrie hears this, I think ruefully. He's not going to be happy at how easily they were all fooled. This is not a win-win situation.

Ida gives me the tour of Madame Ramona's all-black office with the crystal ball, Ouija board, and tarot cards.

We wait. And we wait. Ida knocks on the bathroom door. "Let's go, Izzy."

No answer. It dawns on me; he's just pulled the oldest scam in the world. And we fell for it. Joe hurries into the bedroom. Of course the bathroom door is locked.

Joe rolls up his sleeves. "I'm gonna break the door down!"

As he starts to sprint; shoulders pointing, Evvie grabs him by the arm and pivots him around. "Are you crazy? What do you think this is—like the movies? It's not so easy to knock down a door."

"I can do it," he says, but his voice betrays him.

"You're an old man! The only thing you'll break is your neck."

"He's gone," Ida announces as she walks back into the apartment. "I looked outside and the bathroom window is definitely open, and bye-bye, Bandit."

I sigh. I've watched this scene in a lot of movies, too.

But everyone is smiling. And Joe actually winks at me.

Needless to say, Izzy didn't leave anything in the apartment that will give us his real name or any other information. The Madame Ramona name is obviously phony. The apartment is a rental. Even if Morrie checks out Izzy's fingerprints, I'll bet he has no police record to match them against.

Bye-bye, Grandpa. I wonder where you'll turn up next. You wrote us that getting old was not for sissies, and you were right.

I can't wait 'til Jack gets home so I can tell him that the Grandpa Bandit case is solved. More or less.

And Morrie will have a fit that we let him get away. Oy!

34

An Unexpected Visit

The doorbell rings. Enya, on her way to her kitchen, is startled. Hardly anyone ever comes to her door. Which is just the way she likes it. She peers through her peephole. To her surprise, Abe Waller is standing there, holding a small bouquet of flowers.

She doesn't answer, standing still, almost holding her breath. Maybe he'll go away. What does he wants from me? she wonders.

He rings again.

She hesitates, unconsciously smoothing her skirt down with her hands. He must know she's in here. She can't be rude. As she opens the door she sees Abe glancing at the mezuzah on the right side of her door frame.

He smiles ruefully. "It is a very strange feeling living in someone else's home. I have never lived anywhere without a mezuzah. May I, Mrs. Slovak?"

Of course she knows what he is asking—permission to pay his respects to God. Her second husband, Yacov, whom she met after the war, himself a survivor, put the tiny box up when they moved into the apartment. She protested; she cared nothing about religion anymore. She looks at this pious stranger. Let him do what he wants. She nods.

He touches the sacred parchment scroll gently, then places those fingers to his lips. Then he hands her the flowers, which she accepts in puzzlement.

"What did I do for you to bring me flowers, Mr. Waller?"

"It's what *I* did. I felt I did not treat you kindly in the laundry room the other day. Perhaps I was too abrupt?"

At that moment, Evvie and Joe come out of the adjoining apartment. There is a moment of awkwardness, but quickly and at the same time they all nod. Then Evvie and Joe walk off.

Enya, not knowing what to do, and feeling obliged, says, "Perhaps you would like a cup of tea?"

"A glass of water, maybe." Abe says, following Enya inside.

* * *

"Well, that was interesting," Evvie says to Joe as they head for his car, out to a restaurant to celebrate their capture of Izzy. "Bringing flowers? How romantic."

"I brought you flowers a while ago. You gave them away."

Evvie flicks an imaginary bit of dust off his shoulder. "Don't go there, Joe. That was then and now is now."

With that she flounces into his car before he has a chance to open the door for her.

* * *

Across the way, Jack turns from the kitchen window. "Well, well," he singsongs, "love is in the air. Tra-la-tra-la. Just saw Abe bring flowers to Enya, and Evvie actually touched Joe's shoulder."

I come over, wiping my hands on my apron, and put my arms around him. "It's catching, isn't it?"

He pulls my arms even tighter, closer. "What is?"

"Being a yenta and spying on people. Like everyone else does around here."

He swivels around 'til he's facing me and gives me a playful swat on my rear. Then he goes over to the stove and sniffs what I've cooked for dinner.

"Decisions, decisions," he says. "Food or sex? Sex or food?"

"I thought you wanted to hear more about our Grandpa Bandit story?"

"It can wait." With that, he drags me out of the kitchen and I toss my apron behind me.

* * *

Enya stares at the few photographs on her small kitchen table. They are very old, tattered, practically shriveled up. Abe's empty wallet sits beside them.

Abe points to his photo of a young boy with a bicycle, and says, "We wanted Max to play the violin; he was interested only in sports." He manages a small smile. "I was a musician in the old country."

As he talks about his children, she thinks of the photos on her bedroom wall. For a moment, she is tempted to get them, but she can't bring herself to share them. She politely listens to him, sensing how much it must mean to him to be able to talk about his family. But something won't let her open up to him.

He reaches over to touch her hands, but the moment he does, she pulls away. "Sorry," she says. He gestures by raising both hands aloft, as if to say he understands. "You had children?"

She can barely speak. Her throat seems to be closing up on her. She doesn't want to talk about them. But she doesn't know how to be rude. This very kind man is sharing his pain with her. She whispers, "Rebecca was four and Micah was five. My babies..." The tears start to flow. He hands her a handkerchief.

He indicates the numbers on her arms. "When were you there... Auschwitz?"

She says, "Forty-two to forty-five. Sometimes in my dreams I imagine it never happened..." She moves a teacup around in its saucer, but doesn't drink. "In my nightmares there is no doubt it did."

"You know the strange thing?" Enya understands he is changing the conversation away from the personal to make her feel more comfortable. "I only found out afterward. It was only Auschwitz that tattooed the numbers. None of the other camps ever did."

"I never heard that," she says.

"Your husband. You. What work did you have in Prague . . . before . . . ?"

"Jacov and I both taught at the university."

"I was never there. I never traveled far from Munich."

They sit still for a while. Enya watches the second hand on the kitchen clock move round. She wishes he would go away. Her body is sweating; she wants to wash.

Abe finally gets up. "I will leave now. You must have your dinner to prepare. Thank you for the water. He gathers up his photos and places them gently into his wallet. He walks to the door, and as Enya moves around him to open it, their arms touch for a second. Enya's body goes rigid.

Abe opens the door, bows, and leaves.

Enya slowly returns to the kitchen table and sits down. She lifts the bouquet of flowers from the vase in which she placed them and buries her face in them. She remains there, sobbing until it gets dark.

35

Gladdy Has a Hunch

I wake up abruptly; something in a dream startles me into consciousness. Jack turns, opens one eye, and says, "What?"

I pat his shoulder gently. "Go back to sleep. It's nothing."

The phone rings. Jack groans and puts his pillow over his head. I look at the clock. Eight A.M. Has to be one of the girls. I'm up already, might as well start moving.

I answer the phone in the kitchen so as not to disturb Jack. It's Sophie.

"News," she says. "The pool is fixed and they're putting water in it. Everyone's going to watch."

"Everyone? How many calls have you made?"

"I didn't. Bella called me because Ida called her because Evvie called Ida." And she adds petulantly, "We always used to get up this early anyway to do our exercise."

She's speaking in past tense because since Jack moved in, our early-morning routine has vanished. There's a tiny bit of complaining in Sophie's voice. I have to pay attention to this.

"Okay," I say, "I'll meet you down there soon as I get dressed."

"Don't bother wearing your suit. I don't think we can swim yet. Something about chlorine."

I hang up. Why are we all going to the pool if there's no water? I hum a few bars of "Tradition" from *Fiddler on the Roof.*

As I grind my coffee beans it hits me. Why I woke up so abruptly. I phone Stanley. I know he gets up early to supervise the repair work. Maybe I can catch him before he leaves.

Too late. His wife, Esther, tells me I just missed him.

I say, "When you hear from him, please tell him to find me. I need to talk to him about something important. If I'm not in my apartment, I'll be at the Phase Two pool."

I enjoy my coffee and toast, get dressed, and leave Jack a note. It says, "Not going swimming, but will be at pool. Don't ask. Love and xxxx." I leave the note and a camellia on my pillow. I'm really getting into this living together stuff.

* * *

What a sight! Everyone sits in his or her usual place, facing the pool. Well, not everyone. Our

Canadians won't be back for a while. But here they are, our regulars, staring at a pool slowly being filled with water. Comical, really. Seems as exciting as watching grass grow. Nothing too much is happening.

The difference is we have our new temporary neighbors, and even they have come down for this non-event. First face I see is Louise's. She immediately looks behind me to see where Jack is. Maybe she's hoping we had a fight and he's up for grabs. Not a chance, lady.

Dora Dooley has pulled a patio chair next to Bella and Sophie, even though they try to avoid her existence by chatting with their backs to her. Dora's deep into a *TV Guide* magazine, marking shows she wants to see. Ida knits, ignoring all of them.

Joe has a chaise next to Evvie. He's glued to her side. The way he watches her makes me imagine how a starving man might look at a steak. Evvie pays no attention to him and is engrossed in a book.

Tessie sits on the edge of the pool, her feet dangling in air, as she stares down, watching for the water-level changes. Being the only real swimmer, she can hardly wait until the pool fills. Her hubby, Sol, is a different person since their marriage. The talkative Sol has turned very quiet. As Evvie said to me a while back, she'd love to be a fly on their wall. I'm curious, too.

In between slathering suntan lotion on each

other's backs, Casey and Barbi sit directly in the sun, playing gin rummy.

I note that Enya is not here. However, her new neighbor, Abe, who brings flowers, sits in the shade behind the small wrought-iron gate, away from us, reading a newspaper. Abe is fully clothed, wearing his usual black suit. He doesn't seem to mind the heat. I'm surprised he's even there.

And last and never least, Hy and Lola.

It's as if he's been waiting for me to arrive. "In honor of the return of our pool, I got a new joke, folks."

Sol says, "Hah! Like we care."

Tessie gives her darling a little pinch. "You tell him, honeybunch."

No one shows any enthusiasm at all, but Hy is never bothered by opposition. In fact, he thrives on it. He gets up and emotes:

"A young woman brings her fiancé home to meet her parents. After dinner, the mother tells the father to find out about the young man. The father invites the fiancé to his study for a drink. 'So, what are your plans?' the father asks the young man.

" 'I am a Torah scholar,' he replies.

" 'A Torah scholar. Hmmm,' the father says. 'Admirable, but what will you do to provide a nice house for my daughter to live in, as she's accustomed to?'

" 'I will study,' the young man replies, 'and God will provide for us.'

" 'And how will you buy her a beautiful engagement ring, such as she deserves?' asks the father.

" 'I will concentrate on my studies,' he replies. 'God will provide for us.'

" 'And children?' asks the father. 'How will you support children?'

" 'Don't worry, sir, God will provide,' replies the fiancé.

"Later, the mother asks, 'How did it go, dear?'

"The father answers, 'He has no job, he has no plans, he has no ambition, but the good news is, he thinks I'm God.' "

There are a few small laughs. Abe gets up without a word and starts to leave.

"You insulted him," says Evvie, "using the name of the Lord in vain."

"What's the matter, a man can't take a joke?" Hy says, offended.

As Abe moves out of the perimeter of the pool area, he meets Stanley, who is hurrying in. That stops him. "Is something wrong?" Abe asks worriedly.

"I don't think so, but"—he glances to me—"Gladdy said she needed to see me about something important."

I am now the center of attention. I try to underplay it. "Just some thoughts I wanted to share with him."

Sophie claps her hands. "I bet it's about the skeleton."

"Yeah," says Bella excitedly. "I bet you figured out who he is."

My girls are about to move in my direction as I head toward Stanley. I wave them down. "Relax, everyone. Let me chat with Stanley. If there's anything new to report, you'll hear about it."

They are disappointed. Everyone stares after us as I lead Stanley out of earshot.

* * *

We find a bench to sit at near the duck pond. The ducks are slowly returning after our disaster. I wonder how many were lost forever. We settle ourselves under a tree that is split in half, another result of the hurricane. Stanley shakes his head at all the damage to plants and trees. "So many years this tree was here. I remember we planted it soon after we finished the construction. Now it's dead."

I commiserate with him. He changes the subject. "Never mind, you have information? I thought our case was over."

"Just a hunch, Stanley. Something's been bothering me ever since we came back from Tampa. We finally decided that this Lucy Blake's brother, Johnny, was not our skeleton. But his sister, Lucy, said something that stuck in my head. She questioned the way he died. Falling off the dock immediately after a long voyage? Lucy was informed that her brother definitely left the ship. But what if he didn't? What if somebody wanted to steal his papers? Somebody trying to get into this country from a foreign country? He would wait until they were near port because he couldn't move around the ship before that. Suppose he threw Johnny

Blake overboard the day they docked, and used his papers to get off the ship?"

"A stowaway, you're thinking?"

I nod. "Yes. Once onshore, he could have been moving around, using Johnny's identity, and somehow ended up here and got the job working for you."

Stanley is eager now. "And this stranger is the one buried under the cement."

"Maybe," I say, "and maybe not."

He looks puzzled. "What do you mean?"

"I don't know. But it's something to think about."

Stanley paces back and forth in front of the shattered tree, his hands behind his back. "How can we make sure that it is the same Johnny Blake who is the connection? How can we find out?"

I shrug. "You got back the items you gave Morrie for the testing?"

"Yes. As a matter of fact, this morning. They are in my apartment. I was trying to figure out what to do with them. I almost threw them away."

"I'm glad you didn't. Would you please bring them to my apartment? I want to look closely at them. Perhaps there's something we've missed."

We reach my building. I'm about to go upstairs and Stanley is starting to head for Phase Six, when we run into Abe again. He's standing at his mailbox. He must be eager for something to arrive. The mail doesn't come for another hour.

Abe asks Stanley, "Is there a problem?"

Stanley pats him on the shoulder. “Everything is under control, old friend. This brilliant lady doesn’t give up easily.”

Abe gives me a bright smile. “That is good news indeed.”

36

Putting It Together

We're seated around my dining room table eating lunch. Everyone's a little nervous. This is the first time the girls have gathered in my apartment since Jack moved in. They are on their best behavior. Sitting up tall, like elegant ladies, eating slowly, positively dripping with good manners. Jack is cramping their natural style.

"Would you please pass the salt?" Sophie asks ever so politely. Their usual behavior is boardinghouse style—reach over and grab.

Bella daintily lifts the salt shaker with pinky held high and passes it to Evvie, who gives it to Ida, who places it in Sophie's outstretched hand. What a performance.

Jack smiles and mimics them. "Glad," he says, "would you do me the honor of handing me the pepper?"

"Sure," I say. I lift the shaker and toss it to him. He grabs it and I smile back at him. For a moment, the girls are bewildered, but then they get it and start to relax.

By now I've filled everyone in and we're waiting for Stanley.

* * *

Stanley is excited. He can hardly contain himself. He comes in waving a tattered old envelope. "You are so smart, lovely lady. I never paid attention. The Christmas card to a Lucy Blake came with an envelope. And an address." His hands are shaking as he passes the envelope to me.

I scan it quickly and read, " 'Lucy Blake, P.O. Box . . .' " And I stop, chagrined. "Oh, Stanley, it's a fifty-year-old post office box number!"

The girls get it immediately. Then Stanley's smile fades. "I didn't think."

I pace for a few moments, exchanging glances with Jack. "Hold on, maybe all is not lost. Maybe she'd remember her old number."

Evvie isn't convinced. "You really expect that Lucy woman to remember a post office box number she used almost fifty years ago?"

Sophie chirps, "I remember the first phone number I ever had, when I was twenty. Tivoli two four eight five . . . three."

Ida says, "I lived at thirteen forty-five Manor Avenue, apartment four-J, in the Bronx, until I was sixteen."

"Come to think of it," Evvie says, "I remember

the first driver's license number I ever had." She gets up and pours coffee for all of us.

"Okay, okay," I stop them. "You made your point. Maybe she'll remember and maybe she won't. We'll soon find out."

Bella giggles. "But don't ask me what I just ate for breakfast." Then she says, "I still don't get it. This boy, Johnny, dies because a man kills him for his identity, so why isn't the bad guy the skeleton?"

Jack says, "Let me try to explain, Bella."

Bella practically bats her eyes at him. She's his number-one fan in my motley group of P.I.'s. I know Sophie also adores Jack, and Evvie finally is happy about my relationship with him, acknowledges it as the real thing. I watch for Ida to respond. Is she going to be my only holdout in accepting Jack, who seems to be infiltrating our investigating team? Not a hint does she reveal on her face. Her arms are crossed, however.

Stanley says, "You've obviously done some thinking. Fill me in."

Jack attempts to simplify it. "Lucy Blake told you, her brother Johnny was on a ship coming from South America. A bad guy, probably trying to get into our country illegally, steals his papers and kills him. With me so far?"

Bella practically gurgles.

"The bad guy throws Johnny overboard near shore. Does it just before they dock. The authorities insist Johnny left the ship with all the others. The fake Johnny uses the confusion of docking and rushes off the ship as fast as he can, flashing the stolen papers. After the real Johnny's body washes up, the police figure he must have fallen off the dock. His sister doubts it."

Evvie has to jump in. "Okay, so he wanders around as Johnny Blake and ends up working on Lanai Gardens. It was a dark and stormy night." Evvie smiles; she's imitating a classic mystery novel beginning. "Someone comes to the construction site. And ends up murdered and thrown in the hole."

Bella raises her hand. "Stop. That's what I don't get. How do we know it wasn't the phony Johnny Blake that died?"

My turn. "I'm making that assumption. The bones found do not match the description that Stanley's foreman gave of the man he hired as Johnny Blake. Also, we now realize the impostor has already committed one murder. My supposition is, whoever came upon him that stormy night was the one killed. The bad guy already murdered one man; it wasn't a big jump to suppose he could murder another. Besides, the bones describe a much smaller man."

Good. Here comes Ida, joining in at last. Her curiosity overcomes her misgivings. "But why?"

I lean back and sip my coffee. "That's the big question."

Sophie offers, "A robber came to rob him or to steal building supplies?"

Ida says, "Doubtful. What with how bad the weather was that night."

Jack says, "Perhaps it was someone who was looking for him and finally found him."

I add, "And they had a fight?"

Evvie shakes her head. "So if that's true, now we have two unknown men. The bad guy and the mysterious stranger. How can we possibly figure out who they were?"

Ida says, "Sounds like another dead end."

I say, "I'm hoping Lucy will recognize the post office box number. If so, it will be definite proof the bad guy is connected to this Johnny Blake. We need to narrow that fact down."

Stanley looks at me doubtfully and shrugs.

"It's all we have to go on." I hand him my phone and I turn on the speaker so we can all hear. He takes a card from his pocket and dials Lucy's number.

We're in luck, Lucy's home.

After Stanley explains why we're calling, he repeats the number on the old, crumpled envelope.

For a moment, she's surprised. Then I can almost hear the smile in her voice. "Funny you should ask," she says, "I happen to be very good with numbers. I had that box number for years. Why do you want to know?" But she speaks before we can answer. "The man you found had Johnny's belongings, didn't he?"

Stanley says, "We think so. There was a Christmas card with your name and that post office box number."

"I knew it," Lucy says. "I was sure somebody killed my brother. Please," she begs frantically, "promise me you'll find him, so my brother can have justice."

Stanley looks at me and I nod. "We promise. We will do everything we can to find him."

He hangs up and I'm exhilarated. "Now we have proof!"

Stanley says wryly, "All you have to do is solve the crime. Identify the other dead man and a murderer who's gotten away with it for fifty years."

Everyone looks to me, as usual.

Jack raises his eyebrows. I know what he's thinking. "What has his Gladdy gotten herself into this time?"

37

When Night Falls

First rainy day we've had since the hurricane. It's the three D's out there. Dreary, dark, and depressing. I have every light on in the apartment to chase away the gloom.

I wait for Jack to come home. He's late tonight. Though things have calmed down, I guess there are still many neighborhoods that are far from being repaired and that's where the extra police still guard for trouble.

It's my night to cook. Jack has made our cooking evenings a fun contest. Surprise Night: "I'm not telling you what I'm making, see if you can guess by the way the kitchen smells." No White Food Night; not a bad thing, leaves out lots of starches. Or Competition Night; "Who makes the best lasagna?" Not that we have lasagna two nights in a row. The competition is two weeknights apart.

Instead of *having* to cook, cooking has become fun. *Fun* is the operative word. And he is a fun companion. Why, oh, why did I wait so long? I could have had this life a year ago. Why didn't I follow my own rule of *If not now, when?* I was so afraid to give up what I had in favor of the unknown.

The key turns in the lock and I hear, "Honey, I'm home." He is determined to say that silly thing every time. And I meet him at the door with a kiss and say, "Hard day at the office, dear?" A new tradition.

And of course he heads directly for the kitchen. It's Soup from Scratch Night, and I have a hearty vegetable soup on the stove. To be served with a French bread and Brie. The secret of my vegetable soup is to sprinkle grated Parmesan cheese on it when serving. Jack lifts the lid, takes a spoonful, and smiles his approval.

"You're late. Any problems?"

"Nope. I had to make a stop."

He goes into the living room, where the table is elaborately set. BJ (before Jack), a tacky placemat, paper napkins, and any old silverware. AJ, need I say Martha Stewart would be proud?

He lights the candles in my fancy silver-plated candelabra, which had gathered dust for ten years in the hall closet until now.

And then he places a small box on my plate.

There should be a crash of cymbals. The first four notes of Beethoven's Fifth at least. Something.

I examine the box from every angle. It looks like a small ring box. "Is this what I think it is?" I ask.

"It is," he replies. "Exactly what you said you wanted. A garnet instead of a diamond."

"This is it, then?" I ask, stalling.

He removes the ring from the box and places it on my finger. "Last chance to run. I would get down on my knees, but you'd have to pull me up." He beams. "Hope you like the design I picked. You can always get it reset, though."

It's beautiful, but what engagement ring isn't beautiful? I can't believe how corny I feel. There must be something of a universal subconscious that prompts this response in women when they get "the ring." Tears in my eyes, a blush on my cheeks.

He kisses me. "I'm only marrying you because you love to cook."

I burst out laughing. "You're trapped, too."

"I hope forever."

I bask in the joy of the moment. I wish everyone I love could be so happy.

* * *

They sit on the couch, side by side. Joe eats a TV dinner: roast beef, mashed potatoes, green peas. Evvie eats home-cooked lemon chicken with Brussels sprouts and a salad. They watch *Jeopardy!* Evvie calls out the answers when she knows them. Joe stares ahead and seems to be watching. But he is thinking.

"Evvie," he says. "Can't we divide up the

chores? I can cook one night, and maybe you the next."

"Hah," she says. "When did you learn to cook?"

"I manage."

"You just want me to wait on you hand and foot, like I used to. And that's not going to happen."

He sighs. "I wish we could try to make things pleasant."

"Maybe your apartment will be fixed soon, so this'll be a moot point."

He picks up her plate and his aluminum foil wrapping and brings them into the kitchen. He washes up what little there is. He calls to her, "Want me to go out and get some ice cream?"

"It's raining," she calls back.

"So what?" he says, "I won't melt."

"All right," she says grudgingly. "Make it chocolate almond fudge."

"I know. I know what you like." He grabs his raincoat from the hall closet. And like an eager puppy dog, he races out.

Evvie tries to concentrate on the TV show. She calls out an answer. "Spain." She's wrong. It's Portugal. She shakes her head, disgusted with herself. Why am I so damned stubborn? Why can't I bend a little? He's trying so hard. Stupid. Stupid. Stupid.

* * *

Enya wakes up, disoriented, not knowing where she is. The room is dark. She reaches for the lamp and turns on the switch. She shakes her head to clear it. She had fallen asleep on the couch. Getting up slowly, she makes her way into the kitchen. From her window she sees Joe hurrying past. He is smiling. She puts up the kettle for tea.

Glancing at the clock she realizes it's past dinnertime. What does it matter, she's hardly ever hungry these days. She tells herself she must eat. But what for?

It's the nightmares. They won't stop. Eyes everywhere. The eyes of her husband and the children. Eyes pleading. Eyes filled with dirt and crying. Eyes dying; the light going out. Eyes of an assassin who terrorizes her.

She can't stand it, but what can she do? She needs to talk to someone. Throwing a shawl around her shoulders, she walks outside. She hesitates at Evvie's door. Then, not wanting to disturb her, on impulse she turns next door and rings Abe's bell. Immediately she regrets her action.

Abe, wearing a tallis, his praying shawl, answers and is startled to see her. "Mrs. Slovak, do you need something?"

She moves away, shaking her head. "A bad idea." She goes back into her apartment. How could she think of even going to that man? He's a stranger. And she realizes something about him makes her nervous. She drinks more tea and stares at her white kitchen wall, hoping for serenity.

Fifteen minutes later Abe knocks at her door. This time, he is wearing a jacket. He tells her, "You came to me in need and I should have helped you then and there. Forgive me."

"I'm all right. It was a moment of weakness."

He tries for a smile. "Perhaps I should have brought more flowers. I seem always to be apologizing to you."

She lets him in. She asks herself why. She feels she is not in control of her actions. Once again they sit at the small table, her hands clasped, his on his lap. He waits.

She blurts it out, "It's the nightmares. I see eyes and they are always accusing. I thought I buried those dreams, but they are back." She leans her head tiredly against the white wall.

"There is only one answer. You must forgive and forget, or you will live in agony all your days."

She throws her hands into the air in frustration. "How is that possible? How can I ever forget?" She jumps up, puts her cup in the sink, needing something to do.

He speaks quietly. "You place it in a compartment in the back of your mind. And you lock the door. You find solace in God. Otherwise, there is no peace in you."

"Peace? I don't want peace. And don't you dare say to me that my family would have wanted me to forget. That they would want me to be happy! I've heard it a thousand times, said by people who could never imagine hell on earth. You know better. You lived in the same hell."

Her face is close to his. "I wanted to die with them."

"But God chose you to live."

"And God chose them to die?"

"He had His reasons."

"Oh, yes, And what was His reason for me? To live in agony! There is no limit to the agony I must suffer, and it will never match what my family went through."

"Yet you knocked on my door because you could no longer stand the pain. Enough, Mrs. Slovak. Enya. You've paid your penance long enough."

She shakes her head violently from side to side.

"God would not want you to suffer like this."

She screams at him, "God wanted my babies to suffer?" She drops to her chair, but falls instead to the floor. He reaches down to help her up. She pushes his hands away. She stays there on her knees.

Abe leans down to her and recites gently, " 'When I believed He saved me. I will say of the Lord, He is my refuge and my fortress, my God, in him will I trust.' "

"No! No! No!" Enya shouts. "Leave me alone!"

He drops down on the floor in front of her. "You must forgive. You must forget. You must!" He, recites, louder, with zeal, " 'O Lord my God, I cried unto thee, and thou hast healed me.' "

"Stop it!" she shouts, and covers her ears. "I can't. I won't!"

His voice lifts higher, becomes more passionate. He grabs her shoulders and makes her sway with him. " 'O Lord, thou hast brought up my soul from the grave: thou hast kept me alive, that I should not go down to the pit . . .' "

"Stop it! Stop it!" Enya, unable to bear another moment, pulls away with all her strength and flings her arm out. She slaps his face, accidentally knocking off his glasses. For a moment, they stare into each other's eyes. Both wild with rage and astonishment.

Then Enya faints.

When she comes to, Abe is gone and the front door is wide open.

38

Tremors

"Go on out there, my pretty coward." Jack comes up behind me as I look out the window, and nuzzles me. "You can handle it."

The girls are already outside warming up for our morning exercise. I've reinstated our old routine and they are happy indeed.

"All right, already. I've got it on." I wiggle my ring finger. "But I guarantee it'll open a heap of aggravation."

Today, I intend to wear my engagement ring. It's taken me a few days to work up the courage, because I know what will happen. Instant need to make plans. Instant tumult. I shudder.

I dig my heels in, but Jack gently pushes me out the door.

Ida and Sophie perform their stretches on our landing and I join them in their warm-ups.

Across the courtyard, Evvie and Bella are doing the same. Once that's done, we head downstairs and meet for the rest of the routine of walking the paths.

As we do, we discuss our day's plans. Bella and Sophie are going to a Hadassah luncheon. Ida will teach her baking class. Evvie and I will meet up with Jack at Morrie's office and see what he can do to help solve our skeleton mystery.

I keep waiting for someone to spot the glitter of my ring. But they are looking up and looking down and looking around; Bella, of course, always keeps her eyes on her feet to make sure she doesn't trip.

I need to get this over with. "Look what I have," I say, flashing my garnet ring. I had chosen my birthstone rather than a diamond. First there is a casual glance and then it sinks in. Bella and Sophie grab my hand for closer inspection. Ida's eyebrow goes up. Evvie looks at me, sees my eyes shining, and she is happy for me.

Sophie and Bella then join hands and dance around me, jumping up and down. Next words out of their mouths will be "When's the wedding?"

"When's the wedding?" Sophie asks.

"We need to have a party" will follow as day follows night.

"Yeah," Bella says joyfully. "We need to make you a party."

"Party, party, party," sing my dancing girls.

"Congratulations," Ida says. The words must

be closing down her throat. I know she loves me and wants my happiness, but this is clearly churning up old bad memories for her. Someday I hope she'll feel free to confide in me.

Evvie comes to the little dancing circle and gleefully pulls it apart. She hugs me, with tears in her eyes.

"Okay, okay," I say, "but first walking, walking, walking."

The rest of the walk is plans, plans, and plans.

Evvie glances at me slyly. She knows how much I hate being the center of attention.

* * *

We are on our way to Morrie's, Evvie and I, where we'll meet up with Jack. I've had some of the worst dings taken off the old Chevy, so it doesn't look as awful as it did.

Evvie says from her seat next to me, "What's different?"

"When? Now?"

"Yes."

"I don't know. What?"

"When's the last time we've had time to spend time together alone? Since before the hurricane."

"Come to think of it, we haven't."

"My point, exactly. Now that we have men in our apartments and our lives. In our kitchens, in our bathrooms, in our closets—"

I stop her hyperbole. "Now, now." She would go on forever if I let her, my drama queen sister. I glance at her face. Her lips are tightly pursed.

"Well, you know what's been going on in my life. You just got the latest update this morning. I haven't a clue what you're about. With Joe."

Evvie looks out the window, not answering. Finally, she says, "University Drive is still a mess. The city looks like a war zone."

"Old news. And windows are still shuttered and stores are still closed. Yada, yada, as Seinfeld used to say on TV. You're stalling. Out with it."

She faces me. "Joe doesn't want anyone to know."

"I'm your sister. We don't keep secrets from each other."

She blurts, "He's got cancer and he's decided he wants to spend what time he has left with me!"

I almost lose control of the wheel. I turn to her in anguish. "Oh, Evvie."

Now the two of us are silent.

"I've hated him for years," Evvie says. "Now I'm not allowed to hate him because he's dying."

"What kind of time are we talking about?" I ask softly.

"Maybe six months. Prostate. And now . . . *now,* he starts to be nice to me."

"Can't you forgive and forget?"

"All those years of treating me like dirt. He and his family making me feel small and useless. Dumping me on a New Year's Eve in front of everyone—"

"Ev," I stop the litany from continuing. "I know how much pain he caused, but get a little perspective here. Think of that old saying: I complained because I had no shoes, until I met a man who had no feet."

"Yeah, yeah. I know I should count my blessings."

"Think of Enya and what she went through."

She sighs. "You're right. My new mantra: Forgive and forget."

"Just keep saying that to yourself. Turn things around. Change the negative into positive. Find what's good in him."

"Why do you always have to be so damn smart?"

"Because I am." I smirk. She grins.

We arrive at the police station. Evvie and I hug each other. I wait a few moments until she wipes the tears from her face, and we get out of the car.

* * *

We fill Morrie in, Jack, Evvie, and I, as we sit in his office. He has this habit of tapping his desk when he's impatient, and he's doing it now. I speed up my dissertation. All of it. My trip to Tampa with Stanley, meeting the sister. We track the Johnny Blake line from there to Lanai Gardens. Reminding Morrie that the forensics lab report on the skeleton proves it's not anyone already identified.

Now he pays close attention. "So you have two unsolved murders from fifty years ago. In two different counties." He looks at me.

"I know."

Morrie looks at Jack.

"She knows."

"We need you to take up the slack," I say.

"Nice of you. Thanks for giving me an ice cold case to handle."

I pinch his cheek. "No statute of limitations on murder. We already did the hard stuff, *bubbala*."

Evvie gets her dig in, too. "All you have to do is find out everything about that ship, and how and where the guy got on, and who knew about it. A piece of cake."

With that, we take our leave, with me saying "I know you'll want to get on this right away, so off we go. Ta-ta."

With those long legs of his, he gets to the door before we can. "Not so fast, Gladdy Gold. Don't think I haven't noticed. You aren't getting out of here that easily." He lifts my left hand. "Nice ring. When's the party and when's the wedding?"

Jack, Evvie, and I exchange glances. "I told you so," I say with my grin.

* * *

Denny waits at his truck in front of building Q. Sophie and Bella, all dressed up, hurry to him.

Bella says, "I hope we didn't keep you waiting."

"No problem," he says, opening the door for them. "I got all my chores done already, so I got time."

"Denny, a moment, please."

The girls turn at the sound of the voice. It's Abe Waller, hurrying toward them. He seems agitated. "I have a problem. My faucet just broke off in the kitchen and water is gushing. I'm glad I caught you before you left."

Denny is chagrined. "I'm taking Mrs. Fox and Mrs. Meyerbeer somewhere."

Abe seems upset. "But what can I do with all that water running?" He looks at Bella and Sophie. "So sorry. Didn't mean to interrupt. Where are you lovely ladies going?"

Sophie preens. "Were going to a luncheon. In Margate."

"Margate? Really?" Abe says, "I'm on my way there now myself. May I give you a lift?"

The girls and Denny are at a loss.

"Well, I don't know . . ." Sophie says.

Abe bows to her. "Please, it would be my pleasure. Then Denny will fix my faucet."

That old-country-style charm works. The girls melt.

Abe asks Denny. "Do you need my key or do you have a master?"

Denny says, unsure, "I can let myself in."

"Then it's settled. Ladies, my car is right here. Allow me to escort you."

Bella and Sophie smile at each other. They wave at Denny. "Thanks anyway, Denny," Sophie says. "We'll call when we need a ride home, if that's okay."

Denny nods. "Lots better than a ride in the truck," Bella says, seating herself in the backseat of Abe's comfortable Pontiac.

Sophie sits next to Bella. They giggle. "This is like having a chauffeur," she says happily.

As they drive off, Sophie gives Abe the street address. Abe turns on a music station for them. "Classical all right?" Abe asks.

The girls nudge each other. They are enjoying this. Bella says, "We like anything."

Abe makes conversation. "These have been very exciting weeks, have they not? I, myself, never experienced a hurricane before. Were you frightened? I know I was."

Sophie gushes, "You bet. We were scared out of our wits."

Bella adds, "I thought we were going to die."

Sophie says, "We were lucky. We got to stay with Gladdy and she kept us calm."

Abe turns slightly to them. "Your friend is a very smart woman, is she not?"

Bella says, "She sure is. She knows about everything."

Abe comments, "She even seems very well informed about the skeleton they found."

"Didn't it creep you out?" Sophie asks. "Finding out you lived with a dead guy right under you all those years?"

"Certainly gives one pause," he answers. "My dear friend Stanley told me he and Gladdy went to Tampa and found out the skeleton wasn't really that Johnny Blake person. So, I might assume the trail ends there."

Sophie beams. "Not with our bloodhound-dog leader. Even as we speak, she's at the police station with Detective Morrie Langford, Jack's son. Now they know for sure that the real Johnny Blake is buried in Tampa and she figures someone stole his papers when he was on a boat and then someone must have known the guy and he came to find him . . ."

She's out of breath, so Bella eagerly continues. "And that guy got killed, too. So the way she figures, there are two murdered men. Johnny Blake and the poor guy who became our skeleton." She grins, proud of being able to remember it all.

For a moment, there's silence. Then Abe says, "Yes, your friend is very smart."

Bella smiles with satisfaction. "That killer better watch out—our Gladdy's on his trail."

A few minutes later they arrive at the Chinese restaurant where their luncheon meeting is being held. Abe gets out and opens the doors for them. They thank him profusely.

Sophie and Bella are pleased to see he is watching them walk to the door. Probably to make sure they get safely into the restaurant. "Such a gentleman," Sophie comments.

39

Breakdown

Darkness outside. Darkness in. From where she lies on her bed, Enya dreams she is tied down. A movie appears on all four of her bedroom walls. Black-and-white. No color. Except for the blood. Shouts she knows well. "Achtung! Rause!"

The lights from the towers zigzag, splashing grays and sharp whites from one side of the room to the other. She ducks her head to keep them from finding her.

Schweinhund!

The dogs bark and bare their slobbery fangs.

"Vyhlizet!" *someone cries out to the others in their filthy shack. Look out!*

Inmates who can still move run quickly. Others barely crawl. Confusion everywhere.

The boots march relentlessly. "Achtung!" *Halt!*

The machine guns chatter. Rat-a-tat. Rat-a-tat.

Splazit se! *Hide!*

Schvat se. *Run!*

Nein! Das zaun! *The fence!* Electrfiziertes! *Electric!*

Banging

Tearing.

She needs to run. To hit!

To smash back at them.

She can't . . . She must.

She closes her eyes. She cannot bear to look into his eyes again.

She moans.

She screams.

* * *

Evvie wakens abruptly, hearing the hard knocking on her door. She struggles into her robe and hurries to answer. It's Denny, looking wild-eyed and frightened. "Something's wrong with Mrs. Slovak," he cries.

Denny's apartment is directly below Enya's. He continues breathlessly, "There's banging and screaming. I can hear it from my ceiling. It's scaring me. I don't know what to do."

"Okay," she says, "wait here." She dashes into her living room, where Joe sleeps on the couch. She shakes him awake. He is groggy. "What—"

"Come. I need you," she says. He grabs his robe and they rush outside. At Enya's door she and Joe can hears sounds of things breaking. And Enya shouting.

Evvie pokes Joe. "Go back to my place and call

Gladdy. We may need her help." As he runs, Evvie moves to Enya's door and rings the bell.

Hy and Lola, also in robes, call from their doorway at the other end of the same floor. "What's going on over there? Why is everybody up?"

Evvie says, "We don't know. Go back to sleep. We'll tell you tomorrow."

Hy is about to protest, but Lola pulls him inside. Denny, glad not to get involved, goes downstairs to his apartment again.

Evvie rings Enya's doorbell again and again.

Joe comes out of her apartment. "Gladdy's on her way."

"Joe, grab the master keys on the hall table."

Joe once again is happy to do her bidding.

* * *

It looks as if the place had been robbed and tossed by vandals. Chairs are knocked down. The pillows on the couch have been thrown every which way. Books are ripped and hurled from overturned shelves. The curtains are torn from the living room windows. From the kitchen door Jack and I see dishes smashed, cupboards open, pots and pans flung across the room.

I call, "Evvie, where are you?"

"In the bedroom. Hurry."

We rush to the bedroom, where Evvie and Joe are gently trying to stop Enya as she tears her bed apart. I am surprised—such unnatural strength from so fragile a woman.

"Enya, dear," I say firmly, "let us help you."

Between the four of us we get her to sit on the edge of her bed.

The dresser drawers have already been upended. The bedside lamp lies on the floor, spotlighting the ceiling.

She stares at us, befuddled. "He's come," she says. "I won't let him take anything from my home. I leave him nothing."

I find a blanket to wrap around her. But Enya pulls her arms out in order to grab my hands and clutch them. "I am going crazy. Help me. Madness. All I see is madness! Put me in an asylum in a straitjacket."

From the wildness in her eyes, I'm afraid she's telling the truth. She drops her arms; her eyes seem blank and far away.

Jack says, "I think we should take her to the emergency room."

"Even the smell of him," Enya cries out. "How can I remember? Such a thing as a smell? Can a smell last so long?"

"Who are you talking about?" I ask quietly.

Enya cries out to me imploringly, "He was fatter then. Fat with his importance. How he loved to see the skin cling to our bones. It gave him such an appetite."

We look from one to another, not knowing how to help her. She is shaking now. I'm at a loss to know what to do, other than let her talk.

"His face. The beard. I did not see it because of the beard."

Joe says, "Should I get some whiskey?"

Evvie nods. "We have to try something."

Joe runs out again to go to Evvie's.

Enya asks pleadingly, "Where are his boots? I was always so frightened of his boots."

I say, "Maybe we *should* get her to the hospital."

Enya's eyes seem to whip about. "How is it possible? Such a nice man. Such a religious, good man. What can I be thinking?" She stares at the wall leading to the kitchen. "It can't be. No. It's me. I am crazy."

She is sobbing by now. "It's the scar. Under his eye. It's the scar!"

Jack tries. "Enya, please," he says softly. "Tell us who you're talking about."

She walks out of the bedroom, into the living room. We follow her. She continues walking until she reaches her kitchen.

Joe returns, whiskey bottle in hand. All of us watch as Enya points to the kitchen wall. The one that connects to Abe's apartment.

She wipes the tears from her face, then whispers in an almost childish voice filled with awe, "Shhh, it's him. Don't let him hear you. *Er ist Der Oberführer. Er ist Der Bösewicht,* the evil one with the evil eye. He will be very angry."

40

What Can It Mean?

There's a knock at the door. Jack goes to answer it. It's Mary, our nurse friend who lives right above Hy and Lola. She carries what looks like a doctor's bag. She says, "Lola called me and said there was a problem. Perhaps I can be of assistance."

I'm very glad to see her.

Evvie says, "They shouldn't have wakened you."

Mary shrugs. "Comes with the territory." She glances around, taking in the mess and the near-hysterical woman on the couch, who sits there with a coat around her shoulders.

Joe says, "We were just about to take Enya to Emergency."

Enya rears back, terrified. "No, I don't want to go."

Mary examines her. Takes her pulse, her blood pressure. Listens to her heart.

"Mary."

Enya begs, "Don't let them take me away."

"It's all right, dear," she says. "Maybe you just need to sleep."

Enya nods, childlike. "I haven't been able to sleep."

"Do you have any prescription pills?"

"The doctor gave me some, but I was afraid to take them."

Mary looks to us. "See if you can find them."

Jack and I go into the bathroom and look through Enya's medicine cabinet. We bring back the few bottles we find there and hand them to Mary.

She picks one out. "This will do fine." She tells us, "Mild tranquilizers."

Evvie goes into the kitchen and brings a glass of water. Mary hands Enya a couple of the pills. "These won't hurt you. I promise. And you'll be able to sleep."

Enya takes them and pats Mary on the cheek. "You're a good girl. Thank you." She leans over as if to impart a secret. "He had this terrible scar, you know. It circled his left eye. From a knife fight, perhaps. He was very lucky not to lose the eye."

With that, she lies back and turns her face into the pillows.

"I'll stay with her," Mary says. "You all look exhausted."

Mary walks us to the door. We stand there whispering. Mary asks, "She tore the place apart herself?"

"Yes," I say.

"Hopefully it's not a psychotic episode," Mary says. "Seems like she's having some kind of breakdown. I'll get in touch with her doctor as soon as I can."

We thank her profusely as we go outside. She closes the door behind us.

The four of us stand there, utterly done in. Joe scratches at the bald spot on the back of his head. "Wow, that was bizarre. What got into that poor lady?"

Evvie sighs. "God only knows."

Jack puts his arm around me. "I don't know about the rest of you, but I can't think clearly right now."

"Let's meet in the morning with the girls and discuss this," I say needlessly. With last-minute hugs, we head for our own apartments.

As we head downstairs, I can hear Joe saying, "I don't get it. What's with the pointing at Abe's apartment?"

* * *

"Want me to make some coffee?" Evvie asks as they get inside.

"No, I wanna crash," Joe says, yawning, heading for the living room couch. "I desperately need to sleep."

"Joe," Evvie says quietly. "Sleep with me."

He looks at her for a long moment. "And then the next night back on the couch? No thanks. I feel like a yo-yo."

She goes over and pulls him along to the bedroom. "No more yo-yo. Just yo."

"Yo, toots," he says. Now he's pulling her.

* * *

Back in bed, I find it difficult to relax. I can't even begin to process what just happened. "Maybe we should have taken some of those 'tranks,' too," I say.

"Nonsense," he says. "I'm better than a pill." With that, he puts his arm around me and I cuddle into him, grateful for the comfort he offers.

* * *

By ten A.M. we're gathered in my apartment for a late breakfast. My puzzled girls can't figure out why Jack and I slept so late, until I fill them in on the night we had with Enya. They need only to look at the circles under our eyes to believe it.

We are seated around the dining room table. With seven in that small space, we are crowded together. But no one's complaining as Jack serves us all a wonderful vegetable omelet.

"Take lessons," Evvie tells Joe.

"I already memorized the recipe," he says, smiling at her.

Now it's my turn for eyebrows to go up. These are two self-satisfied après-sex type grins. Hmmm. I sure hope so.

As we dig in, Jack still standing, he says, "Let me try to sum up what we know so far about the two of them. Abe Waller moves in next door to Enya. Enya has nightmares about the camps."

Ida interrupts. "She started having nightmares before he moved in next door, even before the hurricane."

Joe says, "Premonition?"

I say, "Let's table that for a moment."

Jack continues. "They have conversations a few times."

Sophie jumps in. "It looked like a romance brewing like a teapot. Didn't it?" Sophie and Bella exchange nervous glances. I wonder what that's about. Sophie takes seconds of the eggs. Looks like nervous eating to me.

Ida says, "All it means to me is that having talked to someone who also survived the camps brought back her own horrible memories. She's never spoken about her experiences to anyone. She keeps to herself. Obviously she never got therapy. All that guilt-of-the-survivor pain building up for so many years. Now it's come to a head and she's having a nervous breakdown."

I say, "I'd agree with you, but she keeps repeating she recognized him by his eyes. Something about a scar around one eye. She called him by a name. I don't think it was a person's real name. Perhaps some kind of German title? *Der Bösewicht?*"

Jack pours refills of coffee for everyone.

Ida shakes her head. "Crazy talk. It's too much

to believe. Just by coincidence a German soldier from a concentration camp now lives next door to her? And for this sick fantasy, she picks on Abe Waller, a deeply religious Jewish man, for heaven's sakes."

There is silence for a few moments as the girls, while thinking, busily fix their coffee refills with their choice of low-fat milk and/or sugar.

Jack and I both say it in unison, "But what if—"

We stop, surprised at having similar thoughts, and he indicates I should go on. "What if it's true?" I can't believe I'm saying this. "What if he's not Jewish. What if—"

Bella drops her coffee spoon. It clatters to the floor. She looks horrified. She pokes Sophie, who pokes her back and says, "Shh."

"What!" Evvie says, annoyed. "What's with you two? You're like cats on a hot tin roof."

Always the literary one, my sister. Not that they know the reference.

Bella blurts, "That we rode in a car with..." She can't even say his name.

All eyes turn to the two now cowering women.

"Spit it out." Ida says, "Or you'll choke."

Bella is tongue-tied. Sophie is forced to talk. "You remember yesterday, we were off to Hadassah. Denny was going to drive us, but Abe did instead. No big deal."

"You got into a car with Abe Waller?" Ida says, surprised.

"And?" Evvie says, annoyed. "What's with the

two-second explanation? Why didn't Denny drive and why did Abe?"

Sophie, putting her hands on her hips, continues reluctantly. "Abe said a pipe burst in his sink and he needed Denny to fix it right away. And Abe asked where we were off to and then he said he was going to Margate, too, and gave us a lift. End of story."

I pick up the phone and dial Denny's number. Since he is our fixer-upper, I have his number memorized. Denny answers.

"Hi, Denny, it's Mrs. Gold." I listen. "Yes, I think Enya's much better. Thank you for asking. Just have a question. Did Abe Waller have a big problem with his kitchen sink yesterday? I heard it was flooding." I listen again. "Thanks a lot. Bye."

When I hang up, I say, "Denny said the washer came off. It took him a minute to put it back on, and there was never any flooding."

"Wow!" says Joe.

Bella shakes Evvie's arm. "What does that mean? What?"

Jack says, "It means that Abe might have taken the washer off himself and left the faucet running."

Sophie, arms still crossed, says, "So?"

Ida pokes her in the shoulder. "So it means he might have lied, and why do you think he might have done that?"

Sophie says, "I have no idea. You punch me again, I'm gonna punch you back."

Evvie says, "It could mean that he wanted to get Denny away from you so he could drive you to Hadassah."

Bella is practically in tears. "How were we supposed to know that?"

Ida is next. "How come it didn't make you wonder? Abe is not friendly. He never talks to anyone, except for Stanley. Have you ever seen him have anything to do with any of us?"

Sophie says nastily, "Big deal. We needed a ride. He offered."

Jack says gently, "Bella, Sophie, try to remember what you talked about in his car. You did have a conversation, didn't you?"

Bella nods eagerly. She can handle that. "He wanted to know what was happening with the skeleton and we told him Gladdy was still on the case, and he said Gladdy is real smart and we said she sure is and she's at the police station right now telling Morrie what she knows. And then when we got there, he opened the door for us like a gentleman." She stops, out of breath.

"Oh, my God," says Evvie.

"The skeleton?" Joe says, surprised. "He wanted to know about the skeleton? And if he wanted to know about the skeleton, why didn't he ask Stanley?"

"Precisely why he got the girls in his car," I say. "He's already asked Stanley about it too many times. He didn't dare arouse Stanley's suspicion."

Ida mutters under her breath, "He went to the two weakest links."

Sophie glares at her. Bella hangs her head.

We all look at one another. The skeleton. No more coincidences. In my mind I can already connect the dots.

41

The Skeleton Connection

We've gone back and forth on this subject ad nauseam and discussion is still going strong. The noise level is high. Everyone talks at once. Lots of churning emotion in the air. To move around and stretch their cramped legs, the girls remove the breakfast dishes, but that doesn't stop conversation—they use the see-through cut in the wall between kitchen and dining room. Joe moves into the living room area and stretches out on the couch, still close enough to keep up his share of opinions.

"You shouldn't have gone into his car," says Evvie. "Big mouths, both of you."

Ida adds, "And then you don't tell us about it?"

"Enough already," says Sophie, thoroughly disgusted. "You never would've cracked the case if we hadn't. So as far as we're concerned"—she puts her arm around Bella—"without us, you never would've made the skeleton connection!"

"Yeah!" echoes Bella, "we're the heroines here."

"Some heroines. You've put Enya and Glad in danger," Evvie says angrily.

Joe says, "We're close. We'll watch over Enya, won't we, sugar pie?" Evvie nods in agreement.

Ida adds, "And I'm sure Jack will take care of Gladdy."

I glance over at her, listening for her usual sarcasm, but I don't detect any. Maybe she means what she says.

Jack salutes Ida.

We're spinning out of control. I rap on the dining room table. "Enough with the bickering. Let's put our thoughts in order." Jack leans back in his chair, watching me trying, yet again, to keep the girls on track.

Evvie reaches in her purse for the notebook that's always there. "Okay, shoot. I'll get it all down."

"First," I say, "and most important—as far as everyone outside this room is concerned, Enya did not have an . . . episode. She has the flu. All that banging was a call for help. We need a cleanup crew to put her apartment back in some order. Anyone asks questions, repairs are still from the hurricane."

Ida comments, "Lucky you were the only ones to walk in and see the mess. Hey, what about Mary?"

Evvie says, "We can trust her to keep quiet." She glares at Sophie and Bella. "Unlike some others."

Joe says to her, "Don't start again."

"Okay, okay." Evvie backs off.

Ida paces. Everyone watches her do laps around the table. She says, "What did she say, his face was different?"

Evvie says, "That could have been because of the beard." She starts to do stretching exercises. And of course her shadow, Joe, leaps off the couch to follow suit.

Now Sophie moves into the living room area and jumps up and down in place. And here goes Bella, who has to copy her actions.

Evvie adds as she does neck rolls, "And she said that he was big and heavy."

Sophie says, puffing, "So he lost weight by the time he got here."

By now they are all moving in different directions. "Could we all stay in one place?" I ask. "You're making me dizzy. Do you want to take a break?"

Everyone hurries back to their seats. "No, let's keep on," Evvie says.

However, we do take a few minutes to refill coffee cups and water glasses.

"But Abe is Orthodox," Bella says.

Evvie says what I guess some of us are thinking: "What more evil way for a Nazi to hide?"

We are quiet for a few moments, imagining the horror of that.

Jack asks, "What are your thoughts on discussing this with Stanley?"

Again everyone talks at once.

"He'll have a heart attack," says Bella.

"He won't believe us," says Joe. "Not in a million years."

"He'll go right to Abe and tell him!" Ida says. "Stanley will never forgive us."

I hold my hands up. "Okay, table that. We don't say anything yet."

Jack says, "Let's review our logic. The skeleton is unearthed because of the hurricane. Stanley assumes, by where the body was found, that it had to have been buried at the time the condos were built, in 1958. A worker, a guy named Johnny Blake, went missing, so it was deduced that it must be his body. First we suspect some kind of accident. The police tell us, no accident—his head was crushed—it was murder.

"Gladdy and Stanley go to Tampa and find out Johnny Blake died six months earlier than that fateful night, right off the dock near where he lived and his body was found, and buried at a nearby church. His sister, Lucy, says she believes foul play.

"The forensics lab reports what they discover from the bones. Their findings show that it couldn't have been Johnny Blake of Tampa, nor could it be the man posing as Johnny Blake here. However, because of Lucy's P.O. box number, we know for sure there is a definite connection. So now let's call this unknown man X."

I add, "Lucy also tells us the ship her brother was on came from Argentina."

Sophie jumps in. "I read that that's where the Nazis went to hide from being caught as war criminals."

Jack continues. "Maybe X realizes somebody's stalking him in Argentina. So he stows away on the ship and picks Johnny as the one to kill to get a new identity. He throws him overboard and easily makes it off the ship with Johnny's ID. He wanders around and arrives at Fort Lauderdale, gets a job working on building these condos." Jack stops to take a drink from his glass of water.

I continue for him. "But maybe this stalker catches up to him. It could be someone from the camps who wanted revenge for killing his family. A Jewish man named Abe Waller."

Bella gasps. Hearing his name in this manner is chilling.

Evvie can't wait. "X probably murdered the entire Waller family so nobody ever comes looking for the real Abe Waller."

Jack continues. "We can imagine that in the middle of a terrible storm the two men fight to the finish. X is the stronger and he kills Abe Waller. So X has killed two men to keep himself safe."

Ida says fervently, "All right. But why didn't X keep using Johnny Blake's ID?"

Jack says, "My guess is, he kept track of Tampa news and found out about Johnny's body turning up. Here was a golden opportunity. He can't remain Johnny Blake, so now he becomes Abe

Waller. When he leaves Johnny's stuff behind, it probably must be because he couldn't get back into his locker and he figures those old clothes would get thrown out."

Joe says, "Which Stanley, the pack rat, never disposed of. Safe for fifty years until you, Gladdy." He tips an imaginary hat to me.

Ida says, "But why would he do something so crazy and then move in and live where he buried the body? It doesn't make any sense."

I say, "We can only speculate. He comes back a year later, thinner and with a beard and mustache. No one would recognize him as the guy who worked on the construction site. Maybe he decided to hang about awhile to make sure the body wasn't found. Then he just stayed on. It's amazing how utterly realistic he's been playing the part. I mean, why take on such a difficult role? Fifty years of going to temple consistently with Stanley. Not just being Jewish, but Orthodox, the most rigorous and devout form of Judaism. Why didn't he leave when he was sure he was safe?"

Jack says, "Maybe he thought this was the ultimate disguise. No one would ever again recognize him. And he was right."

It gets very quiet and I say, "Time for a reality check. What if we're totally wrong and our imagination made up this entire scenario? What if Enya's behavior *was* irrational and we're reading Abe's actions incorrectly? Maybe Enya, cracking up, is delusional and for some sick, sad reason, she's picked on Abe. And what if Abe's innocent?

This man has lived an impeccable, faith-filled, decent life. What if our carefully built-up assumptions are just that, assumptions—and we are about to destroy a man's life?"

"One thing's for sure," Jack says, "without knowing his real name, we have nothing to go on. We have no proof. It's all conjecture. But I have an idea . . ."

"Well?" says Evvie, never known for her patience. "Tell us. What?"

Jack looks at me and smiles. "We need to buy time. Glad, you're not going to like this, but we have to get people's minds off hurricanes and Enya and skeletons. Something to make Abe—if guilty—think he's safe. Only way to do that is give everyone something else to get excited about. An event that will make them happy. Now we spread the word about our engagement and upcoming wedding. And have a party to celebrate. That will give us time to come up with a plan."

That startles me. I had no intention of having any kind of party, that's not my style. I'm not thrilled with the idea, but Jack makes sense. I dread having to give the pool gang that ammunition. There goes romance. Good-bye, privacy.

* * *

Ida bursts into the laundry room on our floor, in a robe and with her bun unpinned, letting her salt-and-pepper hair fly. "What's with the call to come over here right away? I was just about to take a bath."

Now that our final partner is here, we turn to Evvie, who called this meeting for eight-thirty this evening. As if we hadn't had enough discussion today. She's busily filling a second washer with a load of clothes. "Thought I'd kill two birds with one stone," she tells us.

Ida says, "It couldn't keep 'til morning?"

With four of us girls already crowded in this small space, there's hardly room to move an arm or leg. We all push backward to make room for Ida.

"I had something on my mind," Evvie says, "and I wanted it settled tonight."

I come to my sister's aid: "Ev suggested that we cast our votes for whether we believe Enya is right about her fears. Or whether we don't believe Abe is really a wolf in sheep's clothing, so to speak."

Ida shakes her head. "But why here, now?"

Evvie shrugs. "I didn't want to hurt Joe's feelings by telling him he didn't have the right to vote." She pushes her garments around in the tub so they fit in evenly.

Ida tries to put her hands on her hips. There's no room, so she drops her arms.

Bella and Sophie watch the two of them bicker. Sophie gets bored and she examines her face in the small utility mirror, looking for new wrinkles. Bella plays with the coin lever, pulling it in and out.

"All right already, vote. My bathwater's getting cold. And what's with you and Joe anyway? Since when do you worry about his feelings?"

"Don't ask," Evvie says, looking toward me, who understands.

Sophie says, "My hand is ready to lift up, so let's go."

"Ditto," says Bella, "not that I'm in a hurry to go back to Dora. She's watching the reruns of the shows she watched this morning. I have such a headache from all the TV fighting and kissing and slamming doors."

They all turn to me as usual, their reluctant leader, so I proceed. I guess it's a good idea to see where we stand. "We heard a lot of stuff today and there was plenty to digest. If you're not sure yet, say so. Okay, who believes Enya is right about Abe being the Nazi she knew in the camps?"

Sophie's hand shoots up first. "I believe."

Bella is next. "I believe."

I say, "I believe."

Ida hesitates, and then her hand goes up, too.

Evvie laughs as she raises her hand as well. "I believe, and now all we need is for Tinker Bell to show up."

We all smile at that. A buzzer sounds to tell her the first load is dry.

"We done now?" Ida asks.

Evvie lugs out her dry clothes. "Done."

The secret society meeting is over and it's time to head for our homes. Except for me. Evvie beckons me to stay. She says, "We should go over and tell Enya. She must be on pins and needles. First I gotta finish my laundry."

* * *

It's past ten o'clock by the time Evvie's laundry is done. Lights are out everywhere. Evvie and I tiptoe along the second-floor landing where Evvie and Enya live. I take a quick look at Abe's kitchen window. No light there. Evvie leaves her filled laundry basket in front of her apartment.

Enya's been told we're coming, so she is waiting right at the door.

We slip into her apartment quickly. Enya looks a little better now that Mary is taking care of her.

"I'm so ashamed," she says. "About the way I behaved."

"Nonsense," says Evvie. "You had good reason."

Enya leads us to the living room. Evvie and I sit down on her old horsehair sofa. "Do you want anything?"

"No, thank you," we say.

Enya sits down at the edge of her chair and looks at us like she's a prisoner at the dock, waiting to hear the verdict.

I say, "Enya, we believe you. But we have a very big problem. Without knowing his real name, our hands are tied. We have to have proof."

Enya shakes her head. "If only I could remember. There were so many of them. We never knew their names. But this one, *Der Bösewicht*—we gave him that nickname because he frightened us more than any of the others—he was truly evil."

Evvie adds, "We aren't giving up. We'll find a way to prove you're right."

Enya's tears start to flow. The tension this woman has to be under must be unbearable. She comes over to us and grabs one of my hands and one of Evvie's. "Thank you. Thank you."

Still clutching our hands, Enya is lost in her troubled thoughts for a few moments. "The things they did, he did. I cannot bear to speak of them. I will not put you through having to listen to these abominations." She pauses, wipes the tears from her eyes. "That he has lived freely among us for nearly fifty years horrifies me. That he lived as a Jewish man is unbearable."

She stares into space. How she survived what she went through is almost unimaginable to me. I say, "I know you're exhausted. Try to rest. We'll keep bringing food to you. Stay put. Do not go out, and be very careful before you answer the door."

"I am so frightened. Does he know I recognized him?"

She walks with us to the door. "Bless you for caring."

We hug and kiss her and tiptoe out.

42

Party, Party, Party

Good news travels faster than the speed of light. At least that's the way it seems in Lanai Gardens, Phase Two. This beautiful morning at the pool is the perfect place to hand out invitations to the Gladdy-Jack engagement party, which we had made up a few days ago. Bella and Sophie are assigned one end of the pool to dole them out, as far from Abe as possible. Evvie and Ida take the section that includes Abe, seated as usual behind the little black metal gate in the shade. Watching us, I now realize, always watching us.

My job is to wander about, showing off my ring, wearing a silly grin.

Sophie and Bella have on large, floppy sun hats, and huge wraparound very dark sunglasses, terrified of letting their faces show their fear. Any more mistakes in what they do or say could be dangerous. They're in trouble, as it is, for spilling the beans to Abe. They especially won't look in our alleged Nazi's direction, afraid he can read them like a book.

From what I can see of his eyes, behind the thick glasses, they seem hooded. You don't fool me, *Oberführer.* I know you're watching us like a hawk. But you've met your match in Evvie Markowitz, who is heading over right now to hand you your invitation. I leisurely stroll by to catch the action.

He will try to stare Evvie down, but she, who believes she might have been an Oscar-winning actress had life not tossed her into marrying Joe, won't blink. "This is for you, Abe," says Evvie, playing an older Little Miss Sunshine. "And don't you try to wiggle out of coming." That's said with a waggling hand demonstrating the wiggle. "Stanley and Esther already RSVP'd because they know we're doing it right. Steinberg's kosher restaurant is catering."

Stanley was happy about my news and told me how he and Abe sometimes after temple go out for lunch at Steinberg's, their favorite eating place. Perfect.

Abe manages what I read as a slick smile. "I wouldn't think of missing it."

Tessie arrives at the gate, carrying a now empty soup tureen. I knew she would be passing by, since it was I who planted this idea in her head, to bring the poor "flu" victim some chicken soup.

"How's Enya doing?" I say, not looking at Abe.

I have to keep calling him Abe and thinking of him as Abe or I'll lose my cool.

"A little better," Tessie reports. "Poor thing. I can't believe how high her fever went the other night. Lucky she didn't die."

Well done, Tessie. I couldn't have scripted it better myself. But, of course, we've been spreading that "dangerous case of flu" story with "Enya becoming delirious" for days. Since Tessie knows nothing, she reveals nothing.

Hy, after immediately responding yes to the party, announces, "For this great occasion, a toast." He lifts his Dr. Brown's Cel-Ray tonic bottle and points toward Jack and me, the engaged couple. Jack, from where he lounges, reading a Michael Connolly detective novel, nods. I perform a silly curtsy.

I look around to see the response. Mary and Irving smile happily. Barbi and Casey grin slyly. Tessie sits down next to her hubby and shouts, "Hooray!" Sol shakes his head sadly. I guess marriage isn't agreeing with him. Aha, Louise is sitting there with her mouth wide open in shock. Close your mouth, lady. As my mom used to say, You don't want to let the flies in. Tiny Dora is jumping up and down. I can't believe it, is that a TV clicker in her hand?

Directly across the way, in Denny's garden, he and Yolie stop their planting and pay attention to what's going on. They are thrilled at what they hear.

Tessie takes another look at her invitation. "Wait a minute. This Friday. So fast?"

Hy, annoyed at being interrupted, says, "At our age, who makes long-term plans?"

Tessie, suitably chastened, shuts up.

Hy instructs, "Those who have bottles to raise, get 'em up." Water bottles and juices wave on high. Those without beverages just wave.

"To the engaged couple..." He indicates we should come to him. In order to make this plan of ours look like all is back to normal, we agreed earlier to put up with whatever nonsense comes up. Naturally, it would be Hy who finds a way to torment us. Jack rises from his chaise, and he and I walk over to where Hy is now standing. Jack kisses me and whispers, "Any excuse, babe."

Hy hands Lola his drink and puts one arm across my shoulders and one across Jack's. I grit my teeth.

Hy stares into my eyes and speaks loud enough for all to hear—and believe me, everyone is zoomed onto us and listening. "Here's to the love that lies in a woman's eyes—and lies and lies and lies."

I try to pull away, but he doesn't let me. Everybody laughs. He leers at Jack, whose turn it is. Watch out, Hy, Jack's no pushover.

Hy's eyes practically twinkle. Lola stands behind him, ready to save him from Jack if necessary. He says, "Here's to the happiest days of your life, spent in the arms of another man's wife!"

Hy pulls his hands away, fast. Jack shakes his fist mildly in a pretense of anger.

Hy pulls Lola in front of him for protection. Jack wouldn't hit a woman, would he? "It's your *mother.* In your *mother's* arms," Hy croaks. Then weakly, "She's another man's wife, right?"

Jack, who towers above little Hy, reaches past Lola and runs his hands playfully over Hy's balding head. "Good one," Jack says, laughing.

I'm glad that's finished.

* * *

On our way back from the pool, Evvie, as instructed, knocks on Enya's door. Enya peers through the peephole, then barely opens it.

"Are you all right?" Evvie asks.

Enya nods. "Yes."

"Need anything?" I ask.

"No, I'm fine. Tessie's soup will hold me."

"Just checking. Things are moving along."

"Thank you," she says.

They gaze at each other, lips smiling, but their eyes reveal their fear.

"He was there, wasn't he?" Enya asks.

"He always is," Evvie says. "Listening to every word we say, watching every move we make."

"Be careful. He is the Devil."

"We will."

43

The Plan

Are you crazy?" Sophie asks. "Tomorrow?"

"He'll kill you if he catches you," Bella speaks up, shaking with fear.

"Yes tomorrow," says Joe, who seems to have slid into place as the newest addition to our investigating group, and nobody seems to mind. Neither is Evvie complaining about the fact that Joe sticks to her like flypaper. Hmm, whatever happened to that gooey, disgusting product? I wonder for no good reason whatsoever.

Evvie also agrees. "Yes, let's move it up."

Ida says, "I can't wait. I wish we could do it now. The tension is killing me."

We sit in a secluded area near Denny's beautiful garden. No one is around usually at mid-afternoon. It's rest time or preparing-dinner time or off to early-bird-dinner time. Quiet enough for what we're scheming. We even have knitting and crocheting stuff in our laps in case anyone does come by and is curious.

Evvie says, "Tomorrow, being just before the Sabbath, we know for sure Abe will be at the synagogue most of the day."

"But why would you want to do it on the day of your party? It'll be a zoo." Bella doesn't like any of this. Short notice always makes her nervous.

"That's what I'm counting on," I answer. "People will be too busy to see what we're up to. Besides, I'll be a wreck waiting for the party—I already have my outfit picked out, so at least this will keep me busy."

Joe has a worry. "What if he doesn't go to temple?"

"He always goes on Friday," says Evvie.

Joe can't let it go. "But what if..."

Evvie puts her fingers on his lips. "Shhh, worrywart."

"We can always get him out on a pretense," says Ida.

"Like what?" Sophie asks.

"We can tell him there's a meeting of the Bund," Ida says wickedly.

Evvie, Joe, and I grimace. We're all old enough to remember there was once an actual club of members of the Nazi party right here in our country.

"Kidding," says Ida. "We'll think of something. But there's no reason for him to change his routine."

Bella raises her hand. "But . . . but I have to go to the beauty parlor."

Evvie says, "Bella, honey, you and Sophie always have early-morning Friday appointments. You'll have plenty of time to help us."

I cut in. "Let me say a few words here. I doubt that Abe has been fooled by our charade and I have a very strong feeling that he is up to something. I can't even imagine what he might be planning. Frankly, I'm afraid to guess. I feel we need to move fast and catch him off guard."

"Besides," Ida says, "we can't keep Enya locked up forever. We have to find a way to end this."

"Okay," says Evvie, "let's go over it again. Naturally, as president of the Condo Association, I have, like Denny, a master key of all apartments. We make sure no one's looking, and we sneak in."

I wait for Bella and Sophie to stop squirming, and I say, "Bella and Sophie are on watch, sitting in the back of my car with a cell phone."

Bella raises her hand. "I still don't get that."

Sophie pokes her. "I do. It's right across from Abe's parking spot, so we'll know exactly when he drives in. And he won't see us."

Bella nods slowly, digesting the information again.

I say, "Ida, Evvie, and I do the search. Joe waits with Enya in her Florida room, next door, in case we have to make an emergency exit. If so, we climb from Abe's apartment into Enya's, with Joe's help."

Luckily for us, the hurricane blew out all

our sunroom screens and none of us have fixed them yet.

"What do we tell Enya?" Bella asks.

I say, "We tell her exactly what we're doing."

Sophie asks, "What if you don't find anything?"

"Honestly, I don't know," I say. "We just have to hope we do."

Joe says, "I have a question for you, Glad. What will you tell Jack?"

Before I can answer, a familiar voice is heard behind me. "Tell Jack what?" my beloved asks as he walks up to us. "I've been searching all over for you. What's this, some kind of class?"

Everyone freezes on the spot. I thought I'd be alone when I dealt with Jack on this subject, but no such luck. I take a deep breath. "We've been discussing a plan on how to prove Abe's guilt."

Silence as Jack looks from one anxious face to another.

"Speaking of guilt," he says. "May I make a guess?"

Sophie and Bella nod frantically. They squirm around in their chairs, wishing, I assume, that they were anywhere but here.

"What I read in your faces is that you've already decided on a plan."

More nods from those two. Everyone else remains rigid.

"And since I wasn't included in this get-together . . ." He pauses to address Joe. "Knitter or crocheter?"

Joe shrugs, flashing a silly grin along with it. "Family kibitzer," he explains.

Jack continues, "Perhaps this plan has something not quite kosher about it?"

Sophie and Bella nod again, their heads bobbing up and down like apples in a barrel.

Ida can't stand it anymore. She shrieks at the two of them, "Stop nodding!"

Both heads bow down.

I try to salvage the situation. "Jack, honey, shall we continue this upstairs? Alone?"

"Not really," he says. "Just go on with your meeting." He kisses me on my cheek. "Shall I start dinner, my love?"

"Whatever," I say meekly. Ooh, oh, I'm in hot water now.

* * *

I smell something wonderful cooking as I open the door and stand in the doorway of the kitchen. Jack is busy chopping vegetables.

"Lemon curried chicken?" I ask, in a most docile manner.

"Might be the last meal I cook for you if certain things don't change around here," he says without turning around.

This startles me. He says the words softly, but there's steel behind them. I feel my heart begin to pound. "May the condemned woman say a few words on her own behalf?"

Jack moves over and stirs something in a pot. "Might I suggest some words—like 'We changed our minds and are not going through with this dangerous plan'?"

"Jack, honey—"

"Or 'I hereby promise to discuss my plans with my future husband before, not after, deciding to break the law.' You do intend to enter Abe's apartment without his permission?"

I pause. I cannot tell a lie. "Yes. But Evvie, as condo president, has the right to enter an apartment if she thinks it's necessary."

"If I recall, for it to be legal, the tenant must be given twenty-four hours' notice, and a reason."

I shrug. I know he's right. No way we can do that.

He turns and holds me by the shoulders. "It's one thing to go after an elderly guy robbing banks, which, by the way, was handled recklessly. You should have called for backup."

"But it wasn't clear what Ida was doing. It seemed odd that she was taking us to what seemed like a psychic. And besides, Grandpa wasn't dangerous."

"You couldn't have known that for sure, going to where he lived. He used a gun in those robberies."

I interrupt with desperation, "We didn't know if it was a real one."

"My point exactly. You didn't have enough information. You behaved hastily. And now, in this situation, you're rushing in again, without considering the terrible danger of going into this man's home. If you're right about Abe Waller, and clearly you believe you are, the man you're taking on is a mass murderer. A man trained to kill. And after leaving the camps, he murdered two other men, ostensibly simply to cover his tracks. Don't you think you're a little out of your league?"

"But you said it yourself: We have no name. There's no evidence."

"Let Morrie handle it. That's his job."

"There's no way to arrest Abe. Asking Morrie for help is useless. We don't have enough for him to get a search warrant. This Nazi has outsmarted everyone for fifty years."

Jack drops his hands and looks deep into my eyes and I see such worry in his. "And you believe *you* can outsmart him?"

I don't know what to say. I don't know how to plead my case. He is absolutely right, of course. Am I guilty of arrogance? I feel like I'm walking on quicksand. "Is what we're having called a serious quarrel?"

"You could say that."

I blurt, "Big enough for you to break off our engagement if I don't do what you want?"

He is almost surprised at my outburst. "Careful, dear, you're dealing in absolutes now. Do you want me to lay down an ultimatum?"

I sit down on the kitchen chair and hold my breath. Will what he says next determine the course of the rest of my life? I'm amazed at how scared I am. The silence is so long, I can hear my teeth clench.

He sits down next to me. "I have one last

question." He reaches over and takes my hands in his. "Answer carefully."

I gulp. "Shoot," I say with false courage.

"If I were not in your life, if we'd never met and it was just you and your girls living the way you used to, would you be going through with those plans tomorrow?"

I hesitate and think long and hard. I look him right in those gorgeous eyes. I know I'm getting too emotional, and I could possibly lose this man I love, but I have to make him understand how strongly I feel. "Damned straight I would. As the Jewish people of the world said after the war, 'Never again!' "

Jack doles out our dinner and brings our plates into the dining room, where he has already set the table. I think about what I might lose. I shudder. I ask, and I'm terrified of his answer, "What are you going to do?"

He sits down and says, "You do what you do and I'll do what I do."

With that, he digs in.

Dinner is very quiet; bedtime, even more so.

44

A Date to Remember

I didn't sleep much last night, but when I finally did and woke up after eight, Jack was gone. I'm sure he didn't sleep too well, either. Nor, I imagine, did the girls. What have I gotten us all into? How can I put my sister and my dear friends at such risk? Should I call it off? I can't be angry at Jack. Everything he said was right. But what's my alternative? Tell Morrie to take it over and hope that someday, someway, he'll find out the truth? Doubtful. Besides, will anything we discover be admissible in court? But there is a higher court out there. And the groups, started by Simon Wiesenthal, to this day track down Nazis as war criminals. They won't give up until the last one is dead or caught. But I'll come across as an idiot when I turn in a religious Jewish man in his eighties who has done good deeds all his life, and has papers that prove he is Abe Waller. I'm sure the numbers he tattooed on his arm nearly half a century ago belong to the real Abe Waller. I'm betting he hasn't made a single mistake.

Will Enya dare to come out of her apartment until Abe finally goes back to Phase Six when it's rebuilt? But that could be six months or more. And even then? The voice in my head says this man will not sit still. We haven't fooled him. He is planning something. We must find a clue. I've opened a Pandora's box and I've got to close it somehow. The truth is, I'm terrified. And I'm so tired, I can barely move my aching body.

* * *

We meet, as planned, in Enya's apartment, right next door to his. Everyone looks tired and drawn. Joe, imitating Jack, made us breakfast. It was only cereal and toast, and very kind of him, but no one eats a bite. We drink coffee, too much. Enya has gone to her bedroom to lie down. Needless to say, she is very stressed out.

Ida says, "Jack was sore, wasn't he?"

I nod. "He thinks what we are doing is foolhardy and very dangerous. I have to ask this before we go any further—do you want out? I'm sure it must be on everyone's mind."

The girls, one by one, shake their heads slowly.

Bella shivers. "But what if we fail you?"

"You won't," I say. "You can't miss watching his parking spot."

"What if the cell phone doesn't work?" Sophie asks.

"I've thought of that," I say. "I've brought another one for you. They're both charged and ready. Just make sure you aren't noticed."

"What if someone sees us anyway?" Sophie asks.

Ida answers, "Then make up something, like you're waiting for us and we're late."

Sophie comments, "Yeah, right. Only an idiot sits in the backseat of a hot car doing nothing for an hour."

Ida says, "I rest my case."

For a moment Sophie is angry, then Ida shrugs and grins. "I'm pulling your leg."

We all smile and it relaxes us for maybe a second.

Joe speaks to Sophie and Bella. "I'm volunteering to be your backup. I'm going to be watching from up here, from the living room window. Then, if anything goes wrong, I'll know, too."

Bella sighs, relieved.

"Besides," Evvie says, "hopefully we'll be through in less than an hour."

"Last instructions," I say to Evvie and Ida. "I'm repeating myself, but I can't say it enough: No matter what happens, every single thing you touch must be left exactly as you found it. One tiny mistake and he'll know we've been in there."

They both nod vigorously.

"We better get started. He's already gone two

hours; it looks good to go." In my head I'm wondering where Jack is. But don't go there, I tell myself, I've got to keep my head very clear.

Everyone hugs and kisses. Even Joe. Enya comes out of her room to watch us leave. She seems as frail as an eggshell.

As planned, Evvie goes first, glances around, then quickly uses her master key and slides into Abe's apartment. Ida's next, she looks, too, then I follow.

* * *

"My heart's hammering like crazy," Evvie whispers as we look around Abe Waller's meticulous apartment. The Canadian family, the Dumas, who owns the condo, only uses it as a vacation home, so thankfully there is very little furniture, other than the basics, to deal with.

I blab, also whispering, "Don't miss ice trays, hollow legs of chairs, in bottoms of socks, coffee cans, inside lamps—underneath drawers, for taped stuff. Probably never under mattresses. Too obvious."

I feel a calm coming over me. Now that we're here and committed, I breathe easier. We can handle this. We'll be all right.

We walk slowly from room to room as a first survey. Evvie manages a nervous smile. "You get that stuff from all those mysteries you read."

"You bet," I say.

Ida heads for the kitchen. Evvie, the bathroom, to be followed by the bedroom. I take the living room and then the Florida room. We work slowly and methodically.

I hear Evvie say, "This is so spooky."

For a long while that's the last thing said, as we intensely examine everything. Every drawer, every cupboard. All the places I thought might be hiding places. But nothing speaks of Abe. There were only the possessions left by the Dumas. Surely he must have personal things somewhere. Not even a toothbrush, reports Evvie from the bathroom. How is this possible?

We take a very short break after half an hour to stand in the kitchen for a drink of water. Then, carefully, we wash and dry our glasses and put them exactly where they were.

"Weird," says Ida, "it's as if no one lives here. There doesn't seem to be anything of his own. Not even a piece of mail to be found."

I say, "Well, don't forget, he lost his things in the hurricane."

"Yes, but they were all allowed to go back to Phase Six and get whatever stuff wasn't ruined," Evvie reminds me. "I'm sure he found some things."

"Even if he didn't, it still seems strange. Not a book or magazine? Not a careless shirt, or whatever, tossed over the back of a chair?" Ida says.

"And nothing in the bathroom medicine cabinet? Not even a bottle of aspirin? No dirty clothes in the hamper?" Evvie is incredulous.

"Okay, back to work," I say.

Evvie tries for a joke. "I can't wait to see what his underwear looks like."

We disperse to our areas of search.

A few minutes later Evvie utters a small scream and comes running out. Her eyes glitter. "Get in here, now!"

She runs back to the bedroom with the two of us racing after her. She indicates the open closet door. In the corner is a large suitcase.

"At first I thought it was just parked there, but when I started to move it, it was heavy."

Pull it out," Ida says excitedly. "Maybe that's where he hides his stuff."

"Carefully," I say, "watch exactly how it was placed in the closet."

Evvie tries to lift it. She can't. I help her pull it out. "Fingers crossed," I say as I reach for the snaps to open it.

I try a few times, but it's locked. "Bad luck. I bet he has the key with him."

We are let down.

I feel for an outside pocket. "Wait, there's something..." I pull out a long, narrow, black leather folder and open it.

"Oh, my God," Evvie says, over my shoulder. "Airline tickets. To where? When?"

"Buenos Aires," I read. "Tonight. Late."

"We knew it! We knew he was up to something. He's gonna make a run for it." Evvie jumps up and down in excitement. "No wonder we couldn't find anything personal. Everything he owns must be in here!"

Ida leans over me, squinting without her glasses. "What's his name?" she demands of me.

Disappointed, I tell her, "It says Abe Waller on tickets and passport."

"Damn," says Evvie. "And we dare not break the lock open."

I dig deeper into the fold. Something is lodged down there. I pull it out. It's a small patch of cloth wrapped around a signet ring. Evvie grabs the patch; Ida, the ring.

"There's a large cross on here," Evvie says.

"And one on the ring."

"I've seen this before," Evvie says, "in movies."

"It's called the Iron Cross," I say in wonder. "I read about it a long time ago. I think it's the highest award German soldiers ever get."

We look at one another, happily astonished, big smiles on our faces.

I look on the back of the Iron Cross patch. "We've got him!" I say. "There's a number. I bet somewhere there's a match with his real name. We've got to copy down the number."

Evvie grins happily, grabbing the patch from me so she can examine it more thoroughly.

My cell phone rings. Evvie actually jumps. The three of us stare at the instrument with foreboding. He can't be back! He mustn't! I answer. Sophie and Bella are screaming into our ears. "He just drove in! He's back! Get out! Get out!"

At the same time we can hear Joe shouting Evvie's name from Enya's rear sunporch.

* * *

I feel like I'm moving in slow motion as I shove the black folder back into the side pocket.

Ida is quietly hysterical. "I don't remember which way the suitcase went in!"

Evvie, breathless, pushes it in the corner.

"The zipper part was in back!" I say, terrified now. "Wasn't it?" Evvie's not sure, but we're out of time and we leave it.

We close the closet and run from the bedroom to the Florida room. Please, God, don't fail us now.

What a crazy idea, I think, looking at our escape route. What could I possibly have been thinking! We have to climb through the windows where screens used to be and jump two feet over air to get next door.

Trying to hide his fear, Joe thrusts his arms out Enya's window as far as he can reach, and grabs Evvie by her forearms as she balances herself on the window ledge. She looks down at the empty area between both screened porches.

"Don't look down," Joe says, too late. "When I say three, jump toward me!"

Evvie looks at us, eyes wild, then to Joe.

Ida and I hold our breath as Evvie jumps. Joe pulls her through Enya's side window, but for a moment, it looks like Evvie is flying.

All I can think is, I'm looking at a seventy-five-year-old man's flabby arms, unused to exercise, along with his arthritic hands. Will he have the strength to pull all three of us?

Ida gives me a panicky look, and then focuses on Joe. She bends her knees, waits until Joe has her arms in his grasp. She leaps out and up toward him. She's so fast, the two of them fall backwards into the room.

Now it's my turn, and Joe's arms are shaking from the strain. I call to him, "Joe, get Ev and Ida behind you, and have them both hold on to your waist. Hurry."

He doesn't stop to question me; he understands how weak he is now. He turns inside to tell the girls.

My eyes dart toward the front of Abe's apartment, expecting any second for him to come in and find me there with no place to hide.

Joe turns back to me. "They're ready."

I step out on the ledge. I look down in spite of myself. If I fall I'll probably break my neck dropping two stories, or at least my legs.

I reach my arms out. Joe grabs on to them, gripping me as tightly as he can. He looks at me and I can see the fear there. He counts to three.

I jump.

And miss Enya's window ledge. Suddenly I'm hanging straight down, with nothing but air under me. I feel Joe's arms sliding down my arms, to my hands. I clutch his hands tightly.

"Pull!" Joe screams to Evvie and Ida behind him. "Pull me inside!"

Within seconds I am jerked up the side of the building and into the room, just as Joe loses his grip.

All four of us fall to the floor, one on top of the other, panting breathlessly.

My stomach and legs are scratched and bloody from bouncing off the building. But at least I'm in one piece.

Evvie throws her arms around Joe, laughing and crying at the same time. "My hero," she says, hugging him tightly.

I see Enya standing in the doorway, holding her breath.

"I'm all right," I tell her to allay her fears.

"The bastard came back early," Ida mutters. "Why?"

Joe tries to calm us as well as himself. "But it's okay, you got out safely. And you left everything the way it was. Right?"

"I think so," Ida says unsteadily.

Evvie stares down at her hands. "Oh, no," she cries out. We look at her, still clutching the small patch of cloth in her left hand. The small patch with its distinctive Iron Cross.

45

Engaged

Hearing a commotion coming from downstairs, we hurry to the living room window and stare out and down. A group of people are gathered and chattering directly under us.

Ida says, "They're circling around Abe's car."

"Something's blocking our view. I can't see what it is," says Evvie.

Ida points. "Look over there. It's Abe. And he's talking to Jack!"

Abe is still downstairs? With Jack? What's going on?

Evvie rushes to the front door. "I can't stand it. I've got to see what's happening." She opens the door and rushes out onto the landing.

Ida and I are right behind her. Not only can we see, over the balcony, but we can easily hear. I feel Joe and Enya peeking over my shoulder. I can see

Sophie and Bella standing near my car, watching anxiously.

Jack, my ex-cop, seems to be in charge. I hear him say to Abe, "I can't imagine how it happened." He looks around. "Anybody see how this big thing got here?"

What a sight before our eyes. A huge garbage Dumpster that, according to the letter on its side, belongs to R building has somehow managed to roll forward and smash the front of Abe's Pontiac, denting the hood severely.

Abe is angry, but he's trying to hide it. "How is it possible? That Dumpster is always at the side of the building. How could it get from there to here?"

Lots of surprised shrugs. Apparently, none of the gawkers had seen anything, since no one ventures forth with information.

Evvie whispers to me, "Jack must have done it. He stopped Abe from coming upstairs."

"Yes," I say, choked up. He might not have approved of what I was doing, but he wasn't about to let anything happen to me, either. But I shudder to think what would have happened if Jack hadn't been watching our backs. We've just had a very close call.

"I'm a witness," says a familiar voice behind me. I hadn't even heard Hy approach us from his apartment down the walkway.

We turn. "What?" I say, nervously.

Hy speaks very softly. "Your boyfriend is the culprit. I saw him roll the Dumpster over earlier, and as soon as Abe drove in Jack leaned down behind the Dumpster and pushed it hard. Anybody want to tell me what's going on?"

Oh, no, I think to myself. Not Hy, the town crier!

A chorus of six (which includes Joe) says in unison, "No!"

Hy performs a zipping motion across his lips. "No problem. Your secret is safe with me. If Jack is into car demolition, he must have a very good reason. Let me in on it when you're ready."

He pauses, and grins. "Here's a joke for you. Husband comes home. His wife's wearing a sexy negligee and is all tied up with ropes. She says, seductively, 'You can do anything you want to do.' So he walks back out and goes to play golf." He laughs at his own joke. "I got dozens more. Saving 'em for tonight's engagement party!" With that he struts back toward his open door, where Lola stands watching.

Ida says, "I can hardly wait."

We hear Jack saying in a loud voice, "Just call your insurance company, Abe. Bye, see you later." He's warning us. Abe is climbing up the stairs. We scurry back inside, fast!

Once inside, Joe asks, "What do we do now?"

"Talk to your Jack," Enya says. "He'll know."

* * *

I lie on my couch with a cold compress on my eyes and forehead. I have a bad headache that makes me see stars; it hurts that much. My left eye keeps twitching and it won't stop. Jack brings me another wet towel to exchange for the one I have.

"Feel any better?" he asks.

"No," I groan.

"Maybe if we talk about it, your pain will go away."

"Ouch," I mutter. "I doubt it."

"You can't go to your party like this, so let's try. I'll start first. I want to tell you how *I* feel. Waiting helplessly downstairs while I knew you were in Abe's apartment reminded me of Faye. I finally truly understand—I mean, I thought I understood, but I didn't, viscerally—what Faye felt all those years being married to a cop. She told me she would worry every day, with panic rising—would I come home, still in one piece, or would it be one of my pals from the precinct at the door, to tell her how I died."

I lift the compress and turn my throbbing head to see him better.

"Today, I was Faye. Waiting to see if you came out alive. I couldn't stand it. In all my years as a cop, I was never as afraid as I was this morning."

I weakly reach over to take his hand in mine. "I'm sorry I put you through that. But I felt I had to do it. And we succeeded. We have proof. Finally." I look at him, pleadingly. "Doesn't the end justify the means?"

"Glad, that's not the point. It could have ended very badly, and—"

I interrupt. "But didn't you push the Dumpster into his car? And bought us time to escape? Wouldn't you say you broke the law a bit, too? Didn't the end justify the means then, too?"

He sits me down and pulls me close. "I wouldn't be able to stand it if I lost you."

"Please say you forgive me. Please?"

He crushes me closer. "I do, but promise never to scare me like that again."

"I do. I do." We rock back and forth in each other's arms. This is no time to tell him about how I got scratches on my body.

A few moments later, he asks, "How's the headache? How do you feel now?"

I think about it. My headache is nearly gone. "Better. Much better."

I kiss him long and hard. "I absolutely give you permission to save my life any chance you get."

* * *

I make two phone calls.

"Morrie. Big news. We have the proof we need on Abe." I fill him in on the iron cross without mentioning where and how I got it—later for that. And also about Abe's plane reservations.

Morrie says, "I'll alert the airline not to let him on the plane tonight."

"You've got to catch him before he can get out of the country."

"I'm on it," Morrie says.

The second call is to Stanley. "Can you meet us

at the clubhouse an hour before our party? Without Esther?"

"What? Is something wrong?"

"Yes," I say. "Something is very wrong."

We need to inform Stanley before the police do.

46

Showdown

So here we are in the clubhouse, dressed in our finest. We, who live in sundresses and shorts, had to dig through our closets for cocktail dresses and heels. I'm wearing a peach organza dress, last worn for my daughter Emily's wedding, in New York. It still fits, thank goodness. Evvie is wearing a multi-colored caftan-type dress, all swirly, with lots of folds. Sophie and Bella have matching lemon and lime outfits they bought for a bar mitzvah years ago. Sophie tugs at her dress, realizing she's gained a few pounds since the last time she wore it.

And Ida—well, Ida owns one basic black dress, and that's that. We were going to go shopping, but what with Enya's problem, we decided to make do with what we had. Frankly, I'm just as pleased. I confess, I don't like shopping. And besides, Jack, having never seen me dressed up, whistled when I modeled the peach number to get his opinion.

Jack looks wonderful in a dark suit and tie. Joe, who insists he threw out every tie he owned when he moved here, wears a sports jacket.

We're surrounded by cheerful decorations put up by an energetic, romantic group of Phase Two friends. Lots of balloons and greeting cards with congratulations. There is a large shoji-type screen off to one side with smiling photos they've gathered of me, then Jack, then both of us together. The catered food sits on tables, waiting for the party to begin.

We may be dressed for a party but anxiety is the group emotion. The seven of us are standing, facing the front door, waiting for Stanley. Enya, dressed simply in a beige dress, sits on a chair, all by herself, away from us. There is a strange kind of calm about her. What must she be thinking?

Stanley will arrive any minute. I'm not looking forward to breaking this man's heart.

There's the expected knock on the door and Stanley enters, a puzzled look on his face. "Esther doesn't know why she should stay home and I come an hour earlier."

"You'll explain later," I tell him.

Stanley looks from one face to another. He sees worry, concern, fear, nervousness. "I better sit down." He uses one of the folding chairs facing us. "You all look like somebody died."

Jack moves behind me and rubs my shoulders. I take a deep breath. "Someone did die, but it was fifty years ago. And we found his skeleton recently."

Stanley is ready to smile. "You've solved it, haven't you?" He half stands, about to come forward. "Congratulations."

"Don't!" Evvie blurts. "Please sit back down."

Startled, Stanley lowers his body once more, worry furrowing his brows.

I go on. "Stanley, dear, I have to warn you, it's taken us a while to be able to believe what we now know, and I expect it will be very difficult for you to accept. But we found proof."

Bella nervously needs to get water from the drinks table. I wait until she comes back. This time, she takes a seat. I can see her trembling.

"You know the name of the dead body?" Stanley asks eagerly.

"Yes." I close my eyes for a moment, not wanting to see the expression that will be on his face in a moment. "Abe Waller."

A deadly silence sinks in. Sophie gasps as Stanley clutches the sides of the flimsy wooden chair for support. His face has gone pale.

Bella rushes forward to give him her water, but he shakes his arms in refusal.

"What do you mean?" He is alarmed now. "What can you possibly mean?"

I twist around to Jack and indicate that he should take over.

"It means," Jack says, "that the man who murdered Johnny Blake in Tampa, and took his identity, murdered another man, that night at your construction site. His next victim was a survivor of the camps who tracked down the Nazi who killed his family—"

A new voice interrupts, "Very bad manners to talk about a person behind his back."

We all spin around quickly, to see an unfamiliar man standing in the doorway. He enters and shuts the door behind him. It takes a few moments to realize the large, slightly bent over, clean shaven, no longer bearded man, sporting a barber-styled haircut and wearing a tan suit and tie, is the man we've known as Abe Waller. Now that I can see the face, it's an ordinary face, but it reveals hardness. He's no longer wearing glasses, and the scar that circles his left eye is faded, but still identifiable. I glance at his hands and, to my horror, he's wearing the signet ring.

Stanley looks mystified, unable to comprehend what he sees.

"There I was, ready to take my leave, when I see my dear friend Stanley hurrying to the clubhouse, looking very perturbed. I couldn't resist following him."

Stanley, now realizing who this apparition is, almost falls off his chair as he jumps up. "No!" he shouts, righting himself. "This cannot be."

I look at Enya, who remains calm amid the chaos in the room. Bella and Sophie are clutching each other. Ida and Evvie are rigid, eyes darting. Joe takes a few steps, bringing him next to Evvie. Jack removes his hands from my shoulders and I can practically feel his body move into alert mode.

He takes a stance in front of us. "Jack, dearest," I whisper desperately to his back, "don't do anything foolish."

The man we knew as Abe moves to the side of the room. I see what Jack sees. The Nazi is nearing Enya.

He smiles. "You might as well hear it, from what you call the horse's mouth. As you probably guessed, I came back to Lanai Gardens all those years ago, to make sure Abe Waller's body hadn't been unearthed."

I look at Stanley, hoping he won't have a heart attack. Stanley appears numb.

I wonder what Jack is thinking. We didn't expect this. But we should have.

"Abe" smiles at Stanley, and it isn't a pretty sight. "And lo and behold, the first person I meet standing in front of the pristine building Z is Stanley. I am wearing a fake beard and dark clothes to make sure no one recognizes me as the former Johnny Blake, and Stanley immediately assumes I am Jewish. What an amusing joke. I have a Jewish man's identity in my pocket and now I'm being welcomed with open arms because Stanley thinks I am like him. How can I resist such friendship? I get my brilliant idea. I'll live here among them for a while to make sure no one is looking for Abe Waller and then I'll leave."

My girls, behind me, must be holding their breaths, listening to this, realizing we're in terrible trouble. I hear one of them gasp.

What goes through my mind, based on reading

hundreds of mysteries, is that killers never confess unless they are sure they will leave no witnesses. What will Jack do? What *can* he do? I'm sure the Nazi has a weapon, and Jack will die first! God help us.

As if reading my mind, Abe says, "By the way, allow me to introduce myself. My name is Horst Kolb. Formerly of Munich, Germany."

Enya sighs deeply, and then calmly says, "Formerly *Oberführer* Kolb, known as *Der Bösewicht,* of Auschwitz," as if a great secret has finally been revealed and a huge weight lifted.

Stanley's face turns ashen.

I groan. We are going to die. All of us.

Horst Kolb, as I might as well call him, seems very relaxed, but his clenched fists betray him. "At first I am highly entertained, wearing Jew clothes and going to temple with my new best friend." He glances at Stanley, whose body begins to sway and his lips move in fervent prayer.

Now Kolb looks toward Enya, who hasn't taken her eyes off his face. "But something unexpected happened to me. I don't know when or how," he says with great earnestness. "The religious teachings took, and over the years, as I found God, I felt guilt over the crimes I committed. I became Jewish in my heart and soul. I spent these many years doing penance for my sins. I, too, share your nightmares of the dead bodies, Enya Slovak." He entreats her. "Can you find it in your heart to forgive me?"

Our heads whip back and forth as we look to

Enya, then Kolb. I notice Jack moving forward slightly. Kolb moves, too. Toward Enya. My heart is pounding. This is when he'll pull out the weapon.

Kolb says it again, his tone cooler. "I need your forgiveness."

She says nothing.

"Your fault," he shouts at her, losing control. "If you'd only let it alone!"

Enya finally speaks. Her voice is flat. "There is no room for forgiveness in my heart. Forgive you? Never!"

Kolb is swift. In seconds, he grabs Enya off her chair, and there it is—the gun comes out of his pocket and he presses it to her head.

Sophie screams. Bella whimpers. The girls tumble into one another, clutching at their friends for comfort. I am still watching Jack move a little more. What was it he said this morning? *He was never so frightened in his life?* As I am now.

Jack quickly whispers to me, "When I tell you, grab Stanley and the girls and run for the side door. Warn them if you can. If not, push them."

"Jack, you can't."

"Shh," he says.

Kolb is furious. "Give me back what belongs to me," he shouts at us. "I want the patch!"

Evvie gasps behind me, clutching her purse close to her side.

"We don't have it with us. We hid it," I say, but my trembling voice betrays me.

"Liar," he says.

"I'll kill her if you don't give it to me right now." He pushes the gun farther into Enya's hair.

"Do it," Enya says calmly. "I died the day my babies died. Destroy this shell that feels nothing."

She turns to us. "Leave. Let him kill me. I don't care. I am no longer a victim and he no longer has control over me."

Kolb nudges her with the gun. "If you don't value your life, then I'll kill one of your friends. They care about living."

Enya and Kolb look in each other's eyes. His voice is shrill. "Tell me you forgive me!"

She laughs, but it is a sob. "A good Jew, ready to commit murder?"

To our utter astonishment, Enya raises her hand and smacks him. "May you rot in hell!"

Jack yells, "Run!"

I react instantly. I pull Stanley along and shove the girls and Joe toward the nearest side door, shouting, "Move. Move!" Yet I'm still watching what's occurring behind us.

Amazingly, these things happen all at once. Enya calmly walks away from Kolb, not looking back. Jack picks up a heavy glass ashtray from a side table and lobs it along the floor toward Kolb as if it were a bowling ball. At the same time as Kolb is distracted by the runaway ashtray, Jack races toward him, zigzagging every which way, head lowered, as if he were on a football field, trying to confuse the opposition so they would be unable to pin him down.

As Kolb whips the gun around, trying to aim at the ever-moving Jack, the front door swings open.

"Drop it! Drop the gun!" Morrie Langford says, as he and Oz Washington rush in.

Jack reaches Kolb, tackles him, knocking him down. Jack instantly rolls away. Morrie reaches Kolb and kicks the gun out of his hands. Oz grabs Kolb to his feet and cuffs him. Morrie says, "You are under arrest for the deaths of Johnny Blake and Abe Waller."

Jack catches up to Enya and leads her far out of danger. As he does, he says to Kolb, "Not only doesn't Enya forgive you, but the state of Florida won't, either. Neither will the war crimes commission. They will be very happy to close the books on Horst Kolb, once and for all."

The girls are screaming and crying at the same time.

If I had to guess who among us would faint, I wouldn't have picked Stanley Heyer, whose inert face now lies flat across my shoes.

Jack runs to me and hugs me. "How?" I begin to ask.

He grins. "Something else about me I haven't gotten around to telling you. I was a football jock in college."

And to all of us who complained to the clubhouse hospitality committee that we wanted the ashtrays removed because nobody smokes anymore, give thanks they didn't get around to it yet.

Jack has saved my life again. That's two I owe him.

At that moment, appearing at the open front doors, are the beautifully dressed engagement party guests. They begin to file in.

Hy, looking very dapper in a pearl gray Armani knockoff, looks around eagerly and says, "What did we miss?"

47

The Party

It takes a while to quiet down the incoming guests as Horst Kolb is taken away by Morrie and Oz and other police. Questions fly, and I am sure the girls and Joe answer as best they can.

Outside the clubhouse Stanley and Esther take their leave of us. Jack holds tightly on to my arm, as I'm still shaken from the last few minutes. The Heyers cannot bear to stay, but shakily, they extend their congratulations. Stanley has tears in his eyes. I am thinking as I look at that dear man that it will take a long time for him to recover from this shocking news. A man he knew and trusted as his dearest friend. How difficult it will be to face his congregation. But he surprises me. He tells me that I will always be a heroine to him for what I did. And that brings on my tears.

* * *

We go back inside and there is much hugging and kissing from the amazed guests. A night to truly celebrate. It's wonderful seeing all my friends and neighbors dressed beautifully and wanting to share our happiness. For their sakes, I must put away my feelings about this momentous day to be able to process later. Enya comes to me and embraces me. It's as if she never wants to let me go. I can feel the wetness of her cheeks. Jack gently moves in and kisses her as well.

The engagement party is a huge success. So much color and laughter and happy music. Everyone eats too much and drinks too much. There is something about having looked into the jaws of death that whets the appetite. One is determined to live life to the absolute fullest.

Highlights of the evening:

Enya leads us in dancing the hora. She looks ten years younger as she weaves in and out of the dance, everyone bending and swaying to her direction.

As I walk by him I'm amused to hear Hy, now retelling latecomers the capture-of-Kolb story, building up his part.

"I could have turned Jack in for smashing Kolb's car. I watched him do it but not a peep out of me, no siree. I could see how he was planning to stop the Nazi from going back into his apartment. I was with him one hundred and ten percent!"

Jack and I do a mean East Coast Lindy Hop and finally sit down, out of breath, to much applause.

He's gasping for breath. I grin. "Football star, indeed."

Evvie starts the clapping and everyone follows with the clinking of spoons on glasses. Voices ring out. "Name the date! Name the date!"

We look at one another and then I call out January first, and that gets even more applause.

Morrie and Oz return, their arms filled with presents for us. Naturally, we hug. I try very hard not to whisper I told you so to my future stepson.

He beats me to it. "Well, you were right, Gladdy." His tone a little forced.

"As usual," I say sweetly back.

While we are strolling around outside with our drinks and food, I spy Evvie and Joe having drinks around the pool. Evvie reminds Joe that this is the very spot where he dumped her years ago on that miserable New Year's Eve.

Joe apologizes. "I'm sorry. I'm sorry. A hundred times over I'm sorry."

"I forgive you," Evvie says, and promptly pushes him into the deep end.

* * *

I hear Sol whisper to Barbi and Casey, "I saw what you do through your windows. You should pull your shades down." Egad, is the Peeper back in action?

* * *

I forgot to mention, in all the tumult today, that there was a picture postcard in the mail. It was postmarked Atlanta, Georgia, and has a lush photo of ripe peaches accompanied by greetings from Grandpa Bandit. He wrote, “Seventy is the new fifty. Gray hair is the new black. Hang around long enough and you’ll be a teenager again.” Signed with a drawing of a green feather.

* * *

A great evening was had by all.

In a quiet corner, Jack and I toast one another with champagne. I say happily, “Nothing will ever part us again.”

Acknowledgments

Evan Baker, Ph.D.: thank you for the German words. Much appreciated. And for all the great photos you take.

My New York team:
Caitlin Alexander
Nancy Yost
Sharon Propson

The 580 team:
Camille Minichino
Jonnie Jacobs
Peggy Lucke

As always, to my family and friends for their continuous support.

And
In loving memory of Bronia

Dear Reader:

I hope I had you on the edge of your seat for **Getting Old Is a Disaster.**

The next book coming up in the Gladdy Gold series is **Getting Old Is Très Dangereux.** *A somewhat French title? Will Gladdy go to France?* Mais non, *perhaps France is coming to her. Hmmm? What can that mean?*

Gladdy and her frisky girls, plus Jack, and also Evvie's ex-husband, Joe, have survived some scary moments during the hurricane, but all is right in everyone's world again. Plans for Gladdy and Jack's wedding are swirling excitedly around Lanai Gardens.

But, from out of Jack's past, a mysterious stranger appears from that faraway land and murder follows. Someone seems determined to destroy Gladdy and Jack's happiness. Perhaps even to murder our loving couple.

So watch your local bookstore for the arrival of the new and exciting **Getting Old Is Très Dangereux**, *coming out next spring. Or visit my website, www.ritalakin.com to get updates, not only about the arrival of the new books, but also my schedule of book signings. If I turn up in your neighborhood, please drop by and say hello. And keep those wonderful e-mails coming to me at ritalakin@aol.com. I love hearing from you.*

Rita Lakin

Before Sierra had time to realize what was happening, Ben tackled her,

and she found herself with a hundred and eighty pounds of lean, hard male sprawled on top of her. Not an entirely unpleasant predicament, she decided.

"This is all so sudden," she said. "After all, we've only just met."

"Shh!" His solid chest heaved against her breasts, and when she squirmed beneath him, he pinned her even more firmly with his body and forced her to lie still.

Despite appearances, it suddenly became clear that she was the only person present who found this situation arousing. "Was that a bullet that just came through here?" she asked mildly.

Ben nodded, a wild gleam in his eyes. From her vantage point, Sierra could see a faint, puckered scar on his forehead that had been hidden by his dark blond hair. And she began to wonder just what else this man was hiding from her. . . .

Dear Reader,

With all due fanfare, this month Silhouette *Special Edition* is pleased to bring you *Dawn of Valor*, Lindsay McKenna's latest and long-awaited *LOVE AND GLORY* novel. We trust that the unique flavor of this landmark volume—the dramatic saga of cocky fly-boy Chase Trayhern and feisty army nurse Rachel McKenzie surviving love and enemy fire in the Korean War—will prove well worth your wait.

Joining Lindsay McKenna in this exceptional, action-packed month are five more sensational authors: Barbara Faith, with an evocative, emotional adoption story, *Echoes of Summer*; Natalie Bishop, with the delightful, damned-if-you-do, damned-if-you-don't (fall in love, that is) *Downright Dangerous*; Marie Ferrarella, with a fast-talking blonde and a sly, sexy cynic on a goofily glittering treasure hunt in *A Girl's Best Friend*; Lisa Jackson, with a steamy, provocative case of "mistaken" identity in *Mystery Man*; and Kayla Daniels, with a twisty, tantalizing tale of duplicity and desire in *Hot Prospect*.

All six novels are bona fide page-turners, featuring a compelling cast of characters in a marvelous array of adventures of the heart. We hope you'll agree that each and every one of them is a stimulating, sensitive edition worthy of the label *special*.

From all the authors and editors of Silhouette *Special Edition*,

Best wishes.

KAYLA DANIELS

Hot Prospect

Silhouette Special Edition
Published by Silhouette Books New York
America's Publisher of Contemporary Romance

To Chris:
modern-day prospector,
human alarm clock,
and world's greatest brother.

SILHOUETTE BOOKS
300 East 42nd St., New York, N.Y. 10017

HOT PROSPECT

ISBN: 0-373-09654-2

First Silhouette Books printing February 1991

Printed in the U.S.A.

Books by Kayla Daniels

Silhouette Special Edition

Spitting Image #474
Father Knows Best #578
Hot Prospect #654

KAYLA DANIELS

loves to travel and has visited every state but one. She has lived in Alaska, California, Alabama and New Orleans' French Quarter. Kayla wrote this book while living in Hendricks, Minnesota, where she learned how to square dance, met some distant branches of her family tree and drank about ten thousand cups of coffee up at Irene's Cafe.

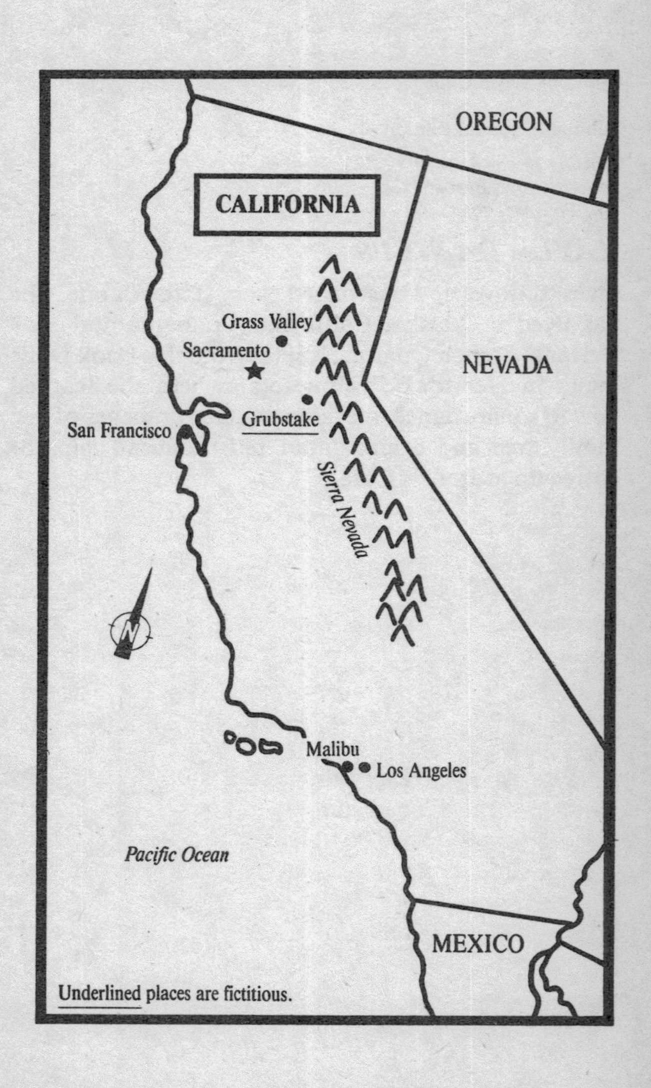
OREGON
CALIFORNIA
NEVADA
Grass Valley
Sacramento
Grubstake
San Francisco
Sierra Nevada
N
Malibu
Los Angeles
Pacific Ocean
MEXICO
Underlined places are fictitious.

Prologue

Sabotage.

The word ricocheted through Ben Halliday's brain like a zinging metal ball in a pinball machine. But the red warning lights on the instrument panel in front of him were flashing a far more ominous message than *Tilt*!

And the danger alarms ringing in his head weren't part of any game.

As Ben struggled to maintain control of the crippled Cessna 210, he forced himself to choke back his outrage, his sense of shock and betrayal. Resisting the urge to curse himself for one careless, possibly deadly mistake, he focused completely on the desperate task at hand: coaxing the small plane down gently enough so that maybe—just *maybe*—he'd survive the crash landing.

He'd only have one shot at it.

With lightning-quick expertise, he scanned the cockpit instruments, automatically noting the rapidly dwindling altitude and air speed. Below him the jagged, snowdrifted peaks of the Sierra Nevada loomed closer and closer, like jaws growing wider and wider just before they swallowed him up.

Ben's stomach lurched sickeningly along with the Cessna. He shoved in the throttle, counting on the increased power to provide more lift. The sputtering engine increased its loud, whining protests, but—as far as Ben could tell—with no effect on the aircraft's relentless downward plunge.

With sweat-slicked palms, he pulled gradually yet firmly on the yoke, trying to bring up the plane's nose and increase the wings' angle of attack. The craft began to yaw wildly from side to side. Ben pumped the rudder pedals, but he might as well have tried to stamp out a forest fire with his feet. Wrestling with the unresponsive controls was like riding a bucking bronco, except that in this case the ground was a long, *long* way off.

"Come on, baby," he urged through gritted teeth. "Stay with me . . . come on, you can do it."

Beads of sweat crawled down his temples as he battled to achieve exactly the right balance. He had to keep the Cessna's nose up, yet at this sluggish speed he couldn't nudge the wing angle too high without sending the plane into a stall.

Ben stole a quick peek at the ground, then wished he hadn't. He was close enough now to make out the individual pine trees that studded the slopes with their sharp green spikes. Swallowing, he choked back the coppery taste of fear rising in his throat. Once he gave in to panic, he'd be a goner for sure.

Adrenaline surged through his bloodstream. Every nerve and muscle in his body was stretched taut with effort, as if he were part of the plane itself and could keep it aloft with his own physical strength.

But all too quickly the rugged landscape approached. Then, to make matters worse, a strong updraft buffeted the doomed Cessna as it veered over a steep drop-off below. The wind currents tossed the plane around as if it were made of paper. Ben pitched forward into the windshield, striking his head with a blow that left him dazed.

He shook his head to clear away the fog. Despite the dizzying stench of gasoline fumes filling the cockpit, he forced several deep breaths into his lungs. Ignoring the sticky warmth he felt oozing down the side of his face, he grappled with the controls, forearm tendons corded like steel cables with the strain.

He darted his eyes to the ground again. Hopeless as it seemed, he had to pick someplace to set this baby down—a highway, a meadow, a damn *parking* lot, for God's sake.

"Fat chance," he mumbled. Where in this forbidding, mountainous terrain was he going to find a place flat enough even to *attempt* a landing? As he scanned the ground ahead, all he could see were more mountains, more stream-filled ravines, more of those damn tall pine trees waiting to impale him....

Wait a second.

Ben's frantic, searching gaze snagged on a break in the trees up ahead. Some kind of open field, perhaps?

Or another deep, rocky gorge gaping up at him....

Gingerly he turned the yoke to the left, praying the ailerons would respond and bank the plane in the direction of that opening.

They didn't.

"Figures. Well, why should *they* work when nothing else does?" Ben growled.

But using every scrap of his considerable piloting ability, he was able to cajole enough of a response from the disabled controls to steer the aircraft more or less toward the clearing.

Now the plane was skimming over the tops of the snow-dusted trees, so close that Ben could see the individual needles. His heart thudded in his ears, drowning out the tortured gasps of the engine.

"This is it... this is it," he muttered, chest heaving, head throbbing, muscles tensed to the limit.

For a few moments, time slowed to a glacial crawl as he neared the break in the trees. He was committed now to this course, and if the opening turned out to be another canyon...

"Hurrah!" he crowed hoarsely when the most beautiful sight in the world crept into his field of vision. The snow-covered, boulder-strewn ground below was hardly the ideal landing spot, but at least it was roughly horizontal.

Ben's burst of triumph vanished as quickly as it had exploded—because the plane was traveling much too fast. Because the controls were virtually useless.

Because, in all probability, Ben Halliday was about to die.

A maelstrom of emotions churned through him: rage, frustration, regret and, finally, an aching sadness.

"I'm sorry, Ma," he whispered. "You counted on me, and I let you down."

He yanked back on the throttle as the plane skidded over the clearing, but he was still going too fast... too fast . . . the field wasn't wide enough . . . the trees ahead were too close. . . .

At the last instant the engine sputtered one final cough and died, and a white roar of silence filled Ben's ears as the thick, prickly trees reached out their branches to snatch him. . . .

Either the whole crash was over incredibly quickly, or Ben had blacked out on impact. In any case the next thing he knew, he was opening his eyes and squinting cross-eyed at a dense canopy of pine trees overhead.

He didn't know how long he'd been out cold, but one fact was certain: he had to get away from the plane before the fuel tank exploded. The mangled interior of the cockpit was barely recognizable. Ben grasped the edge of the opening where the door had once been and tried to heave himself upward.

"Ow!" He let loose a stream of curses as a javelin of pain shafted up his left leg. Moving more cautiously, he rested his weight on his right leg and shoved. Perched on the threshold of his wrecked Cessna, he paused, gasping with effort and agony.

The letter.

Damn it, he had to get that letter. No matter what the cost.

Without hesitation he turned and crawled painfully back through the crumpled cockpit, searching for his coat. He had to find it. The letter was in one of its pockets.

Concentrating on the search, aware that with each passing second he was in greater danger of being blown to smithereens, Ben allowed one small, detached corner of his brain to take inventory of his injuries. From the stabbing in his chest that accompanied each breath, he figured several ribs were broken. His left leg was a virtual dead weight whose excruciating pain sent waves of nausea through him. Something was wrong with his head, but whether this was from the earlier blow or from the crash, he couldn't tell.

There it was! He spotted a corner of his coat wedged under a tangle of glass and metal. Panting, he tugged and cursed until the coat tore free. With shaking hands he fumbled through the inside pocket to make sure the letter was still there. Crimson drops plopped onto the tan suede.

Clenching the letter between his teeth, Ben scrabbled his way back to the gaping hole in the other side of the cockpit. His brain registered a tortured, recurring sound, but it wasn't until he'd clambered out of the plane and dragged himself to the nearest stand of trees that Ben realized the groans were erupting from his own chest.

For a moment the agony was so great, he thought he'd pass out. But he had to hang on for a while longer, just long enough to hide the letter.

Because as sure as day followed night, Quentin Jericho's henchmen wouldn't be far behind him.

Ben propped himself on his elbows and stuffed the letter inside his shirt.

Then the plane exploded.

When Ben came to, he was sprawled some ten feet away from where he'd been before. An eerie orange glow bathed the landscape, and the loud snapping of burning glass and metal punctuated the steady roar of the flames.

Ben's face felt hot, as if he had a bad sunburn. But the scorched feeling was a caress compared to the red-hot pokers jabbing the rest of his body.

In a sudden panic, he grabbed his chest. Thank God. The letter was still under his shirt.

Refusing to surrender to the pain yet, he lifted his head to scan his surroundings. He needed a rock, a hole in a tree—*someplace* where he could stash the incriminating piece of paper.

As he raised himself onto his elbows, a galaxy of black dots peppered his vision, and gray, cottony mist swirled through his brain. "No, damn it," he muttered, clenching his teeth. "Not yet . . . not yet . . . gotta hang in there . . . just until . . . until I can hide the . . ."

The next time Ben opened his eyes, he was gazing up at the homeliest face he'd ever seen. Even through the fading daylight and gently falling snow, he could make out widely spaced eyes beneath a drooping straw hat...enormous nostrils...big pointy ears...and breath that would wilt skunk cabbage.

Ben blinked, shook his head to clear his pain-blurred vision, then blinked again.

Now, what the hell was a mule in a straw hat doing way up here on this godforsaken mountain?

Chapter One

"'Listen to this, Charlemagne. 'Your mother misses you very deeply. Of course, she doesn't say it in so many words, but I know that your stubborn persistence with this reckless escapade weighs heavily upon her heart.'"

Sierra Sloane thrust the letter in front of Charlemagne's eyes. "Do you believe this? Wait, wait—it gets better. Listen."

Charlemagne chewed placidly on a mouthful of weeds and listened.

"'Naturally your decision to throw away a promising career for the sake of some wild-goose chase has been a big disappointment to me, as well. I know you and I have had our differences in the past, Sierra, but I beg you to think of your poor mother's feelings, and please reconsider your impetuous decision, which I know was made in a moment of sentimental weakness.'"

Sierra mashed up the letter and flung it back over her shoulder. "What a bunch of baloney!" She paced back and forth across the campsite, shaking her chestnut curls in exasperation. "For one thing, I know darn well that Mother is the one person in the world who sympathizes with my decision. She'd do the same thing herself if she could."

She scooped up the crumpled paper and shook it in front of Charlemagne's nose. "Do you know what this is?"

Charlemagne didn't reply.

"I'll tell you what this is. This is Daddy's latest scheme to drag me back to Los Angeles and that corporate oppressor of the human spirit they call Sloane Enterprises." She flung her arms wide in a dramatic gesture of helplessness. "What is this now? Plan A? Plan B? C, D or E? Good heavens, I've lost track by now. We could be all the way up to Plan Z, for all I know."

Charlemagne yawned sympathetically.

"Wanna know what I think of this latest scheme of his? I'll show you." With brisk determination, Sierra snatched up a dozen rocks lying around the campsite and pushed them into a rough circle.

"Thinks he can pull my strings by making me feel guilty, does he? I'll show him what I think of his sneaky tricks," she muttered, tossing handfuls of sticks and brush into the circle of stones. Rummaging through the saddlebags draped over a branch of a nearby tree, she found her pieces of flint and crouched down by the makeshift hearth.

"I'll show you what this letter's good for," she announced, tossing the crumpled wad down with disdain. "Kindling! How 'bout a nice fire, Char? I kind of fancy pancakes for breakfast this morning, don't you?" She clinked the pieces of flint together again and again, her tongue protruding with concentration.

"Looks like we might be in for a storm today, anyway. Look at those dark clouds heading this way! A fire will feel real good . . . if I can just . . . get it started. . . ."

Clink. Clink. Clink.

"Yup, looks like summer's nearly over, Char. Feel that wind! Why, I can practically *smell* autumn in the air!" Clink. Clink.

"Come on, one little spark . . . one measly little spark . . ."

Clink.

"Oh, hell." She tossed the flints aside in disgust. "Well, even if I *had* gotten a spark, it's probably too windy to start a fire. I'd never get a flame going in this gale."

Sierra pushed herself to her feet and tucked the flints back into the saddlebag. Wind whipped her hair into her eyes as she scratched behind Charlemagne's ears. "You gonna be okay if the weather gets a little rough?" she asked. "Here, let's make sure your hat's tied on tight. Wouldn't want it to blow away." She slapped the mule affectionately on his flank. "Looks like a good day to stay inside," she said, scanning the western horizon, where she could already see distant flashes of heat lightning.

She slung the saddlebags over her shoulder and headed for the tent, which was pitched at a rather lopsided angle. "Hmm," she muttered, studying the tent critically, her eyes darting to the fast-approaching storm.

She fished her rock hammer from one of the saddlebags and skirted around the tent, pounding in the stakes more securely. "Guess that'll have to do," she said finally as the first spatters of rain hit her shoulders.

Inside the tent she tossed her gear aside and collapsed cross-legged onto her sleeping bag. With a sigh she reached into a plastic bag and scooped a handful of nuts, raisins and sunflower seeds into her mouth.

"Yum, yum," she mumbled, chewing mechanically. "Trail mix for breakfast." She sighed. "Again."

Raindrops tattooed against the tent, increasing in force like the rat-a-tat-tat of a snare-drum crescendo, individual beats merging into one steady, deafening stream of sound. Sierra shivered, though the air temperature was fairly warm. For the first time since leaving Los Angeles two months ago, she was keenly aware of her isolation. Not that she was lonely or anything. Just . . . alone.

A huge gust of wind screamed up the mountainside and slammed into her tent. Sierra flinched. Drawing her knees up close to her chest, she huddled with her arms wrapped around her legs as the storm howled outside.

Somewhere very close by, she heard an ominous creaking noise. Then another. And another.

"Uh-oh," she said.

Ben tugged the hood of his gray rain slicker up over his head and hunkered down behind a tangle of brush. Peering at the campsite, he nodded with satisfaction. This was the place, all right. He'd recognize that mule anywhere.

Now the only problem was how to make sure the old prospector was alone. The fewer people who saw Ben, the better. He'd had a devil of a time tracking down Caleb Murphy without drawing any attention to himself. He hadn't dared ask anyone in town where the old miner was camped out these days, for fear of leaving behind a clue for one of Jericho's goons.

Ben shifted uncomfortably as the ghost of his months-old injury gnawed at his leg. He'd never really believed before that the weather could affect a person's aches and pains, but ever since he'd risen early this morning and sniffed rain in the air, his left leg had been acting up again. He'd hoped today's hike would banish the stiffness, but the throbbing from his thigh down to his calf had only grown worse. Gritting his teeth, Ben willed himself to ignore the pain as he'd learned to do during those long months of physical therapy.

Well, he could live with pain, but he wasn't sure how long he could stand the maddening wetness creeping beneath his collar and into his boots as he crouched below the dripping trees. And the fierce wind, though not cold, lashed through his slicker and combined with the dampness to make him even more miserable.

Maybe he was being overly cautious. Chances were Murphy was alone inside that tent, anyway. Why not simply saunter over and knock on his door—or his tent flap, as the case might be?

The prospect of shelter from the sodden outdoors was a temptation Ben couldn't resist, even though the tent didn't look like much of a shelter. Murphy must have put it up in an awful hurry, by the unsteady looks of it. Well, any port in a storm, Ben thought as he levered himself painfully to his feet.

At that moment a ferocious gust of wind shoved him toward the tent. But before he'd taken three steps, Ben froze and watched in astonishment as the entire tent seemed to expand like a balloon and then collapse.

Even more amazing were the muffled cries that emanated from inside the tangled folds. Amazing not only for their highly inventive profanity, but also for the fact that they were uttered in a high-pitched voice that Ben couldn't imagine coming from the grizzled prospector's vocal chords.

After watching the helpless thrashing for several moments, he decided to risk tweaking Murphy's pride by coming to the rescue. He loped across the campsite and tried to find the tent's opening—not an easy task with all the wild flailing going on inside.

"Hold on a second! Don't move—you're only making matters worse! I've got it— there!" Ben hoisted the tent opening and peered inside to find himself face-to-face with the most exasperated, the most adorable female he'd ever seen.

It was hard to say which of them was more startled.

The woman's enormous, thickly lashed eyes seemed to fill her face. Rich, brown eyes flecked with gold—eyes a man could lose himself in if he wasn't careful. Unruly reddish brown curls framed her heart-shaped, pixieish face, which glowed fiery pink at the moment from her frustrated efforts to free herself from the collapsed tent.

Her cheeks grew even redder as she absorbed the surprising fact of Ben's appearance, and her lips parted as she sucked in a little gasp of air.

His eyes darted immediately to those lips—full, rosy lips that were a strangely seductive contrast to her otherwise delicate features. Suddenly he was awash with the overwhelming urge to taste those lips, to explore her mouth with his own and discover what other delicious surprises she might have in store.

The unexpected flood of desire caught Ben off guard, coming as it did after months of recovery and rehabilitation when his only physical craving had been to escape the pain. For a moment he forgot his soggy feet, his aching leg and the purpose for his presence.

Then a droplet of water plopped onto the tip of her pert nose. She blinked and tossed her head. The defiant uptilt of her fragile chin showed another intriguing contrast. "Who the hell are you?" she demanded crossly.

Ben rocked back on his heels. "What kind of welcome is that? I'd expect a little more gratitude from someone I just rescued from the clutches of a man-eating tent. *Woman*-eating, I should say."

"I didn't need your help. I was doing perfectly fine without you."

"Oh, really?" Ben chuckled. "If I hadn't come along, you'd still be trying to find your way out of this tent. But if you'd rather I left you to your own devices—" He made as if to leave, dropping the tent flap to the ground.

"No, wait!" She scrambled out of the toppled tent. Pushing back her damp curls, she bit her lower lip and studied Ben for a moment. "Look, I'm sorry," she said finally, sounding as if those words didn't pass her lips very often. "You took me by surprise, that's all." Then a sheepish grin teased the corners of her mouth. "I guess I was kind of embarrassed about my tent falling down." She stuck out her hand. "Sierra Sloane."

He grasped her hand, then did a double take. "Sierra?"

"As in Sierra Nevada. That *was* going to be your next question, wasn't it?" she asked, peering mischievously at him from beneath rain-spangled lashes.

"You've been asked that a few times before, I take it." Her slim fingers nestled cozily against Ben's palm.

Reluctantly he released her hand. "You've certainly come to the right place, with a name like that."

"Hmph. I know people who'd disagree with you," she said, throwing back her head with a defiant gesture he was already coming to recognize.

Her remark raised another question. What the devil was this gorgeous *young* woman doing way up here in old Caleb Murphy's tent? Ben scanned her slim figure from the muddy tips of her worn leather boots to the frayed collar of her plaid shirt. She barely came up to his shoulder. Now that he took a closer look at her, he realized how young she really was. Hardly more than a teenager, he'd guess, despite the undeniably womanly curves her disheveled garb couldn't disguise. Her fresh-scrubbed complexion with its faint dusting of freckles across her nose made him think of a high-school cheerleader. Peaches and cream. Apple-pie wholesomeness.

So what the hell was she doing mixed up with a man four times her age?

"Why are you glaring at me like that?" she asked suspiciously, propping her hands on her hips.

"How old are you, anyway?"

Her dark eyebrows shot toward the sky. "What are you, the census taker?"

"Humor me."

"I'm twenty-eight, not that it's any of your business."

Okay, so Caleb Murphy was only *three* times her age. Still, Ben scowled at the images that flitted across his imagination. But she was right. Sierra Sloane's dubious personal life was none of his business. He had a far more vital matter to worry about. "I'm looking for your, uh, companion," he said, inspecting his fingernails.

Her forehead wrinkled in adorable confusion. *"Who?"*

Ben licked his lips. "You know." When it became obvious she *didn't* know, he glanced around helplessly, then jerked his thumb over his shoulder. "I'm looking for the guy who owns that mule. Fellow by the name of Caleb Murphy."

Whatever reaction he'd expected, it wasn't the odd mixture of sorrow and surprise that swept over her face like the storm clouds overhead. She swallowed, and Ben could have sworn the moisture in her eyes had nothing to do with the rain.

"What do you want with Grandpa?" she asked with a slight quiver in her voice.

Ben's jaw dropped. "Grand— You mean, the guy who wanders around the mother-lode country looking for gold? Caleb Murphy? He's your grandfather?"

"Was."

"I beg your pardon?"

She brushed a hand across her eyes, then met his gaze with sad resignation. "Grandpa died almost three months ago," she said evenly, despite a slight trembling of her lower lip.

"Oh, no. Oh, my God." An icy chill swept over Ben. How on earth was he going to get the letter back now? And without that letter, he'd never be able to even the score, to see justice done. All his hopes, his plans, his promises threatened to collapse around him in ruins, like the windblown tent.

Then he noticed Sierra's face and cursed himself for being an insensitive jerk. "God, I'm so sorry," he said, taking one of her hands between his. "I had no idea—I mean, the last time I saw him, he was fine."

Her eyes lit up like a sunrise. "Were you a friend of Grandpa's?"

"No . . . not exactly. But I did meet him once."

Her hopeful interest faded. "Oh." Shrugging, she started to turn away, then stopped when she realized her hand was still imprisoned between Ben's. They both looked down, met each other's gaze, then quickly averted their eyes again.

"Oops." Ben released her hand.

Sierra backed away slowly, then knelt to the ground and began pawing through the tent folds. "I'm sure sorry you came all the way up here for nothing," she said over her shoulder.

Ben rubbed his forehead. What to do now? After everything he'd been through, he couldn't simply give up. Maybe Sierra had come across the letter in her grandfather's things; maybe Caleb had mentioned to her where he'd hidden it.

The trick would be extracting the information from her without revealing too much. Not that Ben didn't trust her; his instincts told him that Sierra Sloane was someone you could count on. But until that letter was safely back in his possession, the less Sierra knew, the better.

Bitter experience had taught him that where Quentin Jericho was concerned, too much knowledge could prove fatal. Once before, Ben had made the mistake of underestimating Jericho's ruthless power. It had nearly cost him his life.

He didn't intend to make the same mistake again.

Ben knelt beside Sierra. "If I offered to help fix the tent, would you bite my head off?"

She laughed. "I might," she replied, "but I'd wait till we had the tent back up to do it."

* * *

Much as she hated to admit it, Sierra was grateful for her unexpected visitor's help. Not that she couldn't have put the tent back up by herself...eventually. But by that time the storm would probably have blown over.

She watched him covertly as he pushed the flap aside and crawled inside the tent to join her. When he tugged off his rain slicker, she got her first good look at him. And suddenly her two-person tent seemed like very close quarters indeed.

The vibrant, male presence that filled the tent sprang from a far more basic source than his six-foot frame, button-straining chest and thickly muscled thighs. Some raw, masculine essence of the man himself seemed to burn up all the oxygen in the tent so that Sierra had trouble catching her breath. Whoever this friend—*acquaintance*—of Grandpa's was, he made all the other men Sierra had ever met seem like pale imitations of the real thing.

She guessed him to be in his early thirties, although her initial impression had been of a man a bit older. Faint creases of what looked like past suffering etched the corners of his eyes and mouth, but did nothing to diminish the bold attraction of his ruggedly carved features. In fact the physical evidence of endured tragedy merely enhanced his appeal. Here was a man who had been tested to the limits and survived.

Rain had seeped inside his slicker hood, plastering a damp fringe of sandy blond hair to his forehead. His eyes, which had appeared slate blue against the backdrop of gray clouds, were a deep cobalt when he returned Sierra's appraising glance. Hastily she busied herself searching through her meager cache of supplies.

"Hungry? How about some trail mix? Beef jerky?"

He slicked back his wet hair. "I don't suppose you've got a pot of coffee stashed away in those saddlebags, have you?"

His husky, baritone voice set her nerves purring. "Hmm, no. I tried to light a fire earlier, but I couldn't get a spark off the flint. Guess it was too wet," she added, omitting the fact that it hadn't been raining at the time.

"Ever hear of matches?"

She snorted. "Grandpa never used matches. He said, why fuss with man-made gadgets when nature provides something just as good?"

Her visitor scratched his head and regarded her with amusement from beneath his sandy eyebrows. "Seems to me you might have got that fire started if you'd used a match instead of banging a couple of rocks together. Or are you on some kind of Girl Scout wilderness survival trip?"

"Don't be ridiculous. Aha!" She pulled a silver flask from the saddlebag and waggled it in front of him. "Now you're going to be sorry you laughed at me."

"I wasn't laughing at you," he said, reaching forward to accept the flask. "I'm trying to figure you out, that's all. But I guess I should introduce myself first. Ben Halliday."

This time when their hands clasped, an odd current of awareness and acknowledged attraction seemed to flow between them. A tingling sensation traveled across Sierra's fingers, up her arm and down her spine. She suppressed a delicious shiver.

"So," she said brightly, "how do you know—*did* you know—my grandfather?"

Ben wiped the top of the flask with his shirt cuff, then tilted his head back and took a swig. Fascinated, Sierra watched his Adam's apple bob up and down. He shuddered and smacked his lips. "Boy, that hits the spot on a day like today."

His fingers brushed hers as he handed back the flask. Without thinking, she took a hefty gulp of whiskey. She might as well have swallowed lighter fluid.

Ben slapped her on the back. "You okay?" he asked, the twinkle in his eye belying the concern in his voice.

Sierra gasped for air, her vision blurred by a film of tears. "Hoo, boy, that stuff is strong!" she coughed, struggling to regain her lost dignity.

"Not your usual brand?"

She threw Ben a haughty look. "It was Grandpa's favorite. And mine, too. It just went down the wrong way, that's all." How she wanted to wipe that amused grin right off his mouth! Or better yet, kiss it off....

"You and your grandfather must have been pretty close," Ben said. His amusement had vanished, and in his casual tone, Sierra detected a hint of wary curiosity. "When I, er, ran into him that once, I didn't realize he was dragging a granddaughter around these mountains."

"Oh, I didn't live with Grandpa," she explained. "At least, not since I used to spend my summer vacations with him when I was a kid."

Ben arched his eyebrows in surprise. "Then how on earth did you wind up living way out here all by yourself?"

"I'm not by myself. I have Charlemagne, don't forget."

"Charlemagne? Who's th—oh, you mean that mule?"

Sierra had to stifle a giggle. The poor man looked confused, to say the least. Confused . . . but cute. "Charlemagne doesn't know he's a mule. Sometimes I forget that myself."

Ben took another swallow from the flask. "Okay. So how did you and *Charlemagne* end up together?"

Sierra played with a frayed thread on her shirtsleeve. "When Grandpa died, he left me everything he owned. I was ready for a change in my life, so I left Los Angeles and came up here to carry on where he left off." She shrugged. "End of story. At least the short, condensed version."

"Someday you'll have to tell me the long, unabridged version," Ben said. His crooked smile sent a rush of warmth and exhilaration coursing through Sierra's bloodstream, more potent than a shot of whiskey. "You're not really trying to make a living by panning for gold, are you?"

The note of disbelief in his voice was an all-too-familiar echo of the skepticism she'd heard from her family, friends and co-workers ever since she'd announced her intentions a few months ago. Despite her resolution to ignore the scoffers, Sierra's defensiveness flared up.

"My life-style may be somewhat unconventional, but it's certainly not some wild-goose chase, if that's what you're thinking."

"I didn't mean—"

"Have you checked the price of gold lately? The forty-niners who mined this area in the last century took the easiest-to-get-at deposits, but they left behind plenty of gold that simply wasn't cost-effective to extract. However, the current high price of gold, combined with advances in modern technology, now makes it economically viable to go after what's left over. A lot of the old abandoned mines are being reopened."

Ben studied her, probing his cheek thoughtfully with his tongue. Then he said, "But you're not taking advantage of modern technology. You're still using a mule and a gold pan, just like the old forty-niners."

"Just like my grandfather," she shot back. "He managed to make a living that way, and so can I. What was good enough for him is plenty good enough for me."

Ben leaned forward, intending to point out the illogic of Sierra's reasoning. Then he noticed the scarlet flush staining her cheeks and the stubborn set of her jaw. Maybe this was one of those times when discretion was the better part of valor.

He drank another leisurely swallow of whiskey and handed back the flask. From what he'd seen so far, Sierra was completely out of her element up here in the wilderness—a babe in the woods chasing some crazy dream because of her misguided devotion to her grandfather.

Ben understood better than most that kind of devotion. He sympathized completely with Sierra's loyalty to a lost loved one's memory. After all, that same brand of loyalty was the driving force that had sustained him through those agonizing months of recovery after the accident. It was the motivation that propelled him out of bed each morning, that had led him to track down Caleb Murphy and brought him instead to this unexpected encounter with the old man's intriguing, impossible granddaughter.

But Ben suspected Sierra's quest for gold sprang from a more complex source than sentimentality. Unless he missed his bet, she was searching for a lot more than precious metal.

And for some inexplicable reason, Ben wished he were going to have the chance to learn more about her. The woman was a mass of contradictions: one minute she was spouting off cost-effectiveness projections, and the next she was scorning plain old matches as some kind of newfangled nonsense.

With an almost wistful hunger that unsettled him, Ben longed to explore the mystery of Sierra Sloane, to dig for answers to the questions that stirred his curiosity. But he had a quest of his own to pursue.

And until he'd seen justice done, he couldn't spend time on detours, no matter how lovely or provocative.

He found Sierra's efforts to squelch her annoyance with his skepticism rather endearing. She took a dainty sip of whiskey, coughed, pushed back her tangled russet tresses and pasted a resolutely polite smile on her face. It was easy to see she was sick and tired of all the flack people had given her lately. "So," she said, "you haven't told me what brings *you* to these parts. What business did you have with Grandpa?"

Here was where Ben had to tread very, very carefully. He had to come up with a plausible excuse for seeking out Caleb Murphy without creating an obstacle course of lies that would trip him up later. He hadn't yet figured out how he was going to wangle that letter out of Sierra, and he wanted to leave as many options open as possible.

Vagueness, that was the key. If he gave elusive enough replies, she couldn't pin an inconsistency on him if he later decided to change his story a bit. Telling her the truth was not an option, of course. What chance would a woman who couldn't light a campfire or stake a tent properly have against Jericho's thugs?

And they'd show up sooner or later—Ben would bet his life on that. Jericho had to suspect Ben had hidden the letter somewhere near the crash site, since it wasn't in his possession after he was airlifted to the hospital in Sacramento. Of course, there was always the chance the letter had been destroyed in the wreck. But that wasn't a chance Jericho could afford to take. And once he found out Ben had returned to this area, he'd dispatch a couple of his goons to retrieve the letter and get rid of Ben. Permanently.

Unfortunately they wouldn't be the kind of fellows who'd have any scruples about eliminating anyone else who might know the contents of the letter. Which was why Ben had to be especially careful not to involve Sierra any further than absolutely necessary. No matter what the price, he would never endanger one curly hair on her gorgeous head.

So he had no choice but to lie to her instead.

"I'm a reporter," he said.

"Oh, really? What paper do you write for?"

Names of various California newspapers shuffled through his brain. Too risky. With his luck Sierra would be related to the editor or something and instantly know he was lying. "Actually I'm more of a free-lance writer. I write for whatever magazine will buy my articles."

"And you came up here to write a story about Grandpa?"

"Yes, that's right," he said quickly. "Your grandfather was quite a colorful character. I wanted to include him in an article I'm writing about modern-day prospectors."

Sierra propped her chin on her fist and studied Ben. "Must be kind of hard to take notes for an article without a tape recorder or a pencil and paper or something."

Was he imagining the suspicious glint in her eyes? Or was she truly puzzled by his lack of journalist's equipment? Whichever the case, Ben realized he'd have to watch his step around Sierra Sloane. She might be a hopeless dreamer and a charming klutz, but she was sharp as a porcupine quill.

"I wasn't planning to interview your grandfather today," he explained. "I didn't think I'd track him down so quickly. I only arrived in Grubstake last night," he added, naming the small town about ten miles away. "I decided not to lug my tape recorder up here until I was sure I could find him."

Sierra continued to scrutinize Ben as if she thought his story was full of holes. He could hardly blame her. What did a cassette recorder weigh, a couple of pounds? His excuse sounded lame even to his own ears.

It was almost a relief when the bullet whizzed through the tent.

Chapter Two

Before Sierra had time to realize what was happening, Ben tackled her. The back of her head hit the ground with a thud, and she found herself with a hundred and eighty pounds of lean, hard male sprawled on top of her.

Not an entirely unpleasant predicament, she decided. Especially when that lean, hard male wore a sexy scowl with kind of a wild gleam in his eye. "This is all so sudden," she said. "After all, we've only just met."

"Shh!" He pressed a finger across her lips. His solid chest heaved steadily against her breasts, but apparently Sierra was the only person present who found this arousing. When she squirmed beneath him, Ben pinned her even more firmly with his body and forced her to lie still.

"Was that a bullet that just came through here?" she asked.

Ben nodded briefly. His head was cocked to one side, like a wild buck alert to danger. From her new vantage point, Sierra could see a faint, puckered scar about an inch long up near his hairline. Previously it had been hidden by the dark blond strands that swept across his forehead. She wondered what other things Ben was hiding from her.

Like, why he was so jumpy, for example. "Look, this has been very enjoyable," she said, "but I'm ready to get up now. I want to go recommend a good marksmanship school to that hunter out there."

"Are you trying to get us killed?" Ben demanded in a hushed voice, his lips barely an inch from hers.

Sierra's pulse picked up speed. She swallowed. "I assure you, that's the farthest thing from my mind," she murmured, unable to tear her gaze from his dark, compelling eyes.

"Good." His breath was a heated caress against her mouth. The tantalizing scent of whiskey teased her nostrils. "Stay here," he ordered quietly, "and stay down until I get back."

Naturally she ignored him, scrambling into a sitting position the instant he pushed himself off her. "Where are you going?" she whispered.

"Now, look!" Ben turned back from the tent opening and jabbed a warning finger at her. "For once in your life, will you please take someone else's advice? Somebody out there is trying to kill us."

"Oh, pshaw."

"Damn it, Sierra—"

"Okay, okay." She held up her hands in surrender. "Go to it, Rambo. I'll play the damsel in distress, if that makes you happy."

The final look Ben fired at her was far more murderous than any possible gunman lurking outside, Sierra decided. On hands and knees, she scooted across the tent and nudged the flap ever so slightly aside so she could watch Ben.

To her surprise he seemed to have disappeared. She had to admit he was pretty good at this cloak-and-dagger stuff. She didn't believe for a minute that he was really a journalist—not unless he'd been a foreign correspondent in a war zone or something. But that didn't make sense, either. You didn't go from dodging bullets and guerrilla attacks to writing human-interest stories about quaint old prospectors.

Maybe he was a Green Beret or an antiterrorist commando. He *did* have that mysterious scar on his forehead. . . .

A sudden rustling in the brush across the clearing caught her attention. A muffled shout reached her ears, followed by the crack of a gunshot. Charlemagne brayed loudly.

"Ye gods, Char! Are you all right?" Sierra dashed out of the tent and rushed to the mule's side. Anxiously she ran her hands over his flanks to inspect him for injuries, but Charlemagne seemed to be all in one piece.

Sierra turned as Ben emerged from the trees, one arm in a choke hold around the neck of a stout, potbellied man with a walrus mustache and a wild haystack of snow white hair. His other arm held a shotgun pointed at his captive's back. "Hold it right here," Ben growled. "You're going to answer a few questions before I turn you over to the sheriff."

Sierra folded her arms. "Oh, very impressive, Mr. Halliday. You've just captured—singlehandedly!—the most-dangerous, most-wanted desperado in these here parts." She shook her head. "My, my, Sourdough Pete in person. I imagine there's quite a reward on his head. I believe he recently escaped from a senior citizens' home in Sacramento, didn't you, Pete?"

"That's right, missy." The prisoner pushed a pair of cracked spectacles up the bridge of his nose. "And I ain't goin' back, d'you hear me?"

The shotgun wavered a little in Ben's grip. "You—you know this character?" he asked.

"Sure do. Pete's an old friend of Grandpa's. His children had him declared mentally incompetent and committed him to a nursing home. But old Pete outsmarted those attendants, didn't you, Pete?"

Pete bobbed his head up and down. "O' course, none of them was *armed*," he said, turning around to give Ben an accusing look.

"Congratulations." Sierra rocked back and forth on her heels, smiling sweetly at Ben. "You've just managed to overpower an eighty-three-year-old man with a hearing aid and a heart problem."

Ben quickly unwrapped his arm from around Pete's neck and stepped back. "He *did* shoot at us," he mumbled, grinding the heel of his boot into the ground. "And he fired at me again when I jumped him."

"'Twere only bird shot, sonny!" Pete glowered indignantly at Ben while he dusted off the sleeves of his dirty red windbreaker.

"I'm sorry."

"What's that? Speak up, boy!"

"I said, I apologize! I thought you were—well, never mind. I was only trying to protect Sierra."

"Whoa, there—hold on! Don't try to blame this on me. I told you it was just some hunter with bad aim. No offense, Pete," she added hastily.

Pete's chest swelled up like a bullfrog's. "Danged gun barrel's outta whack," he said, snatching the shotgun from Ben. "That's why my shot went wild. I was aiming for a squirrel in that tree just past your tent there." He spat a brown stream of tobacco juice on the ground, narrowly missing Ben's boot.

Personally Ben thought Pete's poor shooting had more to do with the nearsighted squint behind those smudged spectacles. But he figured he'd stomped on the old man's pride enough for one day. Not that his own pride was in such great shape, either. The merry sparkle in Sierra's eyes showed how close she was to bubbling over with laughter—at Ben's expense.

Damn it, why did he so hate making a fool of himself in front of her?

Never mind. He couldn't afford to be overly concerned with her opinion of him. This scare with the shotgun had only served to remind Ben of the urgency of his task. He had to retrieve that letter without letting Sierra know what he was after. And he had to do it fast.

As far as he could see, he only had one course of action: make a play for her. Wine her and dine her. Sweep her off her feet.

Winning Sierra's heart and her trust would be the quickest, surest way to get that letter back.

Any normal, red-blooded American male would have drooled over the prospect of cozying up to such a sexy, alluring woman. But the idea left Ben cold. Cold—and disgusted with himself. He'd never deliberately taken advantage of anyone before, and the thought of cold-bloodedly seducing Sierra left a bitter taste in his mouth.

Unpalatable though it was, deceiving her was his only choice.

He forced his lips into an imitation of a smile. "Hey, how about letting me make this...misunderstanding up to you? To both of you. Let's head back into town, and I'll buy you each a big steak dinner."

Ben could see Sourdough Pete's indignation warring with his appetite. "Well," he said, scratching the three-day growth of white stubble on his cheeks, "I reckon that's the least you owe us...." His appetite won. "Sounds good to me," he announced, slapping his hands on the round paunch overhanging his belt. "How 'bout you, Sierra?"

Her suspicious gaze was riveted on Ben. "It's nearly ten miles to town," she said. "Seems kind of far to walk just for one dinner. Especially in the rain."

Ben studied the sky. "Looks like the weather's clearing up. Besides," he said, pointing at the tent, "I noticed you're kind of low on supplies. You'll need to go into town soon, anyway, to stock up." Mentally he crossed his fingers, praying that for once Sierra wouldn't argue with him simply to be ornery.

He found an unexpected ally in Sourdough Pete. "Come on, missy. I got me a hankerin' for some steak, and you could use a little more meat on your bones, too. You're too dang skinny." He winked at Ben. "In my day, when you grabbed a woman, you had somethin' to hold on to."

Sierra rolled her eyes. "Of all the chauvinistic twaddle I ever heard—oh, all right, Pete. Stop mooning at me like some poor starving refugee. Although I don't see why *I* need to come along."

"Why, to keep us menfolk in line, ain't that right, sonny?" Pete slapped Ben on the back with a blow that sent him staggering forward a step. He winced at the sudden jolt of pain that shot up his leg. "Who knows what trouble we might stumble into without a pretty little gal around to keep us on our best behavior?"

"Hmm. I don't know, Pete. My presence doesn't seem to have kept Mr. Halliday out of hot water so far." She cast Ben a saucy grin as she sauntered across the campsite. "I sure hate to take this tent down, after all the trouble it took to put back up."

Watching the sassy sway of Sierra's copper brown curls, Ben shook his head and wondered what the hell he was getting himself in for. He still hated himself for what he planned to do, but as a reluctant grin tugged at the corners of his mouth, he began to think that romancing Sierra Sloane might turn out to be...well...kind of fun.

If she hadn't been so desperate for a bath and a nap, Sierra assured herself, she would never have agreed to let Ben rent her a hotel room in Grubstake. Be Beholden To No Man had been her grandfather's motto. On the other hand, didn't Ben owe her a favor after nearly scaring her and Charlemagne half to death this morning?

That was Sierra's rather groggy reasoning, anyway, as she peered with bleary disgust at her reflection in the bureau mirror. Ugh. Sure couldn't call that nap a *beauty* sleep, she thought, trying to rub out the creases embedded in her cheek by the chenille bedspread. She'd collapsed on the bed the second the hotel-room door had slammed shut behind her.

Despite two months of trekking around the mountains, Sierra still wasn't quite in the peak condition required for a four-hour hike—even if it *was* downhill most of the way. Her thrice-weekly visits to a trendy Beverly Hills health spa apparently hadn't been enough to tone her body into a lean, mean, fighting machine. And now her cushy urban life-style was catching up with her. Muscles groaned in aching protest as she lowered herself gingerly into a tub of scalding hot water.

She closed her eyes with rapture as she slid into the steaming, piped-in, purified water. "Isn't indoor plumbing wonderful?" She sighed. "Not that I'd ever admit it to anyone. Look! Soap! Full of perfumes and artificial colors and all sorts of nasty chemicals. And I don't have to worry about polluting any pristine mountain streams." Stretching her legs, she poked her feet out of the suds and wriggled her toes in ecstasy.

After luxuriating in her bath for as long as possible, Sierra pushed herself stiffly out of the tub and grabbed a towel. A thick, plush, terry cloth towel that made her pink skin glow with pleasure as she vigorously rubbed herself dry.

Even yanking a comb through her tangled damp curls was a treat. Washing hair while camping out wasn't the easiest of chores. She rummaged through her dirt-encrusted duffel bag, tossing clothes over her shoulder to fall like autumn leaves on the floor, the bureau, the bed.

Thank goodness she'd had the foresight to keep one respectable outfit from her previous life. She inspected herself in the mirror, lips pursing in satisfaction at the flattering fit of her dark green corduroy jumper. A bit wrinkled perhaps, but otherwise presentable. The short-sleeved, yellow sweater she wore underneath added just the right jaunty touch of color.

She bent over as if to touch her toes, shaking her hair wildly, then flinging her head back. As she fluffed the springy curls with her fingertips, she couldn't help wondering how Ben Halliday would react to the sight of the new, improved Sierra Sloane.

Then she scoffed at her own reflection. She'd given up all that phony stuff, hadn't she? All the games, the concern for appearances, chewing her nails over what other people thought of her. The only person she needed to impress was herself. Not some alleged journalist who'd seen a few too many action adventure movies.

Still...

She licked her lips to give them a glossy sheen, then pinched her cheeks to flame them with color. Ben Halliday was up to something—of that she was positive. And if a little good old-fashioned flirtation would help her discover what it was, where was the harm? She could bat her long lashes and wiggle her hips as well as the next woman.

Sierra scuffed her feet into a pair of slightly battered sandals, then gave herself a smoky, half-lidded look in the mirror. "Ben Halliday," she breathed huskily, "you don't have a chance."

Flickering candlelight... dry red wine... soft music crooning in the background. The hotel dining room was the perfect setting for a romantic evening with a beautiful, desirable woman, Ben thought.

Except for the definitely *undesirable* presence of one tobacco-scented old prospector, happily devouring a ten-dollar sirloin and regaling Ben and Sierra with the tale of his escape from the nursing home.

"Then, in all the confusion I snuck outside and just walked right off. Them security folks were too busy tryin' to stop the food fight to even notice me."

Ben drummed his fingertips on the white tablecloth and slid his gaze across the table to watch Sierra watching Pete. The shimmering candle flames danced across her features, casting mysterious shadows that made her eyelashes seem even longer and thicker, highlighting the smooth arch of her cheekbones and the sleek hollows of her face. In the dim candlelight, her skin took on a rich golden hue, and her dark hair glinted with hints of copper. The wine in her glass swirled and sparkled as if she clutched a fistful of rubies. When she lowered the glass, her lips glistened with moisture. Almost in a trance, Ben ran his tongue over his lips.

And it wasn't Sierra's wine he imagined tasting.

He'd hardly recognized her when she'd bounced down the staircase into the hotel lobby an hour ago. As she sashayed toward Ben, his admiring glance had traveled from her coy smile to the soft swell of her breasts to the slender curve of her waist. Her jumper clung enticingly to her hips before draping around the best pair of legs he'd ever seen.

Gone was the hoydenish, jeans-clad tomboy, replaced by a *very* feminine, *very* alluring woman. Still as fresh faced and impudent as ever, but with an overlay of sophistication and confident self-possession Ben hadn't noticed before.

His intense fascination with this previously unsuspected aspect of Sierra's personality surprised and alarmed Ben. After all, he was supposed to play the seducer, not the seducee in this little melodrama. *He* was supposed to set *Sierra's* pulse racing and palms sweating, not vice versa.

That was the plan, anyway. The plan did *not* include long walks on the beach or nights before a blazing fire or houses with white picket fences. Ben didn't have time to waste daydreaming about an impossible future.

Let's get this show on the road, he scolded himself.

Beneath the table he slowly inched his boot toward Sierra until he encountered resistance. He deliberately nudged her foot, not enough to dislodge it, but enough so that his meaning would be unmistakable.

Oh, she was a cool one! Her rapt attention to Pete's story never faltered, at least not on the surface. As Ben stroked his toe back and forth across the arch of her sandaled foot, an outside observer would never guess what was happening under the table. Ben bolted his glance to Sierra's face, willing her to turn from Pete and meet his eyes so he could send her visual confirmation of his message.

She propped her chin in her hand, otherwise appearing to ignore Ben. But he was getting to her, no question about it. A tiny vein fluttered in her temple, and he was almost certain her breath had quickened. Ben focused every volt of his mental energy on transmitting over and over again a very succinct, very explicit telepathic suggestion.

Good. He could almost swear a rosy flush was spreading up Sierra's neck and flooding her cheeks. He edged his other boot forward and imprisoned her foot between his.

Now the corner of her mouth curled upward in the beginning of a smile. "How on earth did you manage to start a food fight in the nursing-home cafeteria?" she asked Pete. A cool customer, all right. Ben could barely detect the slight quaver in her voice.

Relishing the memory of her well-shaped, slim calves, he slid his boot languidly up past her trim ankle.

"Piece of cake," Pete replied around a mouthful of baked potato.

"That easy, huh?"

"No, I mean that's how I started the food fight. See, we was having pineapple upside-down cake for dessert that day, and—" With a clatter, Pete dropped his knife and fork onto his plate. "Say, what in tarnation is movin' around down there, anyhow?" He shoved back his chair and peered beneath the table.

Hastily Ben yanked his feet back.

"I coulda swore I felt something nosin' around down there," Pete said with a puzzled frown. "It was startin' to crawl right up my leg, in fact. Didn't you feel it?" he demanded of Ben.

Ben drained his wineglass and shrugged. "Not me, Pete." He picked up his silverware and attacked his steak, feigning sudden hunger.

"How 'bout you, Sierra? Didn't you feel it? I wonder if this here hotel don't have rats or somethin'."

"Gee, Pete, I didn't notice anything. Maybe it was a stray cat. Must have taken quite a liking to you." Sierra tore a dinner roll in half and buttered it. "Of course, I suppose it *could* have been a rat of some kind." Her voice vibrated with mirth. Ben sensed her mocking scrutiny as he popped a forkful of steak into his mouth and tried to chew innocently. Why was it that now, when he longed to be inconspicuous, Sierra shone her attention at him like a spotlight?

It was just like her to act so contrary.

"Hey, I've got a super idea," she said, snapping her fingers. "Why don't you interview Pete for your article?"

Ben lifted the wine carafe and refilled their glasses, grateful for the abrupt change of subject. "My article?"

"You know. Your magazine article," Sierra replied, bestowing the word "magazine" with a sly emphasis that gave Ben the eerie impression she could see right through his journalist's charade.

"Oh, *that* article. Sure, I could do that. I guess." The last thing Ben wanted was to squander precious time with Pete while he should be concentrating on Sierra.

She bit into the buttered roll and chewed thoughtfully. "I mean, it seems a shame for you to go back empty-handed. Pete's been prospecting these mountains nearly as long as Grandpa did. I'm sure he could provide you with plenty of colorful anecdotes."

"I'm sure he could." With a sinking feeling, Ben absorbed Sierra's satisfied smirk and the eager expression on Pete's face. He was trapped. No way was he going to avoid "interviewing" Sourdough Pete for his nonexistent article.

He spent the rest of the meal with his boots firmly planted under his own chair, chewing mechanically while he tried to think up a way to get Sierra alone after dinner.

Surprisingly help came from an unexpected quarter. As the waitress was clearing away their dessert plates, Pete stretched his arms above his head and yawned loudly. "Mmm-*mmm*, that was mighty tasty apple pie. I'm kinda tuckered out, though. Guess I'll go get me some shut-eye." As he tugged off the napkin tucked into his shirtfront, he gave Ben a broad wink.

Good grief, the old-timer was trying to play matchmaker! Ben instantly felt ashamed for not giving Pete enough credit. The old man's courting days might be long past, but he obviously hadn't forgotten what it was like to have a chaperon hanging around.

The poor guy was probably desperate for company. Shut away in an institution by his own relatives, wandering these lonely mountains in a vain search for gold and glory...no wonder he'd seemed so eager for an evening of companionship.

Ben cleared his throat. "Say, Pete, you don't have to leave right this minute, do you? I thought we'd have some brandy with our coffee."

As he rose creakily to his feet, Pete dismissed Ben's suggestion with a wave of his hand. "Naw, it's way past my bedtime, sonny. Besides—" he bent low near Ben's ear and spoke in a loud whisper "—three's a crowd." Then he slapped Ben on the shoulder and sauntered out of the dining room, drawing curious stares from the tourists clustered around other tables.

Ben had half risen when Pete left, and as he settled back into his chair, he shook his head. "Quite a character," he said to Sierra. Then another thought occurred to him. "Say, where's he going to sleep, anyway? He turned down my offer to get him a hotel room, and he doesn't exactly look like he can afford one."

"Save your money," Sierra said, tasting the coffee the waitress had placed in front of her. "Pete hates sleeping indoors. He told me that was the worst part about being in the nursing home. He likes to be able to look up and see the stars when he wakes up at night."

"Then where's he going to—"

"I expect he'll unroll his sleeping bag out back of the hotel and bed down right next to Charlemagne." She smiled distantly, as if recalling some scene Ben wasn't privy to. "Those two are kind of fond of each other."

"You've known Pete a long time, I take it." Ben sipped his own coffee, relaxing for the first time that evening.

"Oh, sure. He and Grandpa go way back, so he was always around when I'd come to visit."

"And where did you come to visit your grandfather *from*?"

She ducked her eyes, studying her coffee for a moment before replying. "Los Angeles."

"Does your family still live there?"

"Uh-huh."

Sierra had turned strangely silent, not at all like her usual loquacious self.

"Brothers and sisters?" Ben prodded.

"Nope."

"And what did you do for a living before you started panning for gold?"

She glanced at him sharply, as if suspecting him of poking fun at her. Then she shrugged, tracing the rim of her cup with one finger. "I worked for a large corporation. I guess you'd call me a junior executive type. You know—staff meetings, profit-and-loss charts, power lunches—the whole rat race."

Ben set his cup down with a noisy clunk. "You?" he asked incredulously. "*You* were a corporate executive?"

Her old defensiveness returned. "Why is that so surprising?" she asked. "Don't you think women are capable of making it in the business world?"

Ben held his hands up in protest. "Hey, I never said that. It's only that . . ." I can't quite picture *you* making it in the business world, he thought, leaving the rest of his sentence unspoken. He didn't want to make Sierra any madder at him. "Somehow I can't picture you sitting in an office all day," he finished instead. "You seem more the outdoor type." A blatant lie. He was willing to bet Sierra had never camped out in her life before embarking on this crazy adventure of hers.

But his response seemed to mollify her. "Yes, well, I couldn't picture myself working in an office for the rest of my life, either. Then, when Grandpa died..." She paused for a moment and gave a quick little sigh before continuing. "It made me examine my own life, question the choices I'd made. Somewhere along the way I think I'd sort of lost sight of the person I was meant to be."

"And who *is* that person?" Ben asked gently, surprising himself with the sincerity of his own question.

"Sometimes I think—and then other times, I—" She broke off with a trickle of laughter. "Maybe I'm not sure of the answer myself," she admitted with a sheepish grin. "But in his will Grandpa left me everything he owned. It wasn't much, I guess. Except for Charlemagne, of course."

"Of course."

"But somehow it meant more to me than all the stocks and bonds and money-market accounts in the world. Because it was everything he had. And he left it all to me. Even though in recent years I neglected him."

"Neglected him how?"

"Oh, you know. After I got to be a teenager, the idea of hanging out with my grandpa didn't seem 'cool.' I had better ways to spend my summer vacations. And then college came along, and then my job...well. You get the picture."

She plucked absently at a thread in the tablecloth. Ben covered her hand with his. "Sierra."

She looked up, startled.

"Your grandfather knew how much you loved him."

Her eyes misted with tears. She looked away, across the room. "I hope so," she said in a soft, shaky voice. "Oh, boy, I sure hope so."

Now Ben thought he understood what had brought this city girl to these rugged mountains. She wasn't searching for gold; she was searching for a way to make up for the past.

Ben squeezed her fingers. "Come on. Let's go for a walk."

She threw him a wobbly smile. "I'd like that."

Outside, the night was balmy, but the faint scent of burning leaves infused the air with the unmistakable snap of autumn. Summer hung on stubbornly, reluctant to surrender its grip on the season.

Somehow Ben hadn't got around to releasing Sierra's hand, and they strolled slowly toward the edge of town, fingers intertwined. Sierra's nerves were humming pleasantly, as if Ben's touch were sending a low-grade electric current singing through her body. Her skin tingled with anticipation. She had a hunch that something exciting was going to happen before this evening was over.

She'd been aware of Ben's impatience during dinner. With secret delight she'd sensed how eager he was to get her alone. Well, that fitted right in with her own plans. Ben had lied to her about his reason for seeking out her grandfather—of that she was certain. So she would be completely justified in using all of her feminine wiles to coax the truth out of him, wouldn't she?

A delicious shiver ran through her at the prospect.

"Chilly?" Ben asked, sliding his arm around her shoulders and drawing her closer.

She snuggled next to him. "No, I'm not cold," she replied a little breathlessly. "It's pretty warm out tonight, isn't it?"

"Warm for late September, that's true. But real fall weather is just around the corner." As they passed through an amber circle of light cast by a street lamp, Sierra could see the concern written in his face. "What will you do when the weather turns cold?"

"Wear warmer clothes, of course."

"What about when it snows?"

"Probably build a snowman."

He squeezed her arm. "Come on, Sierra. You're a city girl from sunny southern California. Surely you don't intend to camp out all winter, do you?"

"My grandfather—"

"I know, I know. Your grandfather did it, and so will you." In the darkness she heard Ben sigh. "Don't take this the wrong way, but are you sure you know what you're doing? Do you have any idea how harsh the winters can be up in these mountains?"

"You sound like you're speaking from personal experience," Sierra said lightly, trying to sidetrack him before they got into another argument. Fighting about her plans for the winter was definitely *not* on tonight's agenda.

"My parents were from Grass Valley, about an hour's drive north of here."

"Is that where you grew up?"

Ben shook his head. "My folks moved to Los Angeles when I was a baby."

"Is that where you live now?"

He hesitated. "That's right."

"What about your parents?"

Ben was silent for so long, Sierra began to wonder if he'd heard her question. Finally he said, "My father died when I was six. Ma passed away early this spring. She'd moved back to Grass Valley a few months before her death."

She turned abruptly, stepping in front of him and placing her hand against his chest. "Oh, Ben, I'm so sorry."

He covered her hand with his; she could feel his heartbeat thumping beneath his shirt. "I guess we've both lost someone we loved recently," he said in a gruff voice.

"Yes." Sierra drew back, and they continued walking. She'd only meant to change the course of the conversation, not put a damper on it. Casting about for a cheerier subject, she pointed to a ramshackle false-fronted building across the street. "That used to be the newspaper office back in the gold-rush days. And see that brick foundation over there? That's all that's left of the old jail."

"You seem to know this town pretty well."

"Oh, I spent lots of time in Grubstake when Grandpa still owned the hotel."

Ben stopped dead in his tracks. "Your grandfather owned the hotel?" His forehead was furrowed in amazement.

"The very one we're staying in."

"But I thought he was—I mean, didn't he always—"

"He didn't start mining until I was about ten. My mother used to help him run the hotel, and then after she got married and moved away, he had a hard time managing without her. I think maybe he sort of lost the heart for it, too. He missed my mother a lot."

"Is your father from around here, too?"

"No. He and Mom met when he was a guest at the hotel. I gather it was quite a whirlwind courtship, and then as soon as they were married, he dragged her off to Los Angeles."

Ben chuckled. "I presume your mother didn't look at it quite that way."

"Well, maybe not. But I know she never got over being homesick for these mountains. That's why she named me Sierra."

"Lucky for you she didn't grow up in the Adirondacks."

She giggled. "Or the Alps."

"Or the Ozarks."

"Or the Himalayas."

"I don't know—Himalaya Sloane." Ben tapped his chin thoughtfully. "Has kind of a nice ring to it, don't you think?"

"You must be tone-deaf."

They had reached the end of town. Sierra led Ben through a small wooded park, steering them past redwood trees and picnic tables, into a clearing where a deserted bandstand loomed against the dark horizon.

"Race you!" she called, dropping his hand and sprinting off.

"Why, you—"

The words drifted to Sierra from far behind. Then she heard the thud of Ben's footsteps, increasing in volume as he chased after her. Her hair flew back over her shoulders; she tossed her head and laughed with exhilaration. Adrenaline pumped through her bloodstream, and she ran faster, but Ben caught up with her just before she reached the bandstand. She heard his steady panting, the rustle of denim, the crackle of leaves and twigs—all growing closer until she felt the heat radiating from his body and smelled the arousing masculine fragrance of sweat and soap.

Then Ben's arms captured her from behind—strong, muscled arms that pulled her back against his heaving chest. Sierra tried to wrestle herself from his grasp, and as his laughter blended with hers, his straight white teeth flashed in the moonlight. Golden strands shimmered in his hair, while his eyes were hidden in shadow. His labored breathing was warm against her cheeks, the scent of wine adding to her sense of intoxication.

"No fair!" she cried. "You cheated!"

"*Me?* You're the one who had the head start!" Slowly Ben's indignant grin faded, replaced by an expression of such sober intensity that Sierra wondered what was wrong.

Then he raised his hand to cradle the side of her face and bring her mouth closer to his. His lips feathered across hers, light as a moonbeam, stirring to life something wild and free inside her. As the deepening heat of their kiss melted his restraint, Ben's mouth grew more ardent, more insistent. When at last he claimed her lips with total, reckless passion, Sierra wrapped her arms around his neck and hung on for dear life as a sudden flood of rapture engulfed her.

Her last coherent thought was that her plan was going remarkably well.

Chapter Three

Ben had nearly forgotten what it felt like to kiss a woman, to hold her in his arms and smell her hair and taste her mouth. First he'd been completely focused on his recovery from the crash. Then his determination to even the score with Quentin Jericho had pushed his interest in women onto the back burner. It seemed like years since the last time he'd allowed himself to revel in such sensual pleasures.

But if his memory served correctly, never before had a simple kiss stirred such deep, intense longing inside him.

He dragged his mouth from Sierra's lips and sought the lush, soft curve of her neck. Her hair brushed against his face, and he inhaled deeply of its floral fragrance. His lips found the pulse beat in her throat, and as he nuzzled her with lazy enjoyment, he felt the vibrations of her satisfaction purring through the slender column of her neck.

When he claimed her mouth again, her lips opened eagerly to admit his exploring tongue. She tasted like apples and sugar, as soft and textured as velvet. Her tongue curled languidly around his, and as she snuggled closer to him, the hardened peaks of her breasts pressed against his chest, arousing him with another unexpected surge of desire.

Something stone-hard and frozen inside Ben began to thaw. The emotional leash with which he'd restrained himself for so long loosened slightly, releasing a raging hunger. Not only hunger for the physical delights of Sierra's body, but also a craving for something he couldn't quite identify—some deeper satisfaction that had eluded him in all his previous encounters with women.

Drawing back for a much-needed breath, he studied her kiss-swollen lips...the way starlight glittered in her burnished curls. Her heavy-lidded eyes gave her a sultry, come-hither expression that made her even more desirable.

"God, you look beautiful in the moonlight," he said in a gravelly voice. Sierra's dark eyes flared, glinting like obsidian. "And everywhere else, for that matter...." Ben's last words were swallowed up as their lips reunited in another searing, hungry kiss.

Ben was sliding his hands along the sides of her breasts before he fully realized what he was doing. Through his passion-fogged senses, he noted Sierra was offering no protests, no resistance to his increasingly bold caresses. In fact she seemed as eager to continue this reckless insanity as he was.

Which was why he stopped.

Tiny lines of puzzlement gathered at the juncture of Sierra's brows. Her lips glistened with the moisture of his kiss, unsettling Ben even further.

It wasn't her smoldering gaze or her bruised-looking lips or her seductive, womanly curves that got to him. It was her basic sweetness, her charming klutziness, her innocent abandon. It was that faint dusting of freckles across her upturned nose, damn it!

How could he deliberately seduce this adorable, enchanting, and all-too-willing victim?

It was too easy. Like taking candy from a baby. Ben would never be able to live with himself if he cold-bloodedly manipulated her to get the information he needed.

On the other hand, maybe he was kidding himself. There'd been nothing cold-blooded about their embrace. In fact Ben's blood had pulsed hot through his veins during their kisses. The last thing on his mind in those wonderful, all-too-brief moments had been the letter he had to retrieve.

So why did he feel like such a cad?

Maybe it had something to do with the confused, slightly hurt look on Sierra's face.

"I'm sorry," Ben said, holding her by the shoulders at arm's length, exerting every scrap of his willpower not to bundle her back into his arms again. "I got a little carried away." He chucked her tenderly under the chin. "You're an awfully sexy lady, you know. And almost impossible to resist. Forgive me?"

The hurt and confusion smoothed from her face, to be replaced by a thoughtful, almost assessing expression. "Sure." She shrugged. "Nothing to forgive." She stepped back and jammed her hands into the pockets of her jumper. "You didn't exactly hear me screaming for the sheriff, did you?"

"No, but still..." Not for the first time in their short acquaintance, Ben wished he could peer behind those big brown eyes and see the wheels turning around in that logic-defying brain of hers. She had a way of studying him that made Ben restless and fidgety, as if she were measuring him against some standard by which he was doomed to fail.

He wasn't used to unfavorable comparisons. He'd been a straight-A student in high school, on the Dean's List at Stanford, then a rising corporate wunderkind with a seemingly limitless future.

He'd been Quentin Jericho's protégé, his right-hand man, his fair-haired boy. Until he'd discovered the evil secret in Jericho's past. The secret that had sent Ben's father to his death and ruined his mother's life.

The secret that Ben had sworn by his parents' memory to avenge.

But first he had to find the letter he'd entrusted to Caleb Murphy after Jericho had engineered his plane crash. The letter spelled out the secret in Jericho's own handwriting. Exposing its contents to the public would destroy Jericho's reputation, his political influence, his corporate empire.

Which was how Ben found himself in this incredibly awkward situation with Murphy's granddaughter.

"It's probably a bad idea, anyway," Sierra said.

"What?" For one confused, alarmed instant Ben thought she'd been reading his mind.

"For us to get involved with each other, I mean."

"What makes you say that?"

She propped her hands on her waist. "What about your journalistic integrity? Your objectivity? I'd hate to be accused of undermining the cornerstone of democracy by subverting the American free press."

"Sierra, what the hell are you talking about?"

She threw up her hands in exasperation. "Your article, remember? You might be tempted to give my late grandfather's story special treatment if you and I became . . . close."

"I hardly think one slanted fluff piece on modern-day gold miners will threaten the foundations of freedom."

"Oh, so you *don't* think it's a bad idea for us to get involved?"

"No. Yes! I—it's not that simple." Ben rubbed the back of his neck and paced to and fro, staring unseeing at the ground.

Sierra sauntered to the bandstand with an outward calm she was far from feeling. Her knees felt wobbly as she sat on the edge of the concrete platform and swung her legs back and forth while she studied Ben.

Though she'd rather endure unspeakable torture than confess it, Ben's kiss had unnerved her far more than she cared to admit. Well, not his kiss, really, but the disturbing surge of desire it had sent cascading through her. Now that the heavenly sensations rippling through her body had receded, Ben's kiss had left Sierra a bit shaky, with a faintly seasick feeling in her stomach—like a hangover after a bottle of champagne.

She was used to being in control of her life and her emotions. With the previous men in her life, she'd always had the upper hand somehow. They'd been perfectly nice men, with perfectly nice careers and perfectly nice manners. They'd sent her flowers and candy, and one had even hired a violinist to serenade her outside her window one night.

They'd made all the right moves, yet something had been missing—some crucial element that could turn her giddy and breathless and make her forget caution and propriety and all the other restraints that had gone rushing from her head the instant Ben Halliday's lips had captured hers.

This roller-coaster, out-of-control feeling was new to her. And she wasn't sure if she liked it. Despite what her father would have called her "impetuous impulses," Sierra had never allowed the whims of fate to rule her existence. Even her decision to throw away her career to follow in her grandfather's footsteps had been entirely logical—from Sierra's point of view, anyway.

But for one insane, passion-crazed moment tonight, she'd been ready to throw caution to the wind and recklessly follow wherever Ben led her. Thank goodness at least one of them had had the good sense to slam on the brakes!

Why, then, did she feel like cursing whatever had stopped Ben instead of feeling grateful?

Under cover of darkness she secretly studied his profile, admiring the craggy angles and solid lines visible in the dim light from the moon. A swatch of hair swept across his forehead above the rugged outline of his features. As he continued his pacing, his wide shoulders and solid chest seemed to displace the night air like the prow of a mighty ship cresting through the ocean. Sierra's glance lingered on his narrow hips, then strayed down his long, muscled legs. At once she saw something she hadn't noticed before.

"Hey, you're limping!" she exclaimed.

Ben halted in his tracks. He looked up at Sierra, then down at his left leg as if he, too, had been unaware of the slight dragging motion. "Oh, that."

"You must have sprained your ankle earlier, while I was outracing you to the bandstand."

His teeth flashed white as he smiled. "No, that's not it. Although I'm sure that didn't help."

As he hobbled toward her, Sierra frowned with concern. "How did you hurt your ankle, then?"

She felt the bunched muscles in his shoulders as he transferred his weight to his arms and lowered himself next to her. A slight hiss as he released his breath was the only clue that the movement had cost him pain.

"Old war injury," he said.

Sierra regarded him skeptically. "*What* war?" she asked. "Or were you drafted in the eighth grade, perhaps?"

Ben chuckled. "That's what I like about you," he said. "Well, *one* of the things I like about you. You make me laugh." Then he paused, and Sierra could almost feel something bleak and bitter settle over him. "I haven't laughed a whole lot lately," he said finally in a distant, musing voice.

"Why not?" she asked softly.

Ben shrugged. "My mother's death hit me pretty hard, even though I knew she was dying. Then right after her funeral, I was in a plane crash."

"A plane crash?" Sierra's voice rose to an astonished squeak. "My God, what happened?"

Ben jerked away slightly, as if he'd caught himself saying too much. "It was nothing. I mean, the plane I was flying had mechanical problems. I was the only one on board."

"So that's how you hurt your ankle?"

He shrugged again. "Not my ankle. More like my entire leg."

"Is that where this came from?" Without thinking, Sierra lifted her hand to Ben's forehead to touch the scar that was invisible in the darkness. Startled, Ben met her gaze. As her fingers brushed against the faint ridge of flesh, his eyes flickered with some mysterious emotion that made her shiver. For an instant they were connected by more than physical contact, as if their souls had reached out and found each other. But the brief encounter was too intense, too revealing. As they both instinctively withdrew, the moment passed.

Sierra pulled back her hand as if scalded.

Ben swallowed. "Yes," he replied in a thick voice, "that's where the scar came from, too."

"Guess I'm not too observant. I—I didn't notice your limp before."

"It comes and goes. Some days I hardly notice the discomfort, while others . . ."

"Your leg must have been pretty badly injured if it still bothers you after all this time."

He made a dismissive motion with his hand. "It could have been worse. At least I'm alive to complain about it."

"I haven't heard you complaining. Did you find out what caused the mechanical problems with your plane?"

"No." He said the word quickly, then pushed himself to his feet. "The plane was almost completely destroyed in the crash. There weren't many clues left to piece together. Come on, I'd better get you back to the hotel." He held out his hand to help Sierra to the ground, releasing her as soon as she was on her feet.

As they walked back to the hotel, a prudent three feet apart, Sierra was more convinced than ever that Ben was lying to her. His answers to some of her questions had been evasive, and he'd been entirely too anxious to change the subject when she'd asked him about the plane crash.

Maybe she was being overly suspicious. After all, nearly losing your life was a pretty traumatic experience. Was it any wonder he didn't care to dwell on the matter?

But what about his flimsy claim to be a journalist? Some sixth sense told Sierra that Ben's real reason—whatever it was—for seeking out her grandfather was somehow connected with the crash.

She stole a sidelong glance at Ben's face as they passed beneath a street lamp. As they stepped off the curb, he winced, and a crazy protective instinct flooded her. Something very bad had happened to Ben Halliday—something besides his mother's death and his own brush with mortality.

The knowledge sent a pang of distress through Sierra. She hated the idea of Ben's suffering any harm or sorrow, and the realization startled her. She'd only just met the man, for heaven's sake. So why should his happiness and well-being suddenly be so important to her?

Nevertheless, her concern for him was a fact Sierra couldn't deny. Ben would never admit he needed help from her or anyone else, of course. He was like Sierra herself in that regard. But why else would he be hanging around, plying her with food and wine and maneuvering to get her alone if he didn't want something from her?

And tonight, when he could easily have taken advantage of her rapturous daze, Ben had proven that he was after more than the obvious quarry.

Being needed was a rather new sensation for Sierra. Her life had been filled with competent, powerful, self-sufficient people who might love or respect her, but didn't exactly *need* her.

Her grandfather had been the exception. But she hadn't realized until it was too late how much the old man had missed her, how important her visits had been to him.

She'd let her grandfather down. But she'd be damned if she'd let down Ben Halliday.

Which made her more determined than ever to pry the truth out of him.

Ben sprawled in a tangle of bed sheets, hands locked behind his head, counting the knotholes in the beamed ceiling and trying to shake off the melancholy that clung to him like fog.

It was the green vase that had started it all. The tall, cut-glass vase on the hotel bureau, brimming with yellow and red chrysanthemums, glinting like emeralds in the sunshine that streamed through the window, had captured Ben's attention the instant he'd opened his eyes this morning.

His mother had owned a green vase exactly like it.

And seeing that identical vase first thing upon awakening had brought it all back to Ben: his mother's final illness... the moment she'd reached for his hand just before drawing her last breath... the shock of stopping by her home just before the funeral and finding the place ransacked.

The green vase had been shattered to smithereens. Everything in his mother's house had been flung open, torn apart, dashed to pieces. Or so it had seemed to Ben's stunned, horrified eyes. He'd known that in the city, burglars often scanned the obituaries, breaking into a home while the grief-stricken family was at the funeral. But here in peaceful, small-town Grass Valley? And what kind of burglar would wreak such systematic destruction without actually taking anything?

His mother's jewelry and silver were scattered on the floor, but hadn't been stolen. It didn't make sense—until Ben knelt to the floor to pick up the wooden clock that had always rested beside his mother's bed.

How many times near the end had she begged Ben to keep the clock after her death? "Always keep it running, so its ticking will remind you of me, even when I'm gone," she'd urged him time and again.

As he picked up the clock, its face cracked, a corner chipped off, Ben noticed it had stopped. Through his grief and bewilderment, his mother's plea echoed in his ears.

Maybe the clock wasn't broken; maybe the batteries had only run down. With shaking fingers Ben pried off the back of the clock.

And found the letter.

He'd understood so much after reading it, like why his mother had made such a big deal about the clock, knowing Ben would eventually have to change the batteries and would find the folded-up letter. He understood that Quentin Jericho's men must have ransacked the house, and why Jericho was so anxious to find and destroy the letter. And he understood at last the air of sorrow that had surrounded his mother as far back as he could remember.

Ben had assumed she'd never got over his father's death, and that was true in a way. But her unhappiness had another source: the secret she'd kept all those years, the secret revealed in the letter, the secret that—in death—she'd finally entrusted to Ben.

With mounting horror Ben had stood in his mother's bedroom and realized how long and how much she'd endured for his sake. It didn't take a genius to figure out that Jericho had purchased Margaret Halliday's silence with her son's future.

Jericho's outward generosity toward the family of his former business partner had been nothing more than a bribe to keep the ugly truth hidden. Jericho had paid for Ben's education, sent him on summer vacations to Europe, launched him on a promising career—all in exchange for Margaret Halliday's silence.

What kind of pain had it cost her, seeing Ben's gratitude and affection for the man who had destroyed his father? How much did she suffer every time she heard Ben refer to "Uncle Quent"?

Even now, months after his mother's death, the guilt still pierced Ben like a knife in the gut.

He had to make it up to her. He had to avenge his father's death by using that letter to destroy Jericho. He'd sworn it on his mother's grave the day of her funeral.

Memories of that horrible day swarmed around Ben's head like a flock of vultures. Right after finding the letter, he'd stormed to the funeral service and practically dragged Jericho outside the church to confront him. Having seen the damning evidence with his own eyes, Ben was still hoping against hope that Uncle Quent could produce a perfectly logical explanation for the whole thing, that he would somehow show Ben how this sordid revelation from the past wasn't what it appeared to be.

Instead Jericho's eyes had flared with shock when Ben informed him what he'd just discovered. His florid face had drained of color seconds before a hooded, sly expression crept across it, telling Ben everything he hadn't wanted to know.

In retrospect, of course, Ben had blown it by losing his cool. If he hadn't rushed to confront Jericho in a blur of pain and outrage, Jericho wouldn't have left the funeral, ostensibly to avoid any further scene with Ben. Jericho wouldn't have had a reason to sabotage the plane that Ben took off in immediately after the funeral. And the letter would have made it safely from Grass Valley to the news media in Los Angeles, instead of turning into some kind of time bomb, hidden God knows where, posing a threat not only to Ben, but also to Sierra now.

Ben's rash actions had nearly cost him his life, and might very well have cost him his only chance to avenge his parents. He wasn't about to make the same mistake again.

He pulled the pillow over his head, trying to bury the guilt, the grief, the anger. He needed cool, logical reasoning to succeed. He'd have to shove his emotions aside and sort them out later when all this was over. Better focus on something else, he decided.

Like how soft and sexy Sierra had felt last night, wrapped in his arms, returning his kiss with a fiery passion that made his loins throb to remember.

With a groan Ben rolled over onto his stomach and tugged the pillow even tighter over his head. But he couldn't smother the memories that tormented him, arousing his body and twisting his heart. In front of his squinched-shut eyes, he kept seeing Sierra's face—those limpid, trusting eyes, that spatter of freckles across her pert nose, her mischievous, alluring smile. How could he even consider seducing her to get that letter back?

How could he avoid it?

Did he even *want* to avoid it?

Now that he'd touched her, kissed her, Ben found himself craving more...much more. His hands clenched reflexively as he relived the brief moment when he'd cradled the provocative swell of her soft breasts—right before his self-loathing had forced him to stop. Was he any better than Quentin Jericho, using people, taking advantage of their weaknesses to further his own selfish aims?

Cursing under his breath, Ben flung the pillow across the room and peeled himself out of bed all in one fluid movement. If only his feelings for Sierra were that simple. Unfortunately his desire for her sprang from a far more complicated source than his quest for revenge. He admired her spunk, even if she wasn't exactly a wilderness-survival expert. He relished her tart wit, even though she frequently aimed it at him.

And he was touched by the vulnerable side that she tried to conceal behind her stubbornness and self-assured bravado.

But he couldn't afford to be detoured by such distractions. He had to learn to ignore them, the way he'd learned to ignore pain. Ben tested his leg gingerly as he hobbled to the shower. What the hell had possessed him to chase after Sierra last night and risk reinjuring his leg?

"Don't answer that," he warned himself in a sleep-rusted voice. Thank God his leg seemed better this morning. No more romping around like some high-school kid chock-full of hormones. The seduction of Sierra Sloane would proceed in an orderly, *adult* manner, with emotions tightly harnessed and Ben's underlying goal firmly planted in his brain at all times.

As he lathered his chest under the stinging, hot needles of water, Ben began to feel more like his old self. Was it any wonder he'd been so overwhelmingly attracted to Sierra? After all those months of rehabilitation and therapy, when his only physical craving had been to escape from the pain, his first encounter with a pretty woman was bound to be rather intense. All that sexual energy, all those urges bottled up for so long—no wonder he'd been swamped by a tidal wave of lust when the dam finally broke.

Thus reassured that Sierra wasn't *really* some kind of sorceress, Ben rolled up the cuffs of a fresh blue chambray shirt, snapped his watchband around his wrist and stepped into the corridor, pulling the door shut behind him. Whistling softly, he strode past several rooms and rapped smartly on Sierra's door.

He ran his fingers through his still-damp hair as he waited. No answer. He knocked again, then tried the doorknob. Locked. He pressed his ear to the door, listening for the rush of the shower, but all was quiet. Either Sierra was a very sound sleeper or she'd beaten him downstairs this morning.

Sourdough Pete was spread-eagled in front of the fireplace when Ben entered the lobby. Behind the front desk Addie Winslow, the hotel proprietress, was frowning.

"Tilt it a little to the left, Pete. No, no—the left! That's it. Hmm." She poked on the glasses hanging by a gold chain around her neck and studied the framed landscape critically.

Pete's cheeks turned a boiled lobster color as he strained to hold the large painting in place over the mantel.

"I just don't know. Try moving it a little to the right." She pulled off her glasses and said, "I can't tell. What do *you* think, Mr. Halliday?"

"I think I'd better give Pete a hand before he hurts himself," Ben said, stepping quickly to the fireplace and relieving poor Pete of his burden.

"Oh, my word, I didn't realize...Pete, I'm so sorry." Addie bustled around the desk and took Pete by the elbow, helping him into a chair. "Can I get you anything? A glass of water?"

"Naw, I'll be all right, soon's I catch my breath."

Ben suspected the old prospector was rather enjoying all the solicitous attention from the widow Winslow.

"Now that you mention it, I guess some water might be nice," Pete croaked in a weak voice. He winked at Ben as Addie hurried off, patting her tidy bun of gray hair and tsk-tsking her way out of the lobby. "Mighty fine figure of a woman," Pete said, shaking his head with admiration after Addie's plump, disappearing form.

Ben chuckled. "You old rascal."

"That's what women like, sonny—rascals." He shook a crooked forefinger at Ben. "You'd best remember that advice, if you hope to get anywhere with young Sierra."

"What about Sierra?" Addie's eyes were bright with interest as she returned with Pete's glass of water.

Ben sighed inwardly. The last thing he wanted was a public discussion of his love life. "I'll hang this painting for you, Addie," he said quickly, "if you've got a hammer and nail."

But Addie was not so easily sidetracked. "I've got them right here," she said, reaching behind the desk and handing Ben the tools. "Sierra sure grew up to be a pretty young thing, didn't she?"

"Mmm, very nice," Ben mumbled noncommittally around the nail held between his teeth. He positioned the painting once more.

"She was always such a lively one. I remember how she used to hang around here when her Grandpa Caleb still owned this hotel. Why, one night when all the guests were asleep, she set little paper cups of water over every square inch of the upstairs hallway so that folks couldn't get out of their rooms in the morning without squishing them."

"I'll bet *that* was good for business," Ben muttered.

"Then another time she rigged all the window shades so that when you pulled them down—"

The rest of her fond reminiscence was drowned out by the pounding of Ben's hammer. "How's that?" he asked.

Addie cocked her head from side to side. "Perfect," she announced. "Thank you ever so much, Mr. Halliday." But her matchmaking was merciless. "I've often said, what Sierra needs is a nice, stable young man—someone who'll steady her down a bit without putting a damper on those high spirits of hers."

Personally what Ben often thought Sierra needed was a keeper.

"Of course, she's got to be careful who she gets involved with, considering who her father is. A girl in her position has to watch out for—oh, what's that word, Pete? Not gold diggers . . ."

"Her father?" Ben asked.

"Gigolos," Pete supplied.

"Yes, that's it, gigolos."

"Who *is* Sierra's father?" Ben repeated.

"As I said, a girl like Sierra—her father?" Addie's forehead wrinkled in surprise. "Why, Maxwell Sloane, of course. Yes sirree, with all that money—"

"Sierra's father is Maxwell Sloane?" A cold prickle like the stab of a thousand sharp icicles crept up the back of Ben's neck. "*The* Maxwell Sloane? Founder of Sloane Enterprises? The man they call *Midas* Sloane, whose touch turns any business venture to gold?"

"Why, yes, that's right. So you can see why that young lady has to be mighty careful about who she gets tangled up with, but I know that when the right young man comes along . . ."

Ben didn't hear the rest of Addie's prediction. His mind was reeling with the implications of what he'd just learned. The knowledge had hit him like a two-by-four right between the eyes, leaving him dazed.

The unpleasant truth was that if he succeeded in making Sierra fall for him and then broke her heart, he'd end up with *two* rich, powerful men determined to kill him. Because Maxwell Sloane was bound to put a price on the head of any man who trifled with his little girl's affections.

Menacing as that prospect was, it somehow didn't disturb Ben as much as the discovery that Sierra had lied to him.

Which was ridiculous, considering that Ben had also lied to her. But *he* had a good reason. What possible motive could Sierra have had for hiding this mind-boggling piece of news?

Ben had thought he knew her. He'd thought they were becoming...well, friends or something. She'd told him about her grandfather. She'd shared her sadness and regrets, and in return Ben had opened up to her, revealing more of himself than he'd intended.

His resentment was completely unreasonable. Sierra owed him nothing—certainly not honesty, not after the way he'd already deceived her. But Ben couldn't help feeling a little . . . hurt. His reaction was unfair. And stupid. But there it was.

In as casual a tone as he could muster, Ben asked, "Speaking of Sierra, do you have any idea where she is right now? I need to discuss something with her."

Pete cleared his throat, disguising what sounded suspiciously like a chuckle. Addie threw him an I-told-you-so glance, then smiled benevolently at Ben. "Why, yes, as a matter of fact I happen to know that she's over at the general store, stocking up on supplies. She mentioned it to me on her way out this morning, in case someone—" she gave the word a slight emphasis "—came looking for her."

"Well, er, thanks," Ben said. "Guess I'll go find her, then."

"You do that, sonny. And remember what I said." When Ben blinked uncertainly, Pete mouthed the word "rascal."

"Oh, yeah. Right." Ben gave Pete a two-fingered salute as he backpedaled out of the lobby. "Well, see you both later."

Pete tugged on one end of his mustache as if trying to rein in a smile. Addie beamed after Ben like warm sunshine.

Ben wished he were anyplace else on earth.

He spotted Charlemagne about halfway down the street, wearing that goofy straw hat and tied up to a fire hydrant. As Ben approached, the mule raised his head, then snorted with supreme disdain. "Good morning to you, too," Ben grumbled. He whisked open the door of the general store and collided with Sierra. Boxes and bundles flew everywhere.

"Hey!" she shouted. "Oh, it's you. I should have known."

Ben knelt next to her. "Sierra, we have to talk."

"Heavens to Betsy, those have got to be the most ominous words in the English language." She reached for a packet of instant-soup mix. "Aren't you even going to help me pick this stuff up?"

"Later." Ben felt something moist and cold nuzzling the nape of his neck. "Damn it." Without looking around, he batted away Charlemagne's nose.

"Looks like somebody got up on the wrong side of the bed this morning," Sierra said cheerfully, scooping up a box of biscuit mix.

Ben grabbed her wrist and pulled her to her feet, knocking her packages to the ground again.

"What's bugging you, anyway?" Sierra demanded as he dragged her beyond the range of Charlemagne's wet, inquisitive snoot.

"I'll tell you what's bugging me," Ben said through gritted teeth. "Why didn't you tell me that your father is one of the wealthiest men in the world?"

Chapter Four

"Oh, that," she said.

"Yes, *that*. How could you neglect to mention your father is Maxwell Sloane—*Midas* Sloane, head of Sloane Enterprises, financial genius, adviser to presidents—"

"I didn't think it was important," Sierra replied, shrugging.

Ben's jaw dropped. "You didn't think it was—"

"Important," she repeated. "Now, would you mind letting go of my wrist? You're cutting off the circulation in my hand."

Ben released his grip, but kept staring at her, feeling as if he'd been hit by a bombshell.

Sierra rubbed her wrist and shook her fingers rapidly up and down. "What a relief! The feeling's coming back. Maybe I'll play the violin again, after all." She looked up and paused. "I don't see what you're getting all bent out of shape for,'' she said. ''What difference does it make who my father is?''

''I thought you were—I thought we—it's just that—oh, never mind,'' Ben finished gruffly. Sierra's genuine puzzlement had deflated his indignation like a sputtering balloon. She was right; he was overreacting. Not mentioning her illustrious heritage had struck Ben as strange at first, as if she were deliberately concealing the truth. On the other hand, even after their short acquaintance, he could see it would be extremely out of character for Sierra to proclaim herself as Maxwell Sloane's daughter to every person she met.

And Ben wasn't about to reveal the other source of his consternation: that Maxwell Sloane would undoubtedly use his vast resources to punish the man who broke his daughter's heart.

Well, he'd have plenty of time to worry about that later. Right now he had to mend some fences. ''I guess I *was* making too big a deal out of it,'' he said, giving Sierra a sheepish smile. ''I was kind of stunned, that's all. Come on, I'll help you pick up your groceries.''

As he knelt to the sidewalk and began to hand Sierra boxes and packets, he could feel her inquisitive eyes boring into the top of his head. Before her simmering curiosity could boil over into a big splash of questions about his sudden change in attitude, he forestalled her with a question of his own. ''I assume that large corporation you told me you worked for was Sloane Enterprises?''

Sierra took the package of pancake mix he handed her and tucked it into one of the saddlebags slung over Charlemagne's sagging back. ''Yep.''

''And how did your father react to your recent . . . change in life-style?''

She snorted. "Don't ask." Then she answered him, anyway. "You wouldn't believe all the nonsense I've had to put up with since the day I announced I was turning in my key to the executive washroom."

"He thought you were making a mistake, did he?"

"A mistake?" Sierra rolled her eyes. "Hardly. More like I'd gone temporarily insane. He thought I was throwing my life away, casting shame and ridicule upon the hallowed name of Sloane, not to mention letting him down personally. My father had given me everything, and I was flinging it back in his face. That's the way *he* sees it, anyway." As she spoke, lines of strain creased her forehead, and her voice grew taut with barely repressed emotion. It was obvious her father's scorn and disappointment had wounded her deeply.

She must love him an awful lot, Ben thought.

He retrieved the last stray box of powdered milk and handed it to her, noticing her flushed cheeks and compressed mouth. As she turned to fasten the buckle on the saddlebag, she tossed her curls and straightened her back with a slightly defiant movement. The sight of her fragile, determined shoulders wrestling with the weight of the world strummed a tender chord inside Ben. When Sierra looked up at him again, her dark eyes glistened, and he had to curb the overpowering impulse to sweep her into the comfort of his arms and banish her troubles with kisses and caresses.

Their eyes met for only an instant before she ducked her head in obvious embarrassment. Her cheeks flamed even more brightly as she mustered a weak smile. "My father's tried every trick in the book to lure me back to L.A. First he threatened to disinherit me. Then he tried to bribe me with a big promotion and a new Mercedes. His latest ploy was the old guilt routine—trying to convince me that my mother cries herself to sleep every night because of me. Ha! He should know better than to try *that* one."

"Why is that?"

"Because Mom's the one person on earth who actually sympathizes with the choice I've made. She loves these mountains, and misses Grandpa as much as I do. Mom understands me." Sierra let her breath out in a long sigh. "I only wish my father did."

Ben reached over and grazed her cheek with the back of his finger. "He'll come around someday."

"Not him. Why, he's as stubborn as *I*—well, let's just say he's pretty darn stubborn."

Ben's eyes twinkled. "I know exactly what you mean." If Maxwell Sloane was half as obstinate as his daughter, the man could give lessons to mules.

He'd spoken in an amused tone and was startled by the sudden flicker of uncertainty in Sierra's expression. Then the color drained from her face, and confusion clouded her eyes. She fell back a step.

"Sierra—?" Ben moved toward her, but she twisted deftly aside, eluding his outstretched hand. "Sierra, what is it? What's wrong?"

She busied herself untying Charlemagne, allowing her hair to fall forward and curtain her face. "Nothing. Nothing's wrong. I've got to go, that's all. There's gold in them thar hills and all that."

"You mean you're leaving? Now? But why? I thought we could—"

"Come on, Char. Quit nibbling on Mr. Halliday's collar. We've imposed on him enough as it is. Say goodbye and we'll be on our way." She tugged on the mule's rope.

"Sierra, what the hell— ow! Damn it!" he shouted as Charlemagne trod unceremoniously on his right instep. Limping, Ben trailed them down the dusty street. At the rate he was going, he'd be lucky to have one good leg left by the time this adventure was over.

He caught up with them at the corner, planting himself directly in Sierra's path so that she had little choice but to stop. But he couldn't force her to meet his eyes. She stared stonily over his shoulder as if he weren't there.

Ben felt her slipping away from him, as if the warm rapport they'd established were rapidly disintegrating beneath their feet. He was desperate to reach her, to pull her back before it was too late. And he was honest enough to admit it wasn't just because Sierra was his only way of getting the letter back.

He gripped her shoulders. "Sierra, whatever I've done, whatever I've said, I didn't mean to upset you. I'm sorry. I want to make things right between us." He swallowed. "Won't you at least give me a chance?"

Her eyes darted back and forth as if she were closely observing some internal struggle. Ben held his breath. At last she looked at him, but her shuttered glance was hardly reassuring. "Okay," she said. "Maybe we *should* talk." She shrugged his hands off her shoulders.

"How 'bout if I buy you breakfast?"

"I'm not hungry," she said, contradictory as always. "But I wouldn't mind some coffee."

"Great."

"I'll meet you at the cafe across the street in fifteen minutes."

Ben's relief evaporated. "You're not going to skip out on me, are you?"

The gaze she sent him was cool and assessing. "No," she replied slowly. He would have felt a lot better if she hadn't added, sotto voce, "Not yet, anyway."

As he watched her tow Charlemagne back toward the hotel, Ben scratched his head, damned if he could figure out why all of a sudden Sierra was treating him as if he had the plague or something.

He was worried. Because it was starting to dawn on him that perhaps even more than the letter was at stake here.

"That rotten, no-good, lousy sneak," Sierra muttered as she tied Charlemagne to the back-porch railing of the hotel. She hoisted off the saddlebags and dumped them onto one side of the porch. Then she kicked them for good measure.

Now that her daze had worn off, she was furious. Anger, after all, was easier to cope with than hurt.

All the puzzle pieces had started falling into place when Ben had made that remark about knowing how stubborn her father could be. Well, what he'd actually said was that he knew what she meant about her father. But that little slipup was like an innocent-looking piece of yarn, unraveling Ben's whole story once Sierra's mind started plucking at it.

She'd insisted on fifteen minutes before meeting him for coffee because she needed time to organize and assemble all the bits and pieces, all the clues pointing to the inescapable conclusion that Ben Halliday was a conniving, low-life skunk.

The whole scheme was so obvious now, she felt like a fool for not recognizing it before. And if there was one thing Sierra hated, it was feeling foolish.

She scooped up a couple of fallen apples from beneath the tree she'd climbed and played in as a child. Absently handing one to Charlemagne, she reviewed the incriminating points.

First was Ben's suspicious claim to be a journalist. She hadn't believed *that* part for one minute, which was some consolation, anyway. He hadn't come to find Grandpa; he'd been looking for *her* all along. And at last she'd figured out the reason why.

Then there was all his phony concern. Did she know anything about panning for gold? What about wilderness survival? What was she going to do when winter came?

Sierra mimicked Ben's questions in silent disgust. Charlemagne, chomping lazily on his apple, seemed to be doing the same thing.

At last she understood Ben's reluctance to reveal any of his personal history, although she *had* pried out the informative nugget that he was from Los Angeles. That fit neatly in with the rest of it. He'd practically admitted knowing her father, hadn't he?

Sierra plopped herself down on the edge of the porch and banged her feet viciously back and forth. She'd fallen for Ben's smooth, sweet-talking charm hook, line and sinker. But now she understood his flattering interest in her...why he'd pursued her so relentlessly over mountain and stream.

Ben Halliday was nothing but a cog in her father's latest scheme! He'd been hired to romance her, to seduce her back to Los Angeles and the safe, secure, deadly dull boardrooms of Sloane Enterprises.

He was getting paid to sweep her off her feet.

And he'd damn near succeeded, too. Thank goodness she'd seen through his masquerade before it was too late.

Then Sierra's indignation faltered; her stomach gave a sad, sickening little lurch. She handed Charlemagne the other apple. Her triumph ebbed, leaving a bitter taste in her mouth and a weariness in her heart. She closed her eyes. "Darn it," she whispered. "I really liked him."

Then her eyes flew open, and she whipped her head around guiltily, making sure no one had overheard her confession. The only witness crunched his apple and pretended he hadn't heard.

Sierra shoved herself to her feet, dusted off her derriere and shook her curls out of her face. Doing her best to stoke up a furnace of outrage, she marched toward the cafe, heading for the showdown.

She found her opponent seated in the back booth, poking his fork through a pile of congealed-looking scrambled eggs. He rose halfway to his feet and beamed at her approach, but Sierra could see worry lurking behind those treacherous blue eyes.

Good. Let him suffer.

She lowered herself primly across from him. "Coffee, please," she told the waitress.

Ben leaned forward. "Sure you don't want some breakfast? The food here's terrific."

"No. Just coffee." Sierra glanced disdainfully at Ben's meal. How would he know how the food tasted when all he'd done was push it around his plate?

She gazed idly at her reflection in the metal napkin holder until the waitress set her coffee down and refilled Ben's cup. Ben gulped his coffee as if it were liquid courage. Setting the cup down, he gave Sierra a little half grin, twisting his mouth to one side in a boyish kind of way she'd once found rather endearing. Resolutely she steeled her heart against his perfidious, endearing expressions.

Ben cradled the cup between his palms. "So," he said brightly, "are you going to tell me why you're so mad at me?"

Obviously he'd decided to brazen this out by feigning complete innocence. The low-down rat. Well, the old charm routine wasn't going to work this time.

Smiling sweetly, Sierra let him have it with both barrels.

"I know who you are and what you want," she said.

Ben's hands jerked, sloshing coffee over his fingers. As he pried a wad of napkins from the holder, Sierra could see his devious brain working fast and furiously. His face was pale, making his shifty eyes seem even bluer than usual. Obviously she'd been right about him.

Yet the knowledge gave her no satisfaction.

When he'd mopped up the last puddle of coffee, Ben met her laser-beam gaze. "I'm not sure what you mean," he said.

"Quit playing games, Mr. Halliday. The jig is up. The party's over. The fat lady sings."

Ben gaped at her, then burst out laughing. "You know, in my entire life I've never met anyone even remotely like you."

"No? Well, I've met plenty of men like you, unfortunately. Men who'd do anything for money, like lying, like pretending things they don't feel, just because my father—"

"Hold on a second," Ben interrupted. "You mean to tell me you think I'm after your money? That I'm some kind of fortune hunter? For God's sake, I didn't even know who your father was until this morning!"

"You expect me to believe that, after you let it slip that you know how stubborn my father can be?"

"Huh?"

"Don't play dumb with me. I saw through your charade from the beginning. Free-lance journalist, my foot! How come I've never seen you carrying so much as a pencil? Next time my father hires you to do his dirty work, I suggest you bring along the appropriate props!"

Ben blinked. "Dirty work?"

"Oh, please. You want me to spell it out? Fine." Silverware went flying as Sierra swept back her hand in a dramatic gesture. "My father hired you to lure me back to Los Angeles. He paid you to pretend you were interested in me, to make me fall for you so that I'd follow you back to L.A. Don't try to deny it," she said, raising her palm when Ben's mouth fell open. "I've heard enough of your lies." She leaned across the table, so that her face was mere inches from his. Her voice dropped to a husky, dangerous whisper. "I only have one question, Mr. Halliday. Exactly how far did my father expect you to go? What if your hollow words and meaningless kisses weren't enough to sway me? Were you supposed to make love to me as a last resort?"

Ben moved his face even closer, so their mouths were nearly touching. "That's three questions."

Sierra snapped her head back. "Very funny." She slid out of the booth. "We'll see how funny it is when you report back to my father empty-handed. He doesn't accept failure too well." As she made her way down the aisle, she flung over her shoulder, "But of course, you already know that."

She heard Ben scramble after her and felt the curious stares of the other customers. Holding her head high, she sailed out of the cafe and was halfway down the block before Ben caught up with her. He must have slowed down to pay the bill.

His boots thundered on the sidewalk until he fell in step beside her. "Sierra, this whole idea is crazy! You can't possibly believe all those things you said back there."

She stopped dead in her tracks. Ben stumbled, trying to halt his momentum. "I don't hear you denying any of it," she said. But oh, how she wanted to....

He wiped his forehead, looking ill at ease. Glancing up and down the street, he shifted his weight from foot to foot. "Okay," he said finally. "Maybe *some* of it's true. I said *some* of it," he added, dodging in front of Sierra to prevent her from walking off.

She pressed her lips together, partly in disgust, partly to keep from crying. "If you admit *that* much, how do you expect me to believe anything else you say?"

"Because—because...damn it, Sierra!" With a groan of exasperation, Ben seized her by the shoulders, yanked her against his chest and kissed her. Hard.

For an instant she nearly surrendered, so stunned was she by the swiftness of his embrace, so stirred by the passionate intensity of his kiss. It would be so easy to melt into his arms, to lose herself in the magic spell he wove around her. Desperate to believe that Ben might truly care about her, she could almost forget all the evidence to the contrary.

Almost. But not quite.

Sierra sucked in a deep breath. Then she stomped on Ben's foot.

"Ow!"

She jumped back a prudent distance, observing his painful, puzzled wince with satisfaction. "I'd rather kiss a snake," she announced, wiping off her mouth with the cuff of her sleeve. "Although, come to think of it, that's exactly what I just did."

With that, she gathered her indignation around her and swept off down the street, holding her head high. She could only pray that Ben, hopping up and down on one leg, couldn't see her knees wobbling.

Ben sat at the bar of the Paydirt Saloon, nursing a Scotch along with his sore foot. Drinking before noon wasn't his usual style, but ever since meeting Sierra, he'd found himself doing a lot of things he'd never thought he would.

Like lying to people. Like using people. Like letting himself be distracted from his quest by haunting memories of the hurt in Sierra's blazing eyes . . . the unyielding, unforgiving uptilt of her chin...that darn spattering of freckles across her adorable nose.

With a muffled groan Ben drained the contents of his glass and studied his reflection in the ornate, gilt-edged mirror hanging behind the bar. How had he landed in such a mess, anyway? He, who'd always been so firmly in charge of his destiny, who'd always relied on logic, honesty and hard work to achieve his goals.

Somewhere along the path to this particular goal he'd jettisoned his honesty. Then he'd discovered that logic wasn't a particularly useful quality when dealing with Sierra. And now his hard work seemed about as pointless as running a marathon on a treadmill.

As he crunched on his ice cubes, giving up was the furthest thing from his mind. Ben Halliday was no quitter. But the thought of another skirmish with Sierra was positively overwhelming.

"Ready for another one?" The bartender was mopping the carved mahogany bar top with a white towel. "You look like you could use one."

"You're right about that," Ben said, digging into his pocket. "But no, thanks. Gotta keep my wits about me." He tossed a couple of bills onto the counter.

"Gotcha." The bartender winked. "Woman trouble, huh?"

"Trouble doesn't begin to cover it. Trouble would be a Sunday-school picnic compared to—ah, never mind." Ben slid off the bar stool, wincing as he landed. He took a couple of tentative steps, then decided his foot was sufficiently recovered to carry him off in search of Sierra. With a final nod to the bartender, he traipsed across the sawdust-covered floor and pushed through the swinging saloon doors.

The dazzling sunshine nearly blinded him after the bar's gloomy interior. He stepped gingerly along the sidewalk, then, with long-practiced skill, switched off the faint pain signals reaching his brain. His brain had other matters to wrestle with right now. Like figuring out what clever, plausible, totally fabricated story he could tell Sierra to get himself out of the doghouse.

For one instant Ben considered coming clean with her—telling her the truth about the letter and the reasons he'd sworn to destroy Quentin Jericho. Just as instantly, he rejected the idea. He was more determined than ever to shield Sierra from any dangerous knowledge that would provoke Jericho to harm her—or worse.

The thought of Jericho so much as breaking one of Sierra's fingernails filled Ben with such molten, white-hot anger that he had to pause for a moment to clench and unclench his fists and gulp several deep lungfuls of air. By God, if Sierra suffered so much as a stubbed toe because of Jericho or any of his men, Ben wouldn't be satisfied with exposing Jericho for the ruthless villain he was. He wouldn't be satisfied with seeing Jericho behind bars.

If Jericho hurt Sierra, Ben would kill him.

The realization was startling and unsettling, yet so unshakable, so crystal clear that it seemed as much a part of Ben as his own name. But for the time being, he didn't care to examine too closely the reasons for his fierce protectiveness. Because doing so might force him to admit that Sierra already meant more to him than the quickest route to that letter.

By the time he entered the hotel lobby, he still hadn't figured out how to explain and justify his deception to her. Obviously that feeble journalist pretense wasn't going to work anymore—if it ever had. Did he have any choice but to let Sierra keep believing this wild theory that her father had hired Ben to woo her back home where she belonged?

He spotted Addie Winslow behind the front desk, her gray head bent over an open ledger. Speeding up his pace, Ben hoped he could whiz right by without getting snagged into a conversation. He liked Addie, but her bright-eyed curiosity and eager matchmaking were about as welcome as quicksand right now.

When she glanced up over the tops of her spectacles, Ben gave her a brief smile and a quick little wave as he plowed ahead toward the staircase.

But Addie was not so easily bought off. "Hello, Mr. Halliday, I was just wondering—oh, Mr. Halliday? Mr. Halliday?"

With a sigh Ben withdrew his foot from the bottom step. "Yes, Addie?" When he returned to the front desk, he detected a faintly troubled look in her normally twinkling eyes. Worry wrinkled her forehead, and her smile seemed forced when she asked, "Did your friend find you?"

"Who, Sierra? Well, actually—"

"Dear me, no, I'm not talking about Sierra, of course. I meant the gentleman who was in here a while ago looking for you."

A chill rippled down Ben's spine. "Gentleman? What gentleman?"

Addie's smile faltered. "Very nicely dressed he was, in a dark blue three-piece suit. Dark brown hair, I believe—or was it black? And tall. Well, not *too* tall, but not too short, either. He didn't mention you by name, but when he described you, I knew right away who he was talking about. Then when I said, 'Oh, you must mean Mr. Halliday,' why, his whole face lit up with excitement! He must be a very good friend of yours. Anyway I told him you'd gone out for a spell and I didn't rightly know when to expect you back. That's when he told me he was an old friend of yours, but he wanted to surprise you, so he asked me not to . . . say anything. Oh, dear." Addie swallowed. "Look what I've done—gone and spoiled your friend's surprise. I'm so sorry, Mr. Halliday. Perhaps—perhaps you could *pretend* to be surprised when you see him, so your friend won't think I'm nothing but an old blabbermouth?"

The chill along Ben's spine had become a blizzard of fear. "How long ago was he in here?"

The demanding urgency in his voice flustered Addie even more. "Well, now, let me see, I didn't check my watch, so I can't say for certain, but I suppose it must have been . . . oh, now—''

''Addie, *please*.'' Ben closed his eyes, trying to quell the sickening maelstrom of exasperation and apprehension whirling in his stomach. ''Was it more than an hour ago?''

''Oh, no, I don't believe so.''

''Fifteen minutes ago?''

''Oh, longer than that.'' She tapped a crooked finger against her chin, considering.

Ben forced himself not to throttle her.

''If I had to guess, I'd say your friend was in here about half an hour ago. Yes, that's right,'' she added hastily when she saw the expression on Ben's face. ''Half an hour ago.'' She bobbed her head firmly.

''Where did he go when he left?''

''Heavens, I've no idea! I suggested he wait in the dining room—the cook baked some simply scrumptious bread pudding this morning—but he said no, he'd come back later to meet you. Then when I asked if he cared to leave a message, he told me no, that he wanted to . . . surprise you.'' She patted her hair, blushing nervously.

''Don't worry about it,'' Ben said quickly. ''The fact is, I *hate* surprises.'' He leaned forward and brushed a kiss on her dry, powdered cheek, making her blush even more furiously. ''Thanks, Addie.''

With that, he moved swiftly across the lobby and took the stairs two at a time. Friend, indeed. From Addie's vague description, it was impossible to attach a name to the man. But one fact was ominously certain: he was no friend of Ben's.

Ben hadn't told a soul he was coming here. And only one person had the motivation to track him down: Jericho. Had he sent only one emissary, or was there a whole goon squad on the way?

No matter. As Ben dashed down the hallway, he knew what he had to do. Whisk Sierra safely out of the way before anyone discovered her connection to the letter.

He restrained the urge to smash down her door and spirit her off to safety before she had a chance to argue. Better not draw attention to himself until he knew who might be watching. Instead he rapped softly on the door, ready to mumble "room service" if Sierra insisted on making sure it wasn't Ben before she opened the door.

When he got no response, he knocked louder. Damn it, if she was sitting in there sulking...

Despite his intentions Ben found himself hammering on the door with his fist. "Sierra, open up! Please! I've got to talk to you! It's important! For God's sake, I'm begging you—*please* let me in!"

A door opened partway down the hall, and a balding middle-aged man stuck his head out to see what all the ruckus was. At the sight of Ben's glowering expression, he beat a hasty retreat and slammed his door shut.

Get a grip on yourself, Ben thought. *All this racket is like shooting off cannons to announce your presence.*

He rattled the doorknob, then bent to examine the lock. Old and rusted. Probably flimsy. He hesitated. The logical move would be to go downstairs and wheedle the key out of Addie. On the other hand, Sierra played a role in this decision, so logic probably wasn't a consideration. Besides, he was in a hurry.

Bracing himself against the opposite wall, Ben lowered his shoulder and launched himself against the door.

It didn't take long for him to regret his impetuous action. "Aaargh!"

The door gave way, along with his shoulder joint. That's what it felt like, anyway. Clutching his upper arm, Ben scanned Sierra's room, ready to unlease a torrent of verbal abuse as soon as he spotted her hiding place.

Then a twinge of alarm darted through him, obliterating the pain. No sign of her. No saddlebags, no duffel bag, no clothes strewn about the room. Ben stepped quickly to the closet and flung the door open. Empty. He yanked out the dresser drawers, then ducked into the bathroom. The only evidence Sierra had even been here was the rumpled towel draped over the side of the claw-footed bathtub.

Ben returned to the bedroom, breathing rapidly. No sign of a struggle, so he could probably assume that she'd left of her own free will. If one of Jericho's men had dragged Sierra out of here kicking and screaming, surely there would be a path of destruction to rival Sherman's march to the sea. Sierra wasn't likely to have gone quietly.

So things could be worse. Not much, but a little. Ben wiped the sweat from his forehead, then charged out of the room and back downstairs. "Addie," he gasped, gripping the front desk with both hands, "where is she?"

Addie's eyes widened at the sight of Ben's agitation. "Sierra? Why, she checked out, Mr. Halliday. I meant to mention it to you earlier, but then we got talking about your friend, and it just plumb went out of my head."

"Checked out? You mean she's gone? Where did she go?"

"I wish I knew, Mr. Halliday. I don't mind telling you, I've been more than a mite worried about that child." Addie shook her head sadly. "Oh, she was in quite a mood when she left, she was. All het up about something. When I tried to find out what was bothering her, she just waved her hands around and started spouting off about snakes, rats, skunks—why, I couldn't figure out *what* had upset her so! I know she's not exactly partial to creepy crawly animals, but—"

"How long ago did she leave?" Ben interrupted, grinding his teeth. Obviously Sierra wasn't ready to forgive and forget about his little deception.

Addie drew off her glasses and tapped them against her chin. "Oh, now, I believe she was lugging her gear out the back entrance around the time that feller showed up looking for you."

The hair stood up on the back of Ben's neck. "Did my, uh, friend see her leaving?"

"That I couldn't say. There was so much confusion at the time, you see—people coming and going, Sierra all worked up about something . . . then she insisted on dragging Pete along with her. . . ." Addie's ample bosom heaved in a sigh. "I do wish she hadn't kicked up such a fuss about not leaving without him. I know he was looking forward to being in your magazine article. And I must say, it was awful nice to have a man around the place again. Sometimes I think I just can't manage the hotel by myself anymore, that if I could only talk Pete into. . ." She turned pink. "Well, never mind, you're not interested in all that, I suppose."

Ben covered her hand with his. "I'm sure everything will work out, Addie," he said with a reassurance he was far from feeling. "But if you'll excuse me, I've got to try and catch up with them."

"Well, if you find them," she said wistfully, "you tell Pete he's always got a room here, will you?"

"I'll do it first thing," Ben promised. Well, maybe second thing. The first thing he was going to do was give a certain spoiled brat the spanking her father should have given her years ago.

Thank God for yesterday's rain. Ben was no Davy Crockett, but the soft, damp earth yielded a trail of footprints that even Mister Magoo could have followed. After questioning several residents who'd seen the merry little band of travelers pass by, Ben had managed to pick up their trail where they'd left the main road about half a mile out of Grubstake. His childhood Boy Scout training was finally paying off. Of course, it also helped that his quarry included a plodding mule whose hooves gouged deep, muddy craters in the soggy ground that even a city kid like Ben could hardly miss.

He was surprised at how long it was taking to catch up with them. After all, Pete was eighty-three, and Charlemagne wasn't exactly Kentucky Derby material. Sierra must be cracking the whip something fierce. Amazing how a little self-righteous indignation could light a fire under some people.

Every bruised, strained muscle in his body was screaming in protest when Ben clambered atop a narrow, tree-lined ridge and finally spotted them. Spotted their campsite, anyway. In the ravine below, Charlemagne was propped against an elm tree like a lounger in a seedy piano bar, looking just as bored. Tent and saddlebags were piled in a heap nearby, so Sierra and Pete couldn't be far away, either.

Pausing to catch his breath, Ben pondered the best way to approach them. He wasn't exactly expecting a warm welcome and wanted to avoid, if possible, any more injuries to his person.

Sweat plastered his shirt to his back, and as a late-afternoon breeze fanned the top of the ridge, Ben shivered with a sudden chill. The ravine was already in shadow as he carefully scanned the tangled brush below for any clue to Sierra's whereabouts.

He'd just about decided to march boldly into camp and make himself at home when a long, terrified scream rang out.

Chapter Five

He'd recognize that scream anywhere. Sierra.

Ben hurled himself down the slope like a thunderbolt from the heavens. The ravine was steeper than it looked from above, and he half skidded, half flew down the side of the ridge, sending up a spray of dirt and pebbles and starting several miniature avalanches that helped sweep him along.

He was doing a fair job of keeping his balance, however, until a thick root snaked out in front of him. Tripping over the woody tentacle, he plunged headlong down the slope, rolling head over heels until he crashed into the tree Charlemagne was using as a scratching post.

Stars swirled around the mule's head as Ben stared dizzily up at the sky. But the lingering echo of that terrified scream cleared his head immediately. He staggered to his feet, lurching off toward the stand of trees where he thought the scream had come from.

Sierra was half-crouched in a defensive stance next to a dense cluster of bushes. In her upraised hand she clutched a rock, ready to fend off the attacker lurking behind the leaves where Ben couldn't see him.

As he sprang to her rescue, Ben couldn't help admiring what a valiant little fighter she was, what a spunky, brave soul....

He grabbed her in his arms and whisked her away from the bushes. Caught off balance, they both toppled to the ground and whirled over a couple of times before rolling to a halt with Ben's arms still securely pinned around Sierra.

"Get your paws off me," she said, "or I'll clobber you with this rock."

Flabbergasted, Ben didn't move.

"Did you hear me?" she demanded. "Are you going to let me up, or do I have to get rough?"

Any second now, her assailant was liable to pounce on them. Lifting his head, Ben quickly scanned their surroundings, maintaining a firm grip on Sierra. Whoever the guy was, he seemed to have disappeared.

"I mean it," she warned, starting to struggle. "Quit manhandling me, or you'll be sorry."

He was already starting to be sorry.

As he helped Sierra to her feet, she shook off his hand. "Would you mind telling me what that was all about?" she asked, dusting off her jeans.

Ben stared at her, wondering if he'd just entered the Twilight Zone. Maybe one of his numerous recent concussions was making him hallucinate. "You might thank me just a little," he said sarcastically, "for chasing that guy off."

Sierra had a gray smudge of dirt across her cheek when she glanced up at him. "What guy?"

Ben stabbed his finger toward the bushes. "Him! The guy who was about to jump you! I heard you scream, and then I—I—" He folded his arms. "Would you mind telling me exactly what the hell is so funny?"

Sierra, doubled over with laughter, couldn't answer right away. Ben tapped his foot impatiently, sensing that once again he'd made a fool of himself in front of her. When she finally recovered sufficiently to speak, her eyes sparkled with tears of mirth. "You—you thought someone was going to *jump* me?" Her voice choked up as she began to disintegrate into laughter again. At the sight of Ben's scowl, she sobered up. A little, anyway.

"It wasn't a mugger. It was a—a—" She giggled, then cleared her throat and did her best to straighten her smile. "It was a lizard."

Ben blinked, unfolded his arms and examined his fingernails. When he spoke, his calm voice held all the contained fury of a dormant volcano about to erupt. "A lizard?"

Sierra nodded. "Uh-huh." Her chin quivered.

Ben edged toward her. "You screamed bloody murder because you saw a lizard?"

"I didn't scream bloody murder. Besides, it was a *big* lizard."

"A *big* lizard."

"Big and ugly."

He stuffed his hands into his pockets to keep himself from wrapping them around her lovely throat.

"Don't blame *me* because you jumped to the wrong conclusion," she said. "Besides, who on earth would attack me way out here? Some escaped desperado from the state prison? A claim jumper, perhaps?"

"Look, I thought you were in trouble, all right? I didn't stop to make a list of all the possibilities."

Sierra surveyed Ben from the toes of his filthy, scuffed boots to the top of his disheveled blond head. "You were really trying to save me, huh?" She pushed a lock of hair from her face.

"Why else would I have tackled you that way?"

"Oh, I can think of a couple of reasons. Maybe you had orders to hog-tie me and carry me back to L.A. over your shoulder if I didn't come along peacefully." A coy grin lifted the corners of her mouth. "Or maybe overwhelming passion simply got the best of you."

Ben's scowl smoothed into a less-grumpy expression. "I told you before, I wasn't hired by your father. As for your second theory..." He slid his tongue slowly across his upper lip and leaned closer to her. "Time will tell."

Sierra held her ground, though she was torn between the impulse to beat a hasty retreat and the aching desire to throw herself into Ben's arms. Darn his double-dealing hide, anyway! She ought to ignore him, to devastate him with some withering remark, to send him packing back to Los Angeles with his tail between his legs.

Instead she wanted to cover his dirty, scratched face with kisses. She wanted to help him hobble back to camp with his arm draped across her shoulders. She wanted to clasp her hands and sigh, "My hero!" and pledge undying love to her knight in shining armor.

Even though *this* knight's armor wasn't exactly gleaming.

"You're a mess," she said grouchily. "Come on. I've got a first-aid kit, and you can clean up in the stream. I guess I could give you something to eat, too."

"Ever the gracious hostess," she heard him mumble as she led the way back to the clearing. She busied herself with the saddlebags while Ben stripped off his shirt and tossed it over a branch near Charlemagne. Then he apparently thought better of it and prudently hung the shirt on a different tree. Sierra waited till she heard him thrashing off toward the stream before she stole a glance in his direction. She caught sight of a broad masculine back and straight, sturdy shoulders before he disappeared into the brush.

"Hoo, boy," she muttered, fanning her face. Despite the sun's fading rays, she suddenly felt warm.

By the time Ben returned, damp hair slicked back and face clean if somewhat battle scarred, Sierra had wrestled the tent up. But not to Ben's satisfaction, if the way he rolled his eyes was any indication. He didn't say a word, though. Maybe he was learning.

"Will it violate any of your sacred principles if I light this fire with a match?" he asked, dumping an armload of sticks on the ground.

"Suit yourself," she replied, trying not to stare at the glint of golden hair covering the muscular curvature of his chest. "I was collecting those rocks to put around the fire when I spotted that lizard. That very *dangerous* lizard," she added when Ben grimaced. "I picked up a rock and there he was, big as a dinosaur, practically. Ugh."

Ben arranged the rocks in a circle around the stack of wood. "Sierra," he said, pushing himself to his feet with a muffled groan, "don't take this the wrong way, but are you sure you know what you're doing?" He limped over to his shirt and fished a matchbook out of the pocket.

"You're the one who can't start a fire without matches, not me."

"That's not what I'm talking about." Kneeling, Ben struck a match and held it to the kindling until the flame caught. Sierra watched his hands with fascination. Twilight shadows and the fire's glow played across his face, casting its planes and angles into bold relief like a bronze sculpture of some ancient god.

When he scooted next to her, Sierra didn't move away. "I was referring to . . . everything," Ben finished helplessly, waving his arm around the clearing. "I mean, that tent's not much of a shelter *now*, let alone when winter comes. I've yet to see you actually start a fire. And you haven't found any gold yet, have you?"

Her only reply was a narrowing of her eyes and an upward thrust of her chin.

"No, I didn't think so. And you're scared to death of a *lizard*, for Pete's sake! What if it had been a rattlesnake, or a mountain lion, or a grizzly bear—"

"There aren't any grizzly bears in this part of the country," she said reasonably.

Ben sighed. "You're deliberately missing my point."

"Which is?"

He raised his hands in a placating gesture. "All I'm asking is, are you sure you haven't bitten off more than you can chew?"

"Speaking of food, I'm starved. Let's eat."

"Sierra—"

"Hold it right there," she said, holding up a warning finger. "If you and I are going to carry on a civilized conversation, we're going to follow some rules. We will *not* discuss the pros and cons of my chosen lifestyle. We will *not* debate the possibility of my going back to Los Angeles, because that subject is not debatable, as far as I'm concerned. And we will *not* mention Sloane Enterprises. Understand?"

A muscle flickered along Ben's jaw. "Fine."

"Good. Here's the first-aid kit." She lobbed the canvas bundle into his lap. "You look like you could use it."

"You're a regular Florence Nightingale, aren't you?"

"Oh, don't be such a big baby. Here, I'll help you, all right?"

As Sierra yanked out bandages, tweezers, snake antivenom and assorted pills and bottles, Ben glanced around and asked, "Where's Pete?"

She tossed the antivenom aside. "He took off on his own. Seems while we were wasting all that time in town, he heard some rumor about an undiscovered gold strike farther up Bitterroot Creek." She nodded toward the stream.

"How can anyone hear about a strike that hasn't been discovered yet?"

"Go figure." Sierra shook her head in disgust. "I've told Pete time and time again that twentieth-century prospectors have to approach mining scientifically." She doused a cotton ball in rubbing alcohol and began to swab a cut on Ben's chin. "You've got to calculate where the gold deposits are most apt to be, like in a gravel bar along the inside curve of a stream or downstream of a big boulder at a spot where the stream gradient decreases."

"And why's that?"

"Hold still. Those are places where the water slows down. Gold that's being swept along will drop out of the stream when the current isn't fast enough to suspend it anymore."

Ben arched his eyebrows. "I'm impressed."

Sierra shrugged modestly. "I learned it all—"

"From your grandfather." Ben echoed her words in unison.

She smiled at him, and for a moment she forgot what a rat he was. "Here, let me put a Band-Aid on that cut."

Ben studied the small gash at the base of his thumb. "I don't think I need one. It'll heal faster if it's exposed to air."

"Well, at least let me spray some antiseptic on it, then." She cradled his hand in hers, acutely aware of a delightful warm tingling sensation where his skin contacted hers. She met Ben's gaze, then looked down quickly, having ascertained from the gleam in his eyes that he felt something, too. He cleared his throat. "Sierra, whatever you might believe about me—"

She shook the spray bottle vigorously.

"—I want you to know that—"

She closed one eye and took aim.

"—my feelings for you— *ow!*" Ben jerked back his hand. "That stings, damn it!"

Sierra's eyes widened in innocence. "What did you expect? Didn't your mom ever spray this stuff on your skinned knees when you were a kid?"

"Well, yeah. But I don't remember it hurting this much."

"Oh, come on, be a big brave boy, and I'll give you a lollipop when we're through. Now, give me your other hand."

"Forget it. I'll risk the germs."

Sierra groaned. "It's your life. Are you going to leave that nasty sliver in your finger, too?"

"Hmm. Maybe not. Do you suppose you could—?"

She snatched his hand back and went to work with the tweezers.

"Hey, go easy, will you? Ouch! What are you trying to do, amputate the whole finger?"

With a final triumphant twist, Sierra plucked out the sliver and held it up for Ben to see. "Wow! Look at the size of this! I bet it hurt like the dickens."

"Not until you gouged it out," Ben grumbled, inspecting his finger.

"Quit bellyaching." On impulse Sierra grabbed his hand and kissed the sore spot. "There! Is that better?"

His eyes glowed with a strange incandescence. "Much better." He extended his other hand, and she brushed her lips against the small cut. Wordlessly Ben pointed to a graze on his cheek. As if hypnotized, Sierra leaned forward and kissed the scraped skin ever so gently.

Ben touched his lower lip.

"There's nothing wrong with your mouth," Sierra whispered.

"Humor me."

His words were muffled by the melding of their lips as he trapped her mouth with his, tangling his fingers through her hair and pulling her hard against him.

Sierra tumbled into his arms, feeling as if she were sailing over Niagara Falls without a barrel. Instinctively she responded to the smoldering urgency of Ben's embrace, wrapping her arms around his lean waist, falling backward to lie cradled in his arms.

He kissed her over and over again—long, leisurely, determined kisses that barely allowed her to breathe, much less get a word in edgewise. Not that she could think of much to say right now, anyway. The insistent yet tender pressure on her mouth...the way Ben slipped his tongue between her lips to twine lazily with hers . . . filled Sierra with an exquisite floating sensation and emptied her head of any words. The incoherent moans welling up in her throat reflected the confusing, intoxicating effect of Ben's lips, his hands, his heartbeat thudding so close to her ear.

Tentatively Sierra lifted her hand and lightly skimmed his chest, exploring its bristly surface with her fingertips. As Ben dragged his lips from her mouth and buried his face in the sensitive flesh of her throat, she slid her hand to the side of his neck and marveled at the rapid pulse beat her fingers encountered.

Now he was muttering words in her ear, so close, so muffled that she could only catch one here and there. "Precious...sweet...so lovely...ah, Sierra, if only..."

A whipcord of desire, inextricably interwoven with some aching, bittersweet emotion, lashed through her. She arched her back, pressing herself closer against the warm, heaving wall of his chest. Ben wrapped one of his arms even more securely around her, freeing his other hand to roam slowly across the curve of her hip, around her narrow waist, up over the lush swell of her breasts.

Even as a voice inside her head cried a warning, Sierra knew that it was too late. Before she'd fully recognized the danger, Ben Halliday had woven his sensual, irresistible web around her. Now she was as neatly, helplessly trapped as a butterfly in a net. No matter how hard or how fast she beat her wings, Ben had her right where he wanted: completely under his spell. Knowing that his dizzying caresses and wonderful whispered words were bankrolled by her father should have rendered Sierra immune to them. But it didn't.

"Ah, Ben," she mumbled in a half sigh, half groan. "You no-good, sneaky, rotten . . ."

"Flattery will get you everywhere," he responded with a throaty chuckle. His breath tickled her earlobe, making her shiver and snuggle even more cozily into his arms.

With a practiced touch, she noted wistfully, Ben plucked open the buttons of her shirt and eased his hand beneath the velvety flannel. His hands were cool against Sierra's heated skin, and she tensed a bit at the first contact.

"Easy," he crooned. "That's it . . . relax . . . we'll go nice and slow . . . I promise I won't do anything you're not ready for. . . ."

He'd mistaken her slight flinch as nervousness about his increasingly bold forays beneath her clothing. In truth every fiber, cell and nerve ending in Sierra's body was clamoring for Ben's touch, yearning for the rapturous fulfillment of the sweet, anguished longings he aroused. Her eyelids drifted shut as she surrendered herself to his lead, knowing she was slipping into a dangerous oblivion of ecstasy she would later regret . . . and not caring in the least.

Ben sensed the last strands of Sierra's resistance ebbing away, and experienced a brief surge of satisfied pleasure. God, she felt wonderful! Her skin was like silk sliding beneath his fingers; her gossamer kisses were like a healing balm to his battered face and bruised ego. Surely her opinion of him couldn't be *too* low, not the way she curled her slim, soft body around him; not the way she purred deep in her throat when he flicked his tongue across her dainty, shell-like ear; not the way she sucked in her breath with a gentle gasp when he molded his hand around the luscious mound of her breast.

She smelled like grass and fresh air and mountain flowers after a spring rain. Conflicting desires tore at

Ben. He wanted to ravish her, to take advantage of her temporarily befuddled state and possess her with the reckless, almost-savage passion that boiled through his bloodstream.

At the same time a ferocious protectiveness flooded him, intensely poignant and totally unknown in his previous experiences with women. Had this overwhelming, unfamiliar instinct seized him simply because Sierra was so out of her element, so in need of his competent masculine protection?

Hardly. Sierra might never earn any wilderness survival badges, but deep down inside, Ben suspected that when push came to shove, she could take care of herself perfectly well without help from him or anyone else.

No, this crazy impulse to shelter her, to do everything in his power to take care of her and make her life easy had its roots in far more disturbing soil. And Ben knew he'd feel the same protective urge whether Sierra was white-water rafting down the Amazon or safely ensconced at the head of the table in some corporate boardroom.

Yet here he was, entangling her deeper in the complicated mess of his life, exposing her to ever-greater peril as the emotional and physical bonds between them drew tighter. Like a noose around her neck.

Christ, there must be *some* way to destroy Quentin Jericho without endangering this fragile, increasingly precious woman in his arms!

But damned if he could come up with an alternative.

A wave of self-loathing engulfed Ben, magnified by the trusting capitulation apparent in every pliant curve, every trembling response of Sierra's body. When she fluttered her lashes half-open to gaze up at him, the dreamy gloss of anticipation in those translucent brown eyes struck him like an accusing slap in the face.

Ben withdrew his hand from beneath her shirt and pulled Sierra against his chest, tucking her head beneath his chin. After a long moment, during which he concentrated on slowing his breathing and pulse, he drew back and kissed her forehead. Shakily he brushed his thumb across the delicate arch of her cheekbone. "Smudge of dirt," he whispered with a fond smile. Then he puckered his lips and planted a playful kiss on the tip of her freckle-dusted nose.

As she trailed her fingers down his bare chest, Ben closed his eyes with an involuntary shudder. He clasped his hand over hers, unsure how long he could retain his control if she kept touching him like that. Resolutely he began to rebutton her shirt. His fingers felt thick and clumsy, as if they were asleep. As he fumbled with the buttons, he could feel Sierra's eyes focused on him, wide open now, glinting with bewilderment and suspicion.

Finally she swept his hand aside and closed the remaining buttons herself, shifting into a sitting position. Her hair fell across her face like a shield, glimmering with coppery highlights cast by the fire.

Ben reached out and draped her hair back as if peering through a curtain. "Sweetheart—?"

She jerked her head impatiently, tossing her curls back. When she'd finished with the last button, she met his inquiring, apologetic gaze head-on. Her kiss-swollen lips were clamped together in exasperation. "You'd think I'd have learned my lesson by now, wouldn't you?"

Ben hesitated. "I'm not sure I understand what you—"

"I mean, I *know* darn good and well why you're doing this. Good grief, what does it take, a sledgehammer to pound some sense into me?" She shook her head. "I always considered myself a quick study, but where you're concerned I seem to have some kind of mental block."

"Sierra, I can explain—"

"Oh, you don't need to explain! I know perfectly well that this—this—advance-and-retreat, advance-and-retreat business is simply part of your strategy. Well, let me congratulate you. It's certainly working well. Although I guess I don't need to tell you that." She levered herself to her feet from her cross-legged position.

"Will you please let me—"

"God, what a fool I am! What a pushover! One kiss from those magic lips, one peek at that fabulous bare chest, and I'm a goner! Pride, self-respect, self-control—they all go flying out the window. You must think I'm a person of rather easy virtue, but I assure you I'm not. Not till now, anyway. I'm sure my father thought you'd have a much tougher time of winning me over. He'll probably be furious with himself for overpaying you, once he finds out what quick work you made of conquering my resistance."

Unable to squeeze a word in edgewise, Ben watched Sierra pace back and forth in front of the fire, waving her hands in the air, gnashing her teeth and throwing anguished looks at the night sky. More than anything, he wanted to grab her again, to smother her ridiculous rantings with kisses and smooth away her agitation with his caressing hands.

But that would only make matters worse. Ben pushed himself to his feet, barely noticing the aching protest of his muscles. Jamming his hands into the back pockets of his jeans, he vowed to keep a prudent distance from Sierra.

"Are you ready to listen yet? Or haven't you finished your monologue?" he asked.

"I'll tell you what's finished," she retorted. "You and me—*that's* what's finished."

Ben counted slowly to ten. "Okay, since it's all over, can I say just one thing?"

She folded her arms and tapped her foot. "I guess so. But make it snappy."

"Thank you," he said with exaggerated gratitude. "And I'd appreciate it if you'd let me say my piece without interrupting."

She waved her hand in a royal gesture. "Fine. Go ahead."

Ben studied her for a moment as she stood outlined against the fire. He couldn't see her face too clearly against the blazing backdrop, but he could read that defiant stance all too well. He exhaled a drawn-out sigh.

"How do you expect me to make love to you when you think I'm some kind of con man?"

His blunt question drew a faint gasp from Sierra, but she recovered quickly. "I don't *expect* you to make love to me at all," she shot back. "Don't flatter yourself."

"Liar."

She recoiled as if he'd struck her. "I beg your—"

"You accuse me of deceiving you, of pretending to be something or someone I'm not. Then you turn right around and lie not only to me, but to yourself."

He'd caught her off guard for once, and was quick to press his advantage. "Let's both be honest, shall we, Sierra?" He closed the distance between them and grasped her elbows, forgetting his resolution not to touch her again. "Something powerful, something incredible was happening between us just now. Admit it. You wanted me to make love to you." She swallowed, staring up at him with enormous, coffee-colored eyes. Ben thrust his face close to hers, and said through gritted teeth, "You wanted me as much as I wanted you. Don't bother denying it."

Her expression was frozen, only her lips moving as she whispered, "Then . . . why?"

Ben raised his hand, feathering it lightly over her eyebrows, her cheekbones, her mouth, like a blind man seeking an image of her face. "I won't make love to you as long as you're convinced I have some ulterior motive. What's happening between us is real, sweetheart. It's not a game—it's not make-believe. Until you realize that, I have no intention of trying to seduce you. I've never had to trick a woman to get her into my bed, and I'm not about to start with you." He tapped the tip of her nose. "Especially not you."

The words had tumbled out of Ben without effort, without conscious planning. Yet as he spoke them, he realized they were true. He was no longer capable of using Sierra, of taking advantage of their mutual attraction to get the letter back. Maybe he never had been.

Ben had no intention of giving up his search. But he'd been tested this evening. Lines had been drawn, bluffs had been called, and now he knew there was a limit to how far he would go in his quest for revenge. When pushed to the brink, he hadn't been able to cross that final line, to exploit Sierra's passion and emotions to achieve his goal. Tonight she'd offered him the most precious gift imaginable: herself.

And after passing self-judgment, Ben had decreed himself unworthy to accept it.

Sierra's eyes were still locked on his, radiating uncertainty. Somehow he'd managed to render her speechless, but even this amazing feat brought Ben no satisfaction. Their encounter had left him with a bitter taste in his mouth and a throbbing ache in his loins. He longed with a sharp, startling intensity to possess her, but he had no intention of making love to Sierra as long as she suspected him of some hidden motive.

Yet he couldn't tell her the truth without endangering her life.

God, what a convoluted mess this was turning into! *Oh, what a tangled web we weave,* Ben thought. He was certain of one thing, though. When he and Sierra finally came together heart, body and soul, it would be with complete openness, sharing and honesty. Sierra deserved it. And Ben would settle for nothing less.

"You're hurting my elbows," she said at last.

Instantly Ben released her. "Sorry. Guess I got carried away."

"Hmm. Seems to be a nasty habit we've both developed lately." The words were flippant, but her combative fire seemed to have died down. The way she was rubbing her elbows made it appear as if she were hugging herself. Almost absently she continued, "It's too late for you to start back for town. You can bed down out here." She ducked her head into the tent, poked around and emerged with a threadbare green army blanket. "Here," she said, avoiding his eyes as she shoved the blanket at him. "I hope you don't snore."

Ben grinned. "You won't hear it inside the tent."

"I wasn't worried about me. Charlemagne's a very light sleeper."

Was she serious? Or was she gently kidding Ben in an effort to mend the breach between them? With Sierra he was never sure. "I'll try to keep the racket down," he assured her.

"Well. Good. G'night, then." She nodded her head once, hesitating as if about to say something more. Then she pivoted on her heel and disappeared into the tent.

"Pleasant dreams," Ben called after her. He retrieved his shirt from the tree branch, rolled it up and stuffed it beneath his head to use as a pillow. Dragging the worn blanket over his creaking joints, he stretched himself out on the rock-hard ground next to the dying campfire.

With a muffled oath, he rolled onto his side and scrabbled behind him for the sharp pebble digging into his back. Pitching the stone into the darkness, he eased himself back down again. Before long the autumn chill was seeping through the thin blanket into his stiff limbs. He tossed from side to side, searching in vain for a comfortable position that would minimize his physical discomfort and soothe his turbulent thoughts.

Somewhere during the hours after midnight he must have dropped off, because all at once he snapped awake, muscles taut as bowstrings, alert to some new presence nearby. The remaining embers from the fire cast only a feeble glow, but suddenly a dark shape blocked out the stars overhead.

Ben hurled himself to one side, scrambling for a stick, a rock, *something* to use as a weapon.

"Hey, it's only me," came a puzzled, faintly amused voice through the darkness.

Ben froze, blood thudding in his ears. Then he flopped back to the ground with a moan, flinging one arm across his eyes.

"Sorry," Sierra said. "I forgot how jumpy you are."

"Forget it," Ben said thickly. "Was there something you wanted?"

"Well, yeah." She crawled over and seated herself cross-legged next to him. "I couldn't sleep."

"So you decided to share the experience?"

"Oops," she said meekly. "Were you asleep?"

Ben shrugged. "It's something I sometimes do at night. Kind of a hobby."

"Oh. Well, sorry." He noticed Sierra was getting better at apologizing. "I won't disturb you for long, then. I just—I just wanted to say...um..." She cleared her throat. "Thanks."

Ben lifted his arm and peered at her with one eye. Without a moon overhead, the darkness was thick as molasses, but that *was* Sierra over there, all right. "Thanks... for what?" he asked cautiously.

He sensed rather than saw her shoulders rise, then drop. "Thanks for... you know. Stopping. Earlier tonight. When I—when we—well, you know."

Ben toyed with the idea of making her elaborate further, then relented and decided to go easy on her. "Sure. But what changed your mind? I thought you were mad at me."

"I am. I *was*, I mean. Until I started thinking about what you said, about how I wasn't being honest. You were right." He heard her draw in a long, quavering breath. "I wanted you to make love to me, Ben. Even though I knew why you were doing it—"

He pushed himself up on one elbow. "Sierra—"

"No, stay there. Let me finish." She swallowed. "Please."

Ben waited.

"You were right. When two people make love, it has to be with openness and honesty, or it isn't worth anything. I guess I forgot that in the...heat of the moment." She sighed. "Thank you for reminding me."

"No problem." Ben reached up and wrapped one of her curls around his finger. "You see, I kind of forgot that, too. I was reminding myself, as well."

"Anyway." She fiddled with her hands. "That was all I wanted to say. I'll let you go back to sleep now."

Ben watched her slim, shadowy outline as she rose to her feet. "See you in the morning," he said quietly.

Sierra paused, then knelt and tugged the rumpled blanket up over his chest. "See you in the morning," she echoed, her breath a gentle puff of warm air against his skin.

With iron self-control Ben stopped himself from following her back to the tent.

Long after Sierra left, he gazed wide-eyed at the canopy of stars winking above. Only now he had more than the concretelike ground and bone-numbing chill to prevent him from sleeping. The tender, disturbing images of Sierra whirling through Ben's brain also kept him awake.

That...and the loud, sloppy, rat-a-tat snoring of that damn mule.

Chapter Six

Sierra peeked surreptitiously at Ben's motionless form. When she was certain he was still asleep, she whipped out a matchbook from behind her back, struck a flame and lit the pile of sticks she'd just arranged. In no time at all the fire was burning cheerfully, banishing the crisp nip in the air. Soon the pungent, mingled aroma of pine, coffee and burning wood filled the campsite.

She settled herself on the ground next to the fire, drawing up her knees and wrapping her arms around them while she watched Charlemagne breakfasting a short distance away on a tasty clump of foliage.

Inevitably Sierra's gaze drifted back to her slumbering companion. She watched the steady rise and fall beneath the blanket as she thought about last night and how close she'd come to giving herself to a man she knew was a liar and a phony.

It was no use trying to analyze the reasons why she'd been so eager to throw away her principles for the sake of one wild, passionate encounter. The complicated tangle of emotions she felt toward Ben defied logical analysis.

With a sigh Sierra pushed the sleeves of her navy blue sweatshirt up over her elbows. Just when she thought she had Ben pegged as an unscrupulous heel, he had to go and do something nice. Like refusing to take advantage of her temporary insanity last night.

Who *was* Ben Halliday, anyway? Were any of the things he'd told her about himself true? Or were his stories about a plane crash and his mother's recent death merely ploys to gain her sympathy and make her more vulnerable to his advances?

But then why—*why* had he withdrawn last night, right when he had Sierra in the palm of his hand?

Maybe she didn't have him totally figured out yet. But she intended to remedy that situation. Pronto.

"Good morning, sleepyhead!" she sang out gaily when the blanket-covered lump began to move. A muffled grumbling was her only reply.

"Coffee's almost ready. Time to rise and shine!"

Ben opened one eye and peeked at her over the edge of the blanket. "Are you always this cheerful first thing in the morning?" His voice sounded as if he were speaking underwater.

"Heavens, are you always this grouchy when you first wake up?"

"Only when I've been kept awake all night by someone's snoring."

"I beg your pardon! I'll have you know, I do *not* snore."

"Not you." He craned his head around and nodded in Charlemagne's direction. "That—that poor excuse for a—"

"Shh! You'll hurt his feelings. Char's very sensitive."

"Hmm, yes. I can tell by the way he's chowing down those weeds that he's a mule of very refined tastes."

"For goodness' sake, have some coffee. Maybe it'll improve your disposition." Sierra pulled one sleeve down over her hand, using it as a pot holder to lift the coffeepot off the fire. "I've only got one cup, so we'll have to share." She filled a dented tin mug and handed it to Ben. "You can go first," she said generously.

He groped his way into a sitting position, squinting as the sun's low-angled rays hit him head-on. Really, the way that little blond cowlick stuck up on the back of his tousled head was just cute as could be. The blanket fell away to reveal his golden chest, sending a little thrill down Sierra's spine that curled her toes.

"Thanks," Ben muttered, taking the mug from her. His fingers twined with hers for an instant, and now *all* of Sierra's extremities were tingling. As he raised the cup to his lips, she was jolted by a vivid recollection of how those lips had felt on hers. She sucked in a quick breath and turned away.

An instant later a sputtering noise made her look back. "Aaargh!" Ben wiped his mouth on the back of his hand. His normally handsome features were screwed into a picturesque expression of disgust. He inspected the contents of the cup like something left too long in the refrigerator. "What the hell kind of coffee *is* this?"

"Cowboy coffee, what else? You toss in a handful of grounds and boil it up good and strong."

Ben made a disdainful smacking sound with his tongue. "Tastes like some cowboy soaked his boots in it."

"Well, excuse me, but I don't have a long-enough extension cord to plug in my fancy filter-drip coffee maker way out here."

"*You* try it! Don't tell me you think this stuff tastes good."

Sierra snatched back the cup and swallowed with gusto. A big mistake. Somehow she managed to choke down the mouthful of coffee, but not convincingly enough to make Ben believe she'd enjoyed it. "I guess it *is* a little strong," she admitted grudgingly.

"*Strong?* It's scorched! You could mix the ashes from that fire into water, and it would taste better."

"Okay, okay, you've made your—"

"Don't toss it on the ground, for God's sake! You'll kill all the plant life within a ten-foot radius and bring the forest service down on our necks."

"Very amusing." The corner of Sierra's mouth twitched in spite of her annoyance. One thing about her association with Ben Halliday: it was never dull. Infuriating, yes. Disorienting, on occasion. And tempting . . . always. But dull? Never.

"How about some breakfast?" she asked, scrambling to her feet.

Ben cocked a wary eyebrow. "You're not going to try to cook pancakes or anything, are you?"

"Ha! Don't you wish? But no, that takes too long. The morning's half-gone already, and I've got lots of work to do today." She crawled into the tent and grabbed a bright yellow box from her replenished store of food. She backed out of the tent on hands and knees. "How about a delicious Yummee Coconut-Creme Cake for breakfast?" She wiggled the box at a tantalizing distance from Ben.

To her amazement, the color drained from his face. Sierra's smile wavered as Ben stared at the box in her hand with a look of pure revulsion. "Where—where did you get that?" he asked in a strangely flat tone. "I don't recall seeing it with your other supplies from the general store."

Sierra blinked. "I picked it up on the way out of town yesterday. See, I was sort of, um, depressed, because of our little . . . fight, and when I'm depressed I kind of, well, pig out on junk food. I bought tons of this stuff—Yummee Coconut-Creme Cakes, Yummee Nut-Butters, Yummee Chocolate Eclairs— hey, are you all right?" she broke off in genuine consternation. Ben was definitely looking a little green around the gills.

His mouth formed a crooked smile. "Yeah. I'm fine. Really."

"Are you sure? 'Cause you don't look so hot, if you don't mind my saying so. Your eyes look a little . . . glazed."

"It's nothing. I just felt queasy for a second." He raked his hair back from his forehead and inhaled deeply. "I'm feeling better already."

Sierra frowned. "Gosh, I'm really sorry. This is all my fault. I should have guessed you were the type of person who'd get nauseous at the sight of junk food first thing in the morning. If only I'd—"

"Hey, forget it. It's no big deal." The color was returning to Ben's face, making him more incredibly attractive than ever. "I think I sat up too fast, that's all. Made me dizzy for a minute." He grasped Sierra's hand and briefly pressed her fingers to his lips. "I'm fine. Honest."

Distracted by the delightful, lingering sensation of his mouth on her skin, she stammered, "I could, uh, make pancakes or something. Eggs? I think I have some powdered eggs around here somewhere..."

Ben made a face. "Now, that really *would* make me queasy." He threw off the blanket and climbed to his feet. Sierra glued her attention to his straining biceps and his sculpted, hair-matted chest as he arched his back, stretching his arms over his head with a huge, jaw-cracking yawn. "Tell you what," he said, scratching his ribs. "What if *I* cook breakfast this morning? It's the least I can do after—well, after everything I've put you through."

"Sure." Sierra's mouth was dry. "I'll have eggs Benedict, an almond croissant and fruit compote." *With you for dessert,* she thought, licking her lips.

Ben's lazy smile made her mouth water. "Coming right up, madam. Would you care for a champagne cocktail while you wait?"

"Make it a Bloody Mary, would you? And keep 'em coming."

Ben could have used a drink himself. The unexpected appearance of that all-too-familiar, lemon-colored box in Sierra's hand had unsettled him like a magnitude-eight earthquake. He slipped inside the tent and, as he pawed through Sierra's cache for breakfast supplies, he came across practically the entire Yummee product line—cookies, cupcakes, doughnuts, pastries. A veritable treasure trove of sugar, flour, butter, cream and chemical preservatives, guaranteed to raise your blood-sugar and cholesterol levels, harden your arteries and deposit an inner tube of extra pounds around your middle. Sierra must have been planning to eat herself out of a depression and into a stupor.

One undisputable fact about Yummee Foods, though. They all tasted delicious. That was one reason the company had grown from a three-person bakery operating out of a ramshackle Grass Valley storefront into the largest retail purveyor of snack foods in the country.

The other reason was the wholesome family image that Yummee Foods' advertising department so carefully cultivated. In countless magazine ads and television commercials throughout the country, freckle-faced, freshly scrubbed kids in baseball caps and pigtails washed down Yummee Tastee-Bars with foamy glasses of milk that left white mustaches over their upper lips. Perfect storybook families romped at the beach or the neighborhood park with Yummee Fudge Tarts spilling from their picnic baskets. Adorable munchkins brought their mothers breakfast in bed, their little tongues poking out in concentration as they carefully balanced a tray holding a bud vase and a Yummee Banana Cupcake with a birthday candle stuck in it. Yummee Foods was as wholesome, as all-American as Mom and apple pie, baseball and the Fourth of July all rolled into one.

And Ben was intimately acquainted with every gooey confection, every sappy smile that greeted the prospect of sinking one's teeth into a scrumptious Yummee whatever. Because Ben himself had approved many of those ads when he'd been Yummee Foods' director of marketing for the entire West Coast.

And that wholesome, respectable, carefully cultivated public image was the cornerstone of Ben's plan to ruin the man who was cofounder, chairman of the board and the very personification of Yummee Foods.

Quentin Jericho.

See how many hospitals would invite Jericho to cut the ribbon at the opening of their new children's wing once Ben exposed him for the cheating bastard he really was.

See how many charitable foundations would ask Jericho to be the keynote speaker at their thousand-dollar-a-plate fund-raisers after the news media got their hands on that incriminating letter.

See how many mothers would keep plunking those bright yellow Yummee Food boxes into their shopping carts when the tabloids at the checkout stand screamed that Jericho was nothing but a conniving sleazeball.

A back-stabbing, blackmailing, definitely *unwholesome* sleazeball.

Civic groups would organize consumer boycotts, and sales of Yummee Foods would drop off. Stores would panic and reduce the shelf space devoted to Yummee products, sending sales plummeting even further. The price of Yummee Foods stock would tumble right off the profit-and-loss charts. The sprawling corporate empire that Quentin Jericho had built on betrayal and broken dreams would disintegrate and collapse. Jericho would be a pariah—scorned by the wealthy, powerful influence makers, society's movers and shakers, the very same elite he had fought so ruthlessly to join.

He wouldn't die penniless; he was too clever for that. But the public admiration, the respect of his business peers and his jealously guarded image as a benevolent, kindly philanthropist would be blown to smithereens.

Jericho's public disgrace wouldn't bring back Ben's father. It wouldn't make up for his mother's lifetime of unhappiness. But it was the best Ben could do. And the least he could do. He owed it to their memories.

He'd had plenty of time during his lengthy convalescence after the plane crash to work out his plan. At first he'd hoped to find proof of Jericho's criminal wrongdoing. Jail seemed too lenient a sentence if the theory Ben had pieced together were true, but any punishment was preferable to letting Jericho go scot-free.

Unfortunately Ben's hopes of seeing Jericho behind bars evaporated the day he was released from the hospital. He'd made straight for corporate headquarters in Los Angeles after disguising his voice, phoning Jericho's office and learning from his secretary that Jericho would be tied up in a meeting for the next hour.

Once inside the building, Ben had headed quickly for the basement storeroom where all the old company records were kept. Apparently Jericho hadn't issued any orders barring him from the premises, because the young woman behind the counter was most helpful, showing Ben exactly where the old account books from the company's sixth year of business were shelved.

Ben scanned the row of dusty ledgers with a sinking heart. Once again Jericho had been one step ahead of him. But he had to make sure.

"Jennifer? Could you come back here for a second, please?" The woman's high heels clicked on the floor as she walked down the aisle to where Ben stood with a frown on his face.

"What is it, Mr. Halliday?"

"I can't seem to find the volume for the year I want. Maybe you could double-check for me. It's probably right in front of my eyes, and I'm just not seeing it."

She scanned the shelf, then pushed her owllike glasses more securely onto her nose and looked again. "Gee, Mr. Halliday, I don't see it, either."

"Could someone have borrowed it?"

She tapped a pencil against her chin. "Not that I recall, but let me check."

Ben followed her back to the front desk, knowing what she would tell him before she said it. "I can't find any record of someone checking it out." Her eyes were locked on the computer screen, fingers poised above the keyboard.

"Maybe sometime while you stepped out to go to the, uh, ladies' room . . ."

She gave him a slightly offended look over the tops of her glasses. "No one removes anything from here without my permission, Mr. Halliday. When I'm not here, the place is locked up." Then her stern expression wavered. "The funny thing is," she mused, "I could swear that volume was there last month when I did the annual inventory, making sure all the records were in their proper places and so forth." She snapped her fingers. "I'm positive it was there."

Ben knew who'd stolen the set of records. And he was willing to bet the book was now nothing but ashes in some incinerator somewhere.

A tide of hopelessness engulfed him, drowning even his anger and frustration. Those records had been the only surviving physical evidence linking Jericho to that long-ago crime. Only someone who suspected foul play—like himself—might have found discrepancies. Now Ben would never be able to prove that Jericho had framed his father and indirectly killed him.

Now there was only one surviving document with the power to bring Jericho to some kind of justice.

The letter.

Somewhere in the Sierra Nevada wandered an old prospector Ben had been forced to entrust with the only way left to avenge his parents.

He had to find Caleb Murphy. He had to get that letter back.

Ben hadn't found Murphy, of course. But seeing those damn yellow boxes of Yummee Macaroons and Yummee Caramel Nuggets and Yummee Jellee Donuts had renewed his determination to find the letter.

Which was why he had no qualms about searching every square inch of Sierra's tent while she waited outside for him to cook breakfast.

He rooted through her duffel bag, the saddlebags, every nook and cranny of that tottering tent without finding so much as a postage stamp. Either Murphy had stashed the letter in some woodpecker's nest somewhere, or Sierra was carrying it on her person.

Ben couldn't avoid a rueful grin at that second possibility. He'd explored enough of Sierra's clothing to be fairly certain the letter wasn't hidden in a pocket or someplace more intimate. But the first possibility sobered him up. Had the secret of the letter's location died with Murphy? Or had he passed it along as part of his bequest to Sierra?

Ben cursed under his breath. He couldn't simply come right out and ask her about it—not without telling her the whole story and making her a target for Jericho's henchmen. And last night had proven that Ben could never bring himself to cajole the truth from her by cold-blooded seduction.

To make matters worse, time was running out. Thanks to Addie Winslow's gift of gab, Ben knew at least one of Jericho's hired guns was hot on his trail. Sierra might already be in danger if Jericho had discovered her romantic involvement with Ben. And if that were the case, the only way to ensure her safety was by finding the letter and delivering it to the press. Once the whole world knew Jericho's sordid secret, Sierra would no longer pose any particular threat to him.

"Hey, what's taking so long? Are you raising the chickens to lay the eggs for our breakfast?" A blinding halo of sunlight surrounded Sierra as she flung back the tent flap and stuck her head inside. "Forget the eggs Benedict. I'll settle for burned biscuits at this point."

"Ah, but *I'm* the one cooking breakfast, remember?"

She drew herself up on her knees and gave Ben a haughty glare. "Are you implying that *I* would burn the biscuits?"

"Let's just say Smokey the Bear has enough to do without rushing over to investigate any charred smells coming from our neck of the woods."

"You ingrate! After I let you camp out here last night, then made you coffee this morning—"

"Let's not bring up the subject of that coffee, agreed? Now, scoot! Out of my way. You're about to be one of the lucky few privileged to feast upon my extra special, super-duper, award-winning blueberry pancakes."

"Those aren't blueberries—those are raisins."

"That's what makes my blueberry pancakes so unique. Now, why don't you make yourself useful and—and . . . let's see, you could . . . no, how about if you . . . oh, never mind. I've got a better idea." Ben pushed past Sierra, his arms full of pancake ingredients. He paused to smack a quick kiss on her pouting lips. "Why don't you plant your pretty little bottom on that log over there and just *watch* me make breakfast?"

"How about if I plant my pretty little fist in your solar plexus?" she replied sweetly. But she did as he suggested.

And she had to admit the man knew how to cook. After a fabulous, rib-sticking breakfast of pancakes, bacon and hot chocolate, Sierra craved nothing more than to kick off her boots, bask in the sun and indulge in a postprandial nap. Preferably with a certain gorgeous blond chef curled up next to her.

But she couldn't let Ben think she was losing her enthusiasm for the hardworking life of a gold miner. So, after washing the breakfast dishes, she announced her intention of hiking upstream to check out some likely prospecting sites.

As she'd expected, Ben tagged along. Hours later Sierra had to chuckle, imagining what her father would say if he could see the man he'd hired to lure her out of the backwoods actually *helping* her look for gold.

She pushed herself stiffly to her knees and swiped a swatch of curls from her forehead with the back of her wrist. Her feet were soaked, her hands gloved with mud. Well, no one ever said panning for gold was glamorous.

She stole a look at Ben, who stood across the stream, filling a pail with dirt and rocks he hacked off the steep embankment. The day had turned unseasonably warm, and he'd stripped off his shirt. Sierra found herself studying the golden sheen of his sweat-slicked back, the rippling muscles of his thick, corded arms as he plunged the small shovel into the dark, rich earth again and again. . . .

Then Charlemagne sneezed, jolting Sierra from her trance. For a moment she'd forgotten her aching back, her dirt-encrusted hands and the icy water seeping into her boots.

For a moment she'd forgotten that Ben was nothing but a mercenary, that his feigned interest in her would last only as long as her father signed his paycheck.

Yet when he turned and waded back across the stream, something about the way the water swirled and churned around his solid thighs made Sierra catch her breath. Water droplets sparkled across his chest like diamonds, and when he shook a damp lock of hair from his face and sent her a crooked, dazzling smile, she swayed with sudden giddy happiness.

"Find any gold yet?" he called.

"Huh? Er, no, not yet." She wouldn't have believed that anything could possibly improve Ben's appearance, but a day in the sun had bronzed his face and upper torso, enhancing his rugged good looks. It figured. Why couldn't he be one of those people who broil like a lobster? Sierra could practically hear the freckles popping out across the bridge of her nose.

Ben set the bucket of damp earth at her feet and propped his hands on his lean hips. "Striking it rich seems like kind of a slow process."

Instantly Sierra was on guard for more sighs and head shaking, more pleas to give up this craziness for the sanity of civilization. But the twinkle in Ben's azure eyes seemed perfectly innocent.

"It *is* a slow process," she replied cautiously. "But once I find a spot where I can pan out some gold, I'm going to build a sluice box."

Ben made a rocking motion with his hand. "You mean one of those old wooden troughs like the forty-niners used to use?"

She nodded. "I can process a lot more material that way. But I've got to keep taking samples along the stream till I locate a gold-producing site."

"Something that's been bothering me . . . how's the owner of this land going to react when he hears about your bonanza?"

Kneeling, Sierra scooped a few handfuls of dirt from Ben's pail into her dented metal pan. "This is public land we're on, so I should be able to stake a claim to the mineral rights once I decide where I want to mine. Usually all you have to do is post boundary markers and pay a fee to the government. Grandpa used to do it all the time."

She felt Ben's eyes upon her as she dipped the pan into the slow-moving current, swirling the pile of dirt around to float away the lighter material and allow the heavier gold to settle out.

He knelt beside her. "Would you mind if I tried that?"

She glanced sideways in surprise. "Well . . . sure. I mean, no—go ahead." She placed the pan in his hands, then picked out some twigs and larger rocks the current had washed clean. "Swish it around in a circle . . . that's right, slow and easy."

"This is kind of like the way people used to winnow grain back in the old days—tossing it up in the air and letting the wind blow away the chaff."

"Exactly," Sierra replied, tickled by the intent concentration etched in Ben's face. "You can swirl it a little faster than that. If there's any gold, it should settle into the bottom quite nicely." She flicked a handful of small pebbles into the stream.

Ben kept silent, his eyes riveted to the increasingly fine material sloshing around the pan. "I suppose your grandfather taught you how to do this," he said after a few minutes.

"Yup. I was panning gold before I even knew how to walk. My mom would bring me up here, set me on the edge of a stream and stick an aluminum pie plate in my hands."

Ben shook his head, grinning. "I can't quite picture Maxwell Sloane wading through this muck, getting his feet all wet and his clothes muddy."

Sierra tensed. "No, I don't suppose you can." Her tone was as icy as the stream.

Ben froze. "Sierra, I didn't mean that the way it sounded," he said hastily. "I don't have to know your father personally to have trouble imagining him in this environment."

"Let's change the subject, shall we?" It seemed to Sierra as if the sun had hidden behind a cloud, although the sky was still the same intense lapis-lazuli color as before. But she couldn't resist mumbling, "Besides, Daddy never came up here when Mom brought me to visit Grandpa. He was too busy with work."

"Sierra, I'm sorry—"

"Move the pan slower now. You're getting down to the fine sediment. See how black that concentrate is? That's all the iron that's sunk to the bottom."

He peered into the pan. "What do we do now?"

"Tilt out most of the water, then kind of spread the silt over the bottom so we can see if there's any gold mixed in."

Ben studied the pan as if preparing to perform brain surgery. His eyes lit up. "Gold! Hey, look, we found gold! I'll be damned—I never thought—but there it is! Gold!"

Sierra glanced at the pan's contents, then bit her lip to keep from smiling. "I hate to burst your bubble, but that isn't gold."

Ben's jaw dropped in disbelief. "Whaddya mean it isn't gold? I'd like to know what you'd call those little gold flecks, then."

Sierra folded her arms and gave him a Cheshire-cat grin. "Ever hear of fool's gold?"

"Fool's . . . gold?"

"Also known as iron or copper pyrite. Personally I've always thought 'fool's gold' a much more appropriate name. So descriptive, don't you think?"

"Ha, ha." Ben examined the glitter with mingled doubt and regret. "You're sure this isn't the real McCoy?"

"Look." Sierra pulled a Swiss Army knife from her back pocket and wrenched open the blade. "See how brittle this stuff is, how it flakes off? And gold is softer, so I'd be able to scratch it with the tip of this knife."

"Oh."

"And watch." She took the pan from him and leaned over it, positioning her body to block the sun's rays. "See? Gold glitters even when it's not in direct sunlight."

"But this stuff doesn't."

"Nope."

"So it's worthless."

"From a monetary standpoint, yes. But at least we've eliminated this spot as a likely location for any gold deposits." She rinsed the black residue back into the stream. "So we *are* making progress."

Ben's gaze followed the discarded silt as it swirled and dissipated. "I can see you need to be an optimist in this line of work."

"It helps." She shoved on her knees and rose to her feet. "It also helps to be determined."

"Stubborn, in other words."

Sierra laughed. "That's another way of putting it."

Ben unfolded himself from his sitting position. "Well, you've certainly mastered *that* part of it, anyway. And I must admit you've got a great panning technique."

"I learned from the best," she said, strapping the pan onto Charlemagne's back along with the rest of her gear. "Come on, I'm starved. Let's head back to camp and see what I can rustle up for supper."

"I can fix supper," he said quickly.

Sierra fired a withering look over her shoulder. "Just for that crack," she said, "I'm going to try out a new recipe on you."

Despite her threat, Ben whistled a cheerful tune as they plodded back to camp. Sierra dragged Charlemagne along like a child on the way to the dentist. Ben's muscles still ached, but it was the kind of good, satisfied ache he got after an afternoon of racquetball or a day spent painting the outside of his house. Nothing like good old-fashioned manual labor to work out the tension and strip away the pressures of modern living.

He barely noticed the slight stiffness in his injured leg, and the warm sun was like a heating pad on his various bumps and bruises. An entire day without any physical mishaps! Maybe his luck was finally changing. Maybe tonight he'd figure out how to get the letter back, maybe Sierra and he would—

From the corner of his eye Ben caught a flash of black-and-white darting through the underbrush just to Sierra's right. He halted in his tracks. "Hey, be careful, I think—"

Charlemagne suddenly snorted and kicked at the brush, the only abrupt movement Ben had ever seen the mule make.

Sierra whirled around. "What the heck—?"

"Duck!" Ben shouted, backpedaling for all he was worth.

"Char, what's gotten into you?"

"Sierra, watch out—"

"Uh-oh!"

"—for that—"

Sierra shrieked.

An acrid, earthy aroma filled the air.

"—skunk," Ben finished lamely.

Chapter Seven

"I don't suppose you have any tomato juice," Ben said as the merry band straggled back into camp.

"Thirsty?"

"It's the best thing for getting rid of that mule's, uh, smell."

Sierra threw him a wry look. "I *know* that. And yes, I have some. Grandpa always kept it around in case of skunk attacks." She lifted the saddlebags off Charlemagne's back, holding them at arm's length as she draped them over a tree limb.

Leaving Ben gingerly holding the mule's halter, Sierra ducked into the tent and emerged with a large, slightly rusted can of tomato juice, which she proceeded to open with the can opener on her Swiss Army knife.

Ben eyed the can dubiously. "How old is that stuff, anyway?"

"We're not going to drink it—we're going to pour it over Char."

"Better take that hat off first."

"Huh? Oh, good idea." She plucked at the knotted ribbon tying the mule's hat on. "Drat, this thing won't come loose."

"For God's sake, cut it off with your knife. I never saw such a mangy-looking hat in my life, anyway."

Sierra glared at him.

"Don't you think it makes that poor mule look just a little . . . undignified?" Ben asked.

"Grandpa himself put this hat on Charlemagne, and I never wanted to take it off. Okay?" At last she succeeded in working the knot loose. Pinching her nose, she also pinched the hat between thumb and forefinger and hung it on a nearby branch. "Okay, Char—hold still, now."

Charlemagne, however, wasn't about to let himself be marinated without a fight. By the time Ben and Sierra finished rubbing the mule down with tomato juice, they both looked as if they'd been thoroughly doused themselves.

"If I'd known a mule was going to shake tomato juice all over me today, I'd have brought along a change of clothing," Ben grumbled.

Sierra bestowed a sweet smile on him. "Guess you'll have to wear your birthday suit for a while after you rinse out your clothes in the stream."

"You wish."

"Don't flatter yourself."

"Didn't you save any of your grandfather's clothes?"

"What on earth for? I gave them all to Pete." She yanked on Charlemagne's halter. "Come on, you troublesome beast. Let's go dunk ourselves, shall we?" As she headed for the stream, mule in tow, she called over her shoulder, "And I don't want to see you spying on us from the bushes, either."

Ben was about to launch a nasty retort after her when a sudden thought occurred to him. A sly smile crept over his face. "What do you take me for, some kind of Peeping Tom?" he shouted after her good-naturedly.

Then he plunked himself down on the ground, drew up his knees and waited.

At the edge of the stream, Sierra did a quick reconnaissance to make sure she was unobserved. Then she stripped off her clothes and stuck her toe into the water. "Oh, Lord!" she gasped. "Char, you're not going to be too happy about this."

She temporarily forgot the frigid temperature while she struggled to drag the reluctant mule into the stream. "Come on, you ornery critter! Do you want to smell like skunk and tomato the rest of your life? What if some gorgeous lady mule comes along while you reek like this? *Then* you'll be sorry."

Somehow, with a combination of pushing, pulling, pleas and threats, Sierra managed to maneuver Charlemagne into the creek. As she scooped up handfuls of water to splash over the mule's haunches, a vivid flashback forced its way into her mind: memories of the warm, whirling Jacuzzi at her health club in Los Angeles.

She gritted her teeth and banished the image from her mind. "This is much healthier," she muttered. "Gets the old circulation pumping." For good measure she scrubbed her own arms and legs with sand, gulping in quick lungfuls of air as the freezing water swirled around her waist.

All at once Charlemagne decided he'd soaked long enough, and Sierra had to lunge for his halter as he began to thrash toward the stream bank. Somehow she lost her footing on a moss-covered rock, and before she could catch her balance she pitched forward, managing a high-pitched yelp before the icy water closed over her head.

She emerged thoroughly drenched, teeth chattering, limbs quaking from the incredible cold, just in time to see Charlemagne vanish into the trees.

"Sierra?"

With a cry of outraged protest she ducked beneath the water again, clutching her arms over her breasts. "You—you lecherous hyena! Get away from here! You promised not to peek!"

"Calm down, will you?" came Ben's amused voice from behind the bushes at the top of the embankment. "I swear my eyes are closed. But I heard you scream—"

"So of course you thought you had to come to my rescue again." She barely recognized her own voice, so distorted was it by her rattling teeth.

"Guess I was wrong. You obviously don't require any assistance. But tell me one thing—are you planning to put those same clothes right back on?"

Sierra thrust a groan through her clenched jaws. "You rat! Why didn't you remind me to bring a change of clothing down here?"

"Oh, I wouldn't presume to make suggestions," Ben replied in a voice barbed with mirth, "since you've made it quite clear you're perfectly capable of handling your own affairs without any advice from me."

Well, he had her there. Sierra's instinctive response was that she would rather freeze to death in that stream than ask Ben for help. Still, she'd probably pass out first, and he'd no doubt enjoy fishing her dripping, naked body out of the stream.

Through numb lips she squeezed out the words, "Would you *please* go back to the tent and bring me something to wear?"

His chuckle drifted down the slope, and she spent the next several minutes fantasizing about setting Ben Halliday adrift on an iceberg somewhere in the northernmost reaches of the Arctic.

"Here I come, ready or not!"

By now the only remaining feeling in Sierra's body was relief at his return. "Keep your eyes closed, you varmint!"

Ben emerged from the bushes, one hand shading his eyes while the other extended a bundle of clothing.

"Toss it on the ground right there. No, don't come any closer!"

"Oh, for Pete's sake—"

"I mean it! And quit peeking."

"I am *not*—"

"You are too! I can see your beady little eyes between your fingers."

"Hey, maybe you'd like someone else to help you instead."

"Well, if you can't behave like a gentleman for one minute—"

"Gentleman? That's a laugh! You've called me every kind of animal life from pond scum to jackal, and now you expect me to act like a gentleman?"

"Turn your back."

"This may come as a shock to you, but I *have* seen naked women before. I'm not going to lose control at the sight of your gorgeous, sexy—"

"I have absolutely no interest in the history of your love life. Now, turn your back."

Slumping his shoulders with an exaggerated sigh, Ben wheeled around. Sierra paused a moment, then darted out of the stream and scooped up the pile of clothes Ben had dropped next to his feet. In a flash she scampered uphill to the concealing shelter of a thick Douglas fir.

It took several attempts before she could stab her trembling legs into the tan corduroys, her shivering, goose-pimpled arms into the sleeves of her black pullover sweater. Her stiffened fingers refused to cooperate, and she fumbled helplessly with the zipper of her slacks until she heard Ben call, "Need any help?"

Oh, wouldn't he love that? She finally jerked the zipper up, gathered her wits about her and stepped into the open. Ben was watching her from below, his mouth twitching in a devilish grin that made her simultaneously want to shove him into the creek...and to shed her clothes again. Slowly.

She must be suffering from exposure. Her heart was thumping a mile a minute, and her skin prickled with a strange tingling. Probably frostbite.

"Your turn," she announced.

"Whatever you say," Ben replied with a sly grin. He began to strip off his clothes immediately, never taking his eyes from Sierra's. She swallowed. "I'll just, uh, go now, and, er, let you have some...privacy."

"Don't leave on my account." His words trailed after her as she beat a hasty retreat back to camp. The next sounds she heard were a loud splash and an ear-splitting whoop.

By the time she heard Ben rustling through the bushes, Sierra had succeeded in recapturing Charlemagne and tying him up to his favorite tree. Now she was working on starting a fire. If only those matches weren't tucked into Ben's shirt pocket . . .

Bold as you please, he stepped into the clearing with nothing to shield himself but an armload of soggy clothing. Sierra sucked in her breath and quickly turned her back on him, but not before getting a tantalizing glimpse of his boldly sculpted, Norse-god-like physique.

"Haven't you one single ounce of propriety?" she mumbled.

"This was your idea, remember? And a darn clever way for you to ogle my body, too."

"Don't be ridiculous." A light-headed fog drifted over her. "Here. Cover yourself up." She snatched up the green army blanket and flung it backwards over her shoulder.

"Well, as long as you're done gawking at me, I *am* getting a mite chilly."

How peculiar. A minute ago Sierra's teeth had been chattering, but now an odd, unsettling warmth had stolen over her limbs.

"Why don't you light a fire?" Ben suggested.

"Light it yourself," she grumbled.

"Somehow I knew you were going to say that." He crouched beside her, the blanket draped around him like a toga. With a flourish he produced the matchbook. "Lucky for us I had the foresight to take this out of my pocket before washing my clothes in the stream." He pushed the scattered sticks into a pile and ignited them immediately. "I'm sorry, what did you say?"

"Nothing."

"Hmm. I could have sworn you just made some kind of nasty comment."

Ben's thigh was pressing against Sierra's, making her too vividly aware that only a couple thin layers of fabric separated them. She clambered to her feet. "I'd better hang your clothes up to dry." She felt his eyes on her as she moved away.

"I rinsed out yours, too. You left them down by the stream. Guess you were in too much of a hurry."

She ignored his amused smirk, scooping up the wet clothes and hanging them over some bushes. Why couldn't this little run-in with the skunk have happened earlier in the day, so the sun could dry the clothing quickly? An artist's palette of red, orange and lavender splashed across the western horizon, providing a breathtaking view but not much heat. It was liable to be midmorning before Ben was safely garbed in his clothes again. Until then Sierra would have to keep fending off the sensual images and disturbing desires aroused by that sleek male body moving around beneath that damn blanket.

When she returned to the campfire with two packages of freeze-dried beef stew, she seated herself on the opposite side, as far away from Ben as she could get. He arched an eyebrow at the sight of the aluminum saucepan she positioned over the flames. "Is that the same one Johnny Appleseed used to wear on his head?"

"I admit it's seen better days, but it still works. Of course, if you don't dare eat anything cooked in it, I could wolf down all this stew by myself."

"And spoil that girlish figure? I couldn't let you do that."

"Gee, thanks."

"How come you're sitting way over there? That creature squirted your mule, not me. Don't tell me I smell like eau de skunk."

"No..."

"Of course, maybe I should find out what *you* smell like before I invite you to sit next to me." He sidled around the fire and inched up next to her. Before she could dodge out of reach, he buried his face in her neck and inhaled deeply. "Mmm, you smell delicious. All clean and outdoorsy."

"Cut that out," she warned, nearly tipping the pan into the fire. "Or I'll dump this stew into your lap."

"Sierra, Sierra," Ben sighed, drawing back. "I've never met a woman with such violent tendencies. Why can't you be nice to me for even a little while?"

"Because what *you're* doing isn't very nice. Pretending to be interested in me just so you can earn a big bonus from my father."

With a groan Ben fell backward and propped himself on his elbows. "I thought we had that all straightened out. You don't still believe that ridiculous theory, do you?"

Sierra stirred furiously. "What else am I supposed to believe? You drop into my life from out of the blue, tell me a pack of lies and won't fess up when I finally figure you out."

"Look, maybe I haven't been perfectly straightforward with you—"

"Ha! *That's* an understatement."

"—but I swear to you, I've never met your father, never worked for your father, didn't even know who your father *was* when I met you."

She continued stirring, trying to scrape the burning stew off the bottom of the pan.

"Sierra? You do believe me, don't you?" Ben crooked a finger around one of her stray curls, lightly stroking the sensitive skin behind her ear.

She shivered, but didn't tilt her head away from him.

"I can't bear for you to think me some kind of...paid stud or something."

Sierra chuckled.

"Well, that's what you think, isn't it?" His low voice tickled her ear. "Let me prove you wrong." He drew his finger lightly down her backbone. "Believe me, there's no way I could fake what I feel for you. There isn't enough money in the world."

A delicious languor enveloped Sierra, radiating from the pressure of Ben's hand splayed across the base of her spine. Her eyes closed, and her head rolled back. Oh, what heaven it would be to succumb to the sweet yearnings Ben stirred inside her! How easy it would be simply to shove aside her doubts and surrender to the magic of his touch....

The smell of burning stew jarred her from her treacherous thoughts. "Yipes!" With a clatter she knocked the pan aside, nearly spilling the contents into the flames. "Ouch, darn it! I need a pot holder or something."

"Here, use this." Ben pressed a corner of the blanket into her hand, and without thinking, she pulled it forward to wrap around the pan's handle. She nearly dropped the stew again when she turned and saw how much of Ben she'd inadvertently exposed. Flickering flames and the sunset's dying glow burnished his nude male torso, emphasizing the lean, sturdy lines of his muscular build. The blanket slashed across his thighs, revealing his long, golden-haired legs and leaving very little to the imagination.

Sierra's imagination ran amok, anyway. She averted her gaze, but not before she saw the sizzling sparkle in Ben's eyes and the sexy quirk of his mouth. "Why, sweetheart, if you'd prefer me without the blanket, all you have to do is ask." He leaned forward and purred in her ear, "No need to resort to all this subterfuge."

"What I'd prefer is this camp without *you* in it," she retorted, flinching from the low rumbling vibrations that traveled along her nerve endings. "Now, shut up and eat." She slopped some stew into a tin bowl and thrust it in his direction.

She picked up the pan—thank goodness aluminum cooled off so quickly!—and raised a spoonful of stew to her lips.

"Trying to save on dishwashing detergent?" Ben asked.

She paused. "I only have one bowl."

"We could share it."

"No, thanks."

He shrugged, then sampled his stew. He chewed thoughtfully before swallowing. "Up to your usual culinary standards, I see."

Sierra smacked her lips. "Actually it tastes kind of scorched to me."

"That's what I mean."

She lifted her chin. "You can go hungry if you'd rather."

"Well, if that's the only alternative . . ." Ben ladled another bite into his mouth and beamed at her. "Mmm, yummy," he pronounced, licking his lips.

"And would you mind covering yourself up? There's nothing more unappetizing than staring at a hairy chest."

"Quit staring, then."

Sierra blushed to the roots of her chestnut curls, but at least Ben tugged the blanket up around his shoulders so she could finally concentrate on eating.

By the time she scraped the pan clean, Sierra's stomach was filled, but some other part of her still felt empty and unsatisfied. She tried to ignore it by bustling around the camp, rearranging their damp clothing, rinsing out their dishes in a bucket of water she fetched from the creek. All the while she sensed Ben tracking her every move like radar.

Darn him, anyway! Why couldn't he accept that the game was over, go back to the city and leave her alone? But a tiny part of her was glad Ben was so persistent, that he seemed determined to stick to her like flypaper until her father called him off.

Ye gods, he was making her nervous as a turkey on the day before Thanksgiving! She dropped the bowl on the ground, then knocked over the water bucket when she grabbed for it. Now she'd have to schlepp all the way down to the stream again, or else ask Ben to do it.

She'd rather ask Attila the Hun to buy Girl Scout cookies.

When Sierra returned after refilling the water bucket, Ben was lying on his back, hands folded behind his head, watching her. "Boy, this is the life, isn't it? A roaring campfire . . . a galaxy of stars overhead . . . the scent of wet mule wafting on the breeze . . . say, what's for dessert, anyway?" he asked cheerfully.

"Help yourself," she replied with a wave of her hand. "I've got a whole tent full of junk food."

"I've got a better idea," Ben said, pushing himself onto his side and letting the blanket fall across his ribs.

"I'll bet," she said, circling wide to avoid his grasp. "You're just full of suggestions, aren't you?"

"*I* was thinking about that flask of whiskey," he said, placing his hand over his heart. "What were *you* thinking about?"

"Murder," she grumbled, going over to root through the tent. "Here. Let the good times roll." She lobbed the silver flask at him.

"Aren't you going to join me?"

The evening *was* turning a bit nippy. Maybe a little swig of the ol' firewater wouldn't be such a bad idea. For strictly medicinal purposes, of course.

Sierra lowered herself next to the fire, just close enough to Ben so she could take the whiskey from his outstretched hand. As she raised the flask to her lips, she couldn't help envisioning how his mouth had closed around it moments before.

Once again she forgot to sip cautiously and nearly choked as the potent liquid seared her throat. Ben grinned at her, making her far more intoxicated than one gulp of whiskey could have.

When she handed the flask back, a shadow crossed his face. "Your fingers are ice-cold."

"My hands got wet when I refilled the water bucket."

Ben set the flask aside and scooted next to her. Before Sierra could protest, he'd imprisoned her hands between his, rubbing briskly back and forth. "Poor baby. Your fingers feel like icicles."

Actually her fingers felt pretty nice at the moment, but she didn't bother to correct him.

He slid one hand up her arm. "Good grief, it's not just your hands! You're cold all over!"

"I guess it *has* gotten kind of chilly since the sun went down. . . ."

"It's more than that. I think you took too long a swim in the stream earlier."

"That's because I had to wait for someone to bring me my clothes."

"That's only because you forgot them yourself."

"That's only because—" A sneeze cut short her reply.

With a worried frown Ben laid his hand across her forehead. "Hmm. You don't *feel* like you're running a fever. . . ."

"I'm fine," she insisted, batting his hand away. Then she sneezed again.

"Don't try to tell me this is your hay fever acting up all of a sudden. You're coming down with a cold, and it's no wonder—splashing around in a frigid stream all day, sitting out in the night air with nothing on but that flimsy sweater—"

"*You* picked out the sweater—"

"And I'd never forgive myself if you caught pneumonia as a result. Come here." Ben unwrapped his blanket from one shoulder.

"*Eek!* What do you think you're—"

"Get in here where it's nice and warm."

"Ben, no!"

Before Sierra could escape, he'd bundled her into the blanket next to him.

"This is no time for modesty," he told her.

"This is no time for—for— oh, lord." Sierra gulped.

"There, isn't that much better?" Ben rubbed his hands briskly up and down her arms, igniting a delightful, tingling heat that had nothing to do with friction.

"Mmm," she responded, suddenly incapable of verbal communication.

He kneaded her back and shoulders with expert thoroughness, leaving her limp as a rag doll. Warmth invaded every cell in her body. Tension seeped away, replaced by a slowly building fire whose flames licked along her flesh wherever Ben stroked and prodded her.

"Now I know what heaven feels like," she said in a thick voice.

"Sweetheart, heaven feels a lot better than this," Ben growled in her ear. "And I'm going to prove it to you."

"Mmm . . ." Sierra descended into incoherent moaning again as Ben worked his hands down her spine, pushing, squeezing, massaging that fine line between pain and pleasure.

When he slipped his hands beneath her sweater, Sierra didn't utter a peep of protest. She floated lazily, suspended in a dreamlike trance that vaporized any resistance, worry or suspicion. Pure sensation. That was her only conscious awareness, and she reveled in it.

Until Ben circled her waist with his arms and slid his hands up to gently cup her breasts. "Um, Ben . . . just what do you think you're—"

"Shh." His whisper was a heated gust teasing the nape of her neck. "Trying to make you warm." He continued his tender massaging of her pliant flesh, molding her breasts into the hollows of his big hands like an expert sculptor working with soft clay. "Am I succeeding?"

"Hmm?"

"Are you getting warm?" He pressed a kiss into the cleft just above her collarbone.

"Yes . . . warm . . ." Her head fell back to rest against his shoulder, and his bristly jaw prickled against her cheek with delightful abrasion. A tiny pang of disappointment pricked her when he shifted his attention from her breasts to her thighs and began to rub his hands briskly back and forth over her pants.

No doubt about it, she *was* getting warm. Even a bit overheated, perhaps. Whether her rise in temperature resulted from Ben's vigorous massage or the sharing of his body heat or simply the blood-simmering excitement of his nearness, Sierra couldn't tell.

Whatever the source, she was definitely heating up. Maybe getting a little *too* hot. How else to explain this sudden overwhelming urge to strip off her clothes and bare her skin to the night air?

Ben drew her knee up so he could cradle her foot between his hands. His chin rested cozily on her shoulder while he pressed his thumbs into the arch of her foot, then twisted each of her toes between his fingers. A wonderful tingling spread up her calves as he took her other foot and continued his thorough ministrations.

"Such dainty feet," he mused, his vocal chords vibrating against her skin. "There! Have I missed a spot anyplace?"

"Mmm, no, I don't think so."

"What about . . . right here?" He lifted her curls and planted a leisurely kiss on the nape of Sierra's neck, sending a jolt of electricity zapping down her spine.

"No, I think you got that spot before. . . ."

"Then how about . . . here?" He nuzzled her temple.

"Well . . ."

"I *know* I didn't miss these." His hands skimmed beneath her sweater and found her breasts again. He flicked his thumbs across the hardened peaks.

"Oh, God," she moaned.

"Sierra . . ." Ben's voice was muffled as he buried his face in her hair. With one swift, sure motion he spanned her waist with his strong hands and twisted her around to lie across his lap. The blanket fell away, exposing his torso as he cradled her in his arms and gazed down at her. Sierra could see the rapid flutter of his heartbeat as his chest rose and fell.

She wasn't conscious of holding her breath as Ben lowered his head to hers, eyes glowing like fiery cobalt, until his face blocked out the stars and he seized her lips with a passionate urgency that threatened to drive all the air from her lungs.

Dizzy, she clung to him while the constellations reeled overhead. She locked her arms around his neck, weaving her fingers through his coarse golden hair. Ben was her only anchor in the explosive, tumultuous upheaval of her universe, and Sierra hung on to him for dear life. He *was* her life, wasn't he? But no, wait, how could that be? Ben was a double-dealing, unscrupulous scoundrel . . . wasn't he?

Then why did she feel at this moment that she'd gladly, willingly follow him to the ends of the earth, no matter what his reasons for leading her there?

Could it possibly be she was in *love* with this double-dealing, unscrupulous scoundrel?

Instantly Sierra shoved the thought aside as too horrible to contemplate. Because if it were true that she'd somehow fallen in love with Ben, she was in big, big trouble.

But she couldn't so easily ignore the insistent, eager pressure of his mouth on hers, not when he stroked so languidly into the deepest recesses of her mouth before twining his tongue deliciously with hers. Not when the musky male scent of him filled her senses and the caress of his hands on her body sent her soaring into orbit.

Not when every molecule in her body was clamoring for his touch, straining toward him with agonizing, rapturous anticipation.

When Ben finally raised his head, his lips glistened with moisture, his eyes flared with wild, urgent intensity. His breath came in ragged gusts. "Sweetheart," he gasped, placing his hand alongside her face. His fingers trembled slightly. "Sierra, you feel so wonderful, you're so warm and sweet...." A shadow of regret or sorrow drifted across his handsome, tormented face. "Ah, darling, if only... if only..."

The rest of his words were smothered between their lips as he bent his head to hers for another earth-shattering, heart-wrenching kiss. Then, almost before Sierra realized it, Ben had loosened her clothing and cast it aside like a handful of leaves. He caressed her with wandering hands that trailed a path of shimmering desire in their wake. He was like the prince in the Sleeping Beauty fairy tale, only instead of waking her instantly with one kiss, he brought her gradually to life, inch by square inch over every new place he touched her.

Somehow the blanket became entangled around their limbs, and when Ben tugged it impatiently aside to free their movements, Sierra felt the hard, pulsating evidence of his desire. With a slight gasp, she tensed. Ben paused, a look of grim yet tender understanding softening the edges of his features.

"I won't pressure you into anything you aren't ready for," he said in a voice harsh with yearning. "Say the word, and we'll stop." He brushed her chin, then trailed one finger down her throat, along the valley between her breasts, across her belly to the quivering juncture of her thighs. He waited.

Sierra's eyes expanded into dark, wavering pools of excitement and uncertainty. Ben was leaving the decision up to her. Not exactly fair, after he'd spent what seemed an eternity stoking her internal fires to the brink of spontaneous combustion.

She wanted Ben with an aching urgency that consumed her in towering flames, nearly blinding her to the consequences of such reckless indulgence. Yet he hadn't taken advantage of her obvious weakness. Surely that meant that somewhere inside, Ben Halliday possessed at least a spark of integrity, a flicker of decency.

Maybe he wasn't rotten to the core, after all. Maybe he was even a man . . . worth loving.

It was that possibility more than any other consideration that decided for her. Sierra refused to believe that she could have fallen so completely under the spell of a man with absolutely no redeeming qualities. Something fundamentally honest about Ben, something basically good and honorable and true beckoned her.

Her lips barely moved as she whispered, "Don't stop, Ben. Don't . . . stop."

Joy, relief, expectation flared in his eyes. "Never," he replied, shifting his arm beneath her shoulders to lay her gently on the blanket. "I'll never, ever stop. . . ." His face blurred into a kaleidoscope of whirling sensations, desires and emotions as he lowered himself on top of Sierra. He entwined his legs with hers, and she surrendered to the delirious pleasure of his long, hard body pressed against her heated flesh.

She clutched handfuls of his hair when he dropped his mouth to her breasts and drew moist, lazy circles with his tongue. When he flicked teasingly across her taut, straining nipples, she couldn't stifle the cry that erupted from her throat.

She writhed against him, seeking release for the smoldering pressure building up in her abdomen. Only Ben could free her from this maddening, desperate desire and send her soaring to heights of pleasure she could barely begin to imagine. . . .

Then, with a groan of anguish, Ben pushed himself off Sierra and rolled away. "I can't do it," he said in a strangled voice. "Damn it, it's not right! I just can't do it." He buried his face in his hands, shaking his head. A smothered stream of curses escaped through his fingers.

Sierra stared at him with mounting horror and humiliation. After she'd practically begged him to make love to her, he was spurning her rash, foolish surrender! What an idiot she'd been, what a lovesick, passion-besotted—

"I'm sorry." Ben smoothed back his tousled hair and looked at her. Suddenly Sierra realized she was stark naked, and the idea didn't hold nearly the same appeal it had moments ago. "Sierra, the thing is—"

She grabbed the blanket and flung it around herself as she jumped to her feet.

"Hey, wait a second! Where are you going? *I* need that blanket!"

Sierra was about to shoot a scornful reply over her shoulder when she saw Ben scrambling after her. The prospect of being pursued by six feet of lean, naked masculinity was more than she could deal with at the moment.

Quickly she unwrapped the blanket and hurled it at his head, hoping to block his vision while she scooped up her sweater and pants. By the time Ben finished thrashing around and emerged from the scratchy folds, Sierra was backing toward the tent, covering herself as best she could with her hastily retrieved bundle of clothing.

"You keep away from me, Ben Halliday, you—you slinking weasel! You slithering snake! You—you—slimy barracuda!"

"Barracuda?"

"I mean it! Stay back! Don't come any closer!"

"Sierra, for God's sake, you have to let me explain—"

"I don't have to let you do anything!" Her backward retreat came to a temporary halt when she bumped into the tent.

"Sweetheart, there's a perfectly reasonable explanation for this, if you'll only stand still and listen—"

"Don't you 'sweetheart' me. I'm warning you, Ben Halliday, I've got Pete's shotgun around here someplace, and I know how to use it!" She ducked her head and backed into the tent. The vision of Ben clutching the green blanket around his waist like a hula skirt would have struck Sierra as vastly humorous under any other circumstances. But right now she was too unnerved by the determined slant of his brow, the exasperated scowl on his face.

"Don't you dare follow me in here! Get out! Get out, I tell you!"

Ben kept advancing with the relentlessness of a bulldozer. Sierra licked her lips, darting her eyes from side to side as she searched frantically for an escape route out of this trap.

Then she tripped over an open box of Yummee Cocoa Crunches and toppled backward, arms cartwheeling through the air, clothes flying in all directions. She landed with a jarring thud that knocked the breath out of her.

Ben dove on top of her, pinning her wrists to the ground and imprisoning her with the unyielding length of his body. A muscle rippled along his clenched jaw, and when he spoke, his breath rustled the wisps of hair curling at her temples.

"For once—just *once*!—I'm going to talk and you're going to listen. Got that? *I* talk, *you* listen. Think you can remember that?"

Sierra glowered at him. "What choice do I—"

"Ah-ah-ah . . . no talking."

Even without words the glare she aimed at Ben certainly got her message across. She chafed under the handcuffs of his fingers, squirming beneath the oppressive weight of his body. When even Sierra had to admit there would be no escape until she allowed Ben to say his piece, she collapsed in surrender.

A temporary truce, however. Because as soon as Ben released her, Sierra was going to kick his scurvy hide out of these mountains, back to Los Angeles and all the way into the Pacific Ocean.

"Okay," she said. "Talk."

Chapter Eight

The tip of Ben's nose itched, but he didn't dare scratch it. If he freed even one of Sierra's wrists, she was likely to take a swing at him.

Now that she'd grudgingly agreed to let him explain why he'd stopped making love to her, Ben hadn't the faintest idea what to say. He wasn't sure he understood it himself. All he knew was that he'd never taken a woman to bed under false pretenses, and he wasn't about to start now. Not with Sierra. She was far too special to him.

For an instant Ben considered spilling out the whole story—the letter, his parents, his crusade for revenge against Quentin Jericho—all of it.

Then he remembered the stark terror of those moments before the plane crash. He remembered the ruthless, evil glint in Jericho's eyes when Ben had confronted him at the funeral and threatened to expose him. And he remembered Addie's innocent warning that at least one of Jericho's thugs was hot on their trail.

Telling Sierra the truth might be the same as signing her death warrant.

She wouldn't be completely out of danger until Ben reached the news media with proof of Jericho's sleazy past. Until then, the less Sierra knew, the better her chances for emerging unscathed from this whole mess.

"The reason I stopped making love to you," Ben said, "is because you don't trust me."

"Why on earth *should* I trust you?" Sierra replied. "You've done nothing but lie to me from the very beginning. Pretending you were looking for my grandfather, then handing me that cockamamy story about being a journalist."

"You're right," he admitted. Sierra's eyebrows flew up in amazement. "I *have* lied to you all along."

"I knew it," she said. But her voice was strangely devoid of triumph or gloating. In fact she sounded rather unhappy. "My father *is* paying you to lure me back to Sloane Enterprises."

"No!" The word came out louder than Ben had intended, startling them both. "That much of what I told you is true. Your father didn't hire me, I've never met the man, and I'm not part of one of his schemes."

Sierra's lips curved into a skeptical frown. "Then just who exactly are you, Ben Halliday, and what the hell are you doing here?"

"I can't tell you."

"Oh, for God's sake." She began to struggle again. "Let me up, damn it. I've heard enough of your double-talk. You must be some kind of politician. Is that it? You're trying to establish personal contact with each of your constituents?"

"I'm not letting you go until I've finished what I have to say." Ben clamped down more firmly on her wrists. Astounding how much stronger Sierra was than she looked.

"But you haven't said *anything*! All you've done is hand me a bunch of gobbledygook, accusing me of not trusting you, then in the next breath admitting you're a liar."

Ben blew a lock of hair out of his eyes. Or tried to, anyway. It fell immediately in front of his face again. "Look, no more lies, okay? I promise."

Sierra smiled angelically. "Okay. You've convinced me. I'm not mad anymore. You can get off me now."

"Oh, no, you don't!"

She batted her long lashes at him. "Why, whatever do you mean? You asked me to let you explain, and I did. You want me to believe you, and I do. What's the problem?"

"The problem is that you still don't believe me, and you're still mad!" he nearly shouted.

She blinked. "Gee, sounds to me like *you're* the one who's mad."

"Mad as a hatter," he mumbled under his breath, "for trying to reason with you."

"I beg your pardon?"

"Nothing. Never mind." Inhaling deeply, Ben tried again. "I *did* come here looking for your grandfather, but not to write a story about him. We had a...business deal of sorts."

"You and *Grandpa*?" Suspicion laced her voice. "What kind of deal? Buying the Brooklyn Bridge? Swampland in Florida?"

"That's between your grandfather and me." Surprisingly Sierra seemed to accept this. Maybe there was still a bit of Fortune 500 left inside her. "The last time I saw Caleb was back in March. I didn't know he...had passed away."

Sierra's throat convulsed slightly as she swallowed.

Ben rushed on, trying to ignore the glitter of moisture in her eyes. "I'm asking you to take my word that I can't reveal any more about our deal than I already have. Believe me, if I could tell you, I would. I'm not going to lie to you anymore, Sierra. What I've told you is the absolute truth, even though it's incomplete."

Her only response was a forlorn sniffle.

"And the other thing I want to make absolutely clear is that I am *not* being paid to trick you, or seduce you, or— oh, sweetheart, don't! Please don't cry!"

The tear leaking from the corner of Sierra's eye and trickling down her temple finally got to Ben. Without hesitation he released her and pulled her into his embrace. When she linked her arms around his neck and pressed her cheek against his shoulder, a profound, protective tenderness surged through Ben, sweeping aside any thought but to comfort her, to keep her safe and make her happy.

Her thin, fragile body quivered against him like a willow tree in the wind. He patted her shoulder, pressed a kiss on her forehead, feeling helpless and strong and happy and sad all at the same time. "There, there," he crooned over and over—meaningless words that soothed more by tone than content.

"I'm sorry," she finally choked into the side of his neck. "I don't usually lose control like that, but I just miss Grandpa so darn much, and sometimes—sometimes when I look at the mess I've made of things, I wonder what he'd say if he could see me now, how he'd shake his head in disgust and—"

Ben drew back to study her tearstained face in surprise. "What are you talking about, sweetie? What mess?"

"Oh . . . you know. You've pointed it out yourself on more than one occasion." She flung her arm around the tent. "Look at this place! We're lucky it doesn't collapse on our heads. I've been scrambling around these mountains for two months, and I haven't found one speck of gold yet. I don't like sleeping on the ground and I hate bugs and snakes and taking baths in the stream and eating crummy freeze-dried backpacking food and I—I can't even start a fire!"

Ben chuckled, drawing her head under his chin again. "Sweetheart, that's not true! Why, only this morning, when I woke up—"

"I used a match!" she wailed. "I snuck one out of your pocket while you were—were sleeping!" Her voice disintegrated into a fresh storm of sobs.

Ben's laughter rumbled deep in his chest. A second later Sierra punched him in the ribs. "What's so funny?" she demanded, indignation vanquishing her sorrow.

"You are," he said, gasping. "I've never in my life met anyone as determined, as obstinate as you are."

"You haven't met my father," she muttered.

Ben didn't miss the significance of that statement, but he wasn't about to be sidetracked. "It's one thing to be a little...inept about living up here, but you don't even *like* roughing it! Why can't you admit this hasn't worked out and go back where you belong? Not necessarily to Sloane Enterprises, or even Los Angeles," he said, whisking a finger across her lips to forestall her outraged protest. "You could move someplace else and start over, find some new career that's more suitable, more enjoyable than slogging around in an icy creek all day sifting through mud."

Sierra giggled. "You're making it sound more glamorous than it really is."

"Well, there you are. Something to consider at least, isn't it?"

A frown creased her brow. "I don't know. I absolutely hate—and I mean *hate*!—the idea of being a quitter, of slinking back to Mom and Daddy with my tail between my legs—"

"Sierra, for Pete's sake, they're your parents! They're not going to say, 'We told you so.' And even if they *do*—" he continued when she gave him an oh-yeah look "—who cares? You can't let other people's opinions dictate how you run your life."

Ben shifted her so she sat on the ground facing him. "Sierra, you have to live your own life. Not your grandfather's."

"But he left everything to me."

"Because he loved you, not because he wanted to trap you into a miserable existence."

She twisted her hands together. "I feel like I'd be letting him down again. I neglected him during his last years, and this seems the least I can do to make up for it."

"Sierra, how is being unhappy going to make up for the past? And I'm sure you didn't neglect your grandfather as much as you think. Didn't you see him on holidays?"

"Well, yes, but—"

"Did you write to him?"

"Writing's not the same as—"

"Did you always remember his birthday?"

"Of course, but—"

"Sierra." Ben clasped her hands in his. "Your grandfather struck me as an intelligent, perceptive man. Even behind that long shaggy beard of his, I sensed that the moment we met. I bet he understood that when human beings grow up, they inevitably grow away from the people they depended on as children. That's simply a fact of life."

Reluctant agreement was gradually displacing the doubt in Sierra's expression.

"Do you think your grandfather wanted to chain you to a way of life you simply aren't cut out for? Do you think it would make him happy to see you suffer?"

"Don't be silly."

"Well, then. Maybe you should rethink some of your decisions."

She chewed on her lip and stared at the floor. In a moment she shrugged one shoulder. "Maybe."

Ben squeezed her hands. "Good. That's all I ask."

She peered at him from beneath knitted eyebrows. "You know, if I didn't know better, I'd think you had some financial stake in persuading me to give all this up."

"Scout's honor." Ben raised three fingers in the Boy Scout salute. With the other hand he made an X across his chest. "Cross my heart. My interest in your well-being has nothing to do with financial gain."

"No? Then what *does* it involve?" she asked with an impish grin.

"Let's just say my interest in you is strictly...personal." He raked her with an appreciative glance. In all the commotion she'd forgotten about modesty, but under Ben's admiring scrutiny, her skin turned pink and she made a grab for the blanket.

"No, don't," he said in a low voice, catching her by the wrist. "Let me look at you."

"Ben," she said helplessly.

He caressed the side of her face, and she tilted her head into his hand, closing her eyes. Releasing her wrist, he traced the outline of her smooth shoulders, her waist, her hips. She was so slender, yet so soft....

When he lifted his hand to her breast, her eyes opened wide and she trembled slightly. As Ben continued to fondle her, Sierra kept her eyes focused on his, her expression transforming from cautious uncertainty to quickening desire. Her eyelids lowered with sultry heaviness; her rosy lips parted slightly as her breath came faster.

Excitement boiled up inside Ben as he kneaded and stroked the creamy mounds, rasping his thumbs across her nipples, reveling in the shivers that racked her body under his touch. His own body responded with a flood of quick, hot passion, and he could barely restrain himself from dragging her down to the ground and taking her with wild, desperate urgency.

Instead he slowly guided Sierra's hand to the hard evidence of his desire, lowering himself to lie beside her. Her eyes brimmed with wonder and longing and secret satisfaction. As she stroked him, hesitantly at first, then with growing confidence, a surge of incredible aching rapture swept through Ben, obliterating the last remnant of his self-control.

Almost the last remnant. As he arched himself above her, Ben paused and managed to grind out, "You do believe me, don't you, darling? That the reason I'm making love to you is because I . . . care about you? Because I want to share these feelings with you?"

A welter of emotions riffled through Sierra's eyes like a shuffled deck of cards. Blood thundered in Ben's ears as he scanned her face for the only answer he could accept, the only response that would allow him to merge his heart, mind and body with hers.

Sierra felt as if she were poised on tiptoe at the brink of a towering cliff. She knew in her heart that if she made love with Ben, her life would never be the same afterward. If he were lying to her again, if he betrayed her after she gave herself so eagerly, so trustingly...

She searched his eyes for a clue to the truth. Would a man who was only using her for some secret purpose hold himself in check as Ben was now? The anguish of overwhelming desire was scrawled plainly across the bold, straining planes and angles of his face. She could see how much his restraint was costing him by the taut cords in his neck and the flickering muscles along his clenched jaw.

What could Ben possibly have to gain by such effort unless what he said was true—that his feelings for her were genuine, his motives so pure that he refused to tarnish them by making love to a woman who didn't trust him?

In Ben's tormented eyes Sierra saw many things, but dishonesty wasn't one of them. As she lifted her fingers to graze his whiskery cheek, she realized with heart-stopping certainty that whatever else Ben Halliday cared about, he cared about her, too.

"Yes," she whispered. "Oh, yes...I believe you, Ben."

His body shuddered as he released a deep breath. He closed his eyes in relief, turning his head to brand a searing kiss into her palm. As he lowered himself toward her, he hesitated one last time. "And you want this as much as I do?"

"As much as you do," she echoed. *More*, she thought. *I love you, Ben.*

Then she forgot this wistful realization as Ben eased himself inside her. She gasped sharply, clutching at his shoulders. His muscles were like taut steel cables beneath her fingers, his heart a thudding, rhythmic accompaniment to her own.

As Ben's hardness filled the soft, molten core of her being, the shared pleasure and fulfillment reflected in his eyes filled an aching void in Sierra's heart—a void she hadn't even known existed before. Somehow the connection of their bodies had also bridged some gaping emotional chasm, astounding Sierra with its profound intimacy and intensity. She sensed what a person born and raised in total isolation from the rest of the world might feel upon first contact with another human being.

She hadn't known what being lonely was until she wasn't alone anymore.

Ben touched his fingers to her face, a brief smile shimmering across the distorted passion of his features before he bent his head to seize her mouth with his. Sierra arched into the curve of his body, matching her movements to his accelerating tempo, marveling at the perfect synchronization of their bodies' responses. Somehow Ben knew the exact moment to be gentle, to pause, to resume his throbbing, thrusting strokes with ever-increasing vigor.

"Sweetheart," he gasped, his breath hot against her ear. "Sierra, this feels so good . . . so right. . . ."

"Oh, yes," she whispered. "Yes . . ."

Whatever doubts she might once have had about the wisdom of their entanglement were banished by the pulsing, smoldering fire building inside her. No matter what the ultimate price for this encounter, she knew the indescribable, unimaginable ecstasy of this moment would be worth it.

Sierra dragged her fingers down the solid, straining wall of Ben's back, familiarizing herself with every square inch of him. When her hands swept across his thigh, she felt a web of scar tissue splayed across his upper leg. As she traced the faint ridges with her fingertips, she remembered Ben's accident and was suddenly possessed by a crazy determination to shield him from any more plane crashes or suffering or sadness.

Then the onslaught of his sensual caresses drove all other awareness from her mind. His hands were everywhere upon her body at once, tangling in her hair, cupping her breasts, skimming across her belly.

Sierra flung back her head as a tortured moan welled up from the very depths of her soul. Ben growled with satisfaction, sliding his hands beneath her hips and pulling her even closer, more intimately against him. "Go ahead and scream," he rasped. "There's no one around to hear us. I want to hear you scream my name. . . ."

His mouth blazed a path of exquisite, soul-shattering delight over her lips, her eyelids, her breasts. As the pace of their lovemaking increased, Sierra felt like a pulsating star on the verge of a supernova, spinning out of control through the galaxy, throbbing, temperature rising, incredible pressure building.

At the exact moment the critical balance was attained, she exploded across the heavens in a blinding conflagration of white-hot, radiant embers. And then she *did* call Ben's name, over and over again, dimly aware that he was shouting her name, too. The agonized rapture warping his chiseled features mirrored her own dazzling ascent into a part of the universe she'd never known existed before.

Together they careened slowly back to earth like two shooting stars falling from the night sky, landing with passions dimmed and cooled, but no less real now that they were stilled.

Sierra lay with her head against Ben's shoulder, listening to the gradual slowing of his breath and the fading thunder of his heartbeat. He turned his head to smile lazily at her as he brushed a damp curl from her forehead. "Comfortable?"

"Mmm, yes. The cold, hard ground never felt so good."

His chuckle rumbled through his chest, vibrating against her ear. "I guess it would have been better in a thick, plush feather bed."

"Nope." She snuggled into the crook of his arm. "It couldn't possibly have been any better."

He kissed her temple. "You're a love, you know that?"

The word stirred something sweet and tender and kind of scary inside Sierra. She took refuge in her usual flippancy. "I'll make you eat those words the next time we're fighting about something."

Ben laughed briefly, but then grew serious. "I don't want to fight with you anymore, Sierra."

"What? And undermine the very foundation of our relationship?"

"Is that what our relationship is based on? Fighting? Arguing? Being constantly at cross-purposes?"

"No . . ." she said slowly. "But you have to admit, that does spice things up a bit."

Ben groaned. "Any more spice, and my ulcers will flare up again."

She craned her neck to peer at him in surprise. "You have ulcers?"

"Used to. I had a pretty high-pressure job, and I'm afraid I wasn't in the habit of stopping to smell the roses, as they say." He shifted his hold around her shoulders, and she stretched her arm to rest lazily across his chest. "While I was hospitalized after the plane crash, they managed to patch up my ulcers along with the rest of me."

Absently Sierra drew one fingertip in circles through his chest hair. "What kind of high-pressure job did you have?"

She really hadn't intended to trick him into revealing more about himself, but his entire body stiffened. Warily he replied, "Let's not talk about that right now, okay?"

"Ben, I didn't mean—"

"Forget it."

"But I don't want you to think that I was trying to—"

"Sierra, I promise, as soon as it's safe, I'll tell you everything about me. You'll probably get sick of hearing me talk about myself."

"What do you mean, as soon as it's safe?"

He cursed under his breath. "Never mind. Can we change the subject now, please?"

"Uh-oh," she sighed, rolling away from him and folding her arms over her breasts. "Here comes another fight."

Ben's hand sneaked out, and his fingers crawled spiderlike down the curve of her waist. "The only thing I want to fight about," he said, "is who's hogging the blanket."

Sierra flinched as if he'd stuck an ice cube on her skin. "Cut that out!"

"Oho, so we're a bit ticklish, are we?"

"No, *we're* not. I don't know about you, but I am definitely *not* ticklish, so— Ben, stop it! Knock it off!"

"Hmm, ticklish here . . . and here . . . and here . . . and how about there?"

Sierra shrieked. "Enough, already! I told you, I'm not—"

Ben rolled on top of her and imprisoned her body with his while he continued his maddening assault. "Admit it! Tell me you're ticklish! I won't stop till you say it!"

"Never!" Dissolving in a fit of hysterical giggles, Sierra resolved to die laughing before she'd surrender. Ben's eyes sparkled with amused determination, and his quick reflexes parried her every attempt to escape. "Okay!" she gasped finally. "I give up! I'm ticklish!"

"What? I can't hear you."

"I'm ticklish!" she howled.

Instantly he rolled off her and propped himself on one elbow to observe her with casual scrutiny. "I thought so," he said.

She thumped him on the shoulder. "You monster! Don't you know that tickling is a form of torture?"

"In that case, let me make it up to you. Come here." With that, he reached across her to grasp the edge of the blanket, using it to pull her into his embrace.

As the scratchy folds enveloped Sierra, joyful laughter bubbled up inside her. She wrapped her arms around Ben and sank eagerly into bliss.

She awoke nestled in Ben's arms, the blanket wrapped around them both like a fuzzy cocoon. The first gray light of dawn allowed her to study the way sleep altered his face, blurring the sharp angles so he appeared younger, more relaxed, but definitely just as handsome.

Fondly she ruffled his hair and whispered, "At least you don't snore."

Without opening his eyes, Ben mumbled, "Wish I could say the same about you."

She pinched his nose. "How unchivalrous! Positively ungallant, if you ask me." She sniffed, then resumed her observation of him with bright-eyed interest. "So, what's the routine here? Am I supposed to fix you breakfast or something?"

He pried open one eye. "Well," he said in a gravelly voice, "if you were any other woman, I'd insist upon it. But considering it's you . . ."

"Monster," she replied good-naturedly. She snaked one arm out from beneath the blanket's warmth and fumbled through the stash of supplies piled behind her. One after another she picked up a box, brought it in front of her eyes and tossed it aside. "Aha! Here we go!"

She plucked a Yummee Macaroon out of its bright yellow box, took a bite and offered the rest to Ben. His eyes were closed again, so she nudged the savory morsel between his lips.

Ben quickly plucked the macaroon from his lips in disgust. "Isn't it a little early for junk food? What time is it, anyway?" He groped for his watch, then squinted blearily at it. "Good lord, it's still the middle of the night!"

"In Hawaii, maybe. Here it's time to rise and shine."

He sank back with a groan. "I hardly slept at all last night."

Sierra pushed herself up on her elbow and poked a finger into his stomach. "And whose fault is that?"

"Oof!" His muscles knotted in reflex as he cocked one roguish eyebrow at her. "Yours."

She pressed her hand against her chest. "*My* fault?"

"Yes, *your* fault." Ben snatched her and nuzzled his face in her neck. "How the hell was I supposed to get any sleep while you were cuddling your sexy, gorgeous body against me?"

"Hmm. You know, *I* didn't get much sleep, either, if you recall."

His low, lascivious chuckle sent delicious shivers zipping down her spine. "Oh, I recall," he said. "I recall quite well, as a matter of fact. But just so I don't forget, maybe you'd better give me a refresher course."

She wedged her hands between the two of them and shoved. "Business before pleasure. And I don't mean monkey business," she warned as Ben made a grab for her again. She dusted her hands, propped them on her hips and gazed down at him with affectionate disgust. "You can catch up on your beauty sleep while I make coffee."

"Sounds good to me," he said with a yawn, turning over and burying his face in his arms. As she retrieved her scattered clothing, Ben said, "Hey, Sierra?"

She poked her head through the neck of her sweater. "Yes?"

His voice was garbled. "The matches are tucked under one of the rocks around the fire."

She threw a grateful glance at his back as she crawled by on her way out of the tent. "Thanks."

"Don't mention it."

Seeing the ashes of last night's fire made Sierra blush as she recalled how the flames had leaped and crackled while Ben removed her clothes. She could still feel his hands roaming over her body, stirring to life something wonderful and exciting within her. As the sun peeked over the tops of the tallest pines, spilling a golden glow over the campsite, the world seemed like . . . well, like a pretty terrific place.

Sierra shut her eyes, threw back her head and spun around and around in circles, reaching up to the sky, reaching out to grasp all of life's fantastic, thrilling possibilities. Laughter flowed from her throat, a sound as light and lilting as the chirping of the finch perched in a nearby cedar.

The smile illuminating her face was like dawn spreading across the mountains. Hugging herself in delight, Sierra reveled in this totally unfamiliar, totally exhilarating flood of deep, fulfilling joy.

She didn't need a treasure map to show her the source of her happiness. At this very moment the source was less than twenty feet from her, well-muscled limbs sprawled across a scratchy green army blanket.

With a heavy sigh of contentment, Sierra gave herself one final hug before kneeling to tackle the task at hand. It seemed a particularly good omen when the fire ignited immediately, flaring to life with a cheery crackle. In no time at all the heavenly aroma of coffee filled the clearing.

Sierra sat cross-legged in front of the blaze, enjoying the time alone, but anticipating the moment when Ben would emerge from the tent and join her. The flames reminded her of the golden glints in his hair; the heat stirred memories of how warm his skin felt against hers. The soft whisper of the burning wood almost sounded like his voice murmuring in her ear.

"Oh, brother," she said, rolling her eyes. "Boy, have *you* got it bad, kiddo!" She pushed herself to her feet, shaking her head. "What do you think, Char?" She untied the mule from his tree. "Am I a hopeless case, or what?"

As she led Charlemagne down to the creek for a morning drink, Sierra couldn't suppress the dart of hope that ricocheted through her heart whenever she thought of Ben. At last their rocky relationship seemed to be on a steady, smoother course. No more sidetracking lies, no more deceptive detours. The barriers of deceit and distrust between them were toppling down. Maybe she didn't know the whole truth about Ben, but she'd learned the most important truth: he cared about her. Maybe he wasn't in love with her the way—she swallowed—the way she was in love with him, but it was a start, wasn't it?

As for the rest of Ben's mysterious past, well, Sierra didn't want to probe that too closely yet. Best not to ask too many questions right now. She had a sneaking suspicion she might not like some of the answers.

"Char, will you hurry it up? I left the pot on the fire, and if that coffee scorches, I'll never hear the end of it." She wrestled the mule back to the clearing, tying him to his tree in case he decided to repeat yesterday's disappearing act.

Stepping back, she frowned. "Something's wrong with this picture." Her forehead cleared. "That's it!" She snapped her fingers. "I forgot to give you back your hat. Hang on a second."

She retrieved the mule's straw hat from its branch, then wrinkled her nose in disgust. "*Phew!* I hate to tell you this, Char, but that skunk really did a number on your hat. I know Grandpa gave it to you, but I'm afraid you're going to have to buy yourself a new one." Pinching the brim between two fingers, she glanced toward the woods, wondering if a straw hat was biodegradable or if it would litter the landscape for generations to come.

Well, straw was a plant, wasn't it? Sort of? She shifted her eyes from side to side, satisfying herself that no forest ranger lurked nearby, ready to pounce on her and haul her off into custody.

Then she grasped the hat like a Frisbee and prepared to sail it off into the brush. At the last second something caught her eye.

Tucked beneath the ribbon that wound around the inside of the hat before dangling through two slits in the brim was a piece of paper. A dirty, crinkled, folded-up piece of paper, to be exact. Sierra wiggled it from underneath the ribbon and turned it over in her hands.

What on earth?

She unfolded it gingerly so the thin, worn paper wouldn't tear. It was a letter. A very *old* letter, from the looks of it. "My dear Margaret," it began. Sierra's eyebrows furrowed in puzzlement. Who was Margaret, anyway? Some long-lost love of her grandfather's?

Her eyes skipped to the bottom of the page. No, the letter was signed by someone named Quentin. "Curiouser and curiouser," she mused, sinking onto a fallen log and crossing one leg over the other. Absently she tossed the straw hat aside.

Then, smoothing out the wrinkled paper, Sierra began to read.

Chapter Nine

A bundle of clothing slammed Ben square in the face when he crawled out of the tent.

As he scrambled to his feet, his confused gaze fell on Sierra—clenched fists pressed to her sides, feet planted firmly apart, brown eyes blazing. "You lousy, conniving, lying snake," she said quietly.

Ben's heart sank. "Darling, I don't know what you're—"

"Don't 'darling' me, you weasel. I see right through your two-faced sweet talk. It took me long enough, but I've finally wised up to you."

Ben swallowed. "Sierra, whatever it is, I'm sure there's a logical—"

"Oh, there's an explanation, all right. The explanation is that you lied to me. Again." She threw up her hands in exasperation. "I guess I should be getting used to it by now, but after last night . . ." Her chin trembled as her eyes brimmed with tears. "Oh, Ben," she quavered, "how could you? How *could* you?" Without waiting for a reply, she pivoted on her heel and fled into the trees.

Ben started after her, then realized that prancing through the woods without wearing a stitch of clothing was probably not the swiftest move he could make. He scooped up his clothes and hopped after her, bouncing up and down on one foot while he tried to insert his other leg into his jeans. "Sierra, wait! Come back!"

Naturally she did neither. Ben couldn't imagine what had lit her fuse this time, but surely it was all a misunderstanding. He fully intended to keep his promise to tell her the truth from now on—at least as much of the truth as was safe. Stumbling after her, he racked his brain for some stray lie that had come back to haunt him, some loose end he'd forgotten to tie up.

What on earth could have happened between the time Sierra was lazily offering him a macaroon and the moment she hurled his clothes at his head?

Ben caught a glimpse of her up ahead, the sun glinting bright copper off her dark curls. Thank God all this outdoor living had strengthened his leg, or he'd never have caught up with her. Not with fury propelling her like a booster rocket.

Vaulting over a fallen log, Ben closed the distance between them and captured her wrist. Immediately she shook him off and whirled to face him like a cornered animal. "Leave me alone," she snarled.

"Not until I find out what the hell has upset you so much."

"What are you going to do, tickle me until I tell you? Wrestle me to the ground and refuse to let me up? Those are your usual tactics, aren't they?"

Ben closed his eyes and counted to ten. "Sierra," he said in a calm, reasonable voice, "I'm not going to force you to do anything. But don't you think you owe me an explanation?"

"Me?" She smacked her palm against her chest. "Owe *you* an explanation?"

He tried again. "After last night I thought—"

"After last night I thought a lot of things, too. All of them wrong." She banged the heel of her hand against the side of her head. "What a gullible fool I was! Oh, when will I ever learn?" She shook her head in disgust.

Not for the first time, Ben wondered what it was about Sierra that stirred up such violent tendencies inside him. He was basically a peace-loving man who rejected brute force as a matter of principle. But right now he wanted to shake Sierra silly.

Instead he decided to try a new tactic. Shrugging, he said, "All right, if you don't want to tell me what's wrong, fine. I respect your right to keep secrets." He slid his hands into his pockets and turned back toward camp, whistling a tuneless refrain.

His strategy worked. "Secrets?" she shouted after him, her voice teeming with outrage. "You dare to accuse *me* of keeping secrets?"

Ben heard the rustle of dried leaves as she tagged after him. He kept walking.

"You're the one with all the secrets, Ben Halliday. Compared to you, *my* life's an open book."

He sauntered along, tilting back his head to study the sky. Looked like it was going to be a pretty nice day.

"Just who are Margaret and Quentin, anyway?"

She might as well have clobbered him with a two-by-four. All the air whooshed out of Ben's lungs; his legs simply stopped functioning, as if they'd suddenly turned to lead. In slow motion he wheeled around and stared at her. "What did you say?" His voice sounded hollow, as if he were speaking into a concrete tunnel.

At the look on his face, some of her indignation faded. "I said, who are Margaret and Quentin?" Now she looked uncertain, like a mischievous child who suddenly realized she'd gone too far.

Ben took one faltering step toward her. "Where did you hear those names?" he asked hoarsely.

Her lower lip pushed forward with slight defiance. "I didn't hear them. I read them."

Ben's heart thumped like a timpani drum. Dear God, could it be? Was it possible—? He moved a step closer. "Where?" he said. "Where did you read those names?"

Sierra studied him for a moment, as if considering whether or not to prolong this interesting inquisition. Then she shrugged, extracted a folded-up piece of paper from her back pocket and held it out to Ben. "Here," she said offhandedly, as if the matter were no longer of much interest to her. "I read the names in this letter. You're mentioned in there, too."

The letter.

As Ben reached for it, his hand seemed disembodied, as if it had absolutely no connection with the rest of him. Shock and disbelief gave time a dreamlike quality, and the seconds before his fingers actually touched the paper seemed to stretch out into eternity.

Amazingly his hand remained steady as he unfolded the letter, scanned it with unseeing eyes and tucked it into his shirt pocket. This one piece of paper had cost him so much, had given him so much. Without the letter Ben would have no chance to avenge his parents' memory.

And if it weren't for the letter, he would never have met Sierra.

Now that he actually had the letter in his possession, Ben found himself somewhat at a loss. He ought to be shouting for joy, punching the air in triumph. Instead all he could focus on was the sad disillusionment on Sierra's face. Her anger had apparently dissipated, leaving her as deflated as a limp balloon. With a sigh she slumped back against a tree trunk, folded her arms and stared unhappily off into the distance.

"Sweetheart," he said in what he hoped was a soothing tone, "I still don't understand why this letter upset you so much."

She refused to meet his eyes. "It's pretty obvious, isn't it?"

"If it were obvious, I wouldn't be asking."

"You're going to make me say it, aren't you?" she asked in a flat voice. "All right, then. Have it your way." She turned her enormous dark eyes on him, and the hurt accusation Ben saw there nearly broke his heart.

"You were only after that letter," she said. "I don't know why it's so important to you, but it was important enough that you were willing to lie to me, to trick me, to use me." She gulped. "You thought that by making love to me, you could somehow get the letter back. Well, I guess your plan worked, didn't it?"

"Sweetheart—"

"Although it's rather ironic, because I only came across it by accident. I had no idea it even existed before I found it hidden away inside Charlemagne's hat this morning."

Ben's jaw dropped. "You mean to tell me that all this time, that crotchety old mule—"

"—had it stashed inside his hat." She peered at him from beneath her long lashes. "I presume Grandpa must have hidden it there?"

"I gave it to him for safekeeping after my plane crashed."

Her eyes widened in surprise. "Your plane crashed around *here* someplace? And Grandpa saw it?"

"He was the first one to find me. Or actually—" Ben scratched his jaw "—Charlemagne was."

That brought a glimmer of a smile to her troubled face. "In the Alps people get rescued by Saint Bernards. In the Sierra Nevada they get saved by mules." Then her forehead furrowed again. "What do you mean, you gave that letter to Grandpa for safekeeping? Safekeeping from what? Or whom?"

For a moment Ben wavered, sorely tempted to tell her everything. He was so close now . . . so close to the day when the truth about Quentin Jericho would be blazoned across every newspaper in the country. He was sick and tired of lying to Sierra. She deserved better than that.

The whole story welled up inside Ben's chest, ready to burst from his throat. Then, in a brutal flash he recalled his confrontation with Jericho right before his mother's funeral service began. His memory dredged up with sickening clarity the pure malevolence, the ruthless determination seared on Jericho's face when he discovered the letter hadn't been destroyed years ago, after all.

Ben shuddered, reliving the wave of shock and revulsion that had swept over him when he saw for the first time what evil his "Uncle Quent" concealed behind his good-natured, benevolent mask.

Ben had to keep protecting Sierra for just a little while longer, until he could rip away that mask in front of the whole world.

"I can't tell you anything about the letter," he said finally.

She eyed him skeptically. "Can't? Or won't?"

He paused. "Won't."

She threw up her arms. "Well, this is a switch! How come you don't just dream up another phony story to satisfy me? Or are all these lies getting to be too exhausting?"

"I swore I wouldn't lie to you anymore, and I meant it." Ben tipped her chin up, forcing her to meet his eyes. "But I can't tell you the whole truth right now. Not yet. It's too dangerous."

She swatted his hand away. "There, that's more like it! I was starting to worry I wouldn't get to hear another one of your fairy tales. Dangerous, indeed."

"It happens to be the truth," he said quietly.

"The truth, huh?" She probed her cheek with her tongue. "Let's see, which version of the truth are we up to now? Version three? Four? Goodness, I've heard so many versions of the truth from you I've simply lost count."

"Sierra..."

She clamped her hands over her ears. "Please, no more, all right? I don't want to end this relationship with one last lie. Although that would certainly be appropriate, wouldn't it? God knows, that's what this whole relationship has been based on."

Ben clenched and unclenched his fists. "I had to hide the truth from you for your sake."

"For *my* sake?" She dropped her hands. "Hey, don't do me any more favors, okay? *My* sake. Too dangerous. Oh, that's priceless," she scoffed. "What on earth could be so dangerous about an old letter?"

Before Ben could reply, Sierra narrowed her eyes and tapped her finger against her chin. "Are Margaret and Quentin your parents?"

"No!" The very idea struck Ben as so horrific, he spit out a denial before he realized that Sierra had just managed to pry another chunk of information from him.

"Then Margaret and this Tom mentioned in the letter must be your parents. And apparently this Quentin person tried to blackmail Margaret into dumping Tom and marrying him. He says in the letter he'll drop the embezzlement charges against Tom if Margaret will leave him. And he urges her to think about poor little Ben, how awful it would be for him to grow up with a father in prison."

Ben groaned inwardly. Sierra nearly had the whole thing figured out, all right. Except for one key piece of information: she didn't realize who Quentin was.

Fresh urgency seized him. He had to get to Los Angeles and contact the press. Fast. Sierra was too smart for her own good sometimes.

Her smug look of triumph melted in sympathy. "Did your father spend time in prison, then? Is that why you hid the truth from me? Because you were ashamed?" She laid her hand on his arm and spoke with earnest intensity. "You don't have to be ashamed, Ben. Your father made a mistake, but he paid for it. And it was all so long ago. . . ."

He focused his eyes where her hand rested on his arm. "You don't understand," he said in a low voice. "My father didn't do anything wrong. The only mistake he made was trusting that bastard Quentin Jer—"

Ben broke off in horror. His resentment and anger had made him reckless, pushing him to the brink of revealing everything and thrusting Sierra even deeper into danger.

But her eyes, searching his face in bewilderment, showed no sign that she'd detected his near slip. Relief washed over him, and with a swift, abrupt movement he pulled Sierra into his arms and buried his face in her hair. He felt her arms slide slowly, cautiously around his waist.

Ben inhaled deeply, wanting to absorb the clean, woodsy scent of her, to imprint on his brain the memory of her small, fragile body cradled against him. Soon, very soon he would have to leave her. He didn't know for how long, or what kind of reception would await him when he returned to set things right with her.

This might be his last chance for a long time to hold Sierra, to touch her. The knowledge made their imminent parting even more bittersweet.

No sense prolonging the agony. The sooner Ben accomplished his mission, the sooner he could return to Sierra. Drawing back, he traced his thumb across the lush, sensual fullness of her lips. Then he pressed his mouth against hers and kissed her gently. "I have to go," he said at last, brushing one of her reddish brown curls off her temple.

Her arms, loosely clasped around him, tensed. A look of startled disappointment dashed across her delicate features, chased by an expression of pained acceptance. She skittered away and stood with her back to Ben. Unhappiness and resignation were written in every line of her posture.

"So that's it, huh?" she said in a dull voice. "You found what you were looking for, and now you're leaving."

Ben stepped closer, intending to grasp her shoulders and turn her toward him. At the last second he paused, then dropped his hands limply to his sides. "I'll be back," he said in a strained voice. "But I have something to do first. Something important. Something that can't wait."

She spun around quickly, and for an instant he saw the naked hurt in her eyes before her anger and resentment disguised it. "But you expect *me* to wait."

"I don't expect it. But I'm *asking* you to wait, yes. Just for a little while longer. Then I'll come back and explain everything to you."

She searched his face with a mixture of hope and frustration. Then something in her eyes flickered and died. Whatever she'd been searching for, she hadn't found it. "You're not coming back at all, are you?" she said softly.

Ben seized both her hands and pressed his lips against her knuckles. "I'll be back, Sierra. I swear it."

She continued as if she hadn't heard him. "Now I finally know the real reason why you pursued me, why you pretended to care for me, why you—" she nearly choked on the words "—made love to me."

Ben shook his head wildly. "You've got it all wrong, sweetheart!" Her anguish was like a knife stabbing him through the chest. "I never *pretended* to care for you! I didn't make love to you just so you'd help me find the letter! Those things I said, my feelings for you—all that was real, Sierra. It was the truth." He gripped her hands even tighter. "I *do* care for you, darling, and I *will* come back. You've got to believe me!"

Tears glittered in her eyes. "Oh, Ben," she said with a strangled sob, "how can I believe you, after all the lies you've told me?"

Then she wrenched away from him and stumbled off into the woods, pressing her hand to her mouth.

"Sierra, please! You've got to give me a chance... you've got to let me... oh, hell." Ben pulled up short and watched her disappear into the trees. Desperation gnawed at his stomach, but his instincts warned him that letting Sierra go was the only way to win her back. Trying to reason with her now would be pointless. He could hardly blame her for not believing a word he said anymore. Now he knew how the boy who cried "Wolf!" once too often must have felt.

But after she'd had a chance to cool off and calm down, Sierra would surely realize Ben hadn't been cold-bloodedly using her. And when he came back from Los Angeles, that would prove to Sierra that he truly cared for her, wouldn't it?

That's what Ben was counting on, anyway. Because he couldn't bear to consider any other outcome.

He removed the letter from his pocket and turned it over in his hands. Then he looked up at the spot where Sierra had disappeared. This letter was their life-insurance policy. Neither of them would be safe from Jericho until the letter was exposed to the blinding spotlight of public scrutiny.

There was no time to waste. Ben hated like hell to leave Sierra without straightening out this mess, but he'd have to postpone that until later, after their lives were out of danger. And he somehow suspected Sierra wasn't exactly in the mood to listen to him, anyway.

Nevertheless, he was still torn by the urgency of getting the letter to L.A. and his reluctance to let Sierra think the worst of him.

But protecting her from Jericho's hired killers had to be his first priority.

That, and avenging his parents, of course. Ben blinked as if coming out of a trance. For a moment he'd almost forgotten his original purpose for retrieving the letter. He studied the paper in his hands. Funny. He'd imagined this moment so many times—the moment when he finally recovered the weapon that would wreak vengeance on Quentin Jericho.

Except in his imagination he'd felt a surge of fierce joy, a dizzying flood of triumph.

Now all he felt was weary relief that his difficult task was almost complete. In place of triumphant joy was a hollow ache, a nagging suspicion that he faced an even more difficult, more desperate challenge ahead: winning Sierra back.

But first he had to see *this* matter through to its conclusion. Ben stuffed the letter into his jeans pocket and ran down a mental checklist. He couldn't think of anything he'd left at Sierra's camp, so there was really no need to swing by there before heading back to town.

Besides, he had a feeling that avoiding Sierra for a while would be a wise move.

Casting one final look of regret over his shoulder, Ben turned and began the long trudge back to Grubstake.

Spiky branches snatched at her hair and clawed her face as Sierra floundered through the woods. The only sounds were the crackle of sticks and leaves underfoot, the harsh rasp of her breathing and the hammering thud of her heart.

She wanted to keep running forever, away from the pain, the lies, the memory of Ben's face hovering so close to hers while they made love. "Stop it!" she shouted, squeezing her eyes shut as if that could somehow banish his taunting image.

Instead she tripped over a gnarled tree-root and pitched headfirst into a prickly snarl of bushes. Once imprisoned in their thorny clutches, she simply couldn't muster the energy to fight her way free, and lay sprawled there, tears stinging the scratches on her hands.

At last, disgusted with her unaccustomed bout of self-pity, she disentangled herself and scrambled to her feet. With one final sniffle, she wiped her eyes with the sleeve of her sweater and pushed her hair out of her face. "Well, that's the end of it," she told herself. "We met, I fell in love, he broke my heart, I went boo-hoo. Now it's over. End of chapter, end of book. *Fini.*"

As she brushed dirt and leaves off her slacks, her lower lip trembled. But she held up her head, gritted her teeth and headed back to camp—at a slower pace this time. Despite her resolve to wash her hands of Ben once and for all, her ears were keenly alert for the sound of his pursuit.

She tried not to be too disappointed when he didn't catch up with her. By the time Sierra arrived back at camp, she realized he was probably gone for good this time. Well, what reason did he have to stick around, anyway? He'd got what he'd come for.

The only problem was, he'd taken away a lot more than that stupid letter.

Sierra fought back her tears, cursing herself for being an idiot. Obviously Ben Halliday wasn't at all the man she thought she'd fallen in love with.

So why did her heart feel like it had been plowed over by a bulldozer?

Damn him, anyway! Now that he'd got his mysterious letter back, he couldn't even be bothered to keep up a pretense. He simply refused to tell her *anything*, even another one of his outlandish stories.

Sierra's harsh laughter snagged in her throat. Who would have thought she'd ever look back on Ben's lies with sentimental longing?

Yet somehow his indifference was even harder to bear. At least he'd needed her before, if only for some secret, sinister purpose. But now Ben had no use for her. No use for her, at all.

Another shaft of grief plunged into Sierra, making her gasp with its intensity. She tossed her head back. Well, who needed Ben Halliday, anyway? Who needed his devastating blond looks, his smooth-talking charm, his arousing, passionate embraces?

With a convulsive swallow, she dammed back a new flood of tears. Then she crawled into the tent and liberated a box of Yummee Coconut-Creme Cakes. But her first bite of the sweet, mushy confection only aggravated her already-churning stomach.

Eyeing the bright yellow box with disgust, she scooted back out of the tent and accosted Charlemagne. "Here," she said, sticking the gooey cake under the mule's nose. "Live it up. You can eat the whole darn box if you want to."

At such a tempting invitation, Charlemagne shook off his usual lethargy. He wolfed down the partially eaten morsel with gusto, then hopefully nuzzled his nose into the yellow box.

Sierra absently fed him seconds. "I guess you were right about Ben all along, Char. You knew from the very beginning he wasn't to be trusted. Here, have another one." She sighed, trying to dislodge the heavy weight compressing her chest. "I should have listened to you in the first place. Everyone knows what good instincts animals have about people."

Charlemagne brayed indignantly.

"Oops! I didn't mean to lump you in with a bunch of animals, Char. Forgive me? Look, here's another coconut-cream cake. Are we still friends?"

After a moment Sierra sighed again. "I *want* to believe that he cares about me, Char. I *want* to believe he'll come back. But I just can't. Dealing with that man is like peeling an onion. I keep stripping away all these layers of lies, but there's always another layer underneath. The truth must be in there someplace, but I'll be darned if I can figure out what it is or how deep it's buried. And I'm sick of peeling onions. They always make me—" she sniffed "—cry."

Impatiently she dashed another tear from her cheek. Charlemagne nudged her in sympathy. With a moan of despair, Sierra dropped the box and flung her arms around the mule's neck. "You're the only friend I have in the world," she wailed. "The only person I can trust. And you're not . . . even . . . a . . . person!" Her voice dissolved in a fresh spate of sobs as she buried her face in Charlemagne's neck.

Charlemagne stood this undignified embrace for as long as he could. Then he snorted and tried to pull away. Sierra raised her tearstained face and wrinkled her nose. "You may be my best friend in the whole world, but as one friend to another, I gotta tell you, pal—you stink!"

She sniffed, then frowned. That peculiar smell wasn't skunk, and it wasn't coming from Charlemagne. She drew back, noting in surprise that the mule's long ears were twitching nervously. This was as close to a state of agitation as she'd ever seen him.

"What's wrong, Char? Do you smell it, too? Do you hear something?"

Then an ominous prickling slithered up Sierra's spine. Too late, she whirled. Something soft and wet clamped down over her nose and mouth before she could cry out. She tried to squirm from side to side, but a hand grabbed a fistful of her hair and yanked her head back in an iron grip.

Instinctively she tried to hold her breath, simultaneously straining to see who her captor was. If this was her father's idea of a last resort, he'd definitely gone too far this time.

Her lungs clamored for oxygen, and when she could no longer resist the overpowering urge to breathe, a sickly sweet, vaguely medicinal odor permeated her senses, seeping into every cell in her body.

Her vision clouded like a TV with poor reception. Through the swirling dots and roaring static, her last conscious thought was, *Ben*.

Then the picture snapped off, and the whole world went black.

Chapter Ten

Ben drummed his fingers impatiently on the front desk of the Grubstake Hotel. With the phone cradled between his neck and shoulder, he watched Addie Winslow bustle back and forth like a duck in a shooting gallery. The woman was upset, and she simply couldn't keep still.

Ben was the person who'd upset her, and for that he was sorry. Well, another name to add to the list of people he'd have to apologize to when this whole ordeal was over.

"Come on, come on," he muttered into the receiver. Addie darted him a nervous glance, and he forced himself to give her a reassuring smile.

No wonder she was nervous, the way Ben had come bursting into the hotel lobby an hour ago, barely taking time to toss a greeting over his shoulder before he dashed up the stairs two at a time.

Exactly four minutes later he'd clunked his hastily packed suitcase down beside the front desk, told Addie he was checking out and asked if he could use the phone to make a few quick calls.

He'd seen the questions spinning through her eyes like pictures in a slot machine. What was his hurry? Where was he going? And, most important of all, what about Sierra?

Addie had had high hopes for their romance, and now here was Ben, fleeing like a refugee from a war zone without so much as mentioning Sierra's name.

No wonder Addie looked so disappointed.

Ben wished he could reassure her and explain that his relationship with Sierra was just alive and well. But he could have used some reassurance himself on that score. He'd hurt Sierra badly, and could only pray she'd give him a chance to make it up to her.

But she'd looked so damn fed up the last time he saw her. What if she'd pulled up stakes by the time he got back, and moved on to someplace where Ben couldn't find her?

The thought set his stomach seething with worry, and he wondered briefly if his ulcers were coming back. He smothered a groan. Sparring with Sierra would give ulcers to the most easygoing man in the world.

Or maybe the unpleasant burning in the pit of his stomach was simply fear. Primitive, uncomplicated, garden-variety fear. Because as soon as he tracked down a plane to rent, Ben was going to fly again.

He'd spent the past hour on the telephone, calling all the rinky-dink airports in the vicinity, trying to find one with an extra airplane lying around. So far he'd had no luck. It was Saturday—a gorgeous, blue-skied, unseasonably warm Saturday, and apparently every pilot within a fifty-mile radius had had the same urge to take the old Cessna or Piper or Beechcraft up for a little spin today.

Ben hadn't flown since the crash, over six months ago. First had come his long recuperation, and then his all-consuming efforts to uncover exactly what had happened between his parents and Quentin Jericho twenty-seven years ago.

Now he was about to take a plane up again, and all he could think of was the overwhelming helplessness he'd felt when the controls had refused to respond . . . those tall, spiky pine trees reaching up for him . . . the terror of knowing he was about to die.

Ben shook his head once, sharply. He wiped his sweaty palms on his shirt. His fear was completely irrational. Quentin Jericho couldn't possibly know which plane Ben was going to rent. And even Jericho wouldn't sabotage every small aircraft in northern California just to be on the safe side.

Yet the thought of climbing into that cockpit, gripping that control wheel and finding nothing between himself and the ground but ten thousand feet of airspace made Ben's heart pound.

But it was a seven-hour drive from here to Los Angeles, and a lot could happen during those seven hours. A truck could run him off the road, for example. Or someone could take a shot at him from another car. All things considered, Ben would no doubt be safer airborne. Now if he could only explain that to his flip-flopping stomach.

"Hey, you still there?" At last the voice at the other end of the line returned.

"Still here," Ben replied. "Have you got something for me?"

"Yeah, we got one that's just had a major overhaul. That's what I was checking on—to see if it was finished. It's a Cessna 210. Ever fly one of those before?"

Ben flinched. A Cessna 210. The same plane he'd been flying when he'd crashed. "Yeah," he croaked. "I've flown one before."

"Great. Now, do you know how to find the airport?"

Ben placed his palm over the receiver and mouthed to Addie, "Pencil and paper?"

Her hands fluttered like nervous butterflies as she searched for something to write with.

Ben scribbled down the directions. The remote mountain airport was about an hour's drive from here, he calculated. "Okay, thanks. I'm on my way." He banged down the receiver. Addie jumped.

"Thanks for everything," he said, bending to pick up his suitcase. At the sight of her woebegone face, he relented. "By the way, I expect to be back soon."

She brightened immediately. "You do?"

Ben nodded. "I have some business to take care of first. But maybe you could keep that same room reserved for me? If it's not too much trouble, that is."

"Oh, my goodness, it's no trouble at all. I'll make a note of it right away. Let me see now, where did I put my glasses?" She located them on the chain around her neck and opened the dusty black ledger. "What day do you expect to return?" she asked, pencil hovering over the page.

Ben backed toward the door. "Gosh, Addie, I can't really say at this point. Look, you go ahead and rent that room if someone wants it, okay?"

Her face fell. "Well, all right, although this late in the year—"

"And if you see Sierra . . ."

"Yes?"

"Tell her I'll be back, okay?"

Her face crinkled into smiles. "I certainly will."

"Thanks, Addie." With one final glance at the lobby, Ben swung his suitcase around and pulled the door handle. As he stepped onto the front porch, he collided with Sourdough Pete.

"Whoa, slow down, buddy!" Ben exclaimed, reaching out to steady the old prospector. "What's the matter, did you finally strike it rich?"

Pete did indeed look rather dazed. "What? No. Matter of fact, I was lookin' for you, sonny."

"For me?" Ben quelled a stab of impatience. He was in a race against time, and Pete had stalled him when he was barely out of the starting blocks. "If it's about that interview for the magazine article—"

"No, no, it ain't that." He squinted at Ben from beneath his shaggy white eyebrows. "Besides, Sierra told me you weren't really a writer, anyways."

Embarrassment joined the host of uncomfortable emotions Ben seemed destined to experience today. "Look, Pete, about that magazine business—"

Pete brushed his explanation aside with one swipe of his gnarled hand. "Forget about it, sonny. I done told a lie or two myself in my day. I'm sure you had your reasons, but they ain't none of my business. Besides, I got something for you."

"Pete, I'm kind of in a hurry, so—"

"Keep your shorts on, sonny. I know it's in here someplace." Ben watched in mounting frustration as Pete rooted through the pockets of his red windbreaker. "An' that feller told me it was important, so you just hold on a second."

Dread began to inch its way up Ben's spine. "What fellow?" he asked cautiously.

"Why, the one who asked me to give you this note," Pete said, whipping out a crumpled envelope.

Once again, Ben felt the dreamy sense of unreality that had crept over him when Sierra had handed him the letter. Only this time it was edged with fear.

Willing his hands to remain steady, he tore open the envelope and drew out the paper inside. As his eyes frantically scanned the message, the envelope fluttered to the ground.

Stunned, Ben read the words a second time, as if he could somehow alter their content by knowing what they said in advance. But the same message taunted him, warned him, threatened him.

No, not him. The threat wasn't against Ben. He wasn't the one whose life hung in the balance, subject to the whims of a merciless cutthroat.

"He's got Sierra," Ben said hoarsely.

"Huh? Who?" Pete tugged on his mustache.

Ben seized his shoulders. "Who gave you this note, Pete? When? And where?"

Pete looked at Ben as if he'd gone plumb loco. "Some feller in a dark suit give it to me in front of the general store, right after I come into town for supplies. He asked if I knew who you was, then told me you was in the hotel and to bring you this note pronto. Said it was a—how did he put it? A matter of life and death."

Ben ground his teeth together. Truer words had never been spoken, unfortunately. "Listen to me, Pete. This is very important." He forced himself to release the miner when Pete stared pointedly at Ben's hands on his shoulders. "Did you see where the man went? Was he alone?"

"He was alone, and I didn't see where he went. I come straight over here to the hotel without lookin' back. Didn't see where he disappeared to."

"You didn't see Sierra anywhere, did you?"

Pete frowned. "Sierra? What's she got to do with this?"

Ben wiped the sweat from his forehead. "She's been kidnapped, Pete." God, he had to force back this panic, had to think clearly, or he wouldn't have a chance. Sierra wouldn't have a chance.

Pete's eyebrows shot skyward. "Kidnapped? What the hell are you jabberin' about, sonny?"

Ben thrust the paper at him. "This is a ransom note, Pete."

Suspicion filtered across his grimy, weather-beaten face, followed by concern and then confusion. "Well, what did that feller tell me to give *you* the note for? Sierra's daddy's the one with all the money."

"He's not after money, Pete. He wants something else. Something *I've* got."

Pete scratched his head in bewilderment. "And what might that be?"

The letter. That damn, troublesome letter that had nearly cost Ben his life and might very well end up costing Sierra hers.

But not if Ben had anything to do with it. Not while he had a breath left in his body. A tormenting vision exploded in his brain—the image of his darling, unpredictable, oh-so-vulnerable Sierra trapped in the clutches of that scoundrel. Ben could just imagine her lying chained in some dank dungeon while Quentin Jericho rubbed his hands together in evil glee.

Then, without warning, Ben's emotional dam burst and fear drenched him, leaving him cold and shivering with the bleakest, most bone-rattling terror he'd ever known.

Suddenly the letter didn't seem so important anymore.

First she heard a monotonous whooshing sound, as if a freeway were nearby. But there were no freeways up here in the mountains, were there?

Then the delicious aroma of tomato sauce and basil tantalized her nostrils. Now she *knew* there was something weird going on.

Groggily Sierra peeled open one eye, wondering who'd put the lead weights on her eyelids. The bright sunlight streaming in the window nearly blinded her. Instantly she squeezed her eye shut again.

Okay, take two.

This time she raised her hand to shade her eyes. Lifting her arm was like pulling the strings on a very heavy, uncooperative marionette. With her hand in front of her face, she opened both eyes very cautiously, squinting through her fingers.

A ceiling. Well, nothing too surprising about that, especially when she realized she was lying on her back. Nothing too informative about that ceiling, though. It couldn't tell her, for example, just where the hell she was.

Figuring *that* out was going to require more drastic action. Levering up off her elbows, Sierra swung herself into a sitting position. She regretted that move immediately.

"Aaargh," she moaned, clamping her palms against the sides of her head to still the painful throbbing inside her brain. The room spun about her like an out-of-control merry-go-round, making it even harder for

Sierra to examine her surroundings through her blurred, half-shut eyes.

This was like being in a carnival fun house. Except that it wasn't exactly what you would call fun.

Nausea swooped through her stomach, and all of a sudden that mouthwatering aroma of Italian food wasn't nearly so appetizing anymore. In fact . . .

She spotted the tray of spaghetti, salad and garlic bread on the nightstand next to the bed she was sitting on. "What, no Chianti?" she muttered. With enormous, groaning effort, she managed to lower the tray to the floor and slide it under the bed.

Drat, she could still smell it. Her stomach lurched ominously.

"Boy, I've had hangovers before," she said in a bleary voice, "but this one beats them all. And I can't even remember what I had . . . to . . . drink."

Wait a second. She hadn't drunk *anything*. She'd been at the campsite, talking to Charlemagne, when—

Chloroform. That was the cloying smell lingering in her nostrils. Someone had actually chloroformed her. And when she found out who, he was going to require some general anesthetic himself.

Turning her head slowly to minimize the little jackhammers attacking her skull, Sierra determined she was, in fact, alone in the room. Which was, in fact, somebody's rather luxurious bedroom.

But not hers. She'd never seen this place before in her life. Which would seem to rule out theory number one: that her father had sent someone to kidnap her and drag her back to her rightful place as the crown princess of Sloane Enterprises.

Time to consider theory number two. Except that Sierra didn't *have* a second theory. Pressing her fingers into her temples, she tried to remember what had happened between the moment someone had served her the chloroform cocktail and the moment she'd awoken in this strange bed with a huge bass-drum headache and a mouth that tasted like a ripe litter box.

It was no use. Her memory of that time frame was a big blackboard. A big *empty* blackboard. The only fragments she could dredge up were hazy and vague—brief flashes of men in dark suits and a glimpse of a . . . helicopter rotor whirring overhead?

Yes, for what it was worth, she was almost certain she'd been brought here in a helicopter. Wherever *here* was.

That was the next puzzle to figure out. Taking a deep gulp of air, Sierra eased herself to her feet and tiptoed to the closed door. She grasped the doorknob, turned it, then rattled it with growing annoyance.

Locked. Somehow that news flash didn't come as a surprise. Well, before she started banging her tin cup and hollering for the warden, it might be prudent to investigate other possible escape routes.

She poked her head into the adjoining bathroom. Marble fixtures, huge sunken tub, expensive tile. But no way out. Then she crossed the plush carpet to the bedroom's single window, an enormous expanse of glass she was almost certain would yield to a persuasive chair bashed into it.

What luck! The window was actually unlocked, sliding open on a well-oiled track in a very cooperative manner.

"Time to blow this scene," Sierra mumbled, hoisting one foot to the sill. "I didn't feel like eating lunch, anyway." She had one leg hanging out the window before she chanced to look down. "Whoa, Nellie!"

Just in the nick of time she refrained from heaving herself through the window...and onto the jaws of some very jagged-looking rocks a good hundred feet below. Heart thudding, she perched half in, half out of the window, pondering her newfound respect for that old adage Look Before You Leap.

So that's what that whooshing sound had been—not a freeway at all, but the rhythmic crash of ocean waves against the rocks. Sierra had to admit, her cell had a fabulous view. Gazing up and down the coast, she could see dozens of expensive homes, many of them propped against the steep shoreline cliff with massive, towering pylons—like the house in which Sierra was currently an unwilling guest.

She tsk-tsked in disgust. She'd been in many homes like this before, and could never understand why some people insisted on defying nature, the tides, coastal erosion and mud slides by constructing their houses where they required propping up, extra reinforcement, sandbagging and constant maintenance just to keep their backyards from sliding into the ocean. Maybe people just did it to prove they could afford it.

At least now she knew where she was. No mistaking one of the most exclusive neighborhoods in Malibu for anyplace else. So she'd wound up back in L.A., after all.

She had no intention of sticking around, however. Too bad the window had turned out to be such an unsatisfactory escape route. And no wonder it hadn't been locked. Dropping to the floor, Sierra strode across the room and hammered her fist against the door. "Fun and games are over," she shouted. "Now let me out of here!"

The noise made her wince, but she hadn't found a bell to ring for the butler. "I said, let me out of here," she yelled. "Unlock this door, or you'll be sorry!"

She pressed her ear to the wood, noting the door was constructed of thick, solid oak. So much for a sharp karate kick to smash it open. Not that she knew karate, anyway.

Was it her imagination, or did she hear muffled footsteps outside? Yes, she was almost positive she recognized the swish of expensive Italian-leather shoes against thick shag carpeting.

Then . . . nothing. She slammed her fist halfheartedly against the door a few more times, but the racket only made her headache worse, and her throat was getting sore from yelling.

Leaning back against the door, Sierra sank to the floor, crossing her arms over her upraised knees. This was really getting irritating. Not scary or anything, but definitely a drag.

Why couldn't people just leave her alone, anyway? Was that so much to ask? First her father kept pestering her to come home, then Ben chased her all over creation so he could get his stupid letter back. Now someone had shanghaied her for some incomprehensible reason.

Hmph. If that louse Ben Halliday could only see the predicament she was in now, he'd sure be sorry for the way he'd treated her.

"Oops, almost waded into a puddle of self-pity there," Sierra scolded herself. "Knock it off. He's not worth it."

She was spared further depressing thoughts by the click of a key in the lock. She sprang to her feet, stirring up a swirl of red dots in front of her eyes. By the time the door swung open, she was planted in the center of the room, hands on hips, feet set firmly apart, indignation blazing.

She couldn't have been more astounded if the Prince of Wales had strolled into the room.

She'd seen this famous, beetle-browed face countless times on the evening news, on TV talk shows, on the covers of magazines. His jet black hair, swept straight back off his prominent forehead, had always struck Sierra as a bit suspicious for a man in his sixties. His well-fed paunch, ballooning out the vest of his dark three-piece suit, evoked an image of Santa Claus that only enhanced his widespread reputation as a kindly philanthropist, a doer of good deeds.

Those twinkling black eyes had certainly never seemed ominous to Sierra. Until now.

"Quentin Jericho," she breathed.

"But of course," he said, closing the door behind him. "Whom did you expect?"

"Expect?" she squeaked. "What do you mean, expect? I didn't expect to be kidnapped in the first place, so how could I expect you or anyone else?"

He shrugged. "It shouldn't have been too hard to figure out, after everything your friend Ben Halliday told you."

His words were like a punch in the stomach. She paused a beat to catch her breath. "Ben?" she whispered. "What's he got to do with this?"

Then all the bits and pieces began to spin and slide into place, like the tumblers in a combination safe. Quentin Jericho. Quentin and Margaret. The letter. Ben.

"You," she said in a shocked voice. "*You're* the one! You tried to blackmail Ben's mother into leaving his father. You had something to do with Ben's father going to prison, didn't you?"

"Blackmail is such an ugly word, don't you think?" Jericho pulled a gold cigarette case from his inside pocket. "And Tom Halliday was an embezzler who got what he deserved. Do you mind if I smoke?"

"Yes."

He lit a cigarette anyway. Sierra stared at his elegantly manicured nails, trying to absorb the implications of this mind-blowing discovery. No wonder Ben had been so desperate to get that letter back. Sierra's corporate instincts were too deeply ingrained for her not to grasp immediately what the consequences would be if that letter were ever made public.

That letter was as explosive as dynamite. It would blast Quentin Jericho's Santa Claus image to smithereens. She'd hate to be the public relations director of Yummee Foods if its sordid contents ever leaked out.

And if Quentin Jericho was the kind of man who could write that letter, he was also the kind of man who wouldn't stand idly aside while his company, his fortune and his reputation were threatened.

Sierra pressed her fingertips to her forehead. So Ben *had* been trying to protect her by being so secretive. He'd been telling the truth when he warned that her life might be in danger.

And if he'd been telling the truth about *that*, maybe he'd been telling the truth about other things, as well.

A warm surge of love flooded Sierra's heart, filling her with tenderness and longing. For a moment she swayed, made dizzy by the overwhelming desire to see Ben again, to find a safe haven in the comfort and security of his arms.

First she had to figure a way out of this mess.

Coughing, she fanned her hand back and forth to dispel the noxious fumes from Jericho's cigarette. Well, they said the best defense was offense, right?

She folded her arms. "Would you mind telling me exactly how *I* fit into the picture?" she demanded.

"Simple." Jericho blew a stream of smoke at the ceiling. "Ben has something I want. Now I have something *he* wants." With an infuriating leer, he bobbed his cigarette at Sierra. "I'm going to offer him a trade."

"Me for the letter."

"Precisely." He let a gob of ash trickle to the carpet. "Ben hands over the letter—I hand over you. A simple business deal."

"You'll never get away with this, you know."

Jericho's jowly, well-tanned face creased with amusement. "You're hardly in a position to make threats, my dear."

"Oh, yeah?" Sierra had vowed never again to take advantage of her family connections, but in this extreme case she decided to make an exception. Fixing Jericho with her haughtiest sneer, she said, "My father will be furious when he finds out about this, you know."

"Your father?" He arched half of the long, dark eyebrow that ran all the way across his forehead.

"Maxwell Sloane, of course," she replied smugly.

Now both sides of Jericho's eyebrow jutted toward the ceiling. "Maxwell Sloane? You're Midas Sloane's daughter?"

"What's the matter, didn't your spies report back that bit of information?"

Anger shadowed his face, then vanished. "I can see I shall have to have a talk with my employees. But no matter." He squashed his cigarette into a crystal ashtray on the dresser. "Ben's a smart boy. He knows better than to go running to your father, the police or anyone else."

"But after I get out of here..." Sierra's eyes expanded with dawning horror. Jericho's nonchalance, his complete lack of concern about any future consequences of this dastardly deed told her everything she needed to know. More than she *wanted* to know. Jericho wasn't the least bit worried about what she might do after he let her go... because he had no intention of letting her go. Ever.

And since imprisoning her in his seaside mansion for the rest of her life seemed a bit drastic even for Jericho, that left only one possible conclusion.

With barely the briefest sideways glance, Sierra hurled herself toward the sturdy oak door. She hardly had time to register the fact that it was still unlocked before Jericho's hand clamped down on her wrist like a guillotine. With surprising strength he whipped her arm behind her back, wedging it into a painful position that made her cry out.

"That was very foolish, my dear," he said into her ear. "Not that you could have escaped, anyway, with Vincent standing guard in the hallway." His breath stank of tobacco, and his cloying after-shave reminded Sierra of the chloroform. "I'll overlook your impulsiveness this time, but I warn you—don't try my patience again with any more useless attempts to escape."

He shoved her onto the bed and, when she glared up at him again, rubbing her wrist, he was standing in the open doorway. Behind Jericho she could see a big thug with no neck and massive shoulders that stretched the seams of his business suit. You had to give Jericho credit; at least the slimy bastard insisted on a tasteful dress code for his employees.

"Don't abuse my hospitality again," he said, "or I might have to become...less hospitable." The ruby signet ring on his pinkie finger seemed to wink at Sierra like an evil eye as he shut the door and was gone.

A geyser of panic erupted inside her, and she flew across the room to pound on the door with her fists, shouting every threatening curse she'd ever heard, plus a few she made up on the spot.

After a few minutes it became obvious this strategy was not going to work. Sierra positioned her ear against the door and held her breath, listening for the slightest response.

Nothing. The damn door was probably soundproof, anyway.

Time to try a new tactic. She rushed around the room, yanking open drawers, whipping pictures off walls, dragging cushions off chairs. There had to be *something* here she could use, some clever tool she could fashion into a means of escape.

Pacing back and forth Sierra racked her brain, trying to recall every Robert Ludlum novel, every cops-and-robbers show, every movie thriller she'd ever seen. The hero *always* found a way out, *always*! All it took was some good old Yankee ingenuity, a dash of luck and nerves of steel.

So how come in real life, the only plan Sierra could conjure up was the old tying-the-bed-sheets-together routine?

She peered out the window, shuddering as a particularly dangerous-looking wave crashed against the rocks so far below. Even if she could somehow screw up the courage to lower herself out that window, she'd need a whole linen closet full of sheets to reach the rocks. And once she got there, what then? Sierra wasn't the world's greatest swimmer, and those waves looked like they could be hiding some nasty riptides. If only this house weren't so isolated from its neighbors, she could scream for help. But the thundering ocean would drown her cries as surely as it would drown *her* if she ever managed to rappel down the steep cliff somehow.

From the corner of her eye Sierra caught a glimpse of herself in the mirror of the antique dresser. Startled, she examined her reflection. Her hair looked like she'd combed it with an eggbeater, her cheeks were streaked with dirt and a lovely purple bruise adorned her left forearm. Scratches covered her face and hands, mystifying her until she remembered her earlier tumble into that prickly bush back in the mountains.

But the most unsettling, unfamiliar aspect of Sierra's appearance was her eyes. She brushed her fingertips against the mirror, then touched her lids to make sure those eyes were really hers.

How strange. Sierra had seen a lot of different emotions reflected in her brown eyes before: joy, sadness, skepticism, coy flirtation. Even suspicion and outrage.

But never had she seen such a chilling expression of primitive, naked fear in her own eyes.

It wasn't until his plane touched down at Van Nuys Airport in Los Angeles that Ben realized he'd made his first flight since the crash. His jitters about climbing into a cockpit again had been swept aside by his fears for Sierra and his guilt about landing her in this predicament.

If Jericho had harmed even one hair on her curly head, Ben would never forgive himself. But he would make Jericho pay.

Careering his rental car onto the Ventura Freeway, Ben headed for one of the winding canyon roads that cut through the Santa Monica Mountains to Malibu. No time to swing by his West Los Angeles home to change out of his bedraggled jeans and shirt. And going to Sierra's father and the police was also out of the question. If Jericho saw or heard them coming, what would stop him from killing Sierra out of pure spite? With his reputation ruined and a kidnapping charge promising a lifetime sentence in prison, the ruthless Jericho would murder Sierra for revenge against Ben—and to have the last laugh. Ben didn't dare underestimate Jericho by taking the risk.

Tires screeched as he swerved the car around the tight curves, ignoring the steep, rocky slopes that plunged away from the road. His mind was focused on one all-consuming goal that blotted out any other awareness: rescuing Sierra.

Reaching the coast, Ben swung north and within minutes was racing up the curving street leading to Jericho's mansion. He slammed on his brakes outside the discreet yet insurmountable wrought-iron gates, pausing to work out his plan of attack.

If a man's home was his castle, Jericho's was a fortress. This place had once been like a second home to Ben, but he'd never noticed before how truly impregnable it was. The front gates, monitored by video cameras, electronic sensors and an intercom, were the only entrance. The twelve-foot brick wall that wound around the border of the estate was topped with shiny coils of barbed wire. Ben recalled with a shudder the pair of vicious, slavering Dobermans that would automatically be turned loose if the sophisticated alarm system should go off.

Funny how it had never occurred to Ben before that a man so obsessed with keeping people out must have something to hide.

He inched the sedan forward and lowered the window. Instantly a red button lit up on the intercom and a flat, uninterested voice erupted from the speaker.

Ben announced his name with no further comment, and almost immediately the massive iron gates swung open. He cruised cautiously up the landscaped drive, scanning his surroundings for any inspiration as to how he could snatch Sierra out of here unscathed.

No reception committee so far. The only person in sight was the uniformed gardener who came every day to manicure the perfect green lawns and carefully trim the bright purple bougainvillea vines and orange hibiscus bushes so they looked artfully junglelike and untended.

Ben parked the car on the circular driveway, bounded up the polished granite steps and raised the heavy brass knocker, intending to bang it loud enough to wake the dead.

Before he could vent his worry and anger on Jericho's eardrums, the huge oak door swung open silently on oiled hinges. Ben recognized Vincent Stockton, one of Jericho's so-called bodyguards. Hired gun was more like it.

Wordlessly Stockton nodded, not an easy trick for someone with no neck. His beefy face conveyed no expression, but his slitted eyes revealed unmistakable gloating. For once in his life he had the upper hand over Ben Halliday, former corporation hotshot.

Stockton grunted and made a motion with his hand that Ben took to mean he was about to be frisked. Heart pounding, he raised his arms. As Stockton patted him down, Ben couldn't help noticing the man's fingers were thick as sausages. Right then and there he eliminated hand-to-hand combat as an option for rescuing Sierra.

Stockton led Ben down the hall and left him alone in Jericho's den, one wall of which was solid glass. As the minutes ticked by, Ben stared at the spectacular view of the Pacific, strode back and forth, settled onto the black leather couch and jumped to his feet again.

He recognized this ploy, of course. Keeping a visitor twiddling his thumbs in the waiting room was a common business ploy to put the visitor at a disadvantage, to give him time to get nervous.

But knowing exactly what Jericho was up to didn't make it any easier for Ben. Tension crouched inside him like a leopard ready to pounce. He wanted to lash out, to knock the expensive crystal lamps off their lacquered tables, to rampage through the mansion, busting down doors until he found Sierra.

Ben had no doubt she was hidden somewhere here on the estate. What better prison could Jericho have found for her?

That panic-laced dread began to suffocate Ben again. How the hell was he going to find her, let alone get her out of here in one piece? Jericho's oceanside villa was as secure as Fort Knox.

And Ben would gladly trade every gold bar in Fort Knox to have Sierra safely back in his arms again.

He sensed rather than heard someone enter the room. When he spun around, knotting his fists in a defensive reflex, Quentin Jericho lounged casually in the arched doorway. He lowered a cigarette from his mouth, tapped it against a cut-glass ashtray and blew a cloud of smoke in Ben's direction.

"Well, well, well," he said. "So the prodigal son returns. Or should I say, prodigal nephew?"

Ben nearly cringed at the reminder of how he'd once called this unscrupulous sleazeball Uncle Quent. "Cut the chitchat," he growled. "Where is she?"

The edges of Jericho's mouth twitched in amusement. "My dear boy, I'm disappointed. Have you forgotten the first rule of business? Never let your opponent see how desperate you are to make a deal."

Ben hadn't forgotten; he simply didn't have the stomach for such subterfuge anymore. He dug his nails into his palms. "I said, where is she?" he forced through his teeth.

Jericho inhaled one last puff from his cigarette, then stubbed it into the ashtray. He gave Ben an oily, superior smile. "I'll be more than happy to return the delightful young lady in question," he said pleasantly, holding out his palm, "as soon as you hand over that letter."

Chapter Eleven

Jericho's blunt demand hit Ben like a punch in the stomach. Even though he'd been expecting it, mention of the letter knocked the wind out of him. For an instant he was certain that Jericho could see the folded paper, tucked under Ben's heel inside his boot.

Ridiculous, of course. Jericho was a man of many talents, but X-ray vision wasn't one of them. Still, Ben couldn't shake the feeling that somehow Jericho sensed the letter was in this very room. And if something in Ben's face gave him away, neither he nor Sierra would ever walk out of this place alive.

He'd never been much of a poker player, but Ben's only choice now was to bluff. "You didn't seriously expect that I'd bring the letter with me," he said to Jericho. "What kind of fool do you think I am?"

Jericho closed his empty fingers around thin air and shrugged. "Perhaps I overestimated the young lady's importance to you. But my sources informed me the two of you were rather...close." He gave Ben a lecherous wink. "Am I to assume you don't think the lady's life is worth that ridiculous piece of paper?"

"I didn't say that." Ben was amazed at how easy the choice was. In fact there *was* no choice. If he could have actually saved Sierra's life by handing over the letter, Quentin Jericho would have torn it to bits by now.

Like a dazzling, golden dawn breaking on the horizon, Ben realized with soaring illumination that losing his last chance to even the score with Jericho was nothing compared to the horrifying prospect of losing the woman he loved.

Trapped in Jericho's lair, confronting the man who had destroyed his father and ruined his mother's life, Ben smiled. The blissful, earth-shattering, indisputable fact of his love for Sierra made everything else seem so clear. He wasn't sure how he was going to save her. But at least he knew what his priorities were.

Jericho frowned as if Ben's smile worried him. He snapped his fingers. "What's it going to be, Ben? The girl? Or the letter?"

Wheels spun furiously in Ben's brain. He knew with cold, dead certainty that Jericho had no intention of letting Sierra go once the letter was back in his possession. How could he? Even if he destroyed the letter, he'd still face kidnapping charges, at the very least.

Besides, Sierra knew too much. If Ben had a corroborating witness to confirm the contents of the letter, Jericho would have a hard time denying Ben's accusations, even without written proof.

On top of everything else, Jericho would face the wrath of Maxwell Sloane if Sierra escaped from this nightmare alive.

Handing over the letter would be the same as signing Sierra's death warrant. And then Jericho would naturally have to kill Ben, as well.

Both their lives were riding on how Ben played out this hand. He decided to stall for time.

"Tell me something," he said, folding his arms with feigned casualness. "Did my father know about this letter?"

Jericho snorted. "What the hell difference does that make?"

"If it doesn't matter, why not tell me? I'm curious, that's all."

Jericho sighed. "He wasn't supposed to, but yes, somehow he found out about it. Either he came across it by accident, or your mother showed it to him."

"How do you know that?"

"Because he came after me like a maniac, that's why!"

A long-ago incident stirred in Ben's memory. "Are you talking about the time the two of you got into that fistfight? Right before Pa went to jail?"

"I should have pressed assault charges against him. But I knew he was heading for prison, anyway."

Everything was starting to mesh, all the bits and pieces from Ben's childhood that hadn't made sense to a six-year-old boy, but that made all-too-horrible sense now. He'd always wondered what had provoked an easygoing, nonviolent man like his father to attack his best friend and business partner.

"You framed Pa on those embezzlement charges, didn't you? You set him up." Ben cut off Jericho's denial. "You might as well tell me. You know damn good and well I don't have any proof. It'd only be my word against yours."

Jericho moved to the teak liquor cabinet, pulled out a bottle of Scotch and poured himself a drink. "Would you like one?"

Ben shook his head.

Jericho swirled the whiskey around his glass before taking a small sip and smacking his lips appreciatively. "In answer to your question, yes, I did 'set your father up,' as you so quaintly put it."

"Just so you could blackmail my mother into leaving him for you."

"Your mother should have belonged to me."

"So you created a set of phony books, opened a secret bank account in my father's name and made it look like he was channeling money into it."

Jericho smiled modestly. "Simple, yet effective."

Cold rage congealed in the pit of Ben's stomach. "And you kept the records, figuring if anyone ever came poking around after my father died in prison, the books would still prove my father's guilt."

"Ah, but you didn't find them, did you?" Jericho asked, wagging his finger. "As soon as I realized you intended to make this unfortunate matter a personal crusade, I removed the book from the company archives myself. I know what a smart boy you are—you might have found something I'd overlooked." He took another swallow of whiskey and smiled. "I can personally assure you, the records have been destroyed."

His triumphant smirk got under Ben's skin like fingernails raked down a blackboard. Although he knew that provoking Jericho was as dangerous as jabbing a stick at a wounded grizzly, he couldn't resist the temptation to take him down a peg or two. "Seems to me you made a big mistake by writing that letter in the first place."

Jericho's face didn't change, but his manicured nails turned white as he clenched his glass. "Yes," he said, "that was a serious mistake." He tossed back the rest of his Scotch. "Chalk it up to the foolish impetuousness of youth. Margaret refused to see me or speak to me after the first time I made my little proposition to her." He spoke into the bottom of his glass, as if watching those distant events playing themselves out once more. "The letter was one last effort to persuade her to see reason."

With a sudden violent gesture, Jericho flung his glass across the room. The expensive, well-crafted glass bounced off the wall without breaking, leaving a trail of liquor to dribble down the paneling. "She told me that letter had been destroyed!" he shouted. He rubbed his hand over his face. "We had a deal. Margaret swore never to use that letter against me, and in return I promised to pay for your education, get you a good job after college, see that you never wanted for anything financially." Jericho's face was a boiled-lobster shade. "I always suspected she kept that damn letter. That's why I sent Vincent to search her house the day of the funeral." His mouth twisted into a sneer. "I should have known better than to believe her when she told me the letter had been destroyed."

"Ma kept her promise," Ben said in a deadly calm voice. "She swore she'd never use the letter against you. She never promised that *I* wouldn't."

"Oh, you were both very clever, weren't you?" Jericho took another glass from the cabinet, filled it, then gulped down more Scotch. "But in the end I'm going to win. Because you're going to give me that letter."

"Let me see Sierra first."

Jericho shook his head. "Not a chance, boy."

"How do I know you haven't—that she's all right?"

"You'll just have to take my word for it." He swayed drunkenly toward Ben. "After all, what choice do you have?"

What choice, indeed? Ben had to admit Jericho had won this round. But the game wasn't over yet.

Not by a long shot.

"All right," he said. "I'll go get the letter. But if I'm followed, the deal's off, understand?" He had to maintain the pretense that he believed Jericho actually intended to trade Sierra's life for the letter.

Jericho waved his hand expansively. "Why should I bother having you followed when I know you'll be back to deliver the letter yourself?"

Ben didn't bother to reply. He pushed past Jericho and strode toward the front door. The *only* door to the outside. And somehow he had to figure out a way to sneak back in past the Incredible Hulk standing guard.

He hated like hell to leave Sierra behind, but he needed time to formulate a rescue plan if he were to have even a slight chance of getting her out alive. Once again his palms went sweaty and his heart thudded painfully as he thought about how scared she must be right now.

Ben had got Sierra into this mess. He had to get her out. Even if she never forgave him.

As he drove through the towering iron gates into the street, he had an idea. A desperate, crazy, reckless idea. But one that just might work....

Once out of sight of the mansion, Ben pulled over to the curb, leaped out of the car and opened the trunk. Then he threw open the car's hood and spent a minute hooking things up. Back inside he rooted through the glove compartment, found a flashlight that would serve his purpose quite nicely and settled back to wait. His eyes never left the rearview mirror.

Perhaps twenty minutes later the vehicle he'd been waiting for appeared. He'd known it would, sooner or later, since this was the only route back to the main road, but relief washed over him nonetheless.

Hopping out of the car, Ben stationed himself in the middle of the street and waved his arms back and forth like a contestant on a game show. The gardener's van skidded to a reluctant stop.

Ben approached the window. "Say, buddy, can you give me a jump? My battery's dead."

The gardener, a middle-aged man in a baseball cap and a khaki jumpsuit, chomped on his cigar and scowled. "I'm in a hurry, bub. Got a schedule to keep."

"Aw, come on, it'll only take a second. I got the jumper cables already hooked up and everything."

"Look, Mac, wouldja mind gettin' outta my way? I told you, I'm in a hurry. Flag down the next guy, huh?"

Life in the big city, Ben thought in disgust. "Look, I'll pay you, all right?" He pulled out his wallet. "Here's ten bucks, okay?"

The gardener shifted the wet cigar to the other side of his mouth and chewed thoughtfully. "Make it twenty, and you got a deal."

"Fine, twenty it is." Ben handed the man a bill and stepped to the front of the rental car while the van pulled alongside. He took the ends of the jumper cables and pretended to be attaching them to the van's battery.

"Hey, come on, what's the holdup?" the gardener yelled, sticking his head out the window.

"I can't seem to get these things connected right," Ben said. "Do you suppose you could have a look?"

"Oh, for Chrissake," he grumbled, climbing out of the van.

Ben stepped aside.

"For cryin' out loud, what's the matter with you? Can't you—"

Ben jammed the flashlight into the gardener's back. "Don't move, don't turn around and don't say a word."

The man froze.

"Throw those cables out of the way and close the hood. Now, very slowly, walk to the back of the van and get inside. Don't try anything funny, or you're history, got it?" The words spilled from Ben's mouth as if he were an actor in some corny gangster movie. He would have felt embarrassed if he weren't so nervous.

He had to stay behind the gardener so the man wouldn't see he was being threatened with a flashlight. Ben followed him into the van. "Now climb into the front seat, but *don't* turn around."

"Afraid I'll see you ain't got a real gun?" the gardener muttered.

"If you turn around, you'll find out for sure how real the gun is. But I don't want you to get a good look at me. If I figure you can identify me later, I'll have to kill you. Got that?"

"Whatever you say, mister. Now what?"

With the gardener at the wheel, they drove back to Jericho's mansion, and while Ben hid behind the front seat, the gardener spoke into the intercom. "It's me again. I forgot a pair of clippers I need."

The gate swung open.

Ben wrapped a rag around the flashlight to conceal it, then directed the gardener to park behind a stand of eucalyptus trees on the far side of the estate. "Now, climb back here and take off that uniform."

"Hey, what the hell is this?"

"Shut up and take it off."

"I bet that ain't even a gun you got there."

"Want to take that gamble? Feeling lucky? Now hurry up, before I pump you full of lead." Ben closed his eyes. Good lord, what cliché was going to come out of his mouth next?

After what seemed an eternity but was probably only a few minutes, the gardener was bound hand and foot with twine and gagged with another rag Ben found. Ben hastily donned the gardener's jumpsuit over his own clothes. Not a perfect fit by any means, but it would have to do. As a final touch he tugged the man's baseball cap down over his eyes.

So far so good. Now if he only had the foggiest idea what to do next.

Sierra held her handiwork at arm's length. Using a tube of toothpaste she'd found in the bathroom, she'd laboriously spelled out the word Help across one of the bed sheets.

As she inspected the results, she shivered. The toothpaste was of the red-gel variety, and the wiggly letters looked as if they'd been scrawled in blood.

After hanging the sheet out the window, she propped her elbows on the sill and stared morosely out at the ocean. The only possible rescuer who could see her makeshift banner from here would be a ship or sailboat passing by. Or maybe a very intelligent seagull.

Well, what other way did she have to attract attention? No one would hear her screaming. A note in a bottle would take too long. Besides, she didn't have a bottle. And considering her success rate at starting fires, smoke signals were definitely out of the question.

How long had she been locked up in here, anyway? When she'd thrown away her career in the rat race, she'd also thrown away her watch. Judging from the sun's low position above the horizon, it must be five or six o'clock in the evening.

As if in confirmation, Sierra's stomach rumbled, reminding her she hadn't eaten since early this morning when she'd gobbled down the Yummee Macaroon that Ben had refused. Of course, now she understood why her supply of goodies disgusted him.

Her heart gave a queer lurch. Goodness, was that only this morning? A million years seemed to have passed since then. She'd awakened in the cozy rapture of Ben's arms, only to face a day full of lies, betrayal and kidnapping.

"I should have read today's horoscope," she mumbled. "I'd never have gotten out of bed."

Although it went against Sierra's grain to sit tight and wait for someone to rescue her—Daddy? Ben?—she couldn't think of a more productive action to take at the moment.

Well, there was *one* problem she could alleviate. Kneeling next to the bed, she reached underneath and pulled out the plate of spaghetti. As she forked cold noodles and sauce into her mouth, she crinkled her nose. Next time she was kidnapped, she would definitely demand a microwave oven in her cell.

Sierra chewed mechanically, watching the sun sink into the sea. Would this be the last sunset she ever saw? She swallowed hard as the food stuck in her throat.

Ben, she thought, *where are you?*

With one final burst of exertion, Ben dragged himself onto the roof and lay there, panting. Using a combination of rope, muscles and a conveniently located jacaranda tree, he'd somehow managed to scale the side of Jericho's mansion. Thank goodness the sprawling, multileveled house was only one story high in this secluded corner.

He'd have made faster progress if he hadn't strained his bum leg again. But a setback in his recuperation was the least of Ben's worries right now.

His immediate problem was figuring out where the hell Jericho was keeping Sierra. Chances were good he'd lock her up somewhere in the back portion of the house, facing the ocean and as far away from the front door as possible.

Shifting himself into a sitting position, Ben raked his hair off his forehead and yanked off his boots. Then he rose cautiously to his feet and started tiptoeing across the flat, shingled roof, crouching as low as he could to avoid being seen from below.

He reached the far edge of the roof and peeked over. Hastily he pulled back. Amazing how far down that rocky shoreline seemed from up here!

Once again he inched his head over the roof eaves, hoping to spot an open window he might be able to climb through—even though the idea of shimmying down the side of the house while dangling over those crashing waves and menacing rocks seemed sheer madness.

Desperate times call for desperate measures, Ben assured himself. But he didn't feel too reassured.

Then he spied something below and off to his left, something flapping in the breeze. He frowned. What on earth?

He sidled closer to get a better look at the strange apparition. The wind refused to cooperate for a minute, but then, in one glorious gust, the breeze billowed out what Ben now saw was a sheet.

By cocking his head he could make out the upside-down letters: Help.

A relieved grin spread across his face. "That's my girl," he whispered.

He fumbled with his coil of rope, unwinding it so one end swung like a pendulum in front of the window. He didn't want to signal her with a noise if he could help it.

Moments later a headful of chestnut curls poked out the window and twisted to look up at him. Ben grinned down at Sierra and waved.

A whole deck of emotions shuffled across her face: surprise, relief, amusement and a profoundly tender expression that reached up and tugged at Ben's heart. But all she said was, "It's about time you showed up."

Ben slanted a finger across his lips as a warning to keep quiet. Sierra formed a circle with her thumb and forefinger to show him she understood. But when he lowered the rope farther, she stared at it blankly.

"Tie it in a loop under your arms," he called softly, hating to raise his voice to be heard over the waves. "I'll pull you up."

Sierra's chin jutted out as she shook her head wildly. "Not on your life, buster." She looked down, then back up at Ben. "You're kidding, right?"

"It's the only way." He jiggled the rope impatiently. "Come on, do you think I'd drop you?"

She sent him a doubtful look. "Well, maybe not intentionally..."

"Sierra, for God's sake, we don't have much time! Tie the damn rope around yourself, climb onto the windowsill, close your eyes, and I'll take care of the rest."

She glanced down again, then swallowed. "Did I ever mention that I'm afraid of heights?"

Ben tried to stem a rising tide of panic. "If you don't give this a try, you're going to wind up at the bottom of the ocean, anyway. Wearing a pair of concrete overshoes." Another line from a gangster movie. If he and Sierra ever got out of this mess, maybe he should try writing for Hollywood.

Sierra appeared to be wavering. Then she asked, "Why don't you just give Jericho the stupid letter?"

That familiar exasperation rose in Ben's chest. "Don't you think I would if I thought he'd really let you go?"

Her expression softened. "You would? You'd really do that for me?"

Ben shut his eyes. "Yes," he replied through grating teeth. "I would. But the question's academic, since Jericho intends to kill us both, either way."

That convinced her. Reluctantly she grasped the end of the rope and disappeared inside the house. Ben played out more rope as Sierra wound it around herself. Finally she crawled onto the windowsill, perching there as if Ben had commanded her to fly and she didn't hold out much hope for success.

"Is that knot secure?" he called.

"I hope so. But I should warn you, I flunked out of knot-tying in Girl Scouts."

"Why doesn't that surprise me?" he said under his breath. "Okay, reach up and loop the rope around each of your hands. Hang on. Ready? Here we go."

Ben braced his feet, took a deep breath and sent up a quick prayer. Then slowly, slowly, he increased the tension on the rope until he felt Sierra swing clear of the window. He shoved aside his awareness of the terror she must be feeling right now, and concentrated every muscle, fiber and tendon in his body on pulling...pulling at a slow, steady rate...refusing to let his imagination picture the woman he loved dangling a hundred feet above certain death.

Sierra's eyes were pinched so tightly shut she wondered wildly whether she'd ever be able to open them again. Her hands were so slick with sweat she could barely keep a grip on the rope. The lower half of her body swayed freely in midair, and although she tried not to think about how high up she was, terrifying images forced their way into her mind, anyway.

Inch by inch she felt herself rising, and with each inch she fully expected to find herself plummeting straight down onto the rocks. She had absolutely no concept of how far Ben had pulled her or how far she had to go—and she wasn't about to take a peek.

Dear God, she *must* be almost there! It seemed as if she'd been hanging forever with this sickening free-fall sensation. The rope cut into her hands and exerted a painful, nearly unbearable pressure around her ribs. When her body wasn't swinging out over thin air, it was scraping against the splintery shingles covering the side of the house.

Then, in one horrible split second, Sierra's worst nightmare came true and she felt herself plunging downward. Her eyes flew open, and her throat constricted with terror, strangling the scream trying to burst from her lungs.

The rapid descent probably lasted no longer than half a second, but to Sierra it felt like half a lifetime. Then, with an agonizing jerk she was suspended in midair again. After another eternal moment, she began to inch upward once more.

Cautiously she dared to look up, fastening her gaze on the edge of the roof less than four feet away...three feet...two feet...one...

Then somehow, miraculously, she was scrambling over the edge, numbly clawing her nails into the roof, struggling to bring her knee up so she could lever the weight of her body onto a solid surface at last.

The world spun around as she collapsed, trying to catch her breath and regain some feeling in her extremities. Then a strong pair of hands dragged Sierra to her feet, and all of a sudden she was in Ben's arms, laughing, crying, sagging against him as if she'd never have the strength to move away from him again.

Ben plastered her tangled hair with kisses, then cradled her face between his palms and kissed her forehead, her eyelids, her cheeks. "Thank God you're all right," he murmured over and over. Then he grasped her shoulders and held her at arm's length. As he scrutinized Sierra from head to toe, his relieved expression hardened into a grim, dangerous scowl. "My God," he breathed, "what have they done to you?"

"Huh?" Sierra blinked in confusion.

"Your face, your clothes..."

She held up her arms for inspection, seeing the scratches, the bruises, the torn sleeves. She could just imagine what her face must look like. "Oh, that," she said, smiling sheepishly. "I had a close encounter with a brier bush this morning. Jericho and his men didn't lay a hand on me. Honest," she insisted when Ben continued to fume.

"They didn't hurt you?" he asked suspiciously.

"Just my dignity."

He enveloped her in his arms again, and Sierra could have sworn she felt him tremble. She tugged at the lapel of his jumpsuit. "What is this, some kind of paratrooper uniform?"

"Not exactly."

"And what's with the baseball cap?"

"Never mind. I'll explain later. Right now we've got to get out of here."

"For once we're in complete agreement," she said. "Will wonders never cease?"

"Come on. No, wait—take off your boots first." Leaning against him, Sierra complied.

They tiptoed back across the roof. "Oh, no—more acrobatics?" Sierra groaned when they reached the far edge. "My mother didn't raise me to be a trapeze artist."

"Will you pipe down?" Ben whispered. "Come on, it's easy. Didn't you ever climb a tree as a kid?"

"I don't think trees were this tall when I was a kid."

"Here's what it boils down to," Ben said as they both put their boots back on. "Climb down that tree...or else."

"Well, when you put it in *those* terms," Sierra grumbled, stretching precariously for the nearest branch.

Somehow they both managed to make it to the ground with only a few additional scrapes to show for it. Ben grabbed Sierra's hand and drew her along behind him in a zigzag course, making sure to keep a tree or hedge between them and the house at all times. Sierra felt like a resistance fighter fleeing through enemy territory.

Ben pulled her down into a crouch, and she noticed a brown van parked behind some eucalyptus trees on the other side of an open stretch of lawn. Ben scanned the area for a moment, then squeezed her hand. "We've got to make a dash for that van," he said. "You run around and get in the passenger side while I'm starting the engine. Then hang on tight. Understand?"

"Sure." Sierra gnawed on her lower lip. "I just have one question."

Ben sighed. "What?"

"Who's that angry-looking man in his underwear running toward the house like his shorts are on fire?"

Ben whipped his head around. "No. Oh, no." He yanked Sierra to her feet. "Come on, sweetheart—run!"

She didn't have much choice in the matter, not with Ben practically pulling her arm out of its socket. She stumbled after him, her free arm pinwheeling in an attempt to keep her balance. They raced toward the van, and Sierra flung herself into the passenger seat just as the engine roared into life. Ben floored the accelerator and cranked the steering wheel, nearly flinging Sierra out of the van. As they sped across the estate, tearing through flower beds and plowing up the manicured lawn, she managed to slam the door shut.

"How are we going to get through those gates up ahead?" she asked through chattering teeth.

Keeping his eyes focused straight ahead, Ben said, "There's a release lever that visitors can pull to let themselves out." As if to demonstrate, he screeched to a halt next to a tastefully concealed metal post about thirty yards from the gates. Cranking furiously, he rolled down the window and speared out his arm to pull the lever. Sierra snapped back in her seat as the van flew into motion again.

"The only problem," Ben said as the imposing iron gates began to slowly swing open, "is that there's an override control inside the house, so if our friend in his underwear has had time to sound the alarm—''

Right on cue the gates hesitated, then began to close like a monstrous set of jaws.

Sierra gripped the edge of her seat when Ben stomped his foot to the floorboard. As the distance to freedom narrowed, so did the gap between the two gates.

She squinched her eyes shut, then peeled open one eyelid. ''Ben,'' she said in a choked voice, ''Ben, we're not going to make it!''

''Duck your head,'' he said sharply. ''I mean it! Get down!''

As Sierra dove for the floor, she caught a quick glimpse of Ben's white knuckles gripping the steering wheel. The engine roar filled her ears, and an oily, scorching odor assailed her nostrils. When the horrendous grating shriek of metal on metal splintered the air and the van lurched like an animal caught in a trap, she was sure they were goners.

Then all of a sudden they were flying forward like a stone from a slingshot, tires screaming, rubber burning. With shaking hands, Sierra climbed up to peer cautiously over the dashboard.

''Not that I'm complaining,'' she said, ''but do you suppose on our next date we could just go to the movies or something?''

Chapter Twelve

Sierra aimed the remote control like a laser gun and zapped off the television.

She had no need and not the slightest desire to watch yet another replay of the taped interview currently filling airwaves all over the country. She'd seen and heard it dozens of times during the past forty-eight hours. Every last detail was painfully etched into her memory.

Sierra tossed the remote control aside, hoisted herself out of the deep, overstuffed cushions of the cream-colored couch and crossed the Aubusson rug to the French windows of her parents' living room. Pushing open the glass doors, she stepped onto the flagstone terrace overlooking the vast metropolitan sprawl of Los Angeles.

The Santa Ana winds were paying their usual late-September visit to southern California, lowering the humidity, raising the temperature and whisking away the grayish brown curtain of smog that frequently hung over the city. Today was what Los Angelenos called a Chamber of Commerce day—one of the rare interludes when pristine cobalt skies formed a dazzling backdrop to the soaring skyscrapers and towering palm trees. Photographers would be out in droves today, snapping as many postcard and tourist-brochure pictures as possible before the smog settled in again.

The glorious day was a mocking contrast to Sierra's bleak mood. As she propped her elbows on the terrace railing, she scarcely noticed the fabulous view from the hills of Bel Air. The hot breeze whipped her curls into a froth around her head, while the sun beat down on her bare arms and legs.

Sierra shivered with unhappiness.

She really had nothing to be depressed about, did she? After all, at least she was alive, and two days ago she'd been wondering if she'd live to see another sunset.

But that damn videotape kept playing itself over and over in her head, tormenting her with those riveting blue eyes, that tousled blond hair, those handsomely chiseled features.

And those devastating, heart-shattering words in response to the reporter's question: "There is absolutely nothing personal going on between Ms. Sloane and myself. Ms. Sloane was simply an innocent bystander in all this, and I can't tell you how sorry I am that she had to get involved."

Innocent bystander, indeed. Sierra snorted. Ben made it sound like she'd been a witness to a traffic accident or something. He'd better hope she never spotted him crossing the street while she was driving, or people would be shaking their heads in dismay and calling *him* an innocent bystander.

"Absolutely nothing personal between Ms. Sloane and myself... sorry she had to get involved."

Sierra clamped her fists over her ears as the taunting refrain echoed through her head again. Bad enough to find out that Ben didn't care for her, after all, but why did she have to learn it from the evening news?

The hours immediately following their narrow escape from Quentin Jericho's mansion had passed in a mad blur of confusion. The clearest images Sierra could single out were the harsh glare of spotlights, the rapid-fire clicking of cameras, the forest of microphones thrust in front of her face when the news media converged on the police station like pigeons flocking to scattered crumbs.

The police, naturally, had been rather dumbfounded when Ben and Sierra, looking like bedraggled survivors from a garbage-scow explosion, had rushed into the station. Their initial skepticism about the wild tale of blackmail and abduction had changed to grudging belief when the desk sergeant, shutting one eye as if to blot out the dirt and scratches adorning Sierra's face, had announced, "Geez, Lieutenant, I can't be a hundred percent positive, but she sure *looks* like the picture of Midas Sloane's daughter in all those celebrity magazines my wife reads."

The desk sergeant scratched his head in mild amazement as he gave Sierra another once-over. "Geez, famous people sure look different in person, don't they?"

Once the police-beat reporters discovered that prominent businessman Maxwell Sloane's daughter was accusing equally prominent businessman Quentin Jericho of kidnapping her, the police station soon resembled the floor of a political convention. Ben hadn't needed to call a press conference, after all.

Less than fifteen minutes after the Sloanes' housekeeper, Hannah, let out a scream at the sight of Sierra's face airing live on the six o'clock news, Maxwell and Rosemary Sloane had marched into the police station and hauled off their daughter.

All the late-evening news programs had broadcast the scandal as their lead story, and by bedtime people all across the country could talk of nothing but the letter, the kidnapping and how years ago Quentin Jericho had framed an innocent man who was later killed in a prison knife fight.

Those who somehow missed hearing the story could open their Sunday-morning newspapers and read all the details over their omelets and blueberry muffins.

The police had nabbed Quentin Jericho as he was scrambling aboard his private Lear jet. The pilot had filed a flight plan for Rio de Janeiro. Vincent Stockton and another of Jericho's henchmen were arrested and charged with kidnapping Sierra and sabotaging Ben's airplane.

So the tragic saga of the Halliday family, begun over a quarter of a century ago, had finally reached its conclusion. Not exactly a happy ending, Sierra mused, since nothing could bring back Ben's father or erase his mother's years of suffering. But maybe the Hallidays would rest easier, now that their son had finally brought Quentin Jericho to justice.

Too bad the saga of Ben and Sierra wouldn't have a happy ending, either. Another sad tide of regret welled up inside Sierra as she gazed unseeing at the lengthening shadows. She swallowed, but the pain lodged firmly in her chest. Would she ever be rid of this hurtful, suffocating pressure?

Not until she could banish the memory of Ben telling the entire world that there was nothing, absolutely *nothing* personal between them.

And though she'd managed to fall in love with Ben in near-record time, Sierra suspected that falling out of love with Ben was going to be a very lengthy process indeed. She wouldn't be the least bit surprised if it took the rest of her life.

A sigh wrenched itself from the bottom of her soul as she turned from the terrace railing and reentered her parents' elegant home.

Funny. She'd never thought of it as her *parents'* home before. Sierra had grown up in this house, so of course she'd always considered it *her* home, as well, even after she'd moved into her own place. But during the months since she'd left Los Angeles, some emotional link had been severed. Now she saw this house with a new detachment, as if she were outside looking in, instead of the opposite.

The realization only confirmed Sierra's previous decision to jump off the corporate ladder, to exit the fast lane. She was more convinced than ever that she didn't belong in Los Angeles anymore.

The only problem was, she had no idea where she *did* belong. Panning for gold wasn't turning out to be the life she was destined for. And she obviously didn't belong with Ben, either.

Yet facing the future without him made Sierra feel like a rudderless boat adrift on a sea of pointless choices. What did it matter where she lived or how she made her living, as long as Ben wasn't part of her life?

She collapsed into the puffy sofa cushions, then guiltily yanked her sneakered feet off the top of the glass coffee table as her parents entered the room.

Rosemary Sloane, a grayer, less-freckled version of Sierra, perched next to her daughter. "How do you feel, dear?" she asked, concern lacing her soft voice as she curved her slim, cool hand against Sierra's forehead.

Sierra mustered a smile. "I'm fine, Mom. Really."

Rosemary frowned as if she didn't quite believe her. "You've been through a terrible ordeal. I still think Dr. Hendricks should examine you."

"Mom, I've been telling you for two days—I'm fine."

"But those scratches, those bruises—"

"Are healing quite nicely, thank you. A couple days from now, and I'll be good as new—ready to battle ruthless evildoers again." She touched the sleeve of her mother's tailored suit. "Mom, I'm only teasing. Wipe that worried look off your face. Daddy, tell her I'm just kidding, will you?"

Maxwell Sloane had a worried look of his own creasing his distinguished features. Distractedly he ran a hand over his expensively barbered, salt-and-pepper hair. "I still can't believe that Quentin Jericho—my God, I've sat next to the man at banquets...once I even presented him with some damn award or other...and he has the audacity, the unmitigated *gall* to *kidnap* my only child—"

Sierra groaned. "Both of you are making too much of this."

"Too *much*?" her parents chorused. They gave each other a what-are-we-going-to-do-with-her glance.

"Dear, if that nice Mr. Halliday hadn't rescued you from that awful man's house—"

"Hey, Mom, what's this damsel-in-distress nonsense? I was well on my way to escaping by the time Ben showed up. I'd have gotten out of there *without* his help. Eventually." Sierra tossed her head and jumped to her feet. "Who needs that grandstander, anyway? Have you seen the way he's been spouting off all over the news? What a publicity hound. Then *you* give him credit for saving my life. Good grief, he was the one who put me in danger in the first place! Now you talk about him like he's some kind of saint or something."

Rosemary's startled look of bewilderment finally registered in Sierra's brain. She stopped pacing and threw her hands into the air. "Oh, what's the use? I'm sorry. I didn't mean to hop up on a soapbox like that."

Rosemary took Sierra's hand between hers. "We're concerned about you, dear."

"I appreciate that, Mom, but I told you—I'm fine. In fact I'm thinking about changing careers again and becoming a stuntwoman. Just kidding, Daddy," she said quickly in response to the flash of alarm in her father's face.

Her mother smothered a smile, but then her forehead wrinkled again. "You may be fine physically, Sierra, but that's not what I'm talking about."

"Oh, no, are we going to start this stuff again? Mom, I thought you were on *my* side! I thought you understood that I wasn't happy at Sloane Enterprises, that I have to live my own life—"

Rosemary hushed her. "I'm not talking about that, either. I'm referring to the way you've been moping around here for two days. You don't smile, you won't eat, and I hear you roaming around the house in the middle of the night." She brushed Sierra's cheek.

"Dear, you seem so unhappy. Won't you tell us what's wrong?"

For an instant Sierra was possessed by the nearly uncontrollable urge to burst into tears and fling herself into her mother's arms. But her problem was more serious than a skinned knee or a broken toy this time. She was an adult now, and was just beginning to realize how much she craved her parents' respect. How could she let them know what a fool she'd been, falling in love with a man who was so transparently using her?

Her parents would still think of her as a child if she confessed her schoolgirl crush, her naive mistake.

She forced down the truth. "Mom, you're sweet to worry about me—*both* of you." She threw her father an affectionate glance. "But it isn't necessary. If I'm a little down in the dumps—it's probably just some silly subconscious reaction to my recent . . . adventure."

Her mother blew a dainty puff of air between her lips and looked unconvinced. "Well, all right, dear. If you say so." She looked pointedly at her husband. "And as long as the subject has come up, your father has something to say to you."

Maxwell Sloane fiddled with his watchband.

"What is it, Daddy?" Sierra asked, bracing herself for another argument.

He snapped his fingers. "Did you hear the bottom fell out of Yummee Foods when the stock market opened this morning?"

"Now darling, that's not what you were going to tell her, and you know it," Rosemary scolded.

Maxwell Sloane sighed and gazed at the ceiling. "What your mother means—what *I* mean, is that if you still don't want to come back . . . that is, if you're still bound and determined to pursue this crazy—"

"Maxwell..." Rosemary warned.

"What I'm trying to say..." He gripped Sierra by the shoulders. "Honey, I promise that from now on I'm going to quit nagging you to come back to Sloane Enterprises." His words were surprising enough, but to her everlasting amazement, Sierra detected a damp sheen in her father's gray eyes. "After all that's happened—after we nearly...lost you—" her father swallowed "—I realize the only thing that matters is your happiness and well-being."

"Oh, Daddy..."

"And if tromping around the mountains looking for gold, or joining the Marines or becoming a damn *stuntwoman* is what makes you happy, then that's what I want you to do, baby."

Sierra flung her arms around her father and buried her face in his lapel. She couldn't remember the last time she'd hugged him, and the familiar, reassuring smell of his bay rum made her feel about six years old. But it was a nice feeling. "Thank you, Daddy," she choked.

Half laughing, half crying, she finally drew back and rubbed her fingers across his smudged lapel. "Oops, I'm getting your nice suit all wet."

"Never mind," he said gruffly, giving her a squeeze. "I've got plenty of suits. But I've only got one daughter."

"Oh, Daddy, that's the sweetest thing you've ever said...." Her voice climbed to a squeak as a fresh spate of happy tears gushed forth. Maxwell Sloane pulled a monogrammed linen handkerchief from his pocket and handed it to Sierra. She blew her nose with a loud honk.

How ironic, she thought. Her father had finally given her his blessing to follow whatever dream would make her happy. And now the one man who could make her happy wanted nothing more to do with her.

Maxwell Sloane patted his daughter helplessly on the shoulder as she continued sniffling. Only they weren't tears of happiness anymore.

The weather had changed abruptly in just the few short days Sierra had been away from the mountains. As she knelt on the edge of Bitterroot Creek, swirling her gold pan, a harsh wind swooped down the ravine and sliced right through her layered blouse, sweatshirt and windbreaker.

Her hands and feet were numb from the freezing water, her back ached and for about the thousandth time that afternoon, she wondered what on earth had possessed her to come back here.

"Well, where else was I supposed to go?" she said as if Charlemagne had asked the question. Inspecting a clump of weeds at the top of the stream bank, the mule made no rejoinder.

"I mean, I've decided L.A. isn't where I want to live anymore. Besides, that town isn't big enough for both Ben Halliday and me." She plucked a handful of pebbles from her pan and pitched them aside with an impatient gesture. "At least here I've got friends—Pete, Addie... you. Maybe Addie will put us up this winter until I decide what to do next." She frowned. "Of course, now that Pete's decided to stay on and help Addie run the hotel... well, you know what they say about three being a crowd."

Swishing most of the black dirt from her pan, Sierra halfheartedly spread the residue over the bottom. "Hmm, too bad there's no market for fool's gold. I'd be a millionaire." She was about to rinse the worthless contents into the stream when she pictured how disgusted her grandfather would be if he could see her sloppy mining practices. She sighed.

With stiff fingers she wriggled her Swiss Army knife from her hip pocket. "Maybe I ought to join the French foreign legion," she mused. "Or sign up for the first manned mission to Mars." She flicked open the blade and poked listlessly at the shiny flecks. "I wonder if they need workers down in Antarctica. Gee, that's weird." She bent closer over her gold pan, shading the glittering specks from the sun. "If I didn't know any better, I'd swear that . . ."

She scratched the tiny flakes with the tip of her knife. Stunned, she rolled back on her heels and sat right down in two feet of icy water. "Well, I'll be a son of a gun," she breathed, staring into the pan.

A shadow fell across her from behind. "Char, you're not going to believe this," she said, "but we just struck gold."

"Honest-to-goodness gold? You really found it?"

Sierra spun around so fast she nearly dumped her precious find into the stream. She didn't know which shocked her more: discovering gold after all this time, or finding Ben leaning over her, sunlight forming a halo around his blond head.

He extended a hand and—when she gripped it in a daze—pulled Sierra to her feet. She stood there dripping, clutching her gold pan, staring at him. He stuffed his hands into the pockets of his leather jacket and gave her a lazy grin. "Aren't you going to come out of the water?"

"What? Oh, er, sure." She waded out of the creek, holding the pan in both hands like a serving tray. "Look what I found."

"So that's the real McCoy, huh?" When Ben lowered his head for a closer view, Sierra inhaled the heady masculine fragrance of leather and denim. His fingers closed over hers to hold the pan steady, but the tantalizing pressure of his touch only made her hand tremble more.

She pried the pan away and stepped back. "What the hell are you doing here?" she demanded.

His eyes flickered with amusement. "I wanted to deliver a present," he said.

"I don't want any presents from you, Ben Halliday, so you can just take your bouquet of flowers or your box of chocolates and—"

"I didn't say the present was for you."

"Oh." She snapped her mouth shut.

"I brought a present for Charlemagne."

"For—but you don't even *like* Charlemagne."

Ben shifted his weight from one long, lean leg to the other. "I think Charlemagne and I got off on the wrong foot, that's all. So I brought him a peace offering." He smiled sheepishly. "Besides, it's the least I could do after he kept the letter safe and sound all those months."

"Hmph." Sierra shoved a cluster of curls from her face. "So where *is* this so-called present, anyway?"

Ben bowed his head in the mule's direction, and when Sierra turned, she spied a brand-new straw hat dangling from a tree branch by a bright red ribbon. "*You* can tie the hat on him," Ben said. "Even though your mule and I are embarking on a new era of peaceful relations, I decided not to press my luck."

"Wise decision," Sierra muttered. "Charlemagne's been known to hold a grudge."

"What about you?" Ben shaded his eyes to study her closely.

"What about me what?"

"Do *you* hold a grudge?"

Her eyes raked him from the toes of his boots to the top of his gorgeous head. "Have you done something for me to hold a grudge about?" Her haughty expression managed to convey both innocence and disdain.

"One or two things. Like lying to you. Using you. Nearly getting you killed. Some people might hold those things against me."

Sierra took a deep breath. "Let's cut to the chase, all right? You didn't come all the way back here just to play milliner to a mule." Her chin inched up a fraction. "Why don't you tell me what you *really* want?"

"Fair enough. As long as *you* quit pretending that nothing's wrong between us."

"Seems to me *you're* the expert on pretending."

"Okay, okay." Ben held up his hands in surrender. "I deserve that. But I also think you deserve an explanation."

"Don't do me any favors."

Ben hissed a long breath through his teeth. Plowing his fingers through his hair, he said, "When I left you here the day you were kidnapped, I promised to come back and explain everything. I'm trying to keep my promise."

Who the hell am I kidding? Ben taunted himself. He'd returned to the mountains with only one purpose in mind: to win Sierra back. And if his success so far was any indication, he had quite a struggle ahead of him.

By bargaining for Sierra's life, Quentin Jericho had inadvertently done Ben a big favor by making him realize how important Sierra was to him. Now he was desperate. He *had* to convince her to give him one more chance.

They faced each other like gunslingers at a show-down. All at once Sierra's anger and defiance seemed to melt away. She carefully set down the pan, then lowered herself to the ground and drew her knees up to her chin. "You don't need to explain," she said quietly, sounding as forlorn as she looked. "I read all the papers and heard all the TV reports. Jericho framed your father for embezzlement, then tried to blackmail your mother into leaving him. She refused, and your father went to prison. He was accidentally killed during a fight between two other inmates." Her dark brown eyes clouded with sadness. "You were only six years old," she whispered.

Ben eased himself onto the stream bank next to Sierra. She brushed her hand against his sleeve. "I'm so sorry, Ben. I can't begin to imagine what you and your mother must have endured."

He captured her fingers and held them where they rested on his forearm. His gaze traveled across the stream, but the scenes he envisioned had taken place long ago. "The three of them grew up together in Grass Valley," he told her. "Jericho and my father were rivals for my mother's hand. She picked my father."

"And Jericho, being the sore loser he was, never accepted her decision."

Ben shook his head. "Who could have suspected the bitterness that lay festering all those years? On the surface, my father and Jericho remained best friends. They even went into business together, starting a small-town bakery that eventually became Yummee Foods." He picked up a small stone and rolled it between his fingers before lobbing it into the creek. "Then, after the company grew so big they had to move operations to Los Angeles, Jericho figured out a way to get even."

"One thing I'm not clear about," Sierra said. "Why didn't your parents expose Jericho when he first wrote that letter?"

Ben shrugged. "You've read the letter yourself, so you know Jericho didn't admit in so many words that he'd framed my father. The letter didn't prove any criminal act."

"Yes, but it would have shown people what a despicable louse Jericho was."

"It wouldn't have mattered back then." Ben picked up a twig and examined it absently. "Yummee Foods was just starting out. No one had ever heard of Quentin Jericho. The letter wouldn't have been the effective weapon it became after Jericho got famous."

"But surely your mother could have revealed the letter years ago."

Ben shook his head. "She made a bargain with Jericho. He swore to take me under his wing and provide me with a good education, a job with a future...all the financial advantages I never would have had otherwise—if Ma would keep the letter secret." He gave a harsh laugh. "But she never promised that *I* wouldn't use the letter against him."

"So you grew up believing that the man responsible for your father's death was your benefactor."

Ben leaped to his feet and hurled the twig aside. "Pretty ironic, huh? Good old Uncle Quent. He was like a father to me after Pa died. God, I actually worshipped that man! He was so good to my mother and me...." Ben slammed his fist into his palm, waiting for the usual surge of bitterness to choke him.

Surprisingly the familiar bile didn't rise up this time. Maybe he didn't need to hate anymore, now that he'd avenged his parents by showing the world Jericho's true colors.

But Ben's usual anger was replaced by a raw, aching emptiness. He'd lost three of the people who were most important to him: his mother and father and the man who'd been an uncle to him.

And he'd be damned if he'd lose the woman he loved, as well.

Grasping Sierra's hands, Ben pulled her to her feet. He slid his hand along her cheek, weaving his fingers through her curls. "Sierra," he pleaded in a husky voice, "I want to make up for all the lies, all the deception." He stroked his thumb over the lush fullness of her lips. "Will you give me one more chance? Please?"

Her gaze was locked on his as if she were mesmerized. Then a shutter clicked into place, and she backed away from him. "Don't play games with me, Ben."

"Sweetheart, I swear I have no intention—"

"What is it you *want* from me?" she asked, her voice rising. "My forgiveness? Fine, you've got it. I accept your apology for involving me in this whole crazy episode. You're absolved of all guilt, okay?"

"That's not exactly what I had in mind."

"That's what you said on TV! 'I can't tell you how sorry I am that she had to get involved.' Well, now you've made your apologies, so why don't you go away and leave me alone?" she cried.

She angled her head so the wind blew her curls across her face. Ben clutched her arm and pushed her tangle of hair aside. "Is that what all this is about?" he demanded. "That damn television interview?"

"You said—and I quote—that there is 'absolutely nothing personal' between us."

Ben cradled her face between his hands. "Sierra, that didn't mean anything!"

"You announced it to the whole world, buster! I'd say that means something!"

Ben flung up his arms. "What was I *supposed* to say to those reporters? My God, we'd just been through a nightmare...I didn't have a chance to talk to you alone afterward, what with the police and then the press swarming all over the place. Then your parents showed up and hustled you away before I knew what was happening. How was I supposed to know how you felt about me? For all I knew, you never wanted to see me again. I wasn't about to tell the whole world I loved you, for Pete's sake!"

Sierra blinked. "What did you say?"

"I said I love you, for Pete's sake!"

The words stunned her as sharply the second time she heard them. A wild flame of joy ignited deep inside her, but was quickly doused by caution. She'd been burned once too often.

"You've said a lot of things to me before that weren't true," Sierra pointed out, trying to keep her voice steady. "Why should I believe you now?"

"I don't blame you for not believing me," Ben said. "But I intend to spend the rest of my life proving it to you."

Sierra gulped. "What do you mean?" she asked slowly.

Ben stepped forward to grasp her shoulders. He slid his hands all the way down her arms to twine her fingers with his. Her eyes flared open as he slanted his head to press a gentle, incredibly tender kiss against her lips.

"Marry me, Sierra," he said, his mouth a mere half-inch from hers.

She caught her breath and staggered back a step, wanting desperately to accept Ben's proposal at face value. She scanned his eyes for some evidence, some proof that he *did* love her, after all, that this wasn't merely the next phase of some secret scheme of his.

In the past Sierra had always been able to tell when Ben was lying to her, even when she hadn't been able to figure out what the truth actually was. And now, incredibly, she saw love blazing in the depths of his eyes, written in every crease and crinkle in his handsome face. The truth shone forth with a powerful, blinding beacon that dazzled her with its miraculous promise.

Despite their muddled, mixed-up history of lies and deception, Sierra was flooded with the crystal-clear certainty that this time Ben wasn't lying, that he'd never lie to her again. . . .

"Never, ever," she whispered with a dreamy smile.

Ben's fingers tightened convulsively around hers as a startled, worried frown crashed over his face. "Sierra, you can't mean that! I know you're still angry, but—"

"Huh? What you are talking about?"

"Don't you think 'never' is too strong a word? Maybe I caught you off guard, maybe if I gave you some more time to think about it . . ."

Her brows knit together in puzzlement. "Think about what?"

Ben's jaw fell open. Dropping Sierra's hands, he dashed the sweat from his forehead and folded his arms. "Excuse me, did I miss something here? I asked you to marry me, and you said—"

"Oh, that." She waved her hand. "Of course I'll marry you."

"You—you will? But then why did you say—what were you—oh, hell, never mind!" Ben grabbed her by the waist and lifted her into the air, whirling her around so fast that the trees kept spinning even after he set her down.

"You won't be sorry, sweetheart...we're going to be incredibly happy together...."

That was putting it mildly, Sierra reflected, if the next few moments were a foretaste of things to come. If she lived to be a thousand, she would never forget the indescribable rapture that spread through her body like wildfire when Ben wrapped her in his arms and kissed her with a fierce passion that made her dizzy.

For the rest of her life the scent of pine would evoke the rushing sound of the creek, the sight of red autumn leaves fluttering to the ground and the exquisite sensation of Ben's eager, possessive lips communicating far more than mere words ever could.

Nestled in Ben's embrace, Sierra knew at last where she belonged.

Eventually she nudged him away. "Give a girl a chance to breathe, would you?" As Ben drew back reluctantly, the wind swept between their bodies, making Sierra gasp as it made contact with her wet clothing. "Oh, my gosh, Ben—now *you're* soaked, too! You shouldn't have hugged me. Didn't you realize I'm all wet?"

He bundled her into his arms again as his laughter echoed across the ravine. "Hold still, will you? Now that I've finally got you back in my arms, I'm never letting you go."

"Well, that could certainly prove awkward in certain situations," she said, giving him a playful poke in the ribs. "By the way..." She circled her arms around his neck and gazed tenderly into his eyes. "Have I forgotten to mention that I love you, too, Ben Halliday?"

He cocked one eyebrow and considered. "Well...now that you mention it, I do believe it's slipped your mind until now." He kissed the tip of her freckled nose. "But I suspected as much, anyway."

"Pretty sure of yourself, were you?"

"Well...yes and no. But after I talked to your mom, I decided I had a pretty good chance of persuading you to spend the rest of your life with me."

Sierra stared at him. "You talked to my *mom*? When?"

"When I came looking for you, of course. After I finally shook off all those reporters, I made a beeline for your parents' house. Pretty swanky digs, by the way."

"If you think we're going to live there after we're married, forget it."

"I assure you, that's the furthest thing from my mind." He nuzzled her neck. "I don't think your father likes me, anyway."

"No? What did you do, break a lamp or something?"

"Let's just say your father was a little reluctant to tell me where you'd disappeared to. I think he's still mad at me for embroiling you in our whole unfortunate escapade. For which I don't blame him at all."

Sierra fidgeted from one foot to the other. "Get to the part where you talked to Mom."

"Oh, yes, your mother. Charming woman. I think she likes me. At least that's the impression I got when she hauled me out of your father's earshot and told me you'd gone back to the mountains. She was awfully concerned about the way you'd been moping around lately. Seemed to think it might have had something to do with me."

"You big egomaniac, you."

"Well? That *is* why you were depressed, isn't it? Because of that stupid remark I made on TV?"

"Ha! That's what you think. I was depressed because the price of gold's fallen off during the last week."

"Is that it? Well, in that case I'm glad I wasn't aware of it. I might not have had the nerve to propose if I hadn't thought you were pining away for me."

"Speaking of marriage, what are we going to do after we're married?"

Ben winked. "Sweetheart, if you don't already know, I'll be more than happy to show you."

She slapped his chest. "I'm not talking about *that*! I mean, where are we going to live? How are we going to make a living? After all, we're both unemployed at the moment."

"Not exactly an auspicious start for a marriage, is it? Maybe we should wait until we're both established in new careers. . . ."

"Forget it."

Ben kissed her soundly. "My sentiments exactly." When he pulled her head against his chest, Sierra could hear the low rumble of his voice. "To tell the truth, I haven't the faintest idea where we'll go or what we'll do. The only thing that matters is that we'll be doing it together."

"Maybe we could open a wilderness survival school."

Pause. "As I said, the only thing that matters—"

"Become acrobats in the circus?"

"—is that we'll be—"

"—together," they finished in unison.

Ben rested his chin on top of her head. "Sweetheart, I know how attached you are to that mule. . . ."

"Say no more." Sierra pressed her finger over his mouth. "I'm sure Addie and Pete will be glad to adopt him."

"You won't miss him too much?"

"I'll miss him like crazy, but I think Charlemagne's earned his retirement. Besides, three's a crowd."

Ben grinned. "For now, anyway."

Sierra beamed in agreement. "For now."

Ben squeezed her tight, then ruffled her curls. Flicking a glance at the gold pan, he teased, "Are you really sure you want to give up your mining career to marry me, now that you've finally found gold? You might be passing up your big chance to strike it rich."

"I've got news for you," Sierra said, stretching up on tiptoe and cupping her hand to whisper in his ear. "I already have."

* * * * *

Silhouette Books®